BEING LOST

Satan's Devils MC - San Diego Chapter #1

COPYRIGHT

Published 2020 by Trish Haill Associates

ISBN: 978-1-912288-73-1

www.mandamellett.com

Disclaimer

This is a work of fiction. Names, characters, businesses, places, events and incidents are either the products of the author's imagination or used in a fictitious manner. Any resemblance to actual persons, living or dead, or actual events is purely coincidental.

Warning

This book is dark in places and contains content of a sexual, abusive and violent nature. It may not be suitable for persons under the age of 18.

PRODUCTION ACKNOWLEDGMENTS

Cover Design by Wicked Smart Designs

Edited and formatted by Maggie Kern @ Ms.K Edits

Proof reading by Honey Palomino

Photographer: Golden Czermak of Furious Fotog

Model: Christopher Clark

DEDICATION

This book is dedicated to the memory of Anthony Onasanya, an ex-colleague of mine aged only fifty-three and who was taken far too soon. I will always remember him with a smile on his face and his loud hearty laugh.

His death, coming at the start of the pandemic was a total shock, to myself and other members of his team.
So I'm dedicating this book to Anthony, to everyone who lost their lives to Covid-19, and to the family and friends who mourn them.

Anthony, old friend, rest in peace.

CAST OF CHARACTERS

Officers

Lost – President

Dart – Vice President

Grumbler – Sergeant at Arms

Salem – Enforcer

Scribe – Secretary

Bones – Treasurer

Blaze – Road Captain

Hard Token – Computer Expert

Patched Members

Brakes

Deuce

Dusty

Keeper

Kink

Niran

Pennywise

Reboot

Smoker

Snips

Prospects

Curtis

Wrangler

Old Lady's and Children

Alex (Dart's): Tyler, Isla

Club Girls

Cindy

Eva

Pearl

Tits

Members Out Bad

Bastard

Crow

DJ

Shark

Rattler

Tinder

Deceased Members

Bird (ex-Prez)

Gator

Poke (ex-SAA) Dispatched to Satan

Snake (ex-Prez) Dispatched to Satan

SATAN'S DEVILS MC

CHAPTER ONE

Lost

"This will be you, one day. When you fuck all this up," the shadowy figure by my side says snidely, pointing to the scene playing out in front of me.

The second version of Snake, stripped of his colours, stands stoically as full-strength brandy is dribbled over his back. His expression doesn't hide that he knows exactly what to expect, as I do myself. I've watched how this plays out often enough, repeated time and time again in my dreams.

Unable to turn away, I stare on as Blade, the Tucson chapter's enforcer, lights the blowtorch and burns off Snake's Satan's Devils' tattoo. I can smell burning flesh, the air so tainted I've got the taste in my mouth. Bile rises in my stomach as I wonder for the hundredth time whether I'd be able to endure the same ordeal as soundlessly as my ex-prez.

Snake only moves when the punch from Drummer, the prez of the mother chapter, forces him to, then rights his head and spits teeth out of his mouth, taking blow after blow. He doesn't beg, doesn't ask for forgiveness or offer excuses, or utters any plea for clemency. Only involuntary grunts and gasps escape until his body is unmoving and prone. The bullet to his head is more symbolic than necessary, I think to myself. The man was already dead.

"It comes to us all," the man in my dream tells me. "I'd like to tell you it doesn't hurt much, but I'm not going to lie. Hurts like a fuckin' bitch. Worst pain of my life." He laughs maniacally. "What will you be like, I wonder? Will you be able to take it? Or will you be like him instead?"

The scene has moved on. Next up is Poke, the ex-sergeant-at-arms, who, unlike his prez, stands screaming, begging for a bullet instead. His shouts grow louder when the blowtorch burns the patch off his back. The sound of his anguish only fading when the hard punches and kicks finally shut him up.

"Will you beg like him, or take it like a man? As one thing's for certain, you're going to fuck up. One day this will be you, Lost."

I turn to look at my tormentor, to tell him I'm not going to fuck up, but the spectre is fading, almost totally gone when his last words reach me. "I'll be waiting for you in Hell, Brother."

I shake my head to clear the vestiges of last night's nightmare away, bringing myself back to the much pleasanter present.

The fresh smell blowing off the ocean reaches my nostrils. Pelicans fly overhead in formation looking like they are a flock of pterodactyls. Seals bask, the more energetic rolling and grunting beneath us, and squirrels pop their heads up from the undergrowth.

"Never get tired of this." Dart shields his eyes from the sun, watching the birds pass.

"That's because you're still a desert boy at heart," I mock him.

"True," he answers with a grin.

"You ever get homesick for Tucson?" I ask my VP. He's made a life for himself here in San Diego over the past three years, but still something drives me to enquire. He'd originally come as my temporary right-hand man when the trouble with the club had blown up, but had stayed and his transfer had become permanent. One important reason was to be close to the specialists treating his adopted son, Tyler, who had had sickle cell disease, but due to a bone marrow transplant, had recovered. Thank fuck. When I'd first met him, he'd been a sickly kid prone to distressing seizures. Now, you wouldn't know there had ever been anything wrong with him.

Dart seems to be considering my question seriously. "Change is everywhere, Lost. Tucson's become a different club over the years—oh, for the better, not the worse. My brothers have almost all found old ladies, something I never thought would happen." He breaks off to chuckle. "Since I left, Heart's got a new woman, and Peg, Rock, Mouse, and even fuckin' Blade have fallen. New faces have come in, some have gone. Things don't stop moving, which is just how it should be." He looks sideways at me. "I didn't know it then, but it had been time for me to move on. I feel the honour the club bestowed on me every fuckin' day. When I first rode into San Diego, I never imagined I'd step into the role of VP. Add to that, I gained a wife and family. I couldn't be fuckin' happier, man. Do I miss Tucson? How could I not? But I've no yearning to return there. I'm exactly where I'm meant to be."

It's much as I feel, without the woman and kids that is. How the fuck did I, the man known for losing everything, end up the president of the Satan's Devils MC San Diego chapter? That question has me beat. I might have been in the role three years now, but I'm still waiting for the other shoe to drop which it's bound to do at some point. Fuck knows, I know that better than anyone.

"How's the baby?" Niran, the man standing to Dart's other side, asks him conversationally.

"Cute as a button and already a bundle of mischief." Love for his one-year-old daughter shines from his eyes. "Tyler is besotted with her, though I can't see that lasting."

Niran chuckles. "The eight-year age difference between them could see him getting fed up with her being in his space. Now she's sweet, but when she starts cramping his style?" He shakes his head.

"You got experience of that?" I seem to recall he was an only child.

But it seems the background research we did on him hadn't led us amiss. "Sister? Nah. I was an only child. But my friend had one much younger. Fought like a cat and a dog in the end. She used to follow him everywhere, cute at first, but not so much when we became teenagers."

Dart harrumphs. "Yeah, I can see that happening. Already it's hard catering for the age gap. Tyler wants to do things any boy of his age does, but it's a hassle taking Isla out. You've no fuckin' idea how much a one-year-old needs."

I slap his back. "Think we do, Brother. Looks like a fuckin' baby store when Alex brings her in—stroller, diapers, formula, changing bag, blankets, spare clothing and toys." My voice trails off as I finish my list.

Dart laughs. "And I wouldn't change it for the world."

"Alex coping okay?" Listing the equipment has reminded me how much work a baby must be.

"Workload's been fairly light, and most of it she's been able to do at home while the baby is asleep." There's a touch of pride in Dart's voice.

So there should be. The Satan's Devils had paid for Alex to complete her studies. Now she's qualified, she's the official club lawyer. Luckily there's not been much trouble lately that has required much more of her help other than reviewing contracts for our businesses. Last time she was called on to help a brother in real trouble was when Truck, from Tucson, got himself locked up. Other than that there was one of Red's crew in Las Vegas who the cops had picked up for having drunk too much and getting into a fight. Alex had stepped in and he'd been let off with a warning. I've a lot of respect for Dart's old lady and I'm glad she's working for the club.

We all stare out at the scenery for a moment. My attention is caught by a kid trying to get too close to the seals who have adopted the beach here, but her dad gets to her in time. The seals are friendly enough as long as no one disturbs them, but they must be tempting for a child.

"Ask," Dart instructs, turning his head the other way, facing Niran head-on. My VP had gotten us all relaxed before addressing the issue that had brought us here. Something Niran hadn't wanted to bring up in front of the club.

Niran was the first black member of the Satan's Devils MC in any of our chapters. As well as being responsible for the Satan's Devils acquiring a new lawyer, Dart had also brought the club into the twenty-first century. When he had gotten together with Alex and had adopted her son as his own, he'd raised the question, what happened if Tyler grew up and wanted to prospect? We'd been a whites-only club up to that point, mainly as no one had ever brought it up. Faced with that query, it hadn't taken long for our outdated bylaws to be changed. Niran had been brought on board as a prospect shortly after and had been patched in after he served his time. He's been sitting around the table for a couple of years now. He's serious, always thinks before speaking and is a fuckin' good man to have at your side. Dart had done good when he encouraged him to join.

I look around Dart, casting my gaze on Niran for a moment. He's been spending time with the sergeant-at-arms, proving like Grumbler, his foremost thought is keeping the club safe. A few months back when Grumbler had landed dirty side down, Niran had done what needed doing without being asked and took over for a while as Grumbler's proxy.

He finally addresses the question he brought us here to ask. "Who was Shark?"

"Shark was one of Snake's men," I tell him, my jaw clenching.

Niran nods. "That's what I thought." He considers his next words carefully. "I wasn't here at the time, but I've heard his name mentioned as if he was fuckin' Satan himself. Didn't want to dredge up what went down, not in front of the club, not without cluing you both in first."

"Appreciate that, Brother." It's never going to be easy to do the unmentionable—bring up names of men who betrayed us in the past. Bringing things thought lost in our rearview into the present is always going to be hard.

Three years ago, the San Diego chapter nearly ceased to exist when it came out that Snake, the president at the time, had persuaded eight other members that the drug trade was lucrative, even though the Satan's Devils had decided years back they didn't want to touch it. Not only that, he'd painted the prez of the mother chapter in Tucson as weak and ineffective and had formed a plot to kill Drummer. Snake's plan—having disposed of Drummer—he himself would have then taken his place. It wouldn't have been a change for the better. I shudder even thinking about it.

Such a mutiny couldn't go unpunished. Snake and his sergeant-at-arms, Poke, had been dispatched to meet Satan, and the other members were sent out bad. Almost half the fucking club lost in one fell swoop. I'd put my hand up expecting to lose my patch. I was guilty, I hadn't seen what was happening, hadn't had a clue how Snake had turned. That I was left wearing my colours was a surprise and one I didn't deserve. And the shocks didn't stop there.

While I otherwise respect the hell out of Drummer, he'd ignored my past, both recent and history, and proposed my move from the VP spot into the prez's seat. Drummer's proposal was met with approval by the decimated club and they voted me in. I suppose there was little choice at that point. Dart, initially only here to support me temporarily, had gained the confidence and respect of the club and he took over my old position as VP.

Dart had been invaluable in keeping this chapter going at a time when I wasn't certain we could survive. The remaining members had nearly chosen to walk away from the club. No one, including me, who wasn't in Snake's inner circle, had had a clue anything was wrong. Until the betrayal came to light, all of us would have pledged our lives for the men we'd ridden beside.

Just surviving those first few months had been hard. The remaining chairs around the table far too spaced out for anyone's liking. Though they'd been tested harder than ever before, our prospects at the time, Al, Lloyd and Dave, had all proved themselves and joined us, taking the road names Deuce, Reboot and Keeper, respectively. Then, a year later, Niran had moved from prospect to member and was brought to the table as well, strangely enough without picking up a road name. Fuck knows why, but none have fallen into place which suit.

Eight men out, four new bloods in. Slowly we're regaining our strength and the trust which had been lost.

But a reference to Snake was enough of a reminder that could threaten to send men's minds back to that dark time, and how the certainty of life continuing without huge potholes in the road couldn't be guaranteed.

"It was a bad fuckin' time." Dart voices my thoughts. "Thought we might lose the club. Even Drummer had had doubts we could pull through. Each man who stayed had lost brothers they trusted with their fuckin' lives."

"Prospects don't know shit, but it was easy to tell the mood of the club at the time." Niran jerks his chin toward the VP. "Wondered what I'd stepped into if truth be told. But everyone pulled together and got there, which is thanks to you, VP, and you, Prez."

I go to refute it but shut my mouth. It's still my view the VP had the most to do with forging a cohesive unit out of the men we had left. Men who were and remain fiercely loyal to the chapter and our way of life. It took more than a moment to stop silently questioning each other as we made sure we had all the bad apples out. We'd taken time to heal, and from the reaction around the table when Shark's name was mentioned, are still healing. It had been Smoker's mention of him at last night's church that found us taking some space to discuss it today. Niran had judged it right—old history was best not resurrected in front of the whole club.

Smoker had simply reported seeing Shark in our town. A man whose presence wasn't wanted or desired, and who had been banned from ever showing his face in this part of California for the rest of his life. Just the mere mention of the sighting had caused the table to erupt. It wasn't time for a reasonable conversation.

"So a man's back in town who shouldn't be here," Niran sums up. "What's your gut feel, Prez? He here to cause trouble for us?"

"I can't rule it out." I stare out over the ocean for a moment. "A sensible man, out bad with our club, would never show his face in San Diego again."

"You want us actively looking for him?"

I think before I reply to Niran. Do I want to waste club resources searching for a man who might already be gone? A man with any brains in his head wouldn't linger here long, however important the reason that brought him back.

"I think it's better to have eyes out and be wary. If he's found, I want to bring him to the compound. Need to have words and find out why the fuck he's returned."

"For a start, I'd like to get up close and personal with him and make sure he got that tat blacked out."

I raise my chin at the VP. He's right. The traitors kept their lives only on the basis they got their Satan's Devils tattoos covered. They'd cried and begged when their cuts, their colours, had been destroyed in front of them. With a blacked-out tat, no club would give them a home, knowing they'd been disgraced and kicked out of their last, except if they were an enemy of ours. As far as I know, we're mostly on the right side of everyone, but there can always be an unknown we are ignorant of.

"If he's still wearing our patch, then he's a dead man walking." Dart bows his head for a moment. "He got family here he could be visiting?"

"I'll get Token to have a sniff around. See if there's anyone still here who's close to him." Hard Token is our computer guy. What he can't find isn't worth knowing. "We'll get Shark checked out, see if we can find a trace of where he's been or what he's been doing."

"Who he's here with or who he's visiting would be useful," Dart agrees. "The man must have a fuckin' good reason to show his face."

"I'd like to know all of that," Niran states. "The club's in a good place now, and if Shark's got some idea about begging to have his patch restored, I'd like to head him off before he causes upset."

"No fuckin' chance of that," Dart growls.

I echo his sentiment. Shark had fucked up good throwing in his lot with Snake and Poke. He wasn't going to get a second chance.

"One other thing, Prez. You mind me shadowing Grumbler?" Niran asks. "I seem to be doing that a lot."

"Long as you make sure he stays shiny side up," I chuckle. But really, it's no laughing matter. Grumbler had hit his head pretty hard when he'd come off. Although we envy our brothers in other states who can get away without wearing one, in California, helmets are mandatory. None of us doubt wearing one had saved his life. He'd had a nasty concussion, as well as breaking his leg and wrist. He's well on the mend now but while he was out, Niran was one of the few who'd put up with him moaning and complaining, and the two had formed a bond. Grumbler still leans on Niran, but I can't complain. We get two sergeant-at-arms for the same price.

"Yeah, two legs are better than one." Dart winks to soften his words as I bark a laugh.

Sometimes I think joining the MC had saved Niran in many ways, by once again making him part of a team. Over time I've watched his bitterness fade. He was a Marine and one who was going to make it his career for life until he'd been home on leave and a woman had crashed into him, knocking him off his bike and he lost his leg as a result. In Grumbler's case his injury means one of his isn't as straight as it was. Doesn't seem to slow either of them down.

True to form, Niran grins to himself. "Better than none," he remarks, flexing his leg with the prosthetic limb. "Anyway, I better get gone. I need to take a run past that house where the woman from Colorado is staying with her son."

"Anyone seen anything of concern?" I haven't been there myself, but every few days one of the brothers rides past the home we shouldn't know about where a middle-aged woman from Colorado and her son have been housed as part of the WitSec program. I doubt if she's had any trouble, officially, no one knows where she is. But Demon, prez of the Pueblo chapter, had managed to get the information and asked us to keep an eye out. They're the mother and brother of one of his member's old ladies. Doesn't seem much of a burden doing a simple enough favour for another chapter.

"Nah," Niran tells me. "Kink rode past a few days ago. House was looking fine, yard kept tidy. Hard to know what's going on inside, but outwardly, nothing to worry about."

We can't do much looking from the outside, and obviously can't draw attention to ourselves by stopping and trying to get closer. We need to keep trouble away, not bring it to their door. Luckily, they've been housed not far from the VP's place, so throaty sounding Harleys taking a shortcut along their road aren't out of place.

I honestly don't expect trouble. People who the feds give protection to are normally in no danger unless they bring it upon themselves. As long as they keep their mouths shut and make no contact with anyone who shouldn't know where they are, they'll stay out of danger. As long as the son keeps his nose clean, too. Hopefully he's learned the lessons of his past which had gotten him into trouble in the first place.

As Niran fastens his helmet on to his head, Dart tells him, "Drop in at my house. Alex will be pleased to see you. Isla's got the sniffles, so she's keeping her home."

"Going stir crazy, is she?" Niran chuckles.

Dart raises his chin. After giving the VP a thumbs up, Niran starts his bike and takes off.

"You did fuckin' good bringing him on board." It's not the first time I've told him that.

He raises his chin in acknowledgement, then observes, "Need to keep an eye out for new prospects. Wrangler's getting close to getting his patch, and we need to keep up our strength."

He's right. We do. But after what happened with Snake, it's not easy for us to trust. It takes a special man to wear a Satan's Devils' patch in any of our chapters, and even harder to gain one in San Diego.

CHAPTER TWO

Patsy

"No luck?" Connor, no, Dan—I'm mainly used to using his new identity as I should be after three months, but sometimes mentally I slip up—looks at me with an eyebrow raised.

I let out a harrumph of disappointment. "The tallest I can find is five foot nine, and that's the wrong shape."

"Couldn't you make do with that?"

Sighing, I explain, "The proportions are all wrong. If I could get a female mannequin that's six foot or more, it would make the photos so much more realistic."

He purses his lips. "Isn't there a way you could get stuff shipped to Beth, then get her to photograph herself wearing it?"

No. The whole reason for moving to San Diego is that no one, not even my beloved daughter, could know where we are. Dan would be dead for real if anyone ever found out.

Beth, now twenty-seven, is nearing six foot two, and was shooting up even before she entered her teens. Growing up, none of the off-the-rack clothes would fit. Tops long enough to drape below her waist would be far too wide, as people saw girls with height as also being wide, whereas she was slender.

Either my daughter would have nothing fashionable to wear, or I'd have to step in and help. It was bad enough her being mocked for towering above everyone else including the boys, but ill-fitting clothing made everything worse. At first, I'd adapted chain-store clothing, taking it in when needed, restyling dresses so she could wear them as tops, and then I branched out and started designing clothes for her myself. I hadn't stopped as she'd grown older and had become quite adept.

One day she'd posted my designs on an Instagram account, and to my surprise, and hers, I started to get a following. While I wasn't interested in making clothes in large quantities myself, my eye for a style that suited taller women had come to the attention of a company that did clothing for the woman who didn't fit in with the definition of 'normal'.

While, technically, I could design on paper, I still prefer making a prototype first so I can see whether the ideas in my head translate to something wearable. Beth used to model for me, but she's unable to do that now.

I push away the laptop I'd been using to Google mannequins and lower my head into my hands. It's been twelve long weeks since I've last seen her, and the pain of missing her hasn't eased. God, I miss talking to her, let alone using her as my muse.

Bethany and I had had an amazing relationship, not just as mother and daughter, but as best friends. Getting on so well meant she'd still been living with me, not thinking of moving out until she met Ink, a member of the Colorado chapter of the Satan's Devils MC. She'd found him while Dan was neck deep in trouble. Funnily enough, Dan had been indirectly responsible for making them realise their feelings for each other, as well as being the reason I'm now facing the possibility of never seeing her again.

I'd had to make a choice no mother should be asked to, which was whether to stay with her twenty-seven-year-old daughter, watch her get married and maybe start a family, or to make a new life with a son five years younger.

Seeing the state my son had been left in, realising how close I'd come to losing him had focused my mind. Dan had made wrong choices when he was eighteen, culminating in being arrested. It was only the knowledge he'd learned that kept him from being behind bars. But you don't snitch on those types of people without risking them taking revenge. He was inches from death when he'd been rescued, so badly beaten it was easy to pretend he'd actually died.

He was being offered a fresh start, a second chance to make something of his life.

He should have learned his lesson; God knows it had been a hard one to learn. Still, I'd worried if I let him go off on his own with no one to set him on the right path, he'd continue making mistakes. He was the one who needed me now.

He was going to have to leave everything he'd ever known behind, start afresh with a new identity and I would not even know where. He'd be as dead to me as if he'd really been in that coffin that day. How could I leave him to do that on his own? Not when I knew Beth was happy and settled. So I chose to accompany my son.

But having made the decision, I had to persuade the federal agent who was Connor's contact.

"You want to go into witness protection with your son. That can't happen."

I've just made one of the hardest decisions in my life, I'm not going to turn back now. "It has to work," I told him. "I'm not abandoning Connor again."

He sighed, his finger idly tracing the ink on the paper in front of him. He shook his head, then looked up. "Think about it, Mrs Foster. As far as everyone knows, Connor died of his injuries. It's not safe for a dead man to be walking around Pueblo, or anywhere in Colorado for that matter. He's only going to stay alive if there's nothing to link him with home."

"I know that. I'm going to disappear with him."

Agent Caruso's eyes hardened. "Alder Cantor is still suspicious about your son's death. He's still out there. If you stay here, you'll be safe. If you leave, then both of you would need to be careful. One slip-up, one attempt to contact your daughter and that's all it would take to bring him to your door. If he finds out that you knowingly cremated an empty coffin, then from what we know of the man, he'll likely take revenge on you both."

There were a few things wrong with that statement. Firstly, the coffin wasn't empty, it contained the body of an anonymous homeless man who ended up with a funeral he could never have expected, surrounded by grieving mourners, courtesy of the Satan's Devils of course. And secondly, why hadn't the feds found Alder yet? With all the resources at their disposal and the evidence provided by my son, they should have had him in custody by now, and Connor wouldn't need to go on the run. As for slipping up, Connor was more likely to do that alone in a strange city and state.

Alder seems to have disappeared into thin air. When he eventually turns up, Connor may need to arise from the dead to give evidence against him. Until then, for their own benefit, the feds would do everything in their power to keep my son safe. Which included, it seemed, separating him from his family.

The agent's mind was on the benefit Connor staying alive will bring to him. Mine was on the welfare of my son. "There's a risk if I let Connor go alone." My voice got an edge to it as I'd tried to get through to the man. "He's lived a criminal lifestyle for four years. What if he finds going straight too hard? What if he falls in with the wrong people?" I failed my son once by not protesting enough when he went to live with his father whose style of living tempted my son to walk well over the wrong side of the line. Now I'd gotten him back, I couldn't make the same mistake again.

It had taken a while, but eventually I'd worn Agent Caruso's objections down and reluctantly he'd agreed and had given me a brief glimpse that he was human.

"So I can go with Connor?" I'd pushed for confirmation.

"Connor Foster is dead," he reminded me. "Dan Forster is currently being moved." He sighed. "If you're intent on following this through, if you've really considered the implications, I'll allow you to go with your son. I have to agree with you on one thing, a criminal lifestyle can be tempting and difficult to stay away from. Your son would benefit from the guidance of his mom."

I'd promised I'd considered all the consequences leaving my previous life would mean and would be able to accept the outcomes that came along with them. As it turns out, I hadn't even scratched the surface. The first came quickly, my telling Beth I was moving away, and of necessity, cutting ties completely. Thank goodness Ink had been there to soften the blow for her, but no one had been there for me. I had no one to support me when I'd discovered that what I'd reasoned sounded easy, putting it into practice tore me into shreds and almost broke me completely.

I could never admit that to Dan or let him see how much leaving Beth pained me. He knows, of course, but I try to make light of it in front of him. I'd made the decision and I had to live with it, it wasn't on him.

I miss my daughter something fierce. My heart aches every day and I still cry myself to sleep often, thinking I'd left her all alone. *Not alone. With Ink, her man, and her MC family.*

It was the right decision but knowing that doesn't make it any easier.

I'd been so used to talking to Beth every day, sharing jokes and insights together, which only women can understand.

Although I love my son, we'd not had the same relationship, particularly in his teenage years when our dealings with each other were so stormy at times to the extent he'd chosen to move out when he became eighteen. Dan had gone to live with his father, unable to believe the man was as bad as I'd made him out to be until he'd been sucked in so deep it was hard for him to climb back out.

Here we are, after a four-year gap, getting to know each other all over again. The positive over the last three months is that I've found he's grown into a man I quite admire. Somewhere along the way, he's acquired a sense of humour that still takes me off guard.

"I'm Beth's height," Dan points out, bringing my attention back from the past. "Long as you avoid the headshot, I can put on a padded bra and model your stuff."

My eyes open wide as I turn to him. He's muscular and tattooed, with long hairy legs sticking out from his shorts.

Suddenly his face cracks as he snorts a laugh. "Your expression, Mom."

"Get out of here." I wave at him, chuckling to myself. Yeah, for a second I thought he was being serious. "You're not going to be of any help. Anyway, you're going to work soon, aren't you?"

He's got a legitimate job that the feds helped him get, just something to tide him over. He works as a security guard in a shopping mall. The money he brings home isn't much but it's at least legal. Next semester he's thinking of going to college but hasn't yet settled on what he wants to do.

Part of the reason he went with his father was that he thought I was always comparing him to his sister and he's right. He and she are very different—she's good with words and numbers and he's good with his hands. I made enough mistakes when I was bringing him up, trying to mould him into something he wasn't, so I'm taking a back seat now. I'm just here to support him in what he wants to make of his life, and to guide him away from anything criminal.

"Yeah, we're open until late tonight."

I'd like to tell him to come straight home but have to remember he's an adult now. I also trust him to keep his head down low and not contact anyone from his previous life. He knows as well as I do that one slip-up and it could bring Alder to our door. Dan doesn't need a reason to fear Alder, Alder's men had given him that themselves when they'd beaten him just short of death.

Alder. As Dan leaves me alone, I think about the man who's made our lives hell.

Phil Foster and I had been married a couple of years before his sister came back into our lives, bringing with her her husband, Alder Cantor. I'd immediately thought she was cowed by her partner. She'd been so meek, subservient when her man was around. I'd mentioned it to Phil, but he seemed entranced by his new brother-in-law who could do nothing wrong in his eyes. When his sister died, even while I thought the circumstance suspicious, Phil remained friends with the man.

Phil had always considered himself Alder's equal, but he was not. Alder could run rings around him. It was about the time that Alder was exerting his influence that I knew our marriage was over for sure. Phil, an accountant, had been cooking the books and had gotten caught. He'd managed to worm his way out of a jail sentence, but not having a legitimate job any longer, went to work with Alder.

Phil, before his death, had been a rich man. But that money went back to where it came from, into Alder's hands. Not that I wanted any of it.

Dan thought he'd been working for his father, unaware that Phil had simply been passing instructions on, until he found out rather than just running protection rackets, Phil was helping Alder supply drugs.

When Dan was arrested because he'd been too violent collecting a debt for his father, he bargained to stay out of jail with the knowledge he'd gained. Of course, the ten kilos of heroin he'd stopped getting to the streets had helped his case. Now instead of the feds not knowing who one of the kingpins was behind the drugs flooding into the United States via Mexico, they now had a name and a description, and many of the routes by which they'd been brought in. Past tense, of course. By giving the information away, Dan had destroyed a large part of Alder's operation.

If Alder knew Dan was alive and got his hands on him again, he'd make him pay dearly for the trouble he had caused him. Alder, as Dan knows only too well, is a man who likes to cause pain.

Dan isn't going to be doing anything to give himself away. That's one thing I don't need to worry about.

While I miss my home in Pueblo, if I had to move anywhere, there could be worse places to be than San Diego. We've been allocated a small house with an easy to maintain front yard, and a small one out back where I can sit in the sun, which seems to shine more often than in Colorado. At least I won't have to contend with snow when winter comes.

It would be perfect were it not for the fact my daughter isn't with me.

"See you later, Mom," is shouted, followed by the front door banging, then the sound of the car Dan drives starting, revving, then fading.

It's then I lower my head into my hands and alone, give into my sorrow. I miss my daughter so damn much. I'd love Beth's advice on the clothes I'm designing, would love her to be here modelling them for me. But that can't be. Dan needs someone on his side in this unfamiliar state and city.

A loud noise reaches my ears. *Grrrr.* It's a motorcycle, one of those loud Harleys. I've no idea why, but they use our road as a shortcut to somewhere. Not every day, but often enough. I swear the sound from the exhausts makes the windows rattle. Can it be legal? Surely not.

Closing my laptop, knowing my unsuccessful search for a mannequin has just made me miss Bethany more, I go to make myself a cup of coffee, feeling lonelier than I ever have. In Pueblo I had friends and a social life, here there's no one I know, and I'm scared of getting out and socialising.

I'm fifty-three years old. I haven't had a man in my life for more than eighteen years since I kicked Phil to the kerb. I'd joked with Beth that maybe I'd find someone when I moved. But how could I seek out a man for myself, and what on earth would I do with him if I found one? My experience with my husband has soured me, and any man I've met since hasn't lived up to my hopes or expectations.

A woman friend would be nice, someone I could share a glass of wine with and gossip to, but she'd want to know my backstory, and I hate lying. I'd be terrified that I'd do or say something and slip up and lead Alder to our door. He'll kill my son and make sure he stays dead this time.

But finding new friends of either sex is unlikely. I work at home and rarely go out, and this doesn't seem a particularly friendly neighbourhood, contact limited to exchanging nods and the odd hello if we're close enough.

To be honest, I'm lonely. I can't even go on Facebook anymore, not that I used to spend much time on it, but if I could, I might find virtual friends if not real ones.

I could set up a fake profile, make friends with Beth...

Too dangerous.

I finish making my coffee and take it into the living room, switching on the television, then switching it off again as the news is too depressing. Instead, I pick up my e-reader and open up the novel I was reading. Since Beth's been living with Ink, I've taken to reading everything I can devour about fictional biker clubs, imagining my daughter and her man in starring roles, well, maybe the supporting ones who don't have sex. I've no inclination to even imagine what Ink and Beth get up to in the bedroom.

I wish I could see them. Or, just talk to them.

I wonder how Mel, Beth's pregnant friend and another biker's old lady is doing? Or Vi, the president's wife? She must be six, seven months pregnant herself. I think of Steph, and wonder how that amazing guide dog of hers is? Then there's Jeannie who's the mother hen to the Colorado club—she was a brusque woman, a bit older than me, but friendly enough.

I count them as my friends as well as my daughter's, but like the rest of my life, it was all left behind in Pueblo, Colorado.

If only there were some way I could talk to Beth. I long to hear her voice. I don't know if she's well, happy, or if something has happened to her. The thought something might, and I'd never find out is horrific.

Perhaps, if I'm clever, I can find some way to get in touch. Just to check she's alright.

No, I tell myself firmly. I mustn't chance it. But I can't quite rid the idea from my head.

CHAPTER THREE

Lost

"What d'you think of this, Prez?"

Pennywise stops me as I'm walking toward the bar. He's got a Harley brochure open in front of him, and he's tapping at something on the page.

"Nice, but pricey." I admire the new model he's pointing out. "Thinking of upgrading?"

"Got to get hold of some money first." He grins. "I can dream, though, can't I?"

Like most of the members, Pennywise lives at the club and has few living expenses. "Perhaps you could work out a payment plan."

"Can you see a bank giving me credit?" he scoffs.

I can't. But that wasn't what I was thinking of. "If you need a new bike, the club can pay upfront, and you can pay us back."

He brightens. "I'll think about that, Prez, thanks. I'll have to work out whether it's a need or a want first."

"Need." Salem, walking past, has overheard. "Your bike's in the fuckin' shop more than you ride it. What is it? Twenty years old? You'd be doing us all a favour if you replace it."

Pennywise grins. "She's a classic."

Salem, our enforcer, snorts and wanders off. "Fuckin' classic," he mutters under his breath.

"You ready, Prez?"

As ready as I ever am, I muse, as I give my VP a chin lift and make my way into church, noticing Pennywise closing the brochure and following.

It's not long before all the seats are taken.

Dart, as my VP, takes his seat to my left, and Grumbler, the sergeant-at-arms, sits to my right. Next to Dart is Salem, and opposite him is the treasurer, Bones. Apart from Salem, who was Snake's enforcer before he became mine, the rest of us officers have only occupied these particular seats for the past three years. We've melded together as best we can after Snake's betrayal.

Due mainly to the work Dart had put in, we hadn't lost one man from the club. Every member sitting around this table appears to have faith in its new top team, and I have to be grateful, if not a bit wary, for that. Why the fuck did they put a man like me in charge? I shake my head daily, wondering why the hell they voted me in.

Not that I'm ungrateful, never that. I love and respect each man sitting around this table, but hell, it's a lot of responsibility. Each day I hope I can live up to the kind of man an MC prez is supposed to be.

Part of which I put into action right now by banging the gavel and starting the meeting.

"Bones. Finance report?"

In the past it was DJ, another out bad member, who handled the books, but it turns out Bones is quite a wizard with numbers which had surprised us.

He sniffs loudly and wipes his hand under his nose, a sinus problem left over from a long-ago coke habit. "Yeah, Prez." Bones passes out something. "The auto-shop with those custom builds—"

"Pimping," Dusty interrupts.

"We do not fuckin' pimp rides," Salem snarls down the table, while everyone else chortles. "You call us a pimp business one more time, Dusty…"

Dusty is unrepentant. He knows he gets a rise out of Salem whenever he calls him a pimp. To my mind, he's skating close to thin ice. One of these days, the enforcer's going to shut him up with his fists.

"As I was saying," Bones glares at Dusty, "I've been able to make some investments with the profits from the shop. Here's the latest report on the interest."

"Looking fuckin' good, Brother," Smoker tells him, then coughs, bending forward over the table. When he recovers, he continues, "I like making money and not working for it."

"What sort of account is it in, Bones?" While I like the club having solid money behind it, I don't like the idea that we can't withdraw it and use it at any time. You never know when funds will be needed.

"We can pull out what we need whenever we want it. I'm moving the money around wherever I think it's necessary."

Bones is our fund manager, and as Smoker pointed out, we're starting to turn a profit without raising a finger. Well, except for Bones' on the keyboard moving money around.

"Salem, how's the work going?"

"Got too much," the enforcer says. "Starting to turn people away. The waiting list for customisation is over a year now."

"Gonna take more people on?" Dart asks.

Salem shrugs before answering, "It's a matter of room. We've got about as many as the shop will hold. If we expand, we could."

"We can speak later," Dart suggests. "Maybe we can get the shop extended. I don't like turning away work."

Salem seems satisfied.

"I've an idea." Niran raises his hand. "Why not do up one of the old hangars, bring the custom builds there? Leaves the shop free to take on more of the regular shit."

Salem leans forward and stares down the table. Slowly his mouth curves. "Good fuckin' idea, Brother." Turning around, he addresses me next. "Be good security wise, too. I know the shops well-alarmed and as secure as we can make it, but some of the work we're doing is on valuable rides."

I can't see anything wrong with the proposal. It's not as if we're short of space. Years back and well before my time, the club took over a disused airfield and adapted one of the hangars to become our clubhouse. "The second hangar's at least been made weatherproof. Yeah, good idea. Look into it, Salem. Okay, what you got, Blaze?"

"Tattoo parlour's doing good, Prez." A short, sharp and concise update, I can't complain about that.

I raise my chin toward Bones, who nods to confirm it.

Brakes takes a moment to tell us about the strip club, requesting funds for redecoration which after some discussion, is agreed. Deuce, who manages our bar and restaurant, also confirms things are going well.

"And the new business?" Dart probes.

It had been Keeper, Dave as he was known while he was a prospect, who'd come up with the idea. When he'd presented a business proposal, we ran with it. It was to have a store which sold biker apparel, helmets, safety glasses, accessories and clothing. Good quality, but we were able to undercut the major retailers by using lesser known brands and cater for people who just wanted a good quality jacket but didn't care what logo was on it. As luck would have it, a store had closed down close to our auto-shop and we snapped it up. It had been big enough to put a small coffee station in it and had become a place for bikers to meet.

"It has started turning a profit, VP." Bones answers Dart's question, jerking his chin toward Keeper.

It looks like church is going to be a short one. No problems. Just how I like it. "Anyone got anything else to bring to the table?" They haven't. I pick up the gavel...

"Prez?"

I wait until Smoker finishes his coughing fit, and then nod. "Any more on Shark?"

The good mood is immediately shattered. "Nah, but just keep your eyes open and ears to the ground. Hopefully he's only made a flying visit and left town. But if you do see him, I want to talk to him."

"Motherfucker will have gone if he knows what's good for him."

I raise my chin toward Snips but hope that conversation has shut down. No need to rehash the betrayal and keep it fresh in our minds. Again, I pick up the gavel.

"Prez?"

I sigh, but it's our data and security guy, Hard Token. He'd picked up his name after he harped on and on about the need for hard tokens to access our businesses. In user speak it meant using a key card system to get in.

"What you got, Token?"

"I waited until we'd finished everything else as I thought this might take more than a minute." So my hopes for a short meeting have just been wrecked. I raise an eyebrow toward him. Token nods. "Had a cryptic message sent to me."

"Cryptic?"

"Well, I don't know who it's from, or how legit it is."

"And what does it say, Brother?" Jeez, this is like pulling teeth.

He taps at the tablet in front of him. "I'll read it. It says *Up the security around the woman and her son that you are watching.*"

There's an intake of breaths around the table.

"Is that it?" Dart snaps. "Did you reply?"

Token shrugs. "No way to reply." He looks around, noticing all eyes are on him. "This wasn't an email, nor an instant message. It didn't appear on WhatsApp or anything like that."

"Well what the fuck is it, and how did you get it?"

Token's face goes hard. "It just appeared on my screen, as if someone took remote control of it for a minute."

"What the fuck?" Pennywise shouts. "Your security shit, Brother?"

Token snarls. "No it's not. Whoever got in left no trace. I don't even know how they did it."

"You cleaned up your system now, Token?"

He rolls his eyes. "No, I did not." I open my mouth to ask what the fuck is he playing at, when he provides the answer. "What I did is put everything we need kept secure behind impenetrable firewalls but left my system as it is. Thought this fucker may get back into contact and left it so the line of communication is still open." Again, he glances at the rest of us. "I don't like it, but to my mind, the how and who isn't as important as the fuckin' message."

He's right. We know where they are because the only other person who knows, besides the feds, is Demon, the Colorado prez, who told us. No one else is privy to that information. I have to wonder whether there's been a leak, and where the hell from if there is.

"The marshals running the WitSec program wouldn't have said anything," I remind them. "They run the program like a tight ship."

"Only lose people when they give themselves away. Perhaps either the mom or son has done that?" Token taps the table as he agrees.

"Isn't the son supposed to be dead?" Dart frowns. "How the fuck could they have found out he's not?"

"Demon organised a funeral. Closed casket, which was incinerated, so everyone should think he's dead," I tell them. "Moving the son was a precaution so no one saw a dead man walking around."

There's another bout of coughing from Smoker, making me want to remind him to kick the habit he's named for. As it's obvious he wants to speak, I wait until he's finished. "It's not easy to remember your assumed name. Maybe one of them gave something away. Or raised suspicions by not answering to it."

"Or they contacted friends or family back where they came from," Blaze, brushing his long dark hair back from his face, suggests.

This is all I fucking need. Our club's been trusted to protect them. Nothing can happen on my watch, not without losing the respect of the other chapters. As always, in the back of my mind, I have a feeling someone is just waiting for me to fuck something up. More to the point, there's my own distrust in my ability to handle shit as I should.

"What do you want to do, Prez?"

What I want to do is go to bed, pull the blanket over my head and forget all my responsibilities. What I don't want is to be the person they turn to, expecting me to have the answers at hand. Been there. Done that. Jumped the wrong fucking way, and there's nothing to say I'd get it right if I'm challenged again. Inwardly I sigh. All I can do is my best.

I rap my knuckles on the table as I think. "It said increase security, not that there was a clear and present danger."

"The only security we currently provide is making sure that nothing looks amiss at the house," Dart summarises. "We could increase the drive-bys, maybe. Or get inside and install mics and cameras?"

"Good idea, but how? We can't just turn up and demand entry, we're not supposed to know who or where they are." Glancing at Dart I raise and lower my shoulders, in return he gives a small shake of his head.

"Who are they hiding from?" Reboot, who I still slip up and

often call Lloyd, leans back in his chair. Reboot got his name from Token who'd gotten fed up with Lloyd taunting him with his own phrase whenever there was a technical problem. When Token had threatened to *re-boot* him right out of the clubhouse, the name had stuck.

He's asked a good question though. I glance at Dart and raise my eyebrow. It's his turn to shrug, then he raises his chin. *Do I tell them? Up to you.*

Yeah. Of course it will be up to me. I'm the prez. The buck stops here. They know about the woman and son which is the part that is secret. Letting them in on the rest of the knowledge that Demon had given to me could help if we've got something heading our way. Taking in a breath, I let it out on a sigh and finally answer Reboot's question. "They're hiding from a man called Alder Cantor. He's into drugs, deep into drugs. He brings them over the border from Mexico. Dan Forster, as the kid's known now, was responsible for fuckin' up his current routes."

"Was he bringing them in via San Diego?" Scribe asks.

I gesture with my hands—*No fucking clue.*

"Maybe it's coincidence," Pennywise suggests. "If he's trying to establish new routes, it could be via Tijuana. Perhaps someone just knows he's too close for comfort and the woman and man need to keep their heads down."

"Who knows they're here?" Dart asks but answers his own question. "The feds, Demon and us. But the feds don't know we know. Demon would just come out and tell us if there was a problem that needed to be faced. Who else knows? And why contact us? The only person searching for a man who he believes dead is Alder. It's crazy as to why he would be searching for a walking corpse in the first place, and, if it were him, what led him to look in San Diego?"

And that, there, is the million-dollar question.

"Let's break this down," I start, getting my brain cells working. "First, if there's a need to increase security, that can only mean Alder's on their trail."

"Could this Dan have made any other enemies? Or his mother for that matter?"

"I can ask Demon." I nod at Grumbler for raising the point. "We might need to do some digging. If Demon knew, I'd have expected him to tell me straight off."

"Apart from the person who warned us, in order for a warning to be required, someone who shouldn't know they are in San Diego does indeed know, and so that begs the question how?"

Thinking, I narrow my eyes at Niran and purse my lips. It's impossible to answer.

"Maybe someone saw them."

I just stare at Snips. The population of San Diego is over one point three million and growing all the time. Needle and fucking haystack come into my mind. I suppose it's possible, but highly unlikely. They're not exactly high profile.

"More likely one of them fucked up, contacted someone they shouldn't have."

At least Salem is thinking logically. That's my gut feeling as well.

My VP is staring down at his hands. After a moment he looks at me. "Wouldn't hurt to check it out, Prez."

"How?" Grumbler asks, reaching down to rub his leg.

"Ask them."

I grimace. "That means we have to come out of the woodwork and let them know we know they're in town." I wonder if they might think it could have been us who have had loose mouths, but I trust every man seated around this table. *You always have,* a little voice in my head reminds me. *You didn't see Snake was, well, a snake in the grass.*

"Nobody here has said anything?" I decide to ask, watching

carefully for anything resembling guilt on their faces. "Let something slip unintentionally?"

I'm gratified when there's not a sudden chorus of denials. Looking down the table, I can see frowns as everyone seems to be considering carefully whether they might have inadvertently betrayed the knowledge.

Kink clears his throat. "Apart from the drive-bys, which I suppose it's possible someone noticed, I don't think any of us have given much thought to the pair. You asked us to look out for them, but not why or who could be on their trail. Haven't got much to let slip in any event. Couldn't even describe them."

There are murmurs of agreement.

"We don't mix much with citizens, and those who come to our parties are here for our cocks, not our information. The club girls and prospects know fuck all about them. I'd say we're watertight, Prez." I nod at Keeper.

"Anyone get the feeling someone's watching us?" Niran looks around. Like him, several men here are ex-services who tend to get twitchy when there's trouble around. If they'd picked up a tail when riding around San Diego, they'd probably have noticed.

"Nah," Salem says. "The hairs on the back of my neck haven't been standing up." Again, there are murmurs of agreement.

"What if someone's fishing?" Grumbler suggests. "What if this contact of Token's guesses they're close to a chapter of the Satan's Devils because of the connection with Pueblo and want to see if they can smoke them out? I don't much like getting anonymous messages."

I scribble a note down, tending nowadays to use pen and paper, eschewing my dependence of technology in the past. "Grumbler's got a good point. I'll contact Drummer, Snatcher and Red and see whether they've been approached as well. I suppose I ought to have words with Demon." I run my hand through my hair. "If we do nothing and something happens to them, Colorado would be after our scalps. But if whoever it is went to the trouble to send an anonymous tip only to us, they know something they shouldn't be knowing. You're right, sergeant-at-arms, it could be a trick."

"It was all done verbally," Dart picks up. "No emails. You arranged everything with Demon using your secure phones."

"Give me yours after church," Token demands. "I want to check your security and antivirus."

"You set it up, Token," I growl.

"Yeah, and advances in technology are being made all the time. I'll install the latest version of antivirus—there's been another update recently—but it is possible you were hacked, which means your calls could have been recorded and listened to."

"Or Demon's," Dart suggests. "That would make more sense. The woman we're supposed to be looking out for is the mother of his member's old lady, and the man, her brother. If someone knew they'd gone, they might have monitored his phone to get information."

"That's another point we can't overlook. The someone who contacted Token must know the son is alive." It's another worrying part of the puzzle which seems to be fragmenting into more and more pieces as we debate.

"But why make a move now? They've been here three months. Why not do something when they first arrived?"

"Might be barking up the wrong tree looking at history," Dart intelligently observes. "The son used to be into some shady business, who's to say he hasn't picked that back up? Might be a recent issue."

"Could he be dealing? Using the info that he had from Alder?" The VP's caught the sergeant-at-arm's interest.

I couldn't rule it out, but, "He'd be pretty stupid to use routes he's already given up to the feds. Unless, of course, he held something back."

Kink looks up. "Apart from the feds who I think we can discount, and Demon, the only people who know the pair are in San Diego and have their address are those sitting around this table. If none of us have let anything slip, and as I'd trust everyone here with my life, I doubt anyone's been loose-mouthed, the only ways someone could have learned are from your phone as Token suggested, or from us driving past the house. Both I'd say are unlikely. I still think it's the bitch herself, or her son. They've stepped out of line." He toys with his long hair for a moment. "In which case, do we let them reap what they've sown?"

I let that question ride for now. If they have brought it on themselves, I'll have to have a discussion with Demon as to whether or not we help them out. My gut feel is that we leave them to deal with any fallout.

"Not going to protect their asses if they've brought trouble on themselves." Dart looks angry, as he voices what's on my mind. "I've got a fuckin' family and don't want men like Alder sniffing around. Nearly lost Alex once, I'm not going to risk losing her again."

"I hear you, Brother." I give him a sharp nod.

Blaze looks around, his eyes narrowed. "I hear you, brothers. But aren't you forgetting one thing? We might not be close neighbours of the Colorado chapter, but they're brothers all the same. I respect their wishes as much as I fuckin' would any of ours." I tilt my head, wondering where he's going with this. "It's fuckin' hard going into WitSec. Sure, they should have been more careful if they gave themselves away, but I can't see how we could step back and not help."

Dart wipes a hand over his face, then he seems to deflate. He turns to me. "Prez, this chapter rode by my side when I needed to save Alex, and my patch was still Tucson's then. Blaze has a good point. They're under the protection of the Satan's Devils, and whatever the reason they're in danger, Satan's Devils should help them out." Dart's the only one of us with an old lady, let alone kids to keep safe. His worry is understandable. What he's said though, strikes a chord.

Smoker coughs, then says quietly, "Hear, hear."

Bones wipes his nose. "The road captain and VP make good points. Don't see how we can keep out of this."

Token raises his chin. "Someone's found out our chapter's involvement, and that's what I don't like. But the immediate question has to be the content of the message. It didn't suggest a threat to us as a club, but instead offered a suggestion. Are we going to act on it?"

Again my hand raps on the table, then I come to a decision. "Okay. First, I'm going to call Demon. Token, got faith in you, Brother, but maybe talk to your counterpart Cadaver in Colorado? Join forces to see if we can smoke this contact out? Demon's got an iron in this fire, so he won't want to be in the dark. Not when it's the family of one of his member's old lady's that's at risk."

"I'm cool with talking to Cad." Token grins. I don't doubt he is, likewise with Mouse in Tucson, and Keys in Vegas. All the tech guys like talking to people who speak the same language.

We need information. At the moment we're working blind and digging through records will only get us so far. I need to go to the source and see what I can find out. "I'll go visit the Forsters and see if the leak came from them. Yeah, Salem, I know what you're going to say. Maybe someone's dangling a threat in front of us because they suspect our connection. I'll take every precaution to ensure I'm not followed, but it's a risk I need to take. I'm not leaving this club exposed without knowing what we're up against." I grin. "Not that I'm exactly up with all the cloak and dagger stuff, but I'll take a car, leave my cut behind, and go visit them under the cover of darkness. See whether either of them has fucked up."

"I can get you a wig as a disguise, Prez."

Now Kink's comment, of course, raises a laugh. As the discussion starts about whether I should be a blond or brunette and whether I should don a dress, I kick back my chair. I'm still shaking my head as I walk out, leaving the rest of them to it.

CHAPTER FOUR

Patsy

Dan's working a late shift again. I put out of my mind what I did that night last week when he was working late, knowing I'll never dare do that again. It hadn't helped much in any event.

It's when he's out in the evenings I feel most alone. Not so much during the daytime as I'd gotten used to Beth being at work. But when she wasn't out with her friends or doing her own thing, we'd curl up next to each other on the couch, open a bottle of wine and watch a movie or some reality show where we poked fun at the contestants. Sometimes we'd just read, or I'd sit sewing while she told me about her day. Doing the same thing on my own is so different. If I'm truthful, even when Dan is home, it's not the same. My son doesn't want to talk about the same things or want to watch the same kind of movies. More often than not, he holes up in his room playing computer games.

I'm not rethinking coming with my son, but what had seemed so easy back then has been infinitely harder than I expected. I feel like I've been put in solitary.

Maybe I should join a club or something, get to know people here? But what club would I join? My one hobby, sewing, has become my full-time job, and having a break is my form of relaxation. A book club? Perhaps, but would I find one who likes the same books as I read? I've no idea what to look for. Fitness classes? I huff a laugh. That's not for me.

Tonight I'm sitting, stuffing chocolates into my mouth while simultaneously feeling guilty for indulging. I'm staring at a program on the television which isn't holding my interest. It's the kind I used to watch with Beth, but without her sassy comments, I find it flat and boring. Instead of concentrating on what's going on onscreen, I'm wondering what I should do with my life now that my best friend, my daughter, isn't in it. I never expected it would be this hard to make a new life. My problem is, my old one was so comfortable. Trying to move on is like breaking in a new pair of shoes which you know will never replace your favourites.

Just as I'm reaching for the television remote to change the channel, I'm startled by an unfamiliar sound, well, at this time of the evening anyway. It's the doorbell chiming.

I'm not expecting anyone.

Maybe it's a solicitor or someone coming to the wrong house? While I don't feel any particular need to worry, it's been ingrained in me to be cautious, so I glance through the peephole before opening the door.

It's a man who I don't recognise, certainly not one of the neighbours who could feasibly have knocked. He's the type that if I'd ever come across him before, he'd have been etched in my mind. Not young, approaching my age, perhaps, but while his hair is greying, his eyes are sharp, and his features handsomely arranged. He looks well built, a tidy beard on his jaw, and his clothes, though casual, are clean. *Who is he?* And more to the point? *Why is he here?* There's something inherently dangerous about him that makes me feel uneasy.

Could he be a friend of Dan's? But he didn't mention anyone would be coming around. He certainly isn't in or even close to my son's age group, and like me, Dan is wary about giving anything about us away, and wouldn't have told anyone our address.

Deciding discretion is the better part of valour, I tiptoe away from the door. *I'll pretend no one's in.*

Returning to the living room, which is at the rear of the house, I switch off the television, then take a seat out of view of the windows.

He'll go away when the door remains closed.

What's that? I strain my ears. I thought I'd heard a sound. I must be imagining things. Then I leap to my feet as I hear something else, the clump of boots on the wooden floor right here in my hall.

I freeze to the spot as I hear a voice grumble, "Your lock is shit. I picked it in like five seconds flat."

He's in my house. A stranger is in my house. I know it, but don't know what the hell to do about it.

"Should have dead bolted it," he admonishes, his words now sounding louder as he rounds the corner and comes into sight.

"I, er… My son wouldn't be able to get back in," I defend while backing away from the stranger who's invaded my home. "And he'll be home any moment now." I fumble with my hands behind me, cataloguing what I've left there. A handy baseball bat would be nice about now, or a dagger or knife, but there's not even a heavy ornament I can hold and get ready to brain him with.

"Soon as you saw a strange man at the door, you should have thrown those fuckin' bolts," he scolds me again.

Hang on. *He's just broken into my house, and he's the one telling me off?*

"Well, I won't be able to keep anyone out if you've broken the lock."

"Didn't need to break in." He pauses then huffs a short laugh. "Well, not by causing any damage." After holding up a credit card he's still got in his hand, he slides it back into his wallet.

I come to my senses. "Get out of my house." My body is shaking, but I manage to keep my voice firm.

While on first sight his appearance and manner doesn't seem threatening, it's not the first time I've had strange men breaking into my house. The last time was when my daughter was kidnapped. I feel my face going white as the blood drains from it and get a dropping sensation in my stomach as I realise this will probably end badly for me. He was right, *why hadn't I thrown that bolt?*

"Who are you? What do you want?" I shoot a look past him, realising my phone is in my purse, and my purse is by the front door. I'd have to pass him to get it. I'm trapped.

He's a big man, six foot I estimate, seeing the comparison between him and the height of the doorway he's standing in. He's muscular and has some tattoos. To my chagrin, my brain goes off on a tangent as I realise I'll have a handsome kidnapper at least—someone attractive to look at while I'm stolen away and sent to my untimely and probably unpleasant death.

"Oh, babe." His eyes land on me. "I'm not here to cause you harm. I'm Lost." His voice is as attractive as he, deep, gravelly. The kind of voice a man should use when he's making love to you in the bedroom.

What? I want to slap myself around the head. This man's just broken into my house using a piece of plastic to open the door. Only criminals do stuff like that, so, de facto, this is a man intent on doing bad things. Coupled with that, it's been nearly twenty years since I had a man in my bed. Getting aroused nowadays takes one of those MC books I've been reading and a session with my BOB. I wouldn't know what to do with a real dick anymore.

"Lost," he repeats with a slight quirk to his mouth, making me blush, wondering whether he can read my thoughts.

Then the word filters through my head. *He broke in to ask for directions?*

Swallowing rapidly, I decide my best course of action is to play along. "Er, wh-where do you want to go?"

He chuckles. "I'm right where I wanna be, babe."

Babe? I don't think anyone's ever called me that. Even my ex wasn't imaginative enough to use anything other than my name. Suddenly, I realise he's used it as he doesn't know where he is, or who I am. I'm starting to think a lunatic's broken into my house, and I must be as crazy as he as I find myself offering my name to replace the term of endearment falling inappropriately from his lips.

"I'm Patsy." There, now he can stop with the babe thing.

He does that raising of the chin thing men tend to do. "Right, introductions done. Can we sit and talk?"

Introductions done? All I know is that he's in the wrong house, and has admitted it, telling me only that's he's mislaid his path. Now he wants to *talk?* That's probably a euphemism, or a new approach for a kidnapper or rapist. Or does he want me to tell him where my valuables are so he can rob me? Well, he's come to the wrong house. I've nothing worth stealing.

Despite the fact he's where he shouldn't be, he doesn't appear overly threatening, which is strange. Though would a would-be rapist walk in with a glowing sign over their head? Alder and Phil were criminals and nothing about their appearance would lead you to suspect their depravities. Nevertheless, while I'm considering whether he's got any evil intent, when he casually sits on my sofa, right in the seat I'd so recently vacated, something inside me snaps.

"Who are you?" I spit at him. "And what the hell do you think you're doing in my house?"

"I'm Lost," he says again, arching an eyebrow as if that explains everything. "And I just want to have a chat with you, babe."

"Don't babe me," I say fast, wanting to keep him at a distance even just verbally. "I want you to leave."

His head moves side to side, and an amused smirk appears. He's placed himself between the door and me. If I tried to run, he'd intercept me, and as for me physically fighting him off? Not a freaking chance.

As I'm summing up my non-existent escape routes, he informs me, "I'm not gonna leave until you start listening. Because, babe, you need to hear what I've got to say."

"Are you some kind of salesman?" I offer the first innocent suggestion that comes into my head. I wonder what he's selling if he is and whether I'd buy anything from him if that would make him leave. Though it's unlikely, his skin is weathered as if he works outside, and his hands… Christ, I had to look at them, didn't I? They lie loosely in his lap, but the position doesn't hide the fact that they're large. And if it's true what they say, their proportions makes me think another part of him is unlikely to disappoint.

Shit. I am not going to go near those books again. They've put too many ideas in my head.

"Sit, babe." He pats the seat beside him, half turning to make me space.

"No." I fold my arms and glare, determined not to go anywhere near this strange man. "I want you to leave. My son will be home shortly," I warn him again.

"Babe." Now he stresses the word as he stands. He stalks toward me. I take a step back, and start circling around, my cunning plan being to get to the door. But he steps this way and that, and belatedly I realise that unknowingly, I've been herded toward the piece of furniture he so recently vacated. I've nowhere to go when my retreat is halted by the back of my knees hitting the sofa. Those hands I admired are closer now, and warm when he places them on my shoulders. "Sit," he says again, this time applying pressure to push me down.

It's the first time a man, other than my son or son-in-law-to-be, has touched me in many years. That, and the shock of this encounter must be the reason why I comply without putting up a fight.

He sits beside me, turning his body so he can watch my face.

There's nothing between me and the door. Am I faster than him? Could I reach the door, grab my phone and, I don't know, run into the street and scream for help?

"No." He shakes his head with another of those half-grins, half-smirks. Mind reading is clearly one of his talents. "Stay where you are, Patsy. I can't go without having this conversation, babe. Shit." He rubs a hand over his face and his mirth fades away. "I'm Lost. Told you that. But that obviously doesn't mean anything to you, so let me explain. I'm President of the San Diego Chapter of the Satan's Devils MC." Again, an eyebrow rises.

My initial thought is that I've fallen asleep and am in a dream world of one of those books that I read, then his words sink in, and I know if he's who he says he is, then perhaps I do need to listen to him. My fear for myself recedes. Satan's Devils have never done anything to worry me, but unease for someone else takes its place. "Has something happened to Beth?" My face pales, going to the only reason I can think of his coming to visit me.

"Not that I know of." He shrugs.

So why is he here? And can I trust he's really who he says he is? "Who's the president of the Colorado chapter?" I ask quickly.

"Demon," he replies without hesitation. "He's married to Violet and they've got a small boy. He's knocked her up again, I believe. Beef is his VP." He is certainly dropping the right names. "Your daughter, Beth, is Ink's, one of their members."

He sounds legit. A burglar wouldn't study up on such facts before invading a house, surely? But if he is a Satan's Devil, the president of the local club no less, and he's not here to bring me bad news about Beth, then, "Why are you here?" My eyes narrow and my brows crease.

His lips press together. "Patsy Foster." As he provides my real name, any remaining blood rushes from my face, and my head drops into my hands. The penny hadn't dropped when he'd mentioned Beth, but now it does. He knows exactly who I am, and who my son is. "Patsy," he says fast, clearly noticing my consternation, "when you moved from Pueblo, Demon spoke to Dan. It was his suggestion you relocate here as it's where a Satan's Devils chapter is. The feds were open to Dan's request, without knowing the reason of course, so here you are, where me and my crew could watch out for you."

Demon did? *Dan told him?* My own lips purse as I wonder how I feel about that. "Does Beth know where we are?"

"No," he says quickly. "And she mustn't, Patsy. Nothing's changed on that score."

But if Demon does...

"No," he repeats more firmly, again reading my mind. "Think, Patsy. At the moment, Beth's safe as no one believes she would know anything about your whereabouts. If Alder thought she knew, what would happen then?"

I give a soft gasp. "He'd use her to find me."

Lost nods. "If he didn't completely buy into the story about Dan being dead and buried, he would. Beth's got to remain in total ignorance of where you are."

"But you're looking out for us?" I put two and two together swiftly. "All those bikes going past…?"

"My boys," he confirms. "But don't worry. My VP lives just up the road, there's nothing unusual in them passing by here."

I suppose I can take a certain comfort in that someone has our best interest at heart. But that raises another question. Surely his appearance could raise a red flag? Why would an MC prez be visiting someone like me? "Are you supposed to be here?"

He shakes his head. "No, you're right, I'm not. Look, babe."

I notice we're back to babe now, having gotten past him knowing my name. I realise I'm starting to like it. "I was supposed to be in the background, knowing about you so I could set Demon's mind at rest. I was never supposed to actually meet you. And things would have gone on that way…" He breaks off, and wipes his hands down his face, tugging at his beard. "The last thing I want to do is to worry you, but we've had a disturbing communication. Someone, and fuck knows who, has been in touch with us. The message told us to increase your security."

What? "Like new locks on the door?" There's not much else I can think of.

He gives a sad shake of his head. "No, babe. Not like that, though that's something you need. Not quite sure how if I'm honest. We don't know what we're dealing with yet. We need to find some facts we can work with. Question for you, babe. And I've got to ask you to be totally honest with me. If I don't know, I can't get to the bottom of this." When he pauses, one of those large hands comes up to cup my face. It's gnarled, not smooth, as if he works on the bike he presumably rides. "You left Colorado suddenly and with no reason. I doubt you would be a target yourself, but you could lead them to someone else, your son. The question is, could someone have discovered Connor Foster wasn't cremated in that coffin?"

My hand covers my mouth as I remember that fateful day when I saw the coffin slide behind the curtain. I knew my son wasn't in it, but it hadn't been hard to show the same sadness as if he were. I hadn't yet made, or even considered, the decision to come with him. At that time, I only knew he had to disappear. I'd never know where he was or what happened to him. I was going to give up my son just as if he were really dead. I hadn't had to force my tears at our forthcoming separation.

"He's dead as far as anyone knows," I say, firmly, believing it has to be so. Alder had had doubts, but I'd thought I'd assuaged them. "If anyone asked Beth what happened to me, she was going to say I'd gone travelling and she wasn't sure where, as I was moving around." It was lame, but we didn't expect Alder to come out of the woodwork to ask, or even bother about where I'd gone. For most people the excuse would have worked. With Beth settled, why shouldn't her mom have some fun?

"I think someone knows he's alive or has serious suspicions. Have you had any contact with your daughter? Or anyone from Colorado? Have they tried to call or talk to you? By email perhaps, or text?"

"No."

"No? Come on, babe. Might not know you, but that look away with your eyes—that tells me you're not telling me the truth. There's something you're holding back, and you need to tell me what it is."

"No one could know." This time the guilt makes me lower my eyes. "There's no way anyone could trace it."

"Trace what?" he asks, his voice hardening.

Evading his hold, I stare at my hands, picking at invisible dirt under my fingernails. His fingers come under my chin again.

"Trace what?" he enquires again, this time with the touch of a growl in his voice. When I still don't reply, he sighs. "Look. I haven't got any kids, but I know it must be fuckin' hard, leaving a daughter behind and not having any contact. Even if she's grown and doesn't need her mom everyday anymore."

"She still lived at home, with me," I offer as justification for my actions before I admit what they were. "I saw her every day. She was my best friend, and I, hers."

"Patsy, tell me. What did you do?" His tone is patient, but there's a tick in his jaw.

I take a breath, then let him know what I did. There was no harm in it. I'd been careful and had covered my tracks. In fact, I'm quite proud of myself. "I bought a cheap phone. I called Beth, just to find out if she was okay."

His eyes close for a second, then he asks, tersely, "Where is this phone now?"

"I dumped it immediately afterward. It wasn't my number. No one could have traced it." I almost finish with *ta da* seeing how clever I'd been. I'd briefly heard my daughter's voice, guiltily, I admit, ending the call after only checking she was alright, and no one was any the wiser.

"You led them right to your door."

What? No. I couldn't have. It's my turn to shake my head. "If it were Alder, and there surely can't be anyone else interested in us, he can't know where we live. He won't even know I called her."

His eyebrows rise. "He'll know. And darlin' if you called from this house—"

"I went to La Jolla," I tell him quickly with a roll of my eyes. "I was nowhere near here." Despite my earlier confidence that I'd done nothing wrong, little doubts begin to settle in.

He breathes out. "Thank goodness for small miracles, but this Alder will know the city you live in, and that will narrow his search."

I don't understand. "But how? How can he trace an unknown number from a phone I never used before nor will use again?"

He breathes deeply before explaining how stupid I've been. "He can't. But he could be tracking calls to hers."

I pull away from him and stand, wrapping my arms around my body. "No, it's impossible. He wouldn't know how."

Lost speaks patiently, as if to a child. "Alder smuggles drugs across the border. If he's what I suspect, he's likely to have a huge transport network, routes he can shift when he knows the border control are stepping up on their searches. I assure you, he'll be utilising every fuckin' piece of technology he can get his hands on, babe. He might not be inclined that way himself, but he'll employ someone to do it for him."

I suppose I'm remembering Alder as the sleazy man who was

married to Phil's sister, not as the man who's become a kingpin in a drug network. At my son's mock funeral, he'd been well dressed, even I could see his suit was made to measure and not off the rack. Of course he'd have minions to do his work for him.

Suddenly, though the room isn't cold, goosebumps arise on my skin as the realities sink in. "If you're right, I've blown Dan's cover." I turn to him anxiously. "What would he know? That I'd called her, or would someone have listened to what was said?" I go over the phone call in my head. The delighted sound of Beth's voice as I'd checked in. Our assurances both of us were okay. I hadn't mentioned Dan, or had I? Suddenly I remember, I certainly had. I'd confirmed both of us were okay and were settling in.

Lost stares at me, a concerned look in his eyes. "From this call, would he know that a dead man was alive?"

I hate to admit it, but it is a possibility. "I called him Dan, not Connor. Maybe anyone listening thought I'd moved to be with a man." I glance at him, but he doesn't look hopeful. "Do you really think he's looking for us, Lost? Is that why you're here? That message you got…?"

"Was a warning, babe. For us to be on our toes. And worst-case scenario? I think Alder knows your son is alive, and that you're both here in San Diego."

I'd messed up, and badly. I'm shaking as I probe to discover just how deep a hole I'd dug. "What are the chances of his finding us? It's a big city, he doesn't know our new family name, and Connor's Dan now. Dan's job only knows his new identity, not who he was before. All our documents are in our new names."

"If I were Alder, I'd get a private investigator looking into you. People buying or renting a house at a time which fits the dates. Heck, new employees starting jobs. What about you? Do you work, babe?"

"I do, but I work from home. I'm a designer, and all my stuff is emailed to the company which uses my designs. And before you ask, Cad, the computer guy back in Colorado, did something to my laptop which hides my IP address and makes it seem like anything I send comes from somewhere else."

Grimacing and again shaking his head, Lost tells me, "I honestly don't know what info he's got, but under the circumstances, I take the message to increase your security seriously."

In which case, I should too. I think of the only people who could help. "Dan needs to go to the feds and get them to relocate us."

CHAPTER FIVE

Lost

From the moment I stepped inside this house, or broke in to be more accurate, I was taken by Patsy. The girls at the clubhouse I can take em' or leave em', and in recent years do the latter. I'm not a man who's turned on by women half my age, preferring someone more mature who I can have a conversation with, and one who's not expecting an athletic man who can keep at it for hours. Nowadays I can manage once, then am satisfied just to cuddle and sleep after.

Truth be told, sex isn't high on my agenda, and I can take it or leave it. I was twenty-two when I got married, thirty-four when we divorced. I hadn't gone crazy when I regained my freedom, too much else was happening for me to think about getting laid.

It's unusual for my cock to perk up at the mere sight of a woman. Today, though, I have to be grateful that my jeans are not particularly tight.

That Patsy wasn't immune to me either was evident. Though she was naturally scared about a strange man being in her house, I sensed there could be a reciprocal interest. It was an intriguing situation, but one I wasn't in any particular hurry to do anything about. Getting my rocks off I can do just as well with my hand in the shower, and it doesn't expect hearts and flowers to follow as a result. Patsy? If I read her right, she's a respectable woman and not one to enter into what could only be an enjoyable interlude jumping into the bed of an MC prez.

Even though I dismissed any thought of exploring this mutual attraction further, I noticed how she flushed when I used the word *babe* instead of her name. It amused me, so I continued.

But now all thoughts of anything to do with sex and a bed has been pushed aside as I consider how to proceed with the predicament she's gotten herself in.

Sure, she'd fucked up and potentially brought trouble on herself. She'd not been as clever as she'd thought when she contacted the daughter she shouldn't have been talking to. But hell, who can blame her? She's a mom, of course she'd want to ease her mind and reassure herself everyone she'd left behind was fine. Problem is, if Alder does indeed know her son is alive, he probably won't rest until he's dead.

Of course her first impulse is to run again, and there's probably a good chance that after a slap on the wrist, the marshals will help them get settled elsewhere. But how long before she slips up again? She's a mother who's desperate to know what's going on in the life of her daughter.

She could be relocated anywhere, or maybe, she wouldn't. I revise my thinking. Maybe this time, the feds would move her son on his own. He's the one the marshals want to protect in case they need his testimony. I doubt she's thought about being split up, but she was the one who'd betrayed them. As far as I know, Dan has kept his mouth shut.

If they did move them both, someone else will have the responsibility of watching out for her. My fear is they'll go to Alaska, or somewhere where there are no Devils or MCs we know and trust. Surely, that's worse than her staying in California, where at least I can have an eye on her?

She's a woman who brings forth all my protective instincts and I already know I'll want to do what I can to help her.

She's naïve. Not about life, in everyday living I'm sure she's competent, but in our world? She doesn't have a clue about security or protecting herself. I suspect Dan isn't much better, else he'd have already changed that lock.

But how can I help them? How can I do this and not involve my club in danger that isn't our business? *Leave it to the marshals. Not my problem.* I try to tell myself that, but my brain seems focused on what assistance I could provide.

I consider what we know and what we don't. The likelihood is that Alder knows the city they are staying in, or at least have recently visited, but not their exact location. Maybe we can prevent him finding out and coming closer? What if we moved them to a new house, or, temporarily, into the clubhouse?

She's standing watching me, waiting for my response.

"I don't think relocating again is the answer."

She briefly closes her eyes. "I admit, moving is the last thing I want to do. I've just gotten settled." She looks around the house that's already showing signs of a woman's touch. "It will be an upheaval for Dan. He's just gotten his job and plans to enroll in college in the fall. But I don't see any other option, Lost. Even the suggestion Alder knows my son isn't dead is terrifying."

I should tell her there are jobs and colleges anywhere, but the words seem to get stuck in my throat. Instead, I point out some home truths to her. "The marshals will want to know how you fucked up, babe. What if they decide you're a risk to Dan? They could move him, but not you."

Now her eyes go wide. "But, but… They wouldn't do that, would they?"

"They very well might," I confirm. "Or could you promise not to fuck up again?"

Her mouth opens, then shuts. "It's hard, Lost. Harder than I expected. I thought as Beth had her own life now, I could leave her alone to live it. But I miss her so damn much. Ink said he wanted a baby with her. I want to be there. I can't bear the thought that I won't be able to help. I may not even know that I'm a grandmother."

I have to appreciate her honesty. "But you must have expected that when you decided to go into exile with Dan," I say, a bit harshly.

"I did," she cries. "But it all happened so quickly. I didn't have long to make up my mind, and Con… Dan, well he might be twenty-two and an adult, but he still needs me. The relief when I said I'd come with him was written all over his face. Beth's five years older, and she's got Ink. I'd feel I was abandoning him if I let him go alone. That was why I made my decision. I knew it wasn't going to be easy, but I had no idea exactly how difficult it was going to turn out. I miss her, Lost. Miss her terribly."

It sounds like a tough choice. My wife and I hadn't gotten around to starting a family. I'd been working so hard building up a business, and she, well, she'd been too busy fucking around. Literally, as I'd later found out.

Patsy turns and walks to the window. Her shoulders hunch. "You're right, Lost. If we move again, I don't know how I'd survive not knowing how Beth's doing. The marshals may not help, as you say, they might move Dan on his own as he's the one they want to keep safe." She swings around. "I want both my children, Lost. I know I'm selfish, but I can't make the choice. Not now I know my sanity is at stake. Beth's not just my daughter, she's my best friend, my confidant. I miss talking to her. Talking to Dan, well, he's a man. It's not the same."

"Have you made any friends here?"

She raises and lowers her shoulders. "I haven't exchanged more than a couple of words with the neighbours, they're not particularly the friendly type. I thought about joining a group or something, but then I got scared. What if I forget what I can reveal, and what I can't? If I talk about what I do, I'm sure to let slip the reason why I make clothes for taller women—that they're for my daughter. How could I explain why I can't see her? I can't risk it, Lost. I'm not that good a liar."

It sounds like a lonely life, I silently observe, not missing that her eyes are glistening. Christ, she should never have moved. She should have left Dan to atone for his sins alone or abandoned him to get into more trouble without her guiding hand. Again I think how fucked up it is for a good woman like her to be forced to choose between her son and her daughter.

Like her, I stand, walking over to the windows and look out into the night. There's only one answer I can come up with—putting Alder in the ground. But the man's a ghost. The feds can't find him, so there's probably no chance we can.

"Why is Alder so fixated on Dan?" I ask, half to myself. "What's it matter that he's alive? Is there something he's not yet told the feds, something he's keeping to himself?"

"Dan wouldn't have held anything back," she replies. "He wanted to keep out of jail, so he told them everything he could."

I wonder if that's true. What if Dan had been involved in something that would implicate him in a serious crime? He might not have come clean about that.

Her face looks tight. "Dan gave the feds Alder's name as the man behind the influx of drugs. Because of Dan, they know who they're looking for. He was forced to go underground. If, or when he surfaces, Dan will have to testify."

"Whether Dan's there to testify won't make any difference to Alder being convicted." Again, I'm thinking aloud. "He was a bystander and not involved. His information pointed the feds in the right direction. A whistleblower if you like. A conviction would have to be based on proving Alder's involvement, and Dan's word alone wouldn't be good enough for that."

"So Alder wants revenge on the man who destroyed his business. He's a spiteful man who holds a grudge."

I consider her offered explanation for a moment. Something doesn't sit right with me. "Alder's a businessman. I'd have thought his concentration would be on rebuilding what he lost, getting his revenue stream flowing again. From what I hear, Dan probably threw a wrench in the works, but didn't halt it."

Sure, a man like Alder would want revenge, but would he put that much effort into getting it? Of course I don't know the man, but it doesn't seem likely. What purpose would it serve unless Dan hadn't done all the damage he could have? If Dan has told the feds everything, what would killing him achieve, other than giving Alder a good night's sleep? He'd be wasting time and resources tracking Dan, when surely, he's got higher priorities? A lot of this doesn't make sense and needs more consideration.

Of course, there's one person who might be able to shed more light on this. "When's Dan back?"

"Ten o'clock," she tells me.

Taking out my phone, I see that's just an hour's time. "I'd like to wait and speak to him, if that's okay with you?"

"You're going to tell him, aren't you?" Her mouth twists as though she's just tasted something unpleasant. "You're going to tell him how I messed up."

"He has to know." I close the gap between us and turn her to face me. "Hate having to tell you this, but the net may be closing in. Do you want him forewarned, or just to go on oblivious to any danger he might be in? He's a grown man, not a kid. He needs to be part of any discussion about whether you stay or go, or whether that's together or alone. It's his life on the line, Patsy. It's got to be down to him."

She stares up at me, then looks away. "I suppose you're right."

"There could be other options we could discuss."

"Such as?"

I don't want to let her in on a half-baked idea. "We'll know more once I've talked to Dan, babe."

The first time I'd called her babe she'd bristled, the second she'd gone red. Since then, she softens, and half smiles each time I say it. During our serious discussion I'd avoided using it, but now we've talked that to death, I want to lighten the atmosphere again. To test out my theory, I repeat the endearment. "So, babe, is it okay if I wait?"

Yup. I was not wrong. *She likes it.* In fact, so much so, it's flustered her, and she hasn't answered my question.

"Have you got a beer?"

"What? Oh, yeah. Dan's got some in the fridge. I'm more a wine girl myself." Words now tumble out one after the other. I grin. She's acting like a gauche teenager, not the middle-aged woman she is. I find I like it.

As she goes off in the direction of what I assume is the kitchen but doesn't quickly return, I think she's probably taking a moment to pull herself together.

I take the opportunity to do the same myself. I'm here on a mission, not to have my interest sparked in a woman who means nothing at all to me. But damn it, while the subject hadn't been pleasant, a discussion about a man who'd nearly succeeded in a previous attempt to kill her son, part of me had enjoyed the debate.

I'm the prez of an MC. I might be older than most of my members, but my cut and my bike still attract attention. I've kept myself in shape over the years. My hair might be grey, but I haven't let myself go. When I ride with my men, it may be because I wear the patch that denotes me as the highest-ranking member, but woman flock to me just like they do the younger men.

I can get laid anytime I want to.

I fucked around when I first got my patch, but soon found what I liked best was having a woman to come home to and not just for sex. It was the holding each other, talking to each other, sharing our days, our successes and tribulations, all the trappings which make a relationship work. There's more to marriage than athletics in the bedroom, much more. What attracts in the beginning becomes just a small part of what matrimony offers.

I'd always thought I'd had a good-enough marriage, until my failures became too great, too much of a burden to be shared.

Truth be told, I don't meet many women my own age. I don't have kids so I don't meet single parents. I don't have hobbies outside of my club, so I rarely meet civilians. Nice women my age tend to shy away from motorcycle riding, leather-clad, tattooed men.

Just for once it's nice to meet someone in the same age group who gives me a second glance.

Still waiting for her to return with my beer, I sigh. I like her, but even if she liked me in that way, there's no way I could go there. Somehow I manage to fool an MC that I'm capable of leading it, and that takes all my time and energy trying to do that right. I can't split my loyalties and take on responsibility for somebody else, someone who'll demand my commitment to her. That I can't fully give, not when I'm married to my club.

"Sorry. I, er..." Whatever excuse she's about to use for her tardiness dies on her lips as she clearly has difficulty uttering a lie.

Taking pity on her, I take the opened beer from her hand. "How do you like living in San Diego?"

"It's warmer than I'm used to," she says, smiling. "I'm looking forward to the winter as it won't be as cold as it is in Colorado." Then her face falls. "If I'm still here then."

"Have you been getting out much? Seeing the sights?"

She sighs and sits down. After waving me to a seat opposite, she takes a sip of her wine. "Not really. My time's been taken up with moving in, setting up the house, making sure Dan's okay, and of course, working. Dan and I have tried to get out from time to time, but I think we're both wary of going out in public."

Their sense of security won't improve now they know Alder knows they're in this city.

"Dan's fully healed now?" I recall her son had taken a nasty beating, stabbed too.

"Physically he's fine."

"Mentally?"

"He's twenty-two, Lost. He's already made mistakes. He'd idolised his dad, then when his eyes were opened, realised what he was. I think he hates himself for staying so long and doing what his dad asked of him. Then, of course, the way it ended, when his dad condoned the way he was treated, and knowing he wouldn't have blinked an eye if Dan had died? It's hard for someone his age to get his head around."

"Your ex is dead." It's a statement, not a question.

She nods. "Don't expect me to feel any grief for him."

I don't. Phil Foster was as evil a man as ever lived. Demon had shared the details with me. Phil had been running a small human trafficking ring when he died. He'd kept women as prisoners in his basement, waiting to be sold. When he'd kidnapped Beth, his own daughter, he was going to sell her as well. The Satan's Devils MC Colorado chapter had been responsible for taking him out.

"So, to answer your question, I haven't really gotten to know the area yet. Now Dan's working, it's a bit lonely sightseeing on your own."

I hear the sound of the front door being opened, properly this time, with a key not a credit card.

"That you, Dan?"

"Who else would it be?" comes the returning shout. "Mom, there's a—" He stops abruptly as his eyes land on me. "Oh fuck."

I cock an eyebrow.

"There's a car parked outside our house." He completes his

original statement. A muscle in his face ticks as he asks with deliberate casualness, "Who are you?"

Standing, I hold out my hand. "The name's Lost. I'm a friend."

"Ain't got no fucking friends in California," he responds, looking down at my outstretched fingers as if my hand was a poisonous snake. "Mom, do you know him? How did you meet?"

Patsy goes to talk, but I wave her down. "Dan," I snap, bringing his attention back to me. "I ride with the Satan's Devils' San Diego Chapter."

"The Satan's Devils?" The name gives him pause, in fact, he barely seems to breathe.

I nod, and go to explain, but I'm not given the chance.

"No one should know we're here, it's too risky." His hands are clenched, and his muscles on his forearm are bunched. He looks like he's getting ready to run, just deciding whether to punch me first before he does.

"I appreciate that. I wouldn't have come if I hadn't had a need."

He's tall, fairly well built, but his muscles are baby ones compared to mine. I might be old, but I'm fast, and experienced. I recognise the expression in his eyes. It's fear. While he stays tense, I relax my posture and point to the seat on the couch beside his mom.

"Why don't you sit, and I'll explain why I've come."

Baulking at my suggestion, he shakes his head. "I want to know now why you're here, and what you know about us, and whether we need to leave?"

It's clear to see he's hanging onto the hope that I only know him as Dan, and his mom by her new surname—Forster, instead of Foster. I dispel him of that immediately, the questions I want answered can't be done on the basis of lies.

"Your mom moved with you, Connor." He stiffens even more

at the use of his real name, so I don't hesitate in continuing. "You left your sister behind. A sister who's older but who very much cares for your mom, and, your mom cares for her."

Connor spares a glance at his mother. "Is this because of you, Mom? Perhaps you should have stayed in Colorado."

"Dan, I—"

I slash my hand through the air. "You going to listen to me?" When his eyes come back to mine, I carry on, "You told Demon where you were heading."

"In confidence—"

"Demon suggested San Diego on purpose. Asked me to keep an eye on you."

"Those bikes we keep hearing, Dan," Patsy butts in, "that's them making sure we're alright."

Dan rolls his eyes. "Like you can tell anything from riding past every couple of days."

"You're right, but we could think about installing motion-triggered cameras." I wipe my hand down my beard as Dan gives me an in to raise what Dart had suggested in church. "Say, if we see anything that shouldn't be here, whoever's watching our security at the time, can get us here fast."

"Motion-triggered cameras?" Patsy exclaims. "So if I went out in the backyard to do naked gardening, someone would be watching me?"

"Babe," I shake my head, chuckling. "Your backyard is not exactly private. I doubt you'd be doing that. But you want to? Just contact me and I'd get the cameras turned off." Or maybe have the feed sent directly to my phone for my personal viewing, and mine only.

I may have many faults, but I've never been someone to get easily distracted. But hell, the thought of Patsy bending over with a watering can in her hand or leaning in to smell a flower, as naked as the fucking day she was born, well, fuck, that has my cock, which nowadays takes a lot to excite it, twitching. I'm also finding it hard to get my mind back on what we were talking about.

Swiftly moving my eyes from her to her son, I address him. “We also keep our ears to the ground. As I told your mother, information has reached us that someone, probably Alder, knows you’re in San Diego.”

Dan reaches out his hand and rests it on the back of the couch, leaning heavily on it. “No,” he breathes. “No one can trace us… unless a leak came from your club?” His half-angry, half-scared eyes fix on mine.

“Wasn’t my club, Dan. We don’t share fuck. I fuckin’ assure you of that.”

“Then how?” His hand forms a fist, which he brings down on the cushion making a dull thud. “How the fuck did anyone find out about us?”

“I messed up, Dan.” Patsy stands and crosses over to him, her hand reaching to rest on his. In a voice that’s not quite steady, she informs him of her mistake. “I needed to hear Beth’s voice, find out if she was okay…”

“Mom? *Mom?*”

CHAPTER SIX

Patsy

Connor's use of that one word coupled with his expression shows utter and complete devastation. I'm gutted, realising how much of a mistake I'd made. Lost pointing out what a fool I'd been hadn't gotten through to me in the same way my son's reaction had. *This was Connor's fresh start.*

After the pain of the last few weeks and the fear that he'd been living with for months before that, fear of the man he at last learned his father could be, and worry he'd never escape his clutches, Connor had felt safe once he arrived in San Diego. He could make himself all over again as Dan, no longer tied to mistakes he'd previously made. No one here knew of his past.

While I'd missed my daughter, I didn't resent that I'd chosen Dan over Beth. The fact that I had, had undeniably formed a new, stronger bond between us. I have to hope my actions hadn't shattered it.

While he'd been growing up, we hadn't shared an easy relationship. I certainly wouldn't win any mom-of-the-year awards, and he was wrong thinking I'd preferred Beth over him, I hadn't. But what I wasn't was the perfect mom, and I'd made a lot of mistakes. What I hadn't seen was that Connor wasn't as naturally academically clever as his sister. He needed an education, and when he didn't get the grades she'd managed at his age, I'd put it down to his being lazy and was on his back about his poor achievements all the time. It was only because I wanted the best for him, but it had backfired. My encouragement had been seen as nagging, and the result was I'd chased him away and into the hands of his father.

Some bridges had been mended when, to make amends, I voluntarily went into exile with him, but now I've betrayed him all over again, by contacting his sister.

"Your mom did the best she could to be careful," I hear Lost explain. "She bought a burner and drove a distance away to use it. She didn't consider that Beth's phone would probably be monitored and thought that was all she needed to do to cover her tracks. Precisely where you live can't be known, just that you're in San Diego."

"I can't believe you were so stupid." Dan rounds on me. "Someone now knows I'm not dead. Do you want to get me killed for real, Mom?"

"Of course I don't," I cry out. "I—"

But he's walked off.

As I move to follow him, Lost takes hold of my arm, a gentle touch, but strong enough that it halts me. "Leave him," he instructs.

"Leave him?" I turn incredulously. "I've got to explain."

"He's a man, he'll work it out," Lost replies confidently. "That's what we do, storm off, give ourselves space to calm down, and then think things through more rationally. I like that in him." He nods after Dan thoughtfully. "Instead of shouting and screaming and saying things both of you would regret, he's taken himself off to cool down."

"He might be packing his bags." I wouldn't blame him if he was filling a suitcase. If I'd brought Alder to our home, we'd have to move like right now.

"He lives in the backyard?" Lost nods over my shoulder. As I turn, I see Dan standing in the beam from the security light in the middle of the grass, his head bowed.

As I stare, Lost leads me out of sight of the window. "Give him some space," he suggests.

"I gave him space when he went to live with his dad. That got us nowhere at all. I thought he'd soon run home with his tail between his legs, but instead he stayed."

"You think it's easy for a man to admit he's wrong?" Lost shakes his head. "Especially at that age, he'd have tried to make what go of it he could. He'd left to make a point to you and wouldn't return until that point had been made. But he was in the wrong place, with the wrong man and unable to do that. In the end, he wanted out, as you know."

"I made so many mistakes with him, Lost. Thought I was making up for them now. Now I've messed up. Look, let me go to him, I have to explain."

"Explain what?" Lost's fingers tighten on the arm he still hasn't let go of. Some primal part of my brain is enjoying the connection between us, but why, I really don't know. Perhaps it's been so long, I'm desperate to have a man's hands on me anyway I can.

"What are you going to explain, babe?" he continues, oblivious to the thoughts in my head. "That you love both your kids equally? That while you're here supporting Dan, Beth is always on your mind? It's not that you prefer one over the other, it's that you're a good mom, and care for them both."

"I—"

I'm interrupted by the voice of my son. "I'm not fucking thinking that, Mom. Get that out of your head. I *know* you care about me. You wouldn't be here if you didn't. But hell, Mom, you must miss Beth. This is the longest you've ever been apart. I *know* you'd like to be part of her life. Fuck it, so would I. But I fucked up and gave up my right to have all my family with me. I've been offered a new start in life and am young enough to take it, but you've been dragged away from everything you've known. Your house you lived in for years is now Beth and Ink's home, you can't speak to your friends, or hold those barbecues when everyone came around. To come with me, you've ripped yourself away from everything, the life you loved as well as Beth."

After the final words of his long speech come out of his mouth, I open mine to tell him it's worth it, but it appears he hasn't finished yet.

"Yeah, you fucked up calling Beth, but all Alder has is the city and state you called from. It's only supposition we live anywhere close by. We've just got to keep our heads down, and hope we stay out of his sights." He grimaces as if he's realised that means staying hidden, only going out when it's essential to do so. It makes him add, "Or, we decide this is the time I use that number to get in touch with the agent they told me to contact in case of trouble. Ask them to move us somewhere else."

"I'm the risk," I tell him, having realised the truth in what Lost had said. "They let me come with you, but only after I begged. Now I've messed up and done exactly what they thought I would, I contacted Beth. They would be in their rights to refuse to relocate me."

Dan looks at me with an expression in his eyes which belie the number of years he's lived on this earth. "Perhaps it's time to face up to hard choices, Mom. I'm the one who needs to pay for what I did. If the marshals will only move me, then maybe that's for the best. You can go back to your life."

"No, she can't," Lost interrupts, brushing a hand through his hair. "Look, I don't know this Alder, but a man doesn't manage to stay one step in front of the feds or arrange pipelines to bring drugs in undetected without having a brain in his head. He knows Patsy, remember? She chose bringing you and your sister up right against living off your dad's ill-gotten gains. He'll know she didn't just abandon you both, not a good woman like her. After losing you, she'd have stayed close to her daughter."

Dan's lips press together. "But she didn't stay with Beth, she left. So following that logic, it's me she's with, so I can't be dead." He shakes his head. "Alder knows I'm alive."

"We can't *know* he thinks that, Dan." I'm clutching at straws, I know.

"I like San Diego," he says tiredly. "I actually like having a job where I don't have to hide from the cops, but I don't know what to do now I'll need to keep looking over my shoulder all the time. When I was 'dead' I could relax and enjoy myself. Work, make friends, do what normal guys of my age do. I could look to my future and think of going to college." He shrugs. "But perhaps I'll just start all over again somewhere else. But, Mom… Look, I know how much you miss Beth."

The expression in his eyes suggests he thinks I'll try to contact her again. He might be right. I might be able to go weeks, months even, but years and never hearing from my daughter again? "All we can hope is this has an end date. Eventually the feds will have to catch Alder. Then it will be safe for us to go home."

Lost snorts. "Not unless Alder is dead. If it's revenge he's after, he'll probably have a long reach even when he's in the pen." As Dan and I exchange dismayed glances, Lost speaks again, continuing in a reasonable tone, "Perhaps there's another option?"

Dan swings around and looks at him hopefully. "What are you talking about? What are you thinking?" I'm glad he asked as I don't have a clue what else we can do other than to stay and risk Alder catching up with us, or one or both of us relocating out of state.

Lost indicates the couch and sits on it. He waves Dan toward the chair opposite him and pats the seat next to him and glances at me.

Accepting his unspoken invitation, I sit, making sure there's a cushion between us. Lost disturbs me in ways I haven't felt for many, many years.

Placing his elbows on his knees, he clasps his hands. "Alder's keeping a low profile, just as you are yourself, Dan. He can't afford to fuck up and show his face. Coming after you means taking risks I'm not sure he'd want to make. Sure, he'd rather you weren't breathing, but this doesn't make sense. The feds want Alder. One sniff he's closing in on you and they could be tempted to use you as bait. Alder must be aware of this, and any move would have to be carefully planned."

My eyes widen. "Could this be down to the feds? Could they have let it be known Dan's not dead?" I gasp at the implications. "Are we being used?"

"Can't completely discount it, but I don't see it's likely. They wouldn't drip feed information, too much could go wrong. Without you being protected, Alder could sneak in under their net. I am wondering whether Dan knows more than he's let on." He raises an eyebrow.

"I know nothing," Dan refutes. He gives me a weak grin. "I'm dead, remember."

"Won't blow smoke up your ass." Lost looks at Dan then me. "As I told your mom, the message we got was cryptic. Might mean nothing at all, but I don't take chances. Which means, I'm gonna act as though someone knows you're alive. Always best to look at things in the worst light. We've been making assumptions your enemy is Alder, but we do need to discover whether anyone else could have you in their sights?"

Dan steeples his fingers beneath his chin. His creased brow shows he's giving the question careful consideration. After a moment, he shakes his head. "I wasn't a choir boy when I worked for Phil, probably made a few enemies when I was debt collecting for him, but they're not the type of folks with the clout to come after me or believe anything other than it was me in that coffin. Alder's the only one who could do that."

"Is there anything you held back when you spoke to the feds about Alder?"

Dan again thinks hard. "I gave them everything I had. I gave away his name, where he lived, the people who worked for him, and the routes I know he used."

"Enough to fuck up his business as we surmised," Lost states. His clasped hands rock up and down. "Any warehouse locations?"

"I didn't know one. But if they picked up the people I named, one of them may have talked."

"One of them may be out gunning for you," Lost reminds him.

Dan nods and agrees. "Could be, I suppose."

"Get me the list of names you gave the feds, I'll get Token, our computer guy, to check them out. See if they're in the pen or walking free men." He gets out his phone and makes a note. "Once we trace them, I can find some connections if they're inside and start asking questions."

"Satan's Devils have men inside?" I ask.

Lost turns and gives me a sad smile. "Not right now. We did, he got sent down a long time back, but he died. We are friendly with other clubs who take more risks than we do, though." He looks back at Dan. "Let's get back to Alder. What's he likely to do? He's still got his contacts over the border and customers this side. Is he able to continue his trade?"

"I fucked it up, but it doesn't mean he can't start over. His supply chain in Mexico is still there. I'd expect that's what he'd do."

Lost makes another note on his phone. "I'll get Token to try and estimate just how much damage was done to Alder, and what the feds did. A warrant is out for his arrest, and they may have been able to freeze any assets in his name, though I suspect he'll have multiple accounts, maybe even untraceable offshore ones."

"I fucked up the entry point he used," Dan points out. "He might find it hard to bring drugs over the border."

"The border is long. He'll find a new way across."

Lost is probably right. But are they forgetting something? "You're talking about the drug trade. What about the girls?" I remember only too well the broken women brought to the clubhouse in Pueblo. I'd been horrified that the same fate—to sell her off as a sex slave—had been planned for Beth as well.

Lost raises an eyebrow at Dan who leans back in the chair. "Phil had trafficked girls. I'm pretty certain he was doing that on his own. A sideline which Alder didn't know about. The feds never questioned me about that in relation to Alder."

"Were Alder and Phil close?"

I huff. "They were brothers-in-law. Thick as thieves from what I remember. Can't see that changing."

"The dynamics had." Dan stares at me. "Phil became more of a junior partner. I think that's why he wanted something for himself."

"It's worth looking into." Lost makes another note. "We'll start digging in that area too. See if we turn anything up." He looks across at Dan. "I agree with you. If Alder came across you, he'd waste no time taking you out of the picture. But I can't see it's worth him putting himself at risk. As for where he is, could he set himself up south of the border?"

"He does have links with the cartel," Dan confirms. "Has to have, that's how the drugs reach him in the first place."

"Okay," Lost stands, getting his car keys out of his pocket, "I'll get back and get Token digging through this shit, see if we can find out more information. I came to warn you, not worry you, okay?"

"Are we safe?" I ask him quickly. "Can I go out for

groceries, and can Dan go to work? Should we go on as we are, or keep our heads down low?"

Lost takes a moment, then tells me, "For now, carry on as usual, but we'll see how this goes. I would suggest I leave a prospect with you, but the reason why I came in the car and without my cut is to hide that the Satan's Devils are interested in whoever lives in this house. You've got links to our chapter in Colorado, so there's a chance they could be watching the club too." His eyes sharpen. "Stay vigilant. I'll leave you my number, and those of my officers. If you see anything suspicious, or think you're being watched or followed, then get somewhere safe, somewhere crowded, and call us. We'll come to you."

It's good advice. I just hope we don't need to take it, I muse as Lost goes to the door.

"You'll tell us if you find anything out?" Dan asks.

"Of course." Lost raises his chin with his reply.

I see Lost out, part of me wishing he wasn't going, part of me wishing he really was what he appeared to be, a man visiting a friend. As I close the door to prevent myself from watching his handsome and shapely for his age figure walk down my driveway, I wished he'd come for something, anything, other than to give me this worrying news.

"Mom, I'm sorry," Dan says contritely when I reappear in the living room. "If I had listened to what you told me about my father, we wouldn't be here now."

He's not too old for a hug it would seem as he opens his arms and I settle into them. "Any apology is on me, Dan. I shouldn't have made that call."

His arms tighten. "Best we accept that we can't change the past or what happened. We just have to deal and move on."

CHAPTER SEVEN

Lost

It's late when I return to the clubhouse. Parking the car, I get out and stretch, rolling my neck to unkink my muscles. I hate driving a cage, even for short distances, feeling trapped without the wind on my face. Living where I do, cars are not such a necessity, we can ride all year, with only rain to deter us. Even then, most of us are hardy enough to ignore what the elements throw at us, preferring to get wet than be caged in.

There are still a few brothers around, I find as I enter, walking in on a common enough scene that I don't raise even an eyebrow. Scribe and Snips have Cindy sandwiched between them; the sweet butt's legs are around Scribe's waist and from the way his pants hang loosely around his hips, his cock is probably deep in her snatch. Snips is bucking his hips against her rear, strongly suggesting his cock is in her ass. Cindy, with her head thrown back in abandon, is clearly one hundred percent engaged and enjoying herself if her cries of encouragement and *harder* are any indication.

In one of the corners, I notice Bones and Blaze are half having a conversation, and half watching the live porn being played out in front of them, while Salem and Pennywise are playing pool.

A bout of coughing informs me Smoker's in the room, his position apparent by the smoke swirling up from the end of the room. Rolling my eyes, I ask Wrangler, who's bartending, for a beer, then walk across to the culprit.

"One," I tell him when I get close, "smoking is going to kill you. And two, you know what was agreed—you fuckin' go outside to smoke."

"Jeez, Prez." He places his hand over his heart. "Warn a brother, will ya? Didn't hear you approach. And Tyler's fine nowadays, and he's not even here."

"Okay," I say deceptively reasonably. "When Dart's old lady brings the baby in and gets a whiff of that smoke, I'll point the finger at you. That will be alright, won't it? As it doesn't matter."

It's a big fucking matter to my VP as everyone knows, and everyone but Smoker goes outside to get their nicotine fix, or to smoke weed. But being an addict himself, Smoker has often said he's unaware of any problem. He long ago lost his sense of smell and has no idea how that odour hangs around.

He growls, then stubs his cigarette out. "Fuckin' kids. Alex should leave them at home." He stands, picks up the box of the offending items, pockets them and his lighter, then walks off.

"You upsetting the man again?" Salem's obviously finished his game and is now coming toward me with a smirk on his face.

"You're the fuckin' enforcer," I tell him. "Isn't it up to you to enforce the rules?"

His lips press together. "You notice how bad his cough is getting?"

Yeah. That's part of the reason I'm coming down so hard on him. If banning smoking indoors gets him reconsidering even one less cigarette, that's got to be better for him. "Kind of hard to ignore. You think it's something serious? Has he seen a doc?"

"Fuck knows. But we all know he smokes too much. How he got his handle back in the day, and that must have been what, thirty years ago, probably plus?"

My eyes follow the path Smoker had taken to the door. The man's fifty-five, only a handful of years older than me, but seriously, he looks like he's lived through at least a decade more.

Salem's looking in the same direction, then his eyes meet mine. "Have you seen him going up the stairs? Noticed the way he pauses halfway up to get his breath?"

Gritting my teeth, I nod. I have. The man should look after his health, but Smoker seems to be ignoring it. "Find out whether he's been looked at," I instruct the enforcer. "If not, we'll have to fuckin' make him see a doctor."

Jeez, when I became the prez, I didn't realise the health and wellbeing of the brothers in my supposedly grown-ass adult MC family were also my responsibility. Snips, now he's got problems with his teeth, but will he go to the dentist? Hell no. We have to slip him something and carry him there. A year back, Blaze had busted his ankle and argued until he was blue in the face that he could still ride until I laid down the law and made him step back. Well, actually I'd gotten Salem to hide the keys to his bike. Brakes had taken over as road captain on a trip to Los Angeles while Blaze, cursing up a storm, stayed behind.

Only last week, Tyler had come running to me for a Band-Aid to cover a scratch on his knee when his mom and Dart were otherwise engaged. Taking a nap in the kid's language, fucking in mine.

Salem gives me a quick grin and slaps my back; it seems he can read my mind. "Being prez ain't all it's cracked up to be, is it?" Then after that remark, he laughs, and jerking his chin toward Pennywise, returns to the pool table for another game.

I sit for a moment, drinking my beer, idly watching as Scribe and Snips pull out of Cindy. She staggers a little, then rights herself. A little bow-legged in my opinion, she walks off in the direction of the club girl's rooms. Both men pull off condoms, knot them, and throw them in the closest garbage can. There they'll lie forgotten until the prospects tidy up in the morning.

"Can I do anything for you, Prez?" Tits has appeared standing in front of me, thrusting out those breasts which, as she often says, cost her a fucking fortune, so she's going to show them off at every opportunity. I prefer a more natural feel myself, but hey, I'm probably old-fashioned.

When I turn her down, she quickly moves off. To be honest, the thought that all my brothers, with only a few exceptions, have sampled the club girls and on multiple occasions means I avoid going there. When I last did, I think I was inebriated.

"Toke!" I beckon to the man when he appears. "Might have some names for you to dig into."

"Sure, Prez." He nods, gestures to my near empty glass, then toward the bar. When I shake my head, he goes off. As Curtis hands him a beer, Snips engages him in conversation. I've missed my chance to update him. But tomorrow will be soon enough.

I finish my drink, stand, flutter my hand up and down in a general good night to anyone still around, then make my way up to my own bedroom.

I'm happy to live at the club. I've got few needs, and the prez's room is more than sufficient to meet them. Back in Bird's day, the president before Snake took the top spot, two rooms had been knocked through to make one big one. I've an area to sit and relax with a television, and speakers through which I can play music when I want. There's an area which is set up like a small home office, and, of course, a large king-sized bed. Not that that's seen more action than me tossing and turning while I'm uneasily sleeping. Too often it seems, I'm haunted by dreams and end up with the sheet twisted around me.

I go to my own attached bathroom, slipping out of my t-shirt and pants as I do. By the time I'm naked and getting into the shower, there's a trail of clothing reaching back to my door. I'll pick it all up. Sometime.

I stand, my face turned into the water spraying down from the shower head, my thoughts returning to earlier this evening. I'm glad I hadn't spoken about my visit to Token, preferring to digest it all myself first and consider what impact if any my rash suggestion of helping them might have on the club. I have to entertain the notion that my dick might have had too much of a say in it.

Patsy's a fine woman, given her age. She's kept herself in shape, that's for certain. Maybe it had been the influence of living with her daughter, but her clothes, while not unsuitable for a woman her age, were young-looking and form-fitting.

The skin on her face isn't as smooth as a young girl's, but hey, who am I to talk about wrinkles? Her eyes are large and seem to draw you in, and that mouth… well, I could think of a few uses I'd like to put it to.

My thoughts find me moving my hand downward, fisting around my cock. I begin to work it while imagining her on her knees in front of me, her full lips stretched around my cock, my hand fisted in her hair. I pump my hips as though thrusting into her, imagining hitting the back of her throat. I tighten my hand, feel my balls churn and my cock swelling, then I'm coming, hard, white ribbons of cum hitting the shower wall.

Aiming the stream of water at the mess, I watch it disappear down the drain. My body feels relaxed, my mind experiencing a slight twinge of guilt at the idea of using her to fuel my release, but hey, what she'll never know won't hurt her.

Sliding under the sheet, I plump the pillows to get them as comfortable as I can, then relax back my head. I fill my mind with Dan and Patsy's problems, wondering what that message meant, who sent it and how much trouble they might be in. Damn Patsy for giving their general location away. All this trouble caused by her need to contact her daughter. But then, given the circumstances, I can't find it within myself to blame her. If I'd had kids, I might well have been tempted to do the same thing myself.

Conscious thought becomes harder, ideas not fully formed appear and disappear before I can take hold of them. My brain slows, I cease thinking at all as sleep overcomes me.

"This will be you, one day. When you fuck all this up." The smell of flesh burning reaches my nostrils as the man in my dream continues to speak. "Will you be man enough to take it? Or will you be a coward like him?" He points to Poke, begging to be saved.

"I'm not going to fuck up," I tell him.

"Of course you are," he scoffs. "You'll fuck up so badly, you'll pay the same price as I did. They'll burn your tattoo off your back and show no mercy when they do. You'll fuck up. You'll destroy this club."

I turn, look him straight in the eye, then take a step back. Snake's eyes are blazing, actually alight with flames shooting out of them.

"I only made you VP as I wanted a pussy who'd be so grateful to walk at my side, he'd do everything I told him without question. Did that well, didn't you, Lost? So fuckin' well, you made them all believe you could walk in my shoes. Don't like it so much now, do you? You don't have the balls for this job. You know it's only a matter of time before you fuck everything up."

"I am not going to fuck up," I protest again. I know I'd give my life before I allowed harm to come to the club. "It was you who almost destroyed us."

"Me?" Snake roars. "I'm a president. You are nothing. Nothing. You're fucking Lost."

He's now a complete ball of fierce orange and red flame. With arms outstretched, he starts to float toward me. I go to move back, but my feet feel like they're encased in concrete. I can't escape as he nears, and I begin to feel the heat...

In my dream, I scream.

I toss, turn, try to rid myself of the images. I can hear myself whimpering, begging him to leave me alone.

I jerk awake. The sheet tight around me shows I've been restless once again. It's still dark, still night, and I should still be sleeping. Instead I untangle myself, turning onto my side.

I know exactly why Snake haunts me. I don't need a therapist to tell me I'm not really being visited by a ghost. It's my subconscious reminding my brain of what I already know, that I'm not a man who deserves to have trust placed in him. I'm a fraud, an imposter.

It was never part of my life plan to join an MC, let alone rise through the ranks and lead it. Part of the problem was I'd played right into Snake's hands. He needed someone he could keep fooled, who wasn't clever enough to guess his plans. Who, as it turned out, had been completely blindsided when things turned sour. I hadn't seen the betrayal coming, but I should have. The dream version of Snake, or rather my own subconsciousness, is right to warn me. The path I choose to go down won't lead where I expect it to take me. When a fork appears in the road, I'm bound to take the wrong direction.

Yet every man here voted me in as the prez. Goddamn them. But I'll give my all to do the job to the best of my ability. I'll always give everything one hundred percent. I'll be damned if I let any man in this club down. *Damned you'll be, alright.*

I hadn't seen through Snake, but he'd seen right through me. Fuck was I a good choice for him to make. Another man might have figured him out, would have realised what was going on. Looking back, all the clues were there. The secret meetings between Snake and Poke, and those between Poke and the other now out bad members. Whispered conversations hastily ending when interrupted. And yet I'd been oblivious to it all.

Can't a man learn from his mistakes?

I sigh deeply. I've got to hope I can.

My eyelids droop even though I try not to give in to sleep again, having no desire to slip back into my nightmare. But it seems he's tortured me enough for one night, as this time I fall into a deep and undisturbed slumber, from which I'm startled awake.

Rap. Rap. Rap rap.

I open bleary eyes and reach for my phone while simultaneously turning my head and glancing at the ancient clock/radio/alarm, a hangover from Bird's time. "Yeah?" *Shit.* I overslept I realise, reading the numbers.

"Prez, you've got that meeting with the insurance company in an hour." Curtis's deep voice booms from the other side of the door. "Bones sent me up to remind you."

Lucky, he did. I would have missed it. "Thanks," I reply.

I listen to his boots thud away down the hallway and roll over onto my back, clasping my hands behind my head, thinking the role of the MC prez is not all it's cut out to be. While being a one-percenter club we don't give a damn about citizen laws, and however much we do our best to live outside them, it's impossible to ignore them entirely as our businesses are open to civilians. At the very least, we have to have public liability insurance covering our buildings and employees. The feds and the cops are always looking for an excuse to say we've fallen foul of the law, so our paperwork is liable for extra inspection. Like anybody who runs any type of business, the MC likes to keep overall costs down. Hence my meeting today to complain about the increase in our premium.

I promise myself a nice long ride once I've finished with the formalities, and I doubt it will take much persuasion for Bones to come along with me. Neither of us likes being cooped up in an office too much. On my part, I did that for far too long in my earlier years. Just look where that had gotten me.

When I joined the MC and put on my leather, I thought I was done with the corporate world. When I was voted in as VP, I found I had not. Now I'm the prez, I've almost as much dealings as I had in my previous life. But my suit-wearing days are long behind me, thank fuck. I don't even possess businessman attire.

An hour later, Bones and I are walking into a glass and chrome building, looking out of place in our t-shirts and worn leather cuts. The man we meet is dressed in smart pants, his short-sleeved button-down has the top button open, and he's wearing no tie. I want to laugh, remembering that's exactly how I used to dress.

The expression of distaste that covers his face is wiped so fast, I could have imagined it was ever there.

"So, Mr Holmes, Mr Kirk. You're here to discuss the renewal quote we recently sent to you." While speaking, he waves us to the seats in front of him and retakes his own behind his desk.

I'd bristled at the use of my government name. Being called Conan Holmes always leaves a bad taste in my mouth, wanting to disassociate myself with anything that man had ever done. I allow myself a moment of internal delight knowing Bones, or *Jerome,* will be equally, if not more, discombobulated by the use of his legal name. He hates being called Jerome, Jerry, or any other derivative with a passion, as many a man has found out to his cost. I can only hope the insurance salesman doesn't try to get on a first name basis, else I'll end up apologising for the blood coming from his mouth.

I jerk my chin at Bones and sit back, letting him as club treasurer take the lead.

He sniffs, takes out the cloth he uses as a handkerchief and rubs at his nose, then, without ado he starts, "Got the renewal quote, but we were disappointed to see the premium has more than doubled and I fail to see why. We've had no claims for the past three years that we've been dealing with your company."

The man, Ken Smart, unless the name plate in front of him is lying, half smirks and launches into an explanation full of complicated words which no doubt he thinks will go straight over two ignorant bikers' heads. I listen with a straight face as he basically tells us they've introduced a new computer system which has a different way of calculating risk. I let him continue his spiel until he runs out of steam and sits back with a satisfied look on his face. "So, therefore, there's nothing I can do." He shrugs, giving a smile which reveals all his glowing white and probably expensively straightened teeth.

Bones sniffs and clears his throat, and I send him a look, *I've got this.*

It's my turn now. Throwing quick fire questions at Ken, I address him in his language, asking about the parameters of the algorithm they use, what factors they've taken into account, and disputing his assessment of the demographics our businesses operate in. Everything he throws back, I counter.

He pulls at the neck of his shirt, his face glowing pink and then red. When finally he runs out of arguments, I finish with my punchline.

"If there's nothing you can do to come up with a more reasonable figure, we'll take our business elsewhere."

His eyes widen as he blusters, "Er, no. I'm sure we can sort something out. I'll run the figures again and see if there's any leeway or room for adjustment."

I've half started to rise, then I sit back down. "Not been here long, have you?"

He doesn't need to reply as he enters data on his keyboard. I'd figured him out when I'd entered the room. He wants to impress his new boss by putting one over on bikers who have no idea of how things work. Instead, he almost did the opposite, coming close to losing an account.

When Bones and I emerge into the sunlight, it's with a quote that's actually lower than what we paid last year.

Bones goes to his bike, then turns to me, shaking his head. "Fuck, Prez. Glad you're on our side and not theirs."

My shoulders rise and fall as I physically and mentally shrug off his words. "I speak the language, that's all."

"Whatever," Bones says. "He'd lost me with his explanation, but you beat him at his own game." He huffs a laugh. "Did you see his fuckin' face?"

I shake my head. I had. But I've had experience of dealing with assholes like the insurance man—trying to take advantage by getting something over on people who in his view were too stupid to understand. We might have a reputation, but our money's just as good as the next man's, and exactly the same colour.

CHAPTER EIGHT

Lost

"Bones is still singing your praises." Dart raises a bottle of beer toward me as if in salute.

I ignore him, wishing the treasurer would stop repeating that story now that it's been a week since we sorted the insurance out. Seven days which have passed without incident. I'd updated the club about what had gone on, and other than increasing the drive-bys we'd agreed to leave things as they stand unless either we get contacted again, or Patsy or Dan need help. Demon hadn't been pleased someone knew their whereabouts and had a few choice words to use about how Patsy had fucked up. But after we'd talked it out, like me, he thought wait and see was all we could do for now. All Alder could know was a call had been made from San Diego. Patsy and Dan could be anywhere in the state, hell, the country and could have been just passing through. Demon too agreed it could be an attempt to smoke them out, and we could lead him straight to them if we gave them our protection openly.

Token had looked into the list of names which Dan had prepared but found nothing that rang any alarms. Most of those named were bit players, who had all been rounded up and were now inside or awaiting trial. Certainly no one with the reach finding Dan would require.

On my part, I'd consciously tried to put the woman and her son to the back of my mind and concentrate on the business of the club.

"How are the two new guys working out in the shop?"

Dart grins, knowing how uncomfortable I am with mis-assigned praise and that I'm changing the subject. "They're good. Fit in well. Niran's idea is proving to be solid."

Yeah, it had been Niran who'd come up with the idea of us making a point to take vets on. He, himself, being one and having been discharged on medical grounds. He knew how it felt to be stateside and find yourself changed, unable to do what you wanted to anymore. Suddenly, you're alone with no team around you and amongst folks who've no idea of what you've been through. Some men join an MC like ours, needing to find a new family. Others drift, not getting the help or support they deserve.

Ex-servicemen often have a trade we can use, or, a genuine desire to learn. We have a few vets working in our auto-shop now, and the bar's staff are all ex-soldiers from one service or another. It works well, and best, they form a team. If they need time to go to the VA, or just simply to sort themselves out, we let them take what they need. In return, they give us loyalty.

Not everyone is a good fit for us, or us for them, but those we have taken on have made it work.

"Hey, there's the man himself." Dart turns and waves at Niran who's just entered the clubroom.

When he beckons him across, Niran points to the bar, then at us, silently telling us he'll be grabbing a drink for himself first. Curtis is ready with one in his hand, so it's only seconds before he comes over.

"We're just discussing the new employees," I explain. "Dart says they're doing okay."

"Sure are," Niran agrees. "I wondered how Ross would cope

at first, but that bionic hand he's got is amazing. Doesn't hold him back at all."

"And Gibbs?" Dart asks. "Any problems?"

"Nah. Sometimes he stares off into space for a while, but he comes back down. He'll do better in time. Which reminds me, I need to get a new prosthesis. I'll need to take some time off to get that sorted."

"Anything wrong?"

Niran shakes his head. "No, but the shape of the stump changes over time, so I need to have a new one fitted."

It goes without saying, he can take all the time he needs. I turn away as my phone vibrates in my pocket. Taking it out, I don't recognise the number that's calling.

"You got Lost."

"Lost, it's Patsy. I, er, you told me to call if something didn't seem right."

"What's up?" I say sharply. "You okay?" Noticing my tone, Dart immediately ceases his conversation with Niran and looks my way.

"I'm at the mall. I think someone's been following me. Dan's at work and I can't risk him losing this job, so I couldn't call him for help. I'm… I'm scared about going to my car. I thought if it really was someone to be worried about, they might follow me home and find out where we live."

Smart thinking. "You sure someone's stalking you?"

"That's the thing, no I'm not. Could just be someone going to the same places as me, but after what you said last week…"

"I told you to be careful, Patsy, so you're doing just what I suggested. If it turns out to be nothing? Great. If not? We'll sort it out. Now, tell me exactly where you are."

She does. I know where she's at and mentally I run through the businesses I remember. There's a coffee shop close by, so I tell her to get there and wait.

Dart's standing with an eyebrow raised.

"Patsy Forster. She thinks she's got someone following her." It's all I need to say.

"Niran, you coming?" Dart asks. "We may have a problem."

Seems he is as Niran stands and joins my VP. As we walk across the room, a few more of the nosy fuckers tag along. I grin. Dart hadn't been particularly quiet and several, it seems, have invited themselves. It's warming that I don't have to issue orders at all. Any of these men will have my back whenever I need it.

"Where we going?" Dart asks, as we go to our bikes.

I name the popular mall she's at. As I swing my leg over the seat, I'm hoping we're setting off on a wild goose chase, and that her senses are on high alert because it was only last week my visit and information had scared her. But if it's made her and Dan more cautious about their surroundings, it wasn't for nothing. Hoping it's a false alarm, I'm rehearsing the reasons why Patsy would be justified to give me a call anytime, and not to feel like she's crying wolf, even if it turns out to be nothing. *Boys wanted a chance at a ride out. It's good practice for them to act like a team. I wanted to see you again, anyway.* Nah, I shake my head under my helmet. I can't say the last to a woman I don't know at all. She'd run a mile if she knew how often I'd used the vision of her to get my dick going. Yeah, my efforts to not think about her hadn't been as successful as I'd hoped.

In truth though, it won't be much hardship to remind myself of those plump lips and generous mouth. Wouldn't hurt anyone if tonight ends the same way as the previous ones had with me rubbing one out in the shower.

When we arrive at the mall and park, five men accompany me as I walk inside, Wrangler being left to watch the bikes. While we're well-known in this part of the city and a man would be stupid to touch our rides, leaving them unattended is not something we want to take a chance on.

Leaving Dart and the others waiting out of sight pretending, or not, interest in the underwear displays in another store front, I enter the coffee shop and spy Patsy at a table near the rear, noticing she's seated with her back against the wall. There's an empty table next to it. Going to the counter, I order a coffee I don't want or need and pay for it. This time in the afternoon, the mall is quieter with the lunch crowd gone. The coffee shop is too. I get served immediately.

I then go to the table next to Patsy.

"He still here?" I ask, without greeting or explanation while looking straight ahead and hiding that my lips are moving by raising my cup to my mouth.

Quick on the uptake, she lowers her head and murmurs toward the table, "I've seen him three times since I came in here, walking past, glancing in. I'm not sure if he could see me."

I couldn't see her until I stepped inside. If he really is following her, he might be lurking so he can pick her up when she steps out.

"You recognise him?"

"I've never seen him before."

"What's he look like?" I ask, taking out my phone.

"About five foot ten? Medium build, white with brown curly hair. He's wearing jeans and a navy t-shirt. I didn't get close enough to see any design."

As she speaks, I tap out the info and text Dart and issue him some instructions as well. "Patsy, you're going to finish your coffee and calmly walk out of here as if you've no worries in the world. Head through the mall and out to the parking lot. I've got men waiting outside. They'll check whether you're being followed or not."

"If I am?" She picks up her empty cup, lifts it to her mouth and puts it back down, then gathers her shopping bags together. As she stands, she catches my eye.

"We'll take care of it," I promise her softly, speaking out of the side of my mouth.

She stands, leaves, and I sit, drinking the coffee that I never touch this time of day, only really enjoying it in the mornings.

Two minutes later my phone vibrates.

VP: She's got a tail

I think for a moment. We could run intervention and enable her to escape, or, we could get some questions answered. The risk in doing that is we'd tip our hand. Weighing it up, I'd prefer to get information. I always hate working blind.

Lost: Pick him up

Linking my hands together, I stretch until my knuckles crack. There I was thinking this was going to be a normal afternoon but instead things have just gotten interesting.

The Satan's Devils MC are a one-percenter club, but we rarely get our hands dirty. The decision I just made could mean there's one less person breathing when the clock chimes midnight tonight, unless we can handle this carefully.

VP: Got him in the parking lot

Lost: On my way

I use the time it takes me to walk from the coffee shop and out into the parking lot to consider what to do. If we can just get away with a bit of bloodletting, then that's what I'd prefer to do. Dead bodies are harder to dispose of. Not that it would be my first, and I'm not afraid of getting my hands dirty—not when it becomes a matter of protecting one of ours. And ours, Patsy is, as she's the mother to one of the club's old ladies. Doesn't matter one bit that she's connected to a different chapter. Cut one of us and we all bleed Satan's Devils blood.

I go to my bike, nod to Wrangler, then bend down and open the concealed compartment disguised as a tool kit. As I straighten, sliding the object I've taken into my cut, a whistle draws my attention as I saunter out into the evening air. It's dusk, and the shadows deepen as I make my way toward the sound which comes from behind a dumpster. As I round the corner, I immediately see the man.

He exactly matches the description Patsy gave me, and I admire how observant she was.

"What do you want with me?" he demands.

The sound of desperation in his voice suggests this isn't the first time he's questioned Dart. That my VP's not yet spoken to him is just as I expected. He'll be waiting for me to take the lead.

I stare at the man who's been stalking Patsy. One thing she hadn't noticed was his age, or that his body is almost imperceptibly but definitely twitching. *A user starting to get angsty for his next fix.* I can work with that.

Dart, Pennywise, Salem, and Niran have him penned against a wall out of the way, the dumpster hiding him from casual sight. As long as no one comes up to throw garbage away, we should have a few uninterrupted minutes to talk.

"I got Curtis on standby to bring a truck if we want to take him back." Dart shows me he's prepared for any eventuality, demonstrating the quick thinking I expect from my right-hand man.

Our captive's eyes home in on me. Whether he can read the patch on my cut or not, he realises I'm the man in charge. "What you doing man? I've got no beef with the Satan's Devils." In vain, he tries to pull away, but Pennywise and Salem have him held tight.

"What's your name?" I ask, casually, unsurprised when he doesn't reply. "Not going to talk?" I jerk my head toward him. "The sooner you cooperate, the sooner you'll be able to go get your fix. So I ask again, what's your name?"

He looks down. His hands are shaking, but whether it's from fear, his need for a top off or something else, it's hard to tell. When he raises his head again, he mumbles the information he thinks I'll settle for. "Jim."

It's a start, and at least it puts him on a more familiar footing. "Well, Jim, how d'ya get your money to supply your habit?" There's a low wall running along beside me. I rest my foot on it and lean over my thigh eyeing him carefully. He doesn't look to me like someone who holds down a steady job. I'm very interested to know how he gets his funds.

A shifty look comes my way, then as quickly as he met my gaze, his eyes move away. "This an' that." Once again, the reply is mumbled.

"Does 'this' include targeting women?" I shift so Jim can see the glint of the gun tucked into my belt.

His eyes widen.

We don't normally carry in our territory unless there's a need. Cops love nothing more than to stop us when riding wearing our colours, and the possession of a gun without a licence is reason enough for us to end up in the tank. Licences are only awarded to people of good moral character in San Diego, and the patch I'm wearing is reason enough to believe I'm not an angel—probably fair enough. But tonight, I've come prepared for anything.

"I don't target women," Jim says a little more strongly, as if willing me to believe his words.

I straighten and casually fold my arms. "Got reports that you were indeed following someone. See, the thing is, Jim, we don't like women being hurt. A woman disappeared from this very parking lot the other week." It's pure fabrication, but he's not to know that. "Not having any more women fall out of sight on our watch. There's a market for women being trafficked, Jim. A market we don't like." I'm trying to paint a picture of Devils' doing their civic duty and having no particular interest in the woman he was following. If he believes me, it might just save his life and spare me from burying his body. While Jim can't see him, I catch the grin crossing Salem's face, and Niran coughs to cover what I'm certain is a snort.

"I'm not involved in anything like that," he spits out. "I'd never hurt a woman." To his credit, the idea appears to fill him with disgust.

"The thing is," Dart's voice sounds beside me, picking up on what I'd said, "you were watched for a while and you were visiting the same shops as she did, and waiting for her to come out of the coffee shop. If that's not homing in on someone, I don't know what is."

"She's old as fuck." His eyes have widened. "No one would traffic someone like her unless they were desperate." As I stiffen, he ignores me and continues, "Look, you've got this all ass backward. I've done nothing wrong. Now, let me go, please." He whines as he begs. "I want no trouble with your club."

"What you want and what you're going to get are two different things," I warn him. "As far as I can see, you were following a defenceless woman half of the day inside, and then out into a deserted parking lot as it was growing dark. If you weren't going to snatch her, what were you following her for? Fancy a bit of older pussy, or did you think she might have money to feed the demon in your head?"

His eyes flick wildly between us, and he doesn't miss the way Niran flexes his muscular arms, nor that he's clenched his fists.

Suddenly, his facial expression changes. I recognise the look, it's sly and calculating. "You're right, I need cash. She looked like she might have a few dollars. I was going to ask her, that's all."

Pennywise tightens the grip on his arms. Jim jerks backwards, realising we're not going to fall for his lie.

"Want me to soften him up?" Salem drawls.

"No, no. Please. If I tell you the truth, will you let me go?" His gaze again lands on my face, and there's a hint of desperation in it.

I shrug. "Depends whether I like what I'm hearing. But I tell you this, Jim, man-to-man like, if I don't like what I hear, you'll never again have to worry about where your next fix is coming from."

I'm getting fed up. We're wasting time when I want to check that Patsy got home safely. The sincerity of my promise clearly shows on my face as the shoulders of the man in front of me slump. "My dealer suggested I could earn some easy money."

"Doing what?" I prompt.

"Finding a woman. If you let me go, I can give you proof."

"What are you going to do if I release you?" I ask instead.

"Get out my phone."

I jerk my head toward Niran, who goes for the pocket where a rectangular shape shows. Gingerly, he pulls out a wallet and the device Jim was after. Another tilt of my chin and Salem and Pennywise release him, and Niran hands him his phone. Dart takes the wallet and starts looking through it.

Jim looks defeated as he eyes Dart, suspecting he's about to be robbed, but the glare in my eyes has him tapping on the screen. He calls up WhatsApp and turns it to face me. On the screen is a picture of Patsy.

"If I find her and discover where she's living, I'll get a thousand bucks. That's decent dough man. I could do a lot with that."

He'd buy a fuckload of drugs if I'm not mistaken. "Why were you asked?"

"It's not just me. The same offer is being made to anyone who buys from my man. I couldn't believe my luck when I saw her today, knew I just had to follow her home. That's it, man, I swear to you. I wasn't going to hurt her, just find out where her place was. I couldn't miss out on the bread. But," he looks around the parking lot as if hoping to see Patsy waiting there and shakes his head, "she's long gone now."

"So you, what?" Dart asks, eerily calmly. "You hang around malls hoping to spot a woman to earn yourself a thousand bucks? Didn't that request strike you as fuckin' suspicious? What did you think was going to happen to her?"

Another rise and fall of his shoulders. "Thought it might be she's run out on her man, and he wants to make sure she's okay."

He'd probably just thought of that as an excuse right now. Junkie like him wouldn't care who he was sacrificing if he got his money. He'd probably sell his mother for the chance to score.

"You could be right." I send Dart a quick look full of warning. If Jim is going to live out the night, he can't know our specific interest in the woman he was following. "Or, you could be wrong. Either way, it's not right."

"Prez?"

As Dart jerks his head, I follow him a short distance away. "He's called Jim Herd. I've taken a picture of his driver's licence. Not sure how bright he is, or whether you've got him off the scent. We let him go…"

He doesn't finish his sentence; he doesn't have to. Last thing I want is anything that links us with Patsy. On the other hand, I'm not happy about killing a man who only wanted money for his next fix.

I take the few steps needed to bring me back to face Patsy's stalker. "Okay, Jim. As we said, we don't like people terrifying women or putting them in danger. We know where you live and will soon know everything about you. We're going to hang onto your phone for now—"

"You can't steal that from me. It's got my contact list in it."

And his dealer on speed dial I would suspect.

"I'll get it back to you tomorrow. This time, same as now. A prospect will come drop it off for you."

His eyes flick between us. His fear of an immediate demise is gone, but we're stealing his lifeline as far as he's concerned. On my part, I don't have to give it back, possession is nine tenths of the law, and a person like him won't run to the cops about the remaining ten percent. But I'm aware I may need to speak to Jimboy again.

So when he asks, "I can trust you?" I nod my head.

Yes, he can trust me on this. I deepen my voice so he takes me seriously. "We'll return your phone when we've checked out your story, and we're letting you off today as you've cooperated. But one word out of your mouth, one fuckin' word that Satan's Devils are protecting the malls and you'll find yourself in a world of pain you wouldn't believe. You'll be pissing blood for weeks and sucking food down a tube. That's if you're lucky enough to be left alive. You hearing me, Jim? You picking up what I'm laying down?"

His eyes widen in horror. "I don't want trouble with your MC. I won't say a word."

"Make sure you don't. We've got eyes and ears in places you'd never believe. Like how we found out about your stalking activities today. We hear one word about us talking to you tonight, and hey, you'll no longer need to feed your habit as you'll be begging for a bullet instead."

"My… wallet?"

Dart hands it back with his money intact, as I pocket the phone. "Get lost," I tell him.

Jim wastes no time, though I notice he checks to make sure all his money is still carefully encased in the leather as he goes off, presumably to score for the night.

CHAPTER NINE

Patsy

I drive home without incident, my hands shaking, knuckles white, as they hold onto the wheel so tightly as I navigate streets I'm only just starting to learn. Stopping at red lights sends fear rushing through me, and I checked I had the locks engaged each time. When I reach my house, I rush inside, not even bothering to scoop up my shopping and bring it along with me.

I pour myself a glass of wine, resisting the urge to gulp it down. I need something to settle my nerves, not to incapacitate me, just in case someone comes to the house and I need to escape.

Then I wait, scared and lonely.

Lost will make contact I'm sure. But until he does, I'm left in limbo, not knowing whether I should try to make plans to disappear tonight. He'd confirmed someone had been following me. What if there were more than one, and undetected, another man had followed me home?

I pace, sip my wine, and think that I'm a middle-aged woman who shouldn't have to worry about stalkers. When I threw in my lot with Dan, I hadn't thought through it wasn't just my daughter

I was leaving, but my safe existence carefully cultivated over the years. I should have expected Dan's past would catch up with him.

But how would they know? Connor Foster is dead and cremated. It's Dan Forster who's living with me in San Diego. I can't blame him. It's my fault. Why did I break and ring Beth?

When the front door opens and closes, I spin around, quickly filled with relief. As soon as he enters the living room, I'm on my feet, rushing to greet him and throwing myself into my son's arms.

"What's up, Mom?" He hugs me for a moment, then gently pries away the fingers gripping him so tightly, pushing me away and holding me at arm's length.

"Someone followed me today." The words come out fast and unfiltered.

"Fuck."

His eyes go wide, then become shuttered with fear. He lets go of my arms and starts to pace, his hand wiping his hair back from his forehead. "Fuck," he repeats. His feet cease movement when he's back in front of me. "What, where? Do you mean they followed you here?" Now his gaze goes to the windows covered by the drawn curtains. "Mom, we need to leave."

Hastily I reassure him, telling him the steps I'd taken, and that Lost had assured me it was safe for me to come home.

"How does Lost know? Was he sure?" Again, his hand brushes through his hair. "Fuck. Someone could know where we are right now." He turns and paces again, his body vibrating in agitation. Suddenly he stops. "This is all my fault, Mom. Why don't you go back to Pueblo? It's me they want, not you. You'll be safe there. I thought we could make a clean break, but that hasn't worked, and I don't want you dragged into my shit."

I can't let him own this when it's down to me. "It's not your fault, it's mine. I was the one who called Beth." Stupid mistake, but I missed my daughter, and thought what I'd done was safe.

"Mom, this isn't on you. I took you away from Beth who's been a better daughter to you than I've been a son. Of course you miss her, and I don't blame you one bit. But perhaps I'm better off on my own. I'll get in touch with the marshals, see if they can move me again, but you go back to Pueblo."

I haven't had him back in my life very long, and I've been enjoying getting to know this more mature version of my son. I shake my head. "I don't want that, Dan. I don't want to lose you. This time, it would be for good." How can I let my son go off on his own, knowing I'll never see him again? He'll be set up in a new town, hell a different state with a new name. Having only just reconnected with him, I don't want to lose him for a second time. This experience will make him obey all the rules, he won't risk picking up a phone. Not knowing whether he's well and thriving would drive me crazy.

"Tell me again exactly what happened today, Mom."

I do, for the second time emphasising that I called Lost. I've just about reached the end of my repeated story, when I get a call from the man I've been speaking about.

"Patsy, I had a talk with that asshole who's been following you."

"What did he say?"

"Shit I've got to wrap my head around."

I swallow back my growl of frustration that he's not telling me anything. Sometimes these bikers keep too much to themselves. I'd found that out in the Colorado club. "Dan wants to contact the marshals, get himself moved again," I tell him.

There's a moment's pause, then, "Is he there? Can I speak to him?"

I pass over the phone, then can only hear one side of the conversation, which seems to involve a few grunts, a mmm hmm and a couple of okays. Dan ends the call.

"Well?" I rise up and down on my heels.

Dan takes in a breath, and his cheeks puff out as he exhales it in a loud sigh. Then his lips press tightly together. "Lost is pretty certain that no one else was involved today, and that we're still safe to stay where we are. But he is sending a couple of men around. They'll stay here tonight. It's just a precaution, but apparently, the man they spoke to isn't the only one who's been looking for us. Lost says tomorrow we're both to go to their compound, and we'll discuss the next steps. He doesn't think we should do anything else just yet."

I spent enough time on the Satan's Devils compound in Colorado to not worry about the prospect of staying with another chapter, albeit, it will be filled with men I don't know. Lost seems okay, and I suspect his club members won't be much different to the ones who rescued both my son and daughter. I trusted the Satan's Devils once, and I can trust them again.

Dan looks indecisive. "I don't know what to do, Mom." His tone and expression make me think of him as a small boy, especially when he grimaces, then admits, "Is it bad to admit that I'm scared? I'm worried that I'll spend the rest of my life looking over my shoulder and worrying that I'll never be able to put roots down and never trust anyone. I thought coming here would be a fresh start, but Alder's obviously got a reach far longer than I'd ever imagined."

For a moment, he's not a man approaching his twenty-third birthday, he's a kid who needs his mom. "If I hadn't called Beth, he'd never have known where to look."

"San Diego's a huge fuckin' city, Mom. We should have been *safe*. It should have taken him years, not weeks to get a bead on us. We shouldn't underestimate him. If he's done it once, he'll do it again."

"Oh, Dan." I take a step closer to him, resting my hands on his arms, and looking up to meet his eyes. "This wasn't what I expected either. I thought we could get away, start a new life. Maybe I haven't tried hard enough."

"It's different, Mom. I'm running for my life, having to start all over again to stay alive. You? You've got everything to live for back in Pueblo. It was always going to be hard; I don't think either of us realised how much it would take."

He's right. He's got a reason to go into hiding, I don't. I can't deny it will be hard to resist the temptation and end up messing everything up again. I can't close my eyes without sending up a prayer that Beth's safe and happy. I'll never stop worrying about her. But Dan? I'd worry about him, too, if I didn't know where he was. At least he's driven by the need to keep his head under the radar. I can't be the reason why he's found and killed.

It's that fear that leads me to tell him, "I don't want to lose you again, Dan, but maybe it's best if you go it alone. Two of us stick out much more than one young man. Maybe you'd have more of a chance if you were on your own."

There's so much hurt in his eyes as he looks at me—pain and regret for the things that he did in the past. For once I'd chosen him over Beth, and now I am being asked to remake that choice.

I hear the sound of a car pulling up outside the house and the engine stops. Wide-eyed, I stare at Dan in horror as he goes to the window and looks out.

Then my phone pings with a text.

Lost: Curtis and Dusty are outside. They're my men.

"It's Lost," I tell Dan. "It's the men he promised he'd send."

Before Dan goes to open the door, he spares me a look, accompanied by the words, "This is what our life will look like from now on. Unless we, or I on my own, move to another location, this is a taste of what it will be like. Fuckin' jumping every time someone knocks on the door. Never knowing if they're friend or foe."

It's a chilling thought. Living in fear is not something I ever expected nor wanted to do, or what I want for my son. I want to spend my life designing clothes, not hiding out from a drug lord or whatever the proper term is to describe Alder now.

Of course my life would be perfect had I not had to make any choice at all and could have both my son and my daughter close. If only their father hadn't been the man that he was. If I'd understood Dan better when he'd been in his teens, he'd never have sought out his dad. So many ifs that don't serve to make anything better, the past cannot be rewritten now.

"I'm Dusty." The strange voice makes me jump, and I turn to acknowledge the man who walks in. He's got shoulder-length blond shaggy hair, and a short beard, but it's his piercing blue eyes that catch my attention. He's tall, slim built, but looks strong. "Curtis." As he introduces his companion with just the one word, the big black man beside him raises his chin toward me. He looks like he could be in the military—tall, shoulders held up, back ramrod straight.

Dusty continues, "I'll stay here tonight, inside. Curtis will be patrolling the perimeter. Both of us will be watching out all night."

"Is that necessary?" I ask. My sympathetic eyes land on the man who seems to have been given a bum job. Sure, it's not cold, but waiting outside the house all night sounds like it will be pretty boring. Or, hopefully.

"Curtis is a prospect who wants his patch." Dusty raises an eyebrow at the man beside him who sends a nod and an easy smile my way, then disappears out the doorway.

"This the couch?" Dusty gives the far-too-short-for-his-body piece of furniture a disdainful look.

"We moved in here and it was already furnished. No choice of mine." I wonder why I'm offering what sounds like an apology. "There is a spare bedroom—"

"I'm not here to sleep, woman," he snaps. "Fuckin' poor bodyguard I'd make if I were napping on the job. The couch will do fine for me."

"There's beer in the fridge, man," Dan offers.

"Oh, and cookies in the cupboard." I bite my lip. "There's not much else I'm afraid." I've found teenagers may grow into men but that doesn't mean they lose their habits of emptying the fridge and pantry of all its contents. The only stuff left are things that need cooking.

"Not here to sleep or to eat, but a beer would be good. Thanks." Dusty tilts his head as though to question where he should be heading. Dan interprets his unspoken query and leads him into the kitchen.

I wonder whether I should offer to take one out to the prospect, but then decide they can sort themselves out. When Dan comes back into the room, he's already deep in conversation with Dusty. A wave of exhaustion comes over me. I've been on edge since noticing I'd picked up a stalker, but Lost taking it seriously, stopping the man and now sending Dusty and Curtis to watch over us has taken the burden from me. I realise I'm starting to crash as the adrenaline fades away. I become aware that my head is pounding, and I want nothing more than to rest it on a pillow.

Interrupting their conversation briefly, I tell them I'm going to bed, then with heavy feeling limbs go through my normal nighttime routine. When at last I slide under the covers, my brain won't switch off, going over and over the events of the evening, and again more what-ifs come to mind.

What if I hadn't been so vigilant? What if I hadn't noticed the man? It had been Lost's insistence on me keeping aware of my surroundings that had put my senses on high alert. Had I not been pre-warned, I might not have taken so much notice of my surroundings nor the people around. If I hadn't been looking, I probably wouldn't have realised I was seeing the same man over and over again. If I'd ignored my first thought that it was a coincidence and I was overreacting, I'd never have called for help.

Even at the time I thought I was imagining things, my palms had become sweaty and my nape had tingled when I'd seen him *yet again*, and the only thought in my head was to speak to Lost.

From Lost's reaction, I was right to, and as it turned out, I hadn't been seeing things that weren't there. If I had, there wouldn't be two Satan's Devils protecting the house right now.

My brain hasn't got the message that I'm tired. Despite the comfort of the bed, instead of letting me sleep, it's whirring with worry instead.

Is Dan right? Should he move on? Should I go with him? What happens if I return to Pueblo? Why had I made contact with Beth? The most important and mystifying of them all, *why was I followed today and by whom?* It had to be someone working for Alder, but why? Does he have proof Dan's alive? It would be him he'd be after, not me. *He was using me to lead him to Dan.*

Could someone else be targeting me for God knows what reason?

I can't think who. No, it has to be Alder. But surely, finding me in that mall must have been coincidence. When I'd left the house, even I didn't really have a destination in mind. I'd gone out after Dan left for work as these four walls were becoming oppressive and decided to while away a few hours doing some late afternoon shopping instead. It was even a mall I hadn't been to before, not a haunt I often frequent.

I'm scared how easily I'd been found and can't think how anyone knew how to locate me.

Finally, I must drop off as I wake to the sounds of banging, clattering and loud voices. There's also the aroma of bacon coming through my bedroom door. Feeling like death warmed over, I sit, rub tired bleary eyes, then reach for my robe. One thing about being a woman in my mid-fifties, I don't have to give a damn about doing much more than running a brush through my bed hair. I've a house full of young men, no one I need to impress. No one who's going to care if I'm wearing makeup or not.

Sliding my feet into my worn, comfy slippers—the ones with the cat's face on them, complete with ears and whiskers, which

Dan had bought me out of his first wages as a joke—I open the door and step out.

When I enter the kitchen, I immediately want to make a retreat, hastily rethinking my decision not to hide that I look like I've just fallen out of bed when my eyes fall on the one man I didn't expect to see flipping bacon on the stove. *Lost.*

Jeez. I don't know exactly how old he is. The grey in his hair suggests he has to be middle-aged, but the view he's presenting with his back to me is more mouth-watering than what he's cooking. The way his ass flexes as he moves this way and that has even my what I thought were non-existent hormones running rampant.

"Morning, Mom." Dan nods as he catches sight of me, showing no reaction at all. Well, he's my son and is used to my morning apparel.

Dusty eyes me up, then down, then gives me a polite, "Hi, Patsy. Sleep well?" as if I'm no interest to him one way or another.

Lost though. Lost turns and looks straight at me. When his eyes peruse my body, parts of me come alive which I'd thought dead. I mean, there's a handsome man in my kitchen, cooking breakfast at my stove. I feel my cheeks glow red under his examination and a tingling starts inside me as his eyes leave my face, travel down my body then fall on my feet covered by my favourite slippers. It's then the bastard smirks. "Nice." He nods downward.

Suppressing the instinct to run back to my room and dress more appropriately in my tightest jeans and best fitting top, I pull my pink fluffy robe tighter around me, and ask through gritted teeth, "Want some help?"

"Nah, I got it. You just take a seat. Dust, why don't you get our host some coffee?"

Host? Pretty damn sure with that title, I should be the one cooking. But I sit, still half asleep, wondering what rabbit hole

I've fallen into as Lost continues to work the stove. As he moves his attention between one pan and another, I begrudgingly admit, he actually seems to know what he's doing.

When Lost serves up the food, Dusty takes two loaded plates and disappears out of the room leaving just the three of us.

Lost must have raided my fridge and freezer I realise when a heaped plate of bacon, eggs and hash browns is placed in front of me. I frown down at it.

"Is everything okay?" Lost asks, sounding concerned. "Not the way you like it, babe?"

"No," I refute fast. "It looks too good. I can't remember a time a man ever cooked for me." I don't think anyone ever has since I was a kid. My ex never did.

"What?" Lost fills his own plate, then comes and sits beside me. "Your son never brought you breakfast in bed?"

"I didn't get the cooking gene," Dan laughs. "But I do make a mean piece of toast."

"Beth would spoil me," I tell them, a pang of loss shooting through me. We'd prepare almost all our meals together, working as a team, each moving around the other with practiced ease, never getting in each other's way, so familiar with what we were doing. I'd barely even had to give her instruction, she'd always second-guess me and have something chopped or taken out of the oven when it was ready.

"You miss her a lot." Lost is eyeing me thoughtfully.

I grimace, seeing the look of regret on Dan's face. "I can't not," I admit. "But I've got to put that behind me. She had me for twenty-seven years, I'm here for Dan now." I decide continuing with this subject is going to see me in tears, so I change it. "What are you doing here so early, Lost? Is it about what happened yesterday? I thought you wanted Dan and I to come to meet you?"

"I did. I changed my mind." He shoves some food in his mouth, chews and swallows it while I look on wondering how come the man can even eat sexily. "And it's not early, it's almost eleven o'clock."

What? I glance at the clock on the oven and see that he's right. Now my attire makes me feel worse than ever. I rarely oversleep. I'm just about to offer an apology when he speaks again.

"I needed to have a talk with you about what you do next."

I open my mouth to ask what he'd discovered when he'd spoken to the man who had been following me, but my son doesn't give me a chance.

"I move," Dan says tersely, sending me a remorseful look. "This is my problem, not Mom's. She should be able to go back to her old life, and I'll get relocated again. Lost, it's great Demon asked you to watch out for us, but no one should have ever known that Connor Foster was alive, let alone where Dan Forster went. So I'll talk to the marshals, get them to change my name again, and then, well…"

Then he'll disappear from my life and won't be able to come back. I put down my fork having lost my appetite.

Lost narrows his eyes. "One choice you've got, obviously. Dan talks to the marshals and get either both of you or just him moved."

"Our only choice," Dan informs him.

"Not true." Lost shakes his head. Unlike me, he's still hungry and takes a moment to chew on a piece of bacon, as Dan and I sit impatiently waiting to hear what in hell other option we've got. I can't think of anything. "What you can do," Lost finally enlightens us, "is stay, face it head-on, and get Alder out of the picture for good."

"Are you talking about taking him out?"

My eyes open wide and go toward my son who'd spoken. Phil had certainly been a bad influence on him as that hadn't been the first thing that had come into my head.

Lost's eyes are stern. "Commit murder? Plan it in cold

blood?" I start shaking my head, ready to say of course Dan hadn't meant that, but stop when he grins. "You're growing on me, kid."

Find Alder and kill him? My eyes flick to one then the other as I realise, they are right. We'll never be free of him while he's still breathing.

CHAPTER TEN

Lost

After I'd spent time talking to that asshole yesterday, I'd done what I normally do. I had retreated to my room to think. I'm not a man who leaps into action, not without considering all the options first.

I tend to look at a problem from one side and then the other, considering solutions then dismissing them, then formulating more. It hadn't taken long to come to the conclusion that Dan and Patsy had had their fair share of running and needed the requirement for them to keep hidden over and done.

That I'd come up with the correct way to play things was confirmed when I'd placed an early morning call to my counterpart in Colorado. Demon had told me something in confidence that moved the goal posts considerably. It seems though the couple wasn't officially announcing it as it was early days, Ink had admitted to his prez that Beth and he had something cooking, something that was going to arrive in seven more months.

If all goes well, Patsy was to become a grandma, and it seemed beyond cruel to keep that from her. Crueller still, perhaps, to let her know about it because she'd be more torn than she is already, wrenched between wanting to be there for Beth, and needing to stay with Dan.

She's a loyal family woman but asking her to live as though she hasn't got a daughter is tearing her apart. I can already see how much she's hurting, and as yet, she doesn't know exactly how much she's going to miss.

So the idea I'd come up with became fixed in my head. It was the right path forward for Patsy and Dan, but that led me to different considerations. It's one thing to offer our protection to them, quite another to put ourselves on the front line.

My problem is, am I right to ask my brothers to take on this fight, now we know who it's likely we'll be going up against?

I'll be putting the club in this Alder's headlights. A man so shady we know little about him, but one powerful enough to evade the reach of the feds. This isn't some two-bit criminal we're dealing with. This is a man who can command an army of druggies at the very least to search for the woman he wanted to locate. One drugged-up man can be overcome easily, but a whole group of men who have brown sugar dangled in front of them can be unpredictable and dangerous, without morals when they're seeking their next fix.

Who else has he got working for him? Even if not partaking in what they're selling themselves, there will be men relying on Alder to supply them with product for sale. Without their brains being fucked, these might be more of a risk if he can get them organised.

If I bring this to the table, I'll be pitting my club against the strength of an unknown army. One thing's for certain—if Alder discovers we're giving sanctuary to Patsy and Dan, he'll be coming for us head-on. I may not understand the reason, may not know how Alder is in possession of the knowledge Connor Foster is still alive, but I do know if Alder's going to the extent of dredging the streets of San Diego for information, he knows and wants him found.

What else can I do but offer them the protection of my club? The idea of leaving them to figure it out themselves doesn't sit right with me.

They could get help from the marshals and relocate once again.

They could. But Alder would still be out there, waiting for just one slip. Patsy deserves to have her life back, and Dan his fresh start. I'm certain that end is the one toward which we should be working.

Or am I? Doubts run through my mind, second-guessing myself, then eventually asking myself the question, am I proposing this for the right reasons? Do I want to keep Patsy close, not because of their relationship to the club, but because my motive is personal?

I've not been interested in a woman for a very long time, but Patsy intrigues me. There's just something about her that calls to me, and I don't know why. I've seen many women around the club, and even in town, when they either see my cut and run, or come onto me, probably because of my president patch. Patsy's different. Something tells me she sees the man, not the motorcycle and title.

Maybe I should let her go and forget all about her. But what if I do and I can't? Since I lost my wife, I've never found another woman who's captured my interest, and especially not one with whom I sense a connection I want to explore.

But is there room for a woman in my life? If we explored that connection and found something there, could I commit to her? Experience has shown me women consume a large part of your life, and I've got the club to consider. Since I moved to the top seat, I've given my all to the Satan's Devils MC, brought men back together and done my best to make sure our businesses run right so everyone stays happy and fed.

Isn't it time to take something for yourself?

I'm not sure that voice is mine, or whether it's Snake offering temptation my way. A woman could make me take my eye off the ball. *It would be safer for me, and for her, if she and Dan just disappeared.*

But what if she went and Alder tracked them anyway? What if she ended up dead? No. That possibility exists, and that's unacceptable to me. I acknowledge I have selfish reasons both for wanting to keep her close and for seeing her drive away.

Thoughts, ideas, a way forward decided then more back-tracking. I spend far too many hours worrying which way I should jump.

Eventually I circled back to the decision I'd made first, coupled with the acceptance that should Patsy demonstrate a reciprocal interest in me, I wouldn't push her away. Not all women are like my ex-wife.

So here I am, at Patsy and Dan's house. I ended up cooking breakfast while waiting for her to awaken, and subsequently to the current conversation.

"It's up to you, Dan." I look at him, having to drag my eyes away from his mom who looks delectable having clearly just rolled out of bed. My cock twitches as I wonder whether she'd look even more disheveled had it been my bed she'd rolled out of. I force myself to concentrate on the man I'm addressing, trying to rid the inappropriate thoughts of his mother from my head. This is not me. I can't remember a woman having such an effect on me in years. I feel more like a horny teenager than a middle-aged battle-scarred MC prez. "You can rely on the authorities, and the marshals will probably get you settled somewhere else." I shrug again. "You'll have to downplay the part your mom played in your discovery otherwise they might see her as a risk. You'll probably be safe enough starting afresh if you keep your head down, and if both of you can resist connecting with your old life, family and friends." I determinedly don't look at Patsy as I've cruelly inferred she's a risk. But I can't sugarcoat it. She fucked up.

Though knowing that doesn't mean I don't feel sympathetic as hell.

He regards me carefully, clearly deep in thought. I give him the moment he needs before he starts speaking, admiring he's not just leaping in. I like a man who can think.

"Or get Alder off our backs for good? We'd need help." Dan's lips press together when he finally comments. He pushes aside his empty plate and leans his elbows on the table. "I lived with my dad, Phil Foster. I…" he glances at his mom apologetically. "For a spell, I was one of his debt collectors. Not proud of what I've done, but I don't back down from a fight and I'm not afraid of facing things head-on. If there's a chance we can take out Alder or get him sent down, I'd like to take it." He glances sideways. "Mom, if we can get him off our backs, life can go back to normal—at least for you."

"Dan, I'm scared. While I agree, I wouldn't have a clue where to start, and you could be putting yourself in danger." Patsy's in agreement with the solution in principle, but I can understand her unease with how it could be achieved.

"Not expecting you to confront Alder." I include both of them in my gaze. "You've got the Satan's Devils on your side."

"No." Patsy's voice is firmer. "We've only just met, Lost. You owe us nothing. I'm thankful that you and your men helped me yesterday, but going after Alder, we can't ask you to do that. He's dangerous." Her brow furrows deeply.

Dan though, well he looks hopeful for the first time this morning. "How?"

"Not got that answer yet, Dan." I reply with an honest answer. "But knowing the destination means we can start mapping out how we get there. At the moment, there are questions but no answers, and it's those we need to be finding." Patsy doesn't look convinced. I direct my next comment to her. "I know you're not asking, but I'm telling you we can help."

Whether there will ever be anything between us, whether

she'll even consider getting to know a man like myself, I want her to be happy. I know that she won't be when she's separated from one of her children. I prefer the option that leaves Alder dead and permanently out of the picture. But in her eyes, while she might have the experience of the Satan's Devils in Colorado, I'm little more than a stranger who's walked in off the street and offered something she's no idea I've got the ability to deliver.

She needs time. "This isn't a decision that should be taken lightly. You both need space to think. What you decide will affect the rest of your lives. In the meantime though, I'm not happy with you staying in this house. I want you both to pack a bag and come to the compound." I grimace. "It's not like staying at the Ritz, but we can protect you better there." At least with Beth being with Ink, Patsy knows something about bikers and clubs.

"I've no problem coming to your clubhouse." She confirms my thoughts, but doubt crosses her face. "I'm worried about getting you involved. I think Dan ought to speak to the marshals as soon as he can."

"I don't," her son says tersely. "Mom, think. You want to be able to at least talk to Beth. To go home—"

"I don't have a home," Patsy all but wails. "I knew what I was stepping into, Dan. There's no going back." I grimace, thinking she'd thought leaving would be easy. In the end, though, she'd found it unbearable not to have contact with her daughter. If she leaves, she may never know that her family is getting larger, and soon she'll be a grandmother.

"Ink and Beth bought my house," she continues. "They'll have changed it—as they should—to make it a home for themselves. I've cut ties, Dan. If it means you're safe, I'll do anything. Even if that means..." her voice breaks, "even if it means I never hear Beth's voice again."

"Mom." Dan's voice is full of emotion.

She looks at him sadly, then turns to me. "Can you give me

that assurance, Lost? Can you promise you'll keep us safe? Or will I be burying my son for real if we stay here and face Alder?"

You're going to fuck it up. You always do. I push Snake's voice out of my head. "I can't promise." I give her the truth. "But at least, come to the clubhouse and take the chance to think this through. It will be safer than your staying here. If after we've discussed everything and decide it's better for you to leave, you've lost nothing but gained a couple of day's breathing space."

"Can't be fairer than that, Mom." Dan implores her with his eyes. "You've no idea how much I want to take back my own name, start a new life, not under this new identity, but as the person I am. Your son and Beth's brother."

Patsy pushes her own plate away. I notice she's only eaten half of it but suspect that's down to the topic of conversation rather than my cooking skills. That's one area where I've never been criticised. She stands, her eyes landing first on me, then on her son. She sighs in resignation. "Okay. If that's what you want, Dan. We'll go to the clubhouse and take a moment to decide what to do."

As she goes to get dressed and pack, and Dan disappears to gather his stuff for their at least temporary move to the compound, I sit, deep in thought.

I think Patsy has been holding her tongue, biting back words she wants to say. That she doesn't voice them makes her go up in my estimation. She must be scared, not just for her son, but for herself too.

It dawns on me that she hadn't taken any persuasion to realise Alder was a clear and present danger to her son. A niggling idea takes hold at the back of my mind, wondering what she knows. Sure, he was responsible for leaving her son beaten close to death, but I'm starting to wonder if she knows more than she's told. She'd known Alder before. It was twenty years or so back, but leopards do not change their spots. I decide I need to have a chat with Patsy, get her somewhere alone... My cock jerks. Jeez. What am I, a kid? Just the thought of one-on-one time with her and my body goes into overdrive.

I'm just looking for an excuse. What more could Patsy offer other than Alder's a nasty piece of work? It's Dan's head that holds the answers to my questions. There must be something he knows that hasn't already been said, and which is why Alder won't stop until he knows for certain Connor Foster is dead.

As I've been lost in my thoughts, Dusty, who'd made himself scarce while we'd been talking, returns and shows he's got a domestic side I hadn't appreciated as he scrapes off the plates and stacks them in the dishwasher, then turns it on.

"What?" He catches me watching him, then shrugs. "You cooked, I clean. Isn't this how it works?"

I laugh, then grow serious again. "No sign of anyone last night?"

"Nothing," he informs me. "Curtis said all was quiet when he was doing the rounds. He didn't see anyone out of place or anything suspicious. You get anything from the dude yesterday to worry you?"

That's the problem. I did. I cast my eye down the hallway where the woman and her son had disappeared. "We'll discuss it later in church."

Catching on to what I'm not saying, Dusty nods. "Sure, Prez."

Fifteen minutes later, Dan appears with a rucksack which looks half empty, followed a quarter of an hour later by Patsy with a case that's bulging at the seams. I grin. All a man needs are a few pairs of underwear and a couple of t-shirts. Women? Well, who knows what they regard as the necessities for a couple of days away.

"I think I've got all I need." Patsy bites her lip as she looks down at her case.

"I'll send a prospect back if there's anything you've forgotten," I tell them. "Ready to go?" I take out my keys and toss them in my hands, now anxious to get moving.

To accommodate Dan's longer legs, he sits shotgun, while Patsy climbs into the rear of the club's truck that I'd brought along. Dusty and Curtis follow in the vehicle they'd brought last night.

In silence, we drive through San Diego. The residential and business areas fall behind as we drive into open country. Soon I make the turn into the gates of the compound and proceed along the roadway alongside the now pitted asphalt which used to be a runway. It's the first hangar that had been converted to a clubhouse. There's not much in the way of luxuries out here, but we've got amazing views out over the sprawling city below. On a clear day, there's a good view of the Coronado Bridge and nearby Navy base.

Three years ago, we were pushed for space until the loss of nine members meant we had a few empty rooms in the main clubhouse. Even with the new prospects we've taken on, we can easily accommodate our two guests.

Dart's been working on plans to add further accommodations to the rear of the second hangar. Optimistic for sure, but hey, the club won't turn away the right kind of new members.

"This is nice." Patsy looks around, saying the right words but from the expression on her face, she was hoping for more.

I sigh, thinking she'd be far happier somewhere like the compound the Tucson chapter has. Years back, they'd bought and restored a burned-out vacation resort complete with a swimming pool. We've got the climate that could do with a luxury like that, but Dart's the only person with an old lady, and comfort takes a back seat for most of us. Often, I think the place needs more of a feminine touch. Of course we've got the whores, but they're in no position to push for the finer things in life.

Yeah, from what I've seen in other chapters, a few more old ladies wouldn't hurt. Still, I'm not leading from the front on that score. By the look on Patsy's face, she'd not be particularly enamoured of where I live should I start something with her. *Start something?*

What the fuck am I thinking?

Patsy might provide me with inspiration for those times I rub one out, but I'll just have to be content dreaming about what she was hiding under that robe. I like the woman, yes. She comes in a package that attracts me, but she's certainly not one-night stand material. No, the man who courts and wins her would have to have something to offer, and that man isn't me.

I'm Lost. I'm not in the market for an old lady, the thought never crossing my mind. I made that mistake once. I'm not going to drag another woman down, nor risk someone making demands on me that take me away from my club.

I heft her case out of the truck and shake my head when she goes to take it from me.

"I got it." I smile at her. She won't be carrying bags while I'm around. "It's not much," I point to the clubhouse ahead, "but it's home."

She laughs softly. "The clubhouse in Colorado is a converted steel mill, it's not much better. But," she turns and stares at the sight in front of her, "your views are to die for."

Perhaps I misread what I thought was a look of distaste. "Doubt if you'll find much difference inside. Our clubhouse runs much the same as the rest. There's a bar, a pool table, offices, then the bedrooms are upstairs."

"Will Dan and I have to share?"

My eyes glaze over for a moment. "No, we've lots of spare rooms nowadays."

Luckily, she doesn't press or ask why.

Dan's hoisted his rucksack over one shoulder. I raise my chin and indicate with my head. They fall in behind me.

As I open the door, a blast of welcome cool air escapes. Ushering them inside, I close it behind me, immediately noticing the clubroom is empty except for the prospect behind the bar. I'd told everyone to be ready to have church as soon as I returned from collecting Patsy and Dan, but as I hadn't arranged a specific time, that's not the reason why no one's around. It doesn't, however, take a genius to work out why the place is deserted.

At the end of the room there's a new addition that was installed three years back. A stripper pole, which is currently being used by a curvaceous but short black woman. On the ground she is beautiful, but there's nothing to give away that she's athletic. On the pole, she's poetry in motion. So fluid, so lithe as one movement turns into the next.

"She's incredible," Patsy breathes, her eyes having locked on the Lycra-clad figure as soon as she entered.

"Wow." Dan's voice is full of admiration.

"Get your fuckin' eyes off my wife," Dart, having magically appeared, snarls. He waits until Dan's looking somewhere else, then his face relaxes as he turns to me and explains, "Alex wanted to practice, so I've got all the fuckers in church."

Alex, the VP's wife, is an amazing pole dancer. She'd had to be to earn money when she'd been on the run from her ex. Her talent had been responsible for originally bringing them together. When Dart had moved from Tucson and accepted his position as VP, certain conditions were attached, one being that we agreed to install a pole for her to practice on. Dart tried to insist we partition off a discrete area in one of the hangars so she could dance without everyone leering at her, but Eva, Cindy, Tits and Pearl wanted to take lessons from her, and the men wanted to watch the sweet butts entertain them with their new skills. So the compromise to having it set up in the clubhouse was that when Alex was using it, every male made themselves scarce—except for the prospects. If they let their eyes stray or had thoughts they shouldn't about the VP's woman, well, they wouldn't be getting their patch.

It wasn't a hardship. Alex tended to use it during the daytime when normally the majority of members would be at work.

"She's looking good," I tell him, softly.

"Huh," he comments, seeming not to expect a man my age to leer after his wife. "Alex thinks she's carrying too much weight after the baby and is trying hard to get her figure back." Dart nods back at Patsy and Dan who's kept his back turned. "I'll get her to look after our guests."

Alex is moving to the music, completely oblivious she's got company. I don't want to bring her out of her zone. "No worries," I tell him, then turn to the prospect behind the bar. "Wrangler. Take Patsy and Dan up to the rooms you got sorted for them." Then I turn to the pair I just named. "The prospect will make sure you've got everything you need."

CHAPTER ELEVEN

Lost

"Thank fuck you're here," Grumbler, well, grumbles. "The VP shooed us all out when Alex appeared. Had to leave my fuckin' beer."

Ignoring the sergeant-at-arms protest voiced as though it's the end of the world, I spy an empty chair. "Where's Blaze?" I ask no one in particular. I notice Token beckoning to Deuce to pass a phone back to him. I recognise it as Jim's and realise he's been passing it around.

Dart explains, "He's doing a full back patch tattoo that he couldn't walk out on."

Deuce raises his hand. "I've got a delivery coming in. I'd like to get back to it as soon as I can."

I take my seat. "Thanks for sparing the time today, but I wanted to bring you all up to speed without delay." I know I sound less like an MC prez and more like a corporate CEO, but it's not my way to berate people for simply existing.

While we all put the club first, part of that is the businesses we run to keep our stomachs fed, so brothers are right to feel annoyed if they're called away from their jobs for no reason.

"Yesterday, Patsy Forster called me for help as someone was

following her. Dart, Salem, Pennywise, Niran and I had a conversation with that someone," I start to remind those who know, and tell some who for one reason or another, may not have picked up on what went down. "I heard enough to be concerned, so for their protection, I've brought Patsy and her son back to the compound." I raise my hand to indicate I haven't finished. "For now, it's only temporary. How long they stay, or what they do next, will need a club decision. It's obvious from the information we got out of the stalker we intercepted that they were in danger of being found if I hadn't done something." I raise my eyes and let my gaze travel around the table. "It seems likely, Alder's net is closing in on Dan."

There are murmurs and shakes of heads, then Token raises his hand. "Want me to give my update?" At my nod, he begins, "I've looked at the phone you took from Jimboy, the stalker, yesterday. I found that he's a member of a WhatsApp group which has about seventy-odd members. It was created about three weeks ago, and its focus seems to be on locating Patsy."

That timing fits with when she tried to call Beth. Alder must have acted fast and got his ducks in a row. There's something about Token's wording that sets off an alarm in my mind, but I can't bring into focus exactly what or why.

Letting it drop for now, knowing my mind will keep working on the problem in the background, I state, "He's got seventy people watching out for her?" It's a lot. If they're scattered all around San Diego, it was only a matter of time before he located her or Dan. Seventy people all anxious to earn a thousand dollars. "How could he get that organised? Have you found anything out about the group members?"

Token frowns. "Many of them use tag names which are unidentifiable, so I've hacked into their accounts. Couldn't do all seventy in the time I had, but most that I looked into have something in common. They're all users, or dealers."

"It makes sense." Dart raises his chin. "Alder runs drugs. We assumed he acted out of Colorado, but maybe he's behind some of the drug trade in Southern California as well and tapped into a network he already had in place."

"We are close to the border," I agree. "Losing his cross-country routes may mean it's less risk dropping them here than taking them across states."

"So what you're saying, Token, is that there's another seventy Jims around?" Salem asks.

Token nods. The enforcer's eyes meet mine and I know he's also thinking, finding her wasn't an *if* but a *when*.

That bell's still ringing in my head. Now it jangles something loose. "You said the focus was on finding Patsy. What about Connor? What mention was there of finding him?" I press the computer guy for more.

"None." Token shakes his head. "The focus is on the woman. Connor isn't given a mention at all."

"That makes no sense." Reboot voices my thoughts. "If that's who he's after and he's got this army of addicts, why not get them looking out for the man himself? If Alder thinks Connor is alive, that's what I'd expect him to do. If he accepts he's dead, there's no reason to go after the woman. If Connor's dead, then the information he had died with him. A dead man can't testify or give away anything to hurt him."

That right there is the niggling thought that had been trying to come to the front of my mind, maybe tardy as I didn't want to even think it. That even if Dan disappeared out of state, she'd remain in danger. But what the hell can she have that Alder wants?

Could Alder be so deranged as to want his revenge on Connor's mother? At the time of his 'death', they'd been estranged. It doesn't make sense, unless he wants her for another reason. Unless I've been working on the wrong assumption all along, and there's someone else gunning for her and not Alder. Wouldn't be the first time I'd made a costly mistake.

"It may not be Alder who's after her." If so, it's imperative I have that conversation with her. But who else would have a team of addicts at his fingertips?

"It is," Token states. "His name was mentioned in the chain of messages. There's no doubt, it was 'find her for Alder.'"

Well, it's somewhat of a relief that the tree I was barking up did indeed hold the squirrel. But why?

"She's an attractive woman," I find myself saying, resulting in dubious looks being sent my way, everyone having seen the photo that Jim had carried around. Well, except from Smoker, Snips and Grumbler who are in the same age bracket as myself, and who, I notice, are nodding appreciatively. With the clean out of the club when Snake was dispatched to meet Satan, we lost a lot of the older members, the remainder all being in their early thirties or less. Reboot, now he's only twenty. I've no doubt most of them don't view Patsy the same way I do, to them she's probably maternal. To me, she's a mature woman, pretty, nice figure, but doesn't pretend to be more or less than she is. But I'll be first to admit, she's not someone you'd expect to be on the arm of a boy toy.

"To an old man like you, I s'pect she looks fit, maybe even to this Alder. But, Prez, I find it hard to believe someone would go to all this trouble just to fuck her."

I have to concede Brakes has got a point. Mind you, running our strip club he's quite a connoisseur of women's bodies and what appeals to men of various ages.

I'm not the only one to think it, as Dusty says with a wink toward his brother, "You would know."

"It's not what you've got, it's what you do with it," Kink offers. "Maybe she's into shit we don't know about. Older women can be fun to top, or bottom for if that's your taste."

And that's where I'm going to draw a line under this particular part of the discussion. With a glare toward Kink—whether she's into the kind of shit he is or not, I'm determined he'll never know—I move this on. Tapping my head, I attempt to put my thoughts into words. “If it’s not her body, it’s either revenge, which doesn’t make sense, or info she could have that Alder doesn’t want to get out.”

“Take us back a bit, Prez.” Salem waggles his hand. “As I understand it, Connor, or Dan as he should be known, is dead and buried. He was moved under WitSec, so no one accidentally saw his face, and kept under wraps in case he was needed to testify when the feds finally catch up with Alder. His mother, Patsy, moved with him at the same time, as she wanted to be with her son.”

“Because she wanted to make sure he kept on the straight and narrow,” I explain. “So yes, she came too.”

“And,” the enforcer continues, “Token says this druggie squad isn’t on the lookout for Dan, which means we’re wrong to assume Alder knows his death was a sham.” He waits for Token’s chin lift, then resumes, “Patsy’s disappearance was straight after her son was buried. What if Alder thinks that wasn’t a coincidence? Could he think Patsy knows something, maybe some message Connor left, and that she was moved by WitSec on her own merits? What if she either does, or he just thinks she has something to tell?”

I don’t immediately reject that notion, but I don’t buy it. I give it a moment’s thought, then shake my head. “I don’t see how she could know anything. The story as I know it is Connor was trying to hide ten kilos of drugs. He was living with his dad and wanted nothing to do with Patsy at the time, but unbeknownst to her, he stored the drugs in her house. When it came to light, she was pretty shocked by all accounts.”

“She was married to Connor’s dad. Maybe she’s got information from when they were together? Something that could bring Alder down.”

I stare at Grumbler, then, again, dismiss it. “But if he knows the feds moved her, he would expect her already to have told everything she knew."

"Unless as Salem said, he thinks she'll appear as a witness, or, it's knowledge she doesn't know she possesses," Pennywise says enigmatically. "It could also be he thinks she's helping them build a case against him, pinning the murder of her son on him."

It's a good point. I'd been focused on what everyone else was thinking, that Alder believed Connor was still alive and wanted revenge, using Patsy only to find him. Was Patsy the target herself? It's certainly starting to look like it.

Could Pennywise have a point? Could Salem?

"Does Alder know the feds moved her?" Dart's frowning now. "How could he? She had no contact with them as far as he knew, but she has gone into hiding. Could he just be worried as to the reason she's gone? He may think as Connor is dead, it's fuckin' strange Patsy rode off into the sunset and left her only remaining family, her daughter, behind."

It was when Patsy had to reassure herself Beth was happy and alive that kicked off Alder's search for her, or as far as we know.

I stare at my VP while thinking we have nothing to go on. "All we know is that Alder is pretty desperate to find her. I need to talk to them both," I decide. "Look, I know you've all got better things to do, so I'll cut to the chase now. If they stay and we have their backs, it could bring Alder down on us, and right now I can't give a measure as to how much danger we could be exposed to. He's got spies, for want of a better word—any addict or dealer. They could be anywhere for all we know."

"Not in the club," Grumbler puts in fast, looking at each man around this table.

"Definitely not," I agree. It's taken a long time for the club to fully come together and trust one another again. You don't have nine of your brothers betray you without keeping an eye on the ones who are left. But we've got there now. Nonetheless, drugs and dealing are dirty words around this table.

"I think what Lost is getting at is that if we extend our hospitality to Patsy, it could bring heat down on the club. I for one vote to protect her." My VP stares me in the eye as others look incredulous.

"Is there any fuckin' doubt?" Smoker's shaking his head. It's the first time he's spoken all meeting, and it triggers a coughing fit now.

My head likewise moves side to side as comments fly from all around me, including Scribe noting things have been far too quiet and boring lately, and taking on a drug lord could make life more exciting. I simultaneously shake my head and roll my eyes.

"Is Dan working?" my VP queries.

He is. I hadn't thought about that. "As a security guard at a mall."

"He'll have to give that up. For now."

He will. But I doubt it was a vocation.

"I can find work for idle hands," Salem offers.

I raise my chin in appreciation. That's better than having the kid just hanging around. "I'll talk to him."

Bones clears his throat. "Is it a coincidence that Shark's reappeared now?"

At the mention of the name, I'm half surprised men don't make the sign of the cross. Their expressions, though, speak volumes. While I hate the name being brought up, Bones had been right to suggest it. After the initial impact of the reminder of the time we'd all prefer to forget, the men's faces turn from angry to contemplative.

"Drugs being the connection?" Scribe looks particularly thoughtful.

I rest my hands on the table. "Shark's got reason to hate us. He's a man adrift without a club and he could very well blame us rather than himself. I don't like that he's surfaced right now, but the only thing about it is timing. I can't see how he could be in with this Alder."

"Worth bearing in mind though, Prez." Dart waves toward Bones, acknowledging that he raised the issue. "Can't disregard anything."

"I'll note it." Scribe picks up his pen.

"I'll kill him if I see him again," Smoker murmurs.

"Not too fast," Salem amends. "We'll need to question him first."

"Another thought, Prez?" Bones raises his chin. "We've seen Shark, what if he's regrouped with the other six of them? What if we've got more than just Alder coming for us?"

Grumbler's hand smashes down onto the table. "They show their fuckin' faces and I'm with Smoker, they're fuckin' dead."

"Painfully," Salem promises, but adds, "but not before I talk to them." The enforcer has his own particular ways of conducting a conversation.

I lower my head into my hands. "Just because there's one bad apple that turned up, doesn't mean there's more. But I take the point, it could be the whole darn barrel. Keep eyes and ears open. I don't think you're right, Bones, but still, we can't just dismiss it." I've had too much bad news already today, like the woman I'd like warming my bed is actively being sought by a drug lord. I pick up the gavel and bang it. "Church dismissed."

Quickly, before anyone can stop me and heap more problems onto my plate, I stand and walk to the door, covering the distance out to the clubroom in just a few short strides. The sound of a thumping beat meets my ears first, not unusual by itself, but I catch movement out of the corner of my eye and come to a dead halt. I'd been making my way toward the stairs, but now I find I won't have to make the climb to find the woman I'm seeking.

I'd thought Patsy might be hiding in her room, unsure of her place in the clubhouse of an MC. Or, if she'd ventured downstairs, I'd find her sitting talking with the only person she knows here, her son. What I hadn't expected to see was her in tight-fitting leggings wrapped around the fucking stripper pole with Alex obviously giving her a lesson.

Sure, she's more ungainly than graceful as Alex tries to tell her what to do. As I watch her attempt to do as instructed, she fails, instead ending up sprawled in a heap on the floor, bent double with laughter.

I watch for a moment as she tries once again, admiring that she's actually quite supple. It's clear she hasn't the faintest idea of technique, but tries valiantly to hold the pole, wrap her leg around it and spin, but she falls once again, and again finds it amusing. It's the sexiest thing I've seen for years. Even more so than watching the strippers who, under Alex's tutelage, have become quite proficient.

The sound of the men filing out of church disturbs her, and she gets to her feet, brushing herself off. When she spies me staring, her face glows red.

Discretely adjusting myself, I walk over, hoping my jeans are disguising the hard-on I'm now sporting.

"I, er… Alex was just showing me…"

"Fuckin' sexy, babe." I lean in close as I speak softly, then I turn to Alex and wink. "So, you're going to make a pole dancer out of Patsy?"

Alex grins, and gestures to herself. "If I can do it, anyone can."

She's putting herself down. I frown, glad Dart hadn't heard her. She'd learned to dance to put a spark into her non-existent love life with her now, thanks to us, dead ex. But whatever she could have done wouldn't have worked—he'd only married her for money and never wanted her for herself. His abuse had worsened, and she'd taken off, running literally for her life. To support her and her sick kid, she'd applied for work at the Satan's Devils strip club in Tucson. While on the surface she hadn't appeared to be stripper material, and certainly didn't want to take off all her clothes, they'd made concessions once they saw how good a dancer she was on that pole. She had customers lined up around the block.

One comment from her ex was all it had taken to make her doubt herself. Now she dances for her own enjoyment, and for Dart's. It's why he's so adamant no other fucker should watch her, but I doubt there's a man here who hasn't sneaked in to watch.

No one could doubt how happy Alex and Dart are together. But it had been touch and go at one point. While Dart was kidding himself his feelings for her didn't run deep, her ex had kidnapped her, tortured her and left her for dead. It was then he realised how much he really felt for her, and luckily, we were there to save her in time.

It's strange how things turn out. That allowance that her parents were paying her ex to stay married to her? Well it stopped when we made sure he wasn't going to bother her anymore or couldn't as he was dead. They weren't going to pay a cent when Alex committed the transgression of marrying a white man. Interracial marriages in their eyes was the ultimate sin.

The reminder that Dart had almost lost the woman he loved by being an ass gives me pause for thought. Am I risking doing the same thing? Should I be thinking of how I might be able to make this work, instead of trying to push my embryonic feelings for Patsy away? I can take things slow, see where it, if there even is a chance of being an it, leads. No need to rush into things.

"I'll never be able to move like Alex." Patsy's grinning as she wipes her chalky hands on a rag seeming to be over her embarrassment. "I'm too old for a start. But it looks fun."

"I'm trying to get back into shape," Alex tells her. "I'm usually here in the mornings. Eva, or Cindy watch Isla—she's my one-year-old daughter—for me, and I have some time to myself. They wear her out so she naps in the afternoons and it allows me to get on with some work."

"Work? What do you do?" Patsy asks with interest.

"She's the club's lawyer," I answer for her. "A fuckin' good one at that."

Patsy's eyebrows rise as she takes in the information, but doesn't comment on it. But I suspect the VP's woman has gone up in her estimation. Instead, she asks a different question.

"Eva? Cindy? Are they old ladies as well?"

Alex giggles at the thought, which makes me grin. "Ah, no. I'm the only one of those. They're club girls, but they're mostly okay. Eva's a nurse which can be handy."

Alex could have been a bitch to the sweet butts, but apart from a rough start with Eva for which Dart takes all the blame, the two have become friends. Alex has never lorded it over them, saying each to their own. Dart's mentioned she got very friendly with the strippers back in Tucson, so understands a girl's got to do whatever she needs to get by. As long as they keep well away from Dart, she appears to have no problem with the girls and what they get up to with the brothers.

Now my dick has decided it's going to behave, I remember why I approached her. "Patsy, I need to talk to you and Dan now. Where is he?"

"Upstairs, listening to music, I think. I'll go and get him."

"Prospect?" I yell, getting Wrangler's attention. "Get Dan to come down here."

I turn back to find Patsy grinning. "Useful." She nods to where Wrangler's taking the stairs two at a time.

A motorcycle engine starts, the sound bouncing off the windows, soon joined by more. Gradually the clubroom is emptying as some members return to whatever they were doing before I'd summoned them for church. Dusty and Scribe have obviously decided to call it a day, as they're already propping up the bar, and Smoker walks past tossing his lighter in his hands as he goes outside to have a cigarette. I notice him glance toward Alex with a slight narrowing of his eyes.

Dan appears quickly, even preceding the prospect down the stairs. I nod at Dart and jerk my head, then the four of us retreat to my office.

"Has anything happened?" Patsy asks anxiously once she sits down.

I stare at her for a moment, regretting that I'm going to demolish the smile that dancing with Alex had put on her face. Taking a breath, I tell her straight, "Alder's looking for you, Patsy."

As far as she's concerned, I've told her nothing new. "I know that. He thinks he'll find Dan if he finds me."

After glancing sideways at Dart, I shake my head and spell it out. "He's not looking for Dan. He's only searching for you. We've found nothing to suggest he thinks Dan is alive."

Dan's brow creases and he sits bolt upright. "Why? That doesn't make sense. What would he want with Mom?" To his credit, he looks dismayed as if the news Alder's searching for his mom is worse than his being the target himself. I find myself liking the kid even more.

Patsy's looking equally confused. "I know nothing about him or his activities. I've avoided Phil as best I could since we divorced over eighteen years ago. As I had sole custody and he didn't want to joint parent, we didn't even meet to discuss the kids. I knew Alder only while I was married, but I always detested the man and even then, had very little to do with him."

"You said Alder came to the funeral, Mom."

"He did." She nods at her son. The pained look crossing her face tells me while the funeral had been a sham, it had still been painful. "It was the first time I'd seen him since before the divorce. He said nothing except not to expect anything from Phil's will, that everything that was Phil's would go to him now. It was amusing as it was only land. Phil's house had by that time burned to the ground."

Dart's hands are steepled under his chin, and his elbows

resting on his knees. He leans forward. "He left you nothing, Patsy?"

"Not a thing. I didn't expect it. We'd been apart more years than we were married, and there was no love lost between us."

The room goes quiet as we're all lost in thought.

CHAPTER TWELVE

Patsy

Apart from this compound being an old airfield and not a steel mill, when I'd gotten out of the truck, it was much as I'd expected. I'd stayed in the Pueblo clubhouse, so wasn't surprised by what I found when I stepped inside. Subtle differences were visible, but it fit in with my image of an MC lair.

The VP's wife's pole dancing had been something I hadn't expected, nor was the respect the men had showed by leaving her to dance by herself. She'd seemed lost in her own world. While noting I'll have to politely introduce myself later at a more appropriate time, I listened to Lost instructing the prospect to take us to our rooms.

He wasted no time, indicating Dan and I should follow him up the stairs. Dan was directed to a room off to one side and he and his bag disappeared. The prospect carrying my much larger one, waved me further along the hallway.

The bedroom that had been assigned to me was plain, I noticed, glancing around when the prospect unlocked the door then left after pressing a key into my hand. It was utilitarian, and not particularly welcoming. There was an adjacent bathroom that's plain and bare with a few cracked tiles, though clean. The bed simply functional, the sheets looked and smelled freshly laundered, though the mattress was thin and worn. But beggars couldn't be choosers, I supposed. It's not a place you'd want to stay in for anything more than its primary purpose, sleeping. After putting away the clothes I'd brought with me in the empty closet and unpacking my bathroom items, I sat on the bed for a while, then decided to get out my e-reader. But I couldn't focus on the words and soon became bored.

After popping my head around the door of the room given to Dan, I saw he was content playing some game on his phone, so I decided to venture downstairs to the clubroom and nose around.

I'd gotten on okay with the bikers in the Colorado Satan's Devils chapter, and nothing led me to suspect I'd find the San Diego members much different, so I only felt a little awkward as I descended the stairs, wondering if, by now, the room would be full of assorted men.

But as I reached the bottom of the staircase, instead of the loud rumble of voices, all I could hear was some muted clanking of bottles from where the prospect was restocking the bar, and music. I realised immediately that Alex must still be dancing.

Would she mind if I sneaked over to watch? I moved closer, not sure whether I should stay or go.

Alex seemed lost in her own world as she put more chalk on her hands and then went back on the pole, contorting herself around it. So rapt by her performance, as I drew nearer, I knocked against a chair and toppled it. After I hurriedly righted it, I saw she'd stopped.

"Hey, come over." She beckoned to me, clearly not upset I'd been spying on her.

"I didn't mean to interrupt."

"You didn't. I was about finished for today. I was just trying to perfect a routine, but I'll leave it for now. I tend to lose sense of time when I'm dancing."

"I'm in awe, you know?" I waved toward the pole. "You're incredible."

She laughed and shrugged. "It's just something I took to. It's easy when you know how."

There was something about this diminutive woman that I was taken by. She's welcoming and friendly. As she pulled on a shirt over her tank top, I waited for her to ask the questions I was sure would come, but she didn't ask anything that I couldn't answer.

"Your room okay? I know it's not much."

"I'm just grateful to have some breathing space. As a stop gap, it's fine. So," I motioned toward her, "baby fat you said? How old's your baby again?"

It was the right question. Like any mom, she was more than happy to talk about her daughter, Isla, and her son, Tyler, who's nine. When she got out her phone to show me a photo, I saw her daughter was beautiful, her skin a gorgeous light coffee colour, and she had dark brown eyes. Her smile was to die for as well.

"She's beautiful," I commented completely truthfully. "Where is she now?"

"Eva's playing with her upstairs."

I glanced at the picture again, looking forward to meeting her in person. A pang went through me thinking Beth could make me a grandmother and I might never know. I'd never have pictures of any grandchildren I had to pass around, unless Dan found a woman and so far, he had shown no inclination to settle down. As tears pricked at my eyes, I made an effort to put such thoughts out of my mind, observing, "She looks like a happy baby."

"Most of the time," Alex responded, drily. "She has her moments though. She's got a stubborn streak a mile wide. So, you ever thought about having a go yourself?" Alex nodded toward the pole.

What woman alive hasn't? "I'm far too old," I told her.

She snorted. "Look at me, I'm hardly what you'd expect

from a pole dancer. You never know what you can do until you try."

I eyed the pole, then Alex, then glanced down at myself. I was wearing leggings and a long stretchy t-shirt, which would probably work.

"There's nobody here. Oh," she added when she sees me look toward the prospect, "ignore him, I do." When she raised a quizzical eyebrow, I suddenly grinned. Well, why the hell not?

Within moments, I was preparing my hands with chalk as Alex sprayed the pole. She showed me some beginner moves, then I tried to copy what she had just done, and failed, spectacularly. But my competitive streak began to kick in, and I was determined to beat this.

Alex didn't laugh as I couldn't get a grip, just encouraged me, saying she had been the same in the beginning. Her confidence persuaded me to try again, a second and then a third go. That attempt was slightly better, and I managed a twirl before sliding down and ending up on my ass. I did it again with the same result.

I started turning to grin at Alex—despite the ignominious ending, it had been a small victory—when instead of landing on her, my eyes found Lost.

He was staring at me, and as I wondered how long he'd been there, my cheeks began to burn, not only with embarrassment, but that he was so obviously trying to adjust himself in his tight-fitting pants. The denim that I'd previously noticed hugging his ass, was now definitely bulging out in the front. *Because of me?*

I couldn't think of another reason. As far as I knew he'd just been in a meeting, and while I had no idea what would have gone on, I doubted it would be anything to get him aroused.

Then he'd told me I was sexy. Me. Sexy.

I hadn't known how to respond. But I didn't have to. Like a switch being thrown, Lost was all business, quickly summoning

Dan then getting us seated in his office. He didn't waste time before dropping a bombshell on me.

Now I'm trying to get my head around it.

I'm stunned at their belief it's me Alder is trying to find. They must have it wrong, and he does suspect Dan's alive. What on earth would Alder want with me? I have no idea.

That Phil had died a rich man and had left me nothing wasn't any more than I'd expect. We hadn't played happy families in a very long time. I'm not sure we ever did. I'd kicked him out and refused to take his ill-gotten earnings not wanting to be beholden to him in any way. If he had left me anything, I'd probably have given it away. Who'd want to touch dirty money earned in dubious ways? Especially now I knew he was into ruining lives, by dealing in drugs, protection money and sex trafficking. No, Phil had never given me anything I wanted to keep, except for my children.

Something, a thought, is niggling at the back of my head, but I can't seem to get hold of it. It's right there, at the edge of my consciousness, dredged up by my busy mind. I'm vaguely aware that Dan's broken the silence, but I concentrate on thinking instead, trying to cast my mind back to a time before it all went wrong and I realised what a crook I was married to.

I'd come in to ask Phil whether he wanted a coffee and found him frantically searching for something instead. "What's the hurry, Phil?"

He spared only one quick glance my way. "I need to get to the bank before it closes."

"Use an ATM if you want to get money out—"

"I don't need fucking money." He kept searching around in his desk. Then he looked up, his eyes narrowing. "Do you have it?"

My brow creased. "Have what?"

His eyes looked upward as if I should be able to guess. "The key for our safe deposit box."

Oh, that. "It's in my jewellery box. What do you need out of it, Phil?" We kept our wills, birth certificates, marriage licence and other stuff in there. As an accountant, one thing Phil did was keep our affairs in order. It's an obvious wife question to ask, what he wants to look at and why.

Phil didn't talk about money, but we always seemed to have enough. Could he be wanting to take out a second mortgage? That's something I should know about.

"I'm not taking anything out. I need to put something in."

"What?"

"For fuck's sake, woman, some of my financial stuff." He huffed as if he shouldn't need to explain himself. "Now get me the key so I can get moving. This needs to be in there today."

Phil hadn't been the best husband, but he wasn't usually so sharp—emotionless would describe him better. That's why it's stuck in my memory. I'd gotten him the key then watched as he'd rushed out of the door. He hadn't taken his briefcase, I'd noticed, nor carried a bunch of papers in his hand. But whatever he was putting inside had to be important, at least to him. I remember questioning him when he'd returned, but he'd said it was something to do with his employment. That would have sounded plausible, except for the shifty look in his eyes. A look I was to become very familiar with.

My marriage had been going downhill for a while, and after that point, it had gotten worse. Phil no longer even pretended to be interested in sex and spent more time in his office with his door not only closed but locked. Something was wrong, but I hadn't known what, until everything had become clear when the police had turned up to arrest him.

Our safe deposit box was rarely touched. I'd left the key with Beth in case she and Ink needed the deed to the house.

"Patsy?" Lost barks.

I give myself a little shake, realising I'd disappeared into my head. "Sorry, I was miles away."

"You look like you've thought of something? Something you should share?"

I press my lips together, then speak, "I'm nothing to Alder. I avoided speaking to the man, and Phil never discussed his legitimate, let alone his nefarious businesses with me. I know nothing, except that my son is alive." Lost raises his chin in encouragement. "Therefore, I have nothing of value. Phil and I parted ways, but as far as he was concerned, he went on to better things. I buried," I glance apologetically at Dan, still having difficulty remembering that day which had almost been for real, "my son. Alder might want revenge on Connor if he were still alive, but he has no reason to take that out on me. He's risking exposure, surely, by trying to come after me at all."

Lost raises and lowers his chin. "But there's something…?"

My face screws up as I reply to Lost. "If Alder thinks I have information he wants, it must be to do with Phil, and that can't be recent. As I said, Phil and I barely spoke after he left. In recent years, I've had nothing to do with him at all. I don't know if it's anything or not, but a memory has just come into my head. It's so long ago now, maybe twenty years back, and could be nothing at all."

"Anything at this point could be useful," Dart puts in. Dan's looking at me quizzically as though thinking back, but he won't remember as he was just two. As I recall, I'd just put him down for a nap.

I shrug and simultaneously shake my head. "Phil and I thought it would be a good idea to get a safe deposit box when we got married. We put in our birth certificates, our wills, and the documents about the house. When the kids were born, we added their birth certificates too, and some of their baby pics, but never anything else. I'd forgotten about it until Phil wanted the key one day to put something in it. It struck me as unusual. It wasn't a big one, so we didn't have room for much else, and I thought we were only using it for the basics. I'd questioned him, but he just said it was some of his employment stuff. It seemed odd then, but I didn't push it. After he moved out, I added the divorce papers." I raise and lower my shoulders again. "Phil knew where the key was, I'd told him I kept it in my jewellery box. He may well have taken whatever it was back out."

Lost looks disappointed. "I can't think it's anything to do with a piece of paper stored twenty years ago in a bank."

"When was it last opened?" Dart asks.

"Not too long ago," I confirm, realising it's probably a red herring. "It's been opened a few times when Beth needed her birth certificate for work. I never noticed anything obvious that I didn't recognise in there. Sorry." I grimace, realising I've wasted their time.

But Lost's eyes sharpen. "You know nothing, yet Alder is desperate to find you. You have nothing of his or Phil's. Did he leave something in your house?"

"It's been twenty years, Lost." I widen my eyes. "When Phil left, he took everything he owned. His office was cleared out. The kids grew up, so the house got changed. I've redecorated everywhere, changed furniture which wore out. His office was used as a playroom for the kids. There isn't anything of Phil's left there."

"That box, Patsy? Did you take everything out when you last opened it? Could there be something in there that's been forgotten all of these years?"

In response, I shake my head. "Lost, no. I didn't take everything out. I know what's in there so there was no need."

Dart raises his chin toward Lost. "What if Phil had dirt on Alder that he wanted to keep hidden away, where Alder would never find it? What if, now Phil is dead, Alder wants his insurance policy back?"

Suddenly Dan's sitting up straighter. "I overheard something once. An argument between Alder and Phil. I'd completely forgotten about it. Phil was trying to get deeper into his business and Alder kept knocking him back. They used to be partners, but Alder was too selfish for that and kept Phil out of a lot of the more lucrative stuff. I was worried at the time as I was still trying to impress Phil and hovered around in case things turned physical. Phil used those exact words. He reminded Alder that he still had an insurance policy."

"So there was something he had over Alder." Lost leans back in his chair and links his fingers behind his head. "And one possible place he kept it was in that safe deposit box."

"Oh, come on," I tell them, my eyes looking around in disbelief. "It's too farfetched to think something's been under our noses this whole time. I've never seen it."

Dart grins. "Wouldn't hurt to look. You still have the key?"

I nod. "I left it with Beth as we moved in a rush. There's nothing secret in there, and if she's going to marry Ink," I break off and swallow thinking I wouldn't be there to witness it, "she needed to have access to her birth certificate."

"You mind her going through that safe deposit box?"

"Of course not. There's no secrets to me."

Lost raises his chin at me, then lifts an eyebrow at his VP. He gets out his phone and taps a pre-set number. He puts it on speaker, and places it in the middle of the desk.

"Demon. It's Lost."

"Lost, what can I do for you, Brother?"

"I've got Patsy, Dan and Dart with me. You're on speaker."

"That means trouble if you've come out in the open, Dan. You at the compound? Are you both safe?"

"Yes to all three," Lost answers for my son, staring at the phone as though he can see the man speaking. He sends me a look full of apology as he drops me straight in it. "Patsy picked up a tail yesterday."

"Jesus." I blanch hearing Demon's censure coming down the phone. "She alright?"

Lost answers for me, "She's fine. She called me. We dealt

with it. But it's not safe to leave them without protection anymore."

"So that fuckin' message you got was legit. Shit."

I start wishing a hole in the ground would open up to swallow me. I shouldn't have called Beth, however much I wanted to hear her voice and reassure myself she was okay. If I hadn't, Alder would never have found out where we are.

Lost sighs, looking my way. "Alder's got eyes all over San Diego. He's got a network of dealers and users, all primed to get a payout if they spot Patsy out and about. Well, yesterday they did."

"They know Connor's alive then." Demon sounds both resigned and business like at the same time, acknowledging the problem and prepared to deal with it.

"Apparently not," Lost interrupts. "It's Patsy he's after. No reason to believe he has suspicions about Dan."

"*Patsy*?" Demon's incredulity comes clearly down the line, clearly having difficulty understanding why a drug lord would be interested in a woman past her prime.

"Yeah. We're trying to figure out why, been knocking it around for a while. We've come up with something. Now it could be grasping at straws, but we could do with your help to check it out."

"Anything you need, Brother."

I admire the way Demon doesn't hesitate without even knowing what task he'll be assigned. It's this loyalty and brotherhood that made me happy Beth had found the right man. One for all and all for one never had greater meaning than when it comes to the men in this MC. That it extends beyond chapters is heartwarming.

"Patsy's got a safe deposit box, goes back to when she first married Phil Foster. Normal shit kept in it, but twenty years back, Phil put something inside, and she doesn't know what. It's a long shot, Brother, but it's possible it's still there. Beth's got a key to that safe deposit box, and I was wondering whether you could get Ink to go with her and see if it's holding a secret? We're pretty certain Phil Foster had an insurance policy, and we're not talking house or car. Only thing that makes sense is that Alder wants any evidence of it buried and gone. Patsy's in danger if he thinks she's got it."

"Fuck. You sure?"

"Nah, Demon, I'm not. Could be barking completely up the wrong tree here, but it's the only fuckin' lead I got. Alder's after Patsy, and we've got no fucking idea why."

"Any risk Alder knows Patsy's with you?"

"No. We stopped the person following her home, and as far as we know, got Patsy and Dan away clean without anyone being any the wiser. But with the network Alder's got, it was only going to be a matter of time before they got hold of her."

Demon's quiet for a moment, then he says, "Be careful, you hear? Lost, I'm well aware you're taking care of what's ours. You need brothers to head down your way, I'm happy to boost your numbers."

Lost smiles, and nods at the phone, then uses words the other man can hear. "Thanks, Demon. I hope we can keep trouble away from our door, but if we can't, I may take you up on that offer."

"I'll be in touch when we've opened the safe deposit box. Patsy, you there?"

"Yes, Demon." I clear my throat. "I'm here."

"This shit with Beth…" he pauses. "Look, I understand you need to speak to her, but you calling her out of the blue on an unsecure phone, well, that can't happen again."

It's at this point I want to slide under the table. I shrink back into my chair, and my voice squeaks when I reply, "I know, Demon. I'm sorry, I—"

"I can appreciate how fuckin' hard this is on you. Her too." He pauses for a second. "Lost's phone is encrypted, mine too.

The clubhouse is clean if Token does as good a job as Cad. We'll make arrangements for the two of you to talk, okay?"

My eyes prick with tears, both at his understanding, and the promise I'll be able to talk to Beth soon. I almost miss what he asks next.

"We find anything in that safe deposit box, I'll get Cad to check it out. You okay with that, Patsy? You got anything personal in there?"

"I'm an open book, Demon. There's nothing secret about me at all."

"Okay. I think we're done here, Lost. I'll get it sorted from our end. Beth's not here today, Patsy, but I'll get her to call you tomorrow, okay?"

I feel like fist pumping the air, but refrain. The smile on my face must say it all, as Lost grins my way. Dan's mouth is curved, and he reaches across and squeezes my hand. *I'm going to be able to speak to Beth again.* I feel my heart beating faster in anticipation.

When I'd left Colorado I was supposed to abide by the rules, and I had every intention of doing so. I had known it was going to be hard, but not even my wildest imagination could have prepared me for the pain of being separated from my oldest child.

Beth's in her late twenties, and it was probably well past time she should have left home and struck out on her own. That she stayed with me as long as she had wasn't because either of us were incapable, but because we'd had a relationship where we were friends as much as anything else.

I suppose I remained protective of her. Both my children are tall, throwbacks to someone far back in my family as both Phil and I were average height. For Dan it had been an advantage, but a girl shooting up to be taller than all the other kids in her class had made her stand out. Children are cruel and would pick on anyone who was different. At school, she'd been bullied.

I'd been helpless. The school hadn't understood, Beth stood head and shoulders above the other students, including many of the boys, so surely, she could look after herself? Beth hasn't got violent tendencies, but in any event, it wasn't abuse in a physical form that she received. It proved impossible to protect her from the snide comments and jeers. They say words don't hurt, they're wrong. The wounds they inflict might be invisible, but they do lasting damage all the same. She'd already been an introverted socially awkward child, now she was ostracised because she was different.

By the time she'd gone to college, her life had changed. Her friends had matured, and she'd grown from an unhappy girl into a confident young woman. But the worry that's sat with a mom for years can't simply be turned off. I was happy she'd stayed under my wing.

When Beth met Ink, I had no idea at the start how long it would last. Beth, I knew, had feelings for him, but whether he reciprocated those I wasn't too sure. The drastic turn of events caused by Dan had shown that Ink really cared—enough so that he was prepared to sacrifice his freedom and go to jail instead of her. Here was a man who I could entrust with my daughter. If it hadn't been for him, for Mel, her best friend and married to a biker herself, for the whole of the Satan's Devils club back in Pueblo, I could never have walked away.

Ink wanted Beth for just who she was. I could see how much he loved her, how he was building a new life with her, coincidentally buying her family home. She'd have the security I used to give her, but as is right, given to her now by her man. In time, they'd have a family.

At this point in her life and in mine, we could finally part. My job as a supportive mother was done. I had nothing to worry about leaving her on her own; her future was mapped out. With only such a brief time to consider matters, I hastily made up my mind, Dan was the one who needed me now.

I didn't realise I'd feel as though I'd been torn in half. I thought I knew, but I hadn't accepted quite how much I'd miss her.

Of course, children move away all the time, but there's always a connection via phone calls or visits. In my case, even the briefest of contact was forbidden. It was as if one of us had died with no funeral, no mourning.

I'd been desperate and I'd broken the rules. Now, it appears, I'm paying the price.

"Patsy?"

A scraping of chairs brings me back to the here and now. I hadn't realised my head had dropped into my hands, nor that said hands are shaking. As Dan stands, he shoots me a worried look, but Lost raises his chin.

Dart's already at the door, and he holds it open for Dan to walk out.

We've been dismissed.

Likewise, I press down on the arms of the chair in preparation to stand to leave.

"Stay," Lost instructs, his voice deep and soothing. "Stay, Patsy. Talk to me."

I don't realise that I'm crying, tears rolling down my cheeks, until Lost passes me a tissue.

When I go to apologise, he stops me. "It's okay to cry, babe."

"I don't know why I am," I sniff.

"I do. It's relief. You can speak to your daughter tomorrow."

I force myself to be sensible. "It's only a temporary reprieve, isn't it Lost? I can talk to Beth now, but there's nothing I can do but stay out of Alder's way. If you're right and he thinks I've got evidence against him, or can bring him down in some way, he'll never stop looking for me."

"We'll start by getting into your safe deposit box and seeing if there's anything inside. If that turns up a blank, we'll start looking for something else. We'll leave no stone unturned."

The more I think about something waiting to be found, the more unlikely it seems. "I can't think there'll be anything there. I'll make the most of being able to speak to Beth now, then we'll contact the marshals and move on." I straighten my back, trying to convince myself I can cope with talking to Beth and facing another goodbye. "It's the only way."

CHAPTER THIRTEEN

Lost

I can understand how much it hurt Patsy to leave everything she'd known behind her, her home and her daughter. I know only too well the pain that losing everything can cause. If proof were necessary, the look on her face, the hope and longing that had covered it with just the promise of a phone call with her daughter was all I would have needed.

She thinks to keep her son safe; they need to disappear again.

But how easy will that be? The marshals are focused on keeping Dan out of Alder's way. They might be mildly interested in what Alder wants with her, but if they want their witness alive, would they want to risk him by also protecting her? Dan's in the clear, he's dead as far as anyone knows, so no one's even searching for him now. Patsy, though, is actively being sought. Would that make her a liability for her son? If the feds got wind of Alder's desperation, might they want to use her to set a trap for the wanted man?

I won't let that happen. No. Patsy will be kept out of Alder's hands, and I've no greater wish than to make it safe for her to be back with her family. Both daughter and son.

As she silently cries, I give her space, passing her the box of tissues so she can help herself.

Leaning my head back, I close my eyes and think over what Demon had previously told me. The decision had been made hastily, Patsy having no time to balance her needs between those of her children. I know something Patsy doesn't, news that up to now hasn't been shared. When Patsy finds out her daughter is expecting… well, I think it will be hard to witness the pain she'll feel not being able to be there, or to share all the moments that a grandmother should.

What pressure would that put on her newly fledged relationship with her son?

Dan had chosen his father and became a stranger to his mom. Patsy obviously felt a responsibility for the breakdown of their relationship and wanted to take the chance to remedy the mistakes she's made in the past. But Dan's a man, he's bound to fuck up again. Will she grow to resent him?

What happens if Dan finds a woman of his own and settles down? What will happen to Patsy? She'll be on her own.

She's so determined to keep everyone out of harm's way that she'll risk her own happiness to do it. I can't see her making that sacrifice again, not when I see how painful being apart from her daughter is.

Watching her blot her eyes once again, she offers me a brave, tenuous smile. I find myself saying, "I want to help you, Patsy."

"You are helping. You've brought us here, and I do admit I feel safer. You're giving me a chance to speak to Beth. Demon's doing whatever he can from his end. That's *everything* right now."

It's nothing at all. Not once she finds out Beth's pregnant.

Now she's got a day to wait before she's likely to hear from Beth. Twenty-four hours or more and each sixty-minute period is bound to drag. It's been a tortuous time since Patsy first called me yesterday, and it's not yet been twenty-four hours. The fear of being stalked, then, while Dusty and Curtis kept her safe last night, that I thought she needed them must have made her more scared. Her only moment of pleasure was that brief interlude with Alex, and I'll need to thank Dart's woman for providing her with that.

But soon after, I'd brought her down to earth with a huge fucking bump, telling her she was the one Alder was after. She's been put through the ringer, all of us trying to work out why her son isn't the target, but her, herself.

I want to take her mind off her problems. Until we hear back from Colorado, or unless Token finds anything, there's nothing more we can do for now.

I notice her tears have dried, and that she's started fidgeting.

"You ever been on a motorcycle, Patsy?"

"Er, what?" My question has flummoxed her, and she takes a moment to process my words.

I grin at her. "On a bike. You want to come for a ride? Personally, I find there's nothing better to clear my head when there are too many thoughts whirling around inside it. Wind therapy never did anyone any harm."

She lets out a short laugh, her eyes going wide as she dips her chin down. "You're joking, aren't you? No, I have never been on the back of a bike and can't say I've ever had any desire to ride one. I think I'm past it now. Just look at me." She waves a hand toward herself.

I almost wish she hadn't made that gesture as my eyes follow the direction of her hand. Sure, she's not got the youthful figure of a woman three decades younger, but as I'd seen from that short demonstration on the pole, she's still supple, and those breasts of hers look like they'll fit just right in my hands. I know from memory her ass is shapely, her hips meaty enough I'd be able to hang onto them with my hands…

I'm glad the desk is between us right now. Though, then again, perhaps it wouldn't hurt for her to understand, she's still desirable to a man. Might perk her up a little. Well, this man, anyway, any other fucker who dares to even think something similar about her will learn his mistake at the end of my fist. *Really?*

Yes, really. *So why am I bothering to fight it?*

I'm no good for her.

She'll be leaving soon.

Everything I think is true, yet somehow, I feel I have to, as they say, seize the moment. Patsy intrigues me like no woman has for a very long time.

Suddenly it's of real importance that I get her on the back of my bike.

"You're not past it," I scoff as I stand. "Come on. Let's go ride."

Maybe it's the dominance in my tone, the suggestion I won't take any refusal, but she pushes herself up from the chair. Then she comes to herself. "It's not safe for me to be seen around."

"You'll be wearing a helmet. Your face can be hidden by a bandana and sunglasses, and no one would think of looking for you riding pillion."

"It's a crazy idea." Her mouth says one thing, her face suggests another.

I work on the spark of interest I see in her eyes. "You object to crazy, babe? You never up to doing something just for the sheer hell of it?"

"Not for a very long time." There's a twinkle in her eyes that makes me suspect her answer will be yes. "Not since I settled down and became a mom."

"Your children are grown, Patsy. You deserve some fun."

Deciding I'm not going to give her a further chance to object, I take hold of her arm and guide her out the door.

Five minutes later, leaving an open-mouthed Dan in our wake and after a few hastily issued instructions, I'm riding down the track and out of the compound, heading up toward the mountains with no particular destination in mind, just knowing I need to feel the wind on my face and her at my back.

At first, she's stiff, awkward, but quickly she begins to move with me like a natural, as though she's been doing this all her life. I love the feeling of her breasts pushed against the leather of my cut, and the way her arms hug my waist. For me, the years drop away. I'm no longer Lost, an MC prez with so much on my plate, I'm just a man with no cares in the world except for enjoying the ride, and the feel of a woman pressed up behind him. Ageless, carrying no burden, all my troubles left behind.

As her tension fades, she starts to relax, her hands wrapped around my waist loosening their death grip. The wind would take my words away were I to speak, so after a while I slow and pull up by the side of the road.

I glance behind me. "Doing okay?"

Her smile tells me all I want to know. Her words, just a bonus. "Why did I wait so long for this, Lost? I feel alive."

I punch down into first again and let out the clutch. If I didn't get moving, I'd give in to my impulse and kiss her. I'm starting to think that will come, but it will have to be the right time and place. I'm wary of chasing away the first woman I've started to have feelings for in years. It's not just the sexy package she comes in, it's her family loyalty, and fuck me if it wasn't for the way she's willing to give anything a try. Pole dancing? Tick. A motorbike ride? Sure, a couple of protests and then she was all in. I suspect she's become so used to living the life of a housewife and mother, she's not given much thought to what she, herself, wants out of life and is capable of should she put her mind to it.

I continue listing the things I admire about her as I ride for another half hour, reaching for, but coming up with nothing I could say would turn me off. Then I pull into a spot where there's a scenic view back down over the city and out over the Pacific.

I tap her knee and turning, ask her to dismount. She does so, balancing one hand on my shoulder. As I put down the stand, she takes off her helmet, hands it to me, then walks to the barrier and looks over, then turns back around and stares up to the mountains, closer to us now than they were back at the compound.

"It's so different here. Hot, dry."

I know she's not talking about between here and the compound. "Colorado more beautiful?"

She shrugs. "Different. There's a stark beauty here too."

There's beauty in front of me as well.

I'm a man who makes mistakes, someone overly cautious as life has taught me to be. The idea I'd had less than an hour ago has only strengthened while we've been riding. *I want her.* But I don't want to fuck this up, so instead of assuming, I state my intention, giving her every opportunity to object.

"I want to kiss you, Patsy." As her eyes widen, I expand, "I want to wrap my hand in your hair, hold you tight and feel your mouth against mine." There's a danger I might never want to let her go, but I keep that part to myself.

"Oh my." Her eyes go wider. "I, er, I haven't been properly kissed for two decades." Her voice is breathy.

"You stayed faithful?"

"Yes, but not intentionally." She shrugs. "I didn't feel I owed him anything, and had no good memories to cherish, but, I, er, well, with two young children I didn't have much chance. I didn't really seek out any opportunities, and none presented themselves. Oh, I was asked out a couple of times, Beth encouraged me to date, but nothing ever came of it." As she turns away to look at the view, this time the ocean, she continues, honestly, "I'm middle aged, Lost. I'm not a young girl."

I've come up behind her, not touching, but close enough with her back to my front that she can feel my breath on her neck as I tell her, "You're still a woman, Patsy."

She shrugs. "Sometimes I feel like I'm just a mom."

"It's time to live for you now." *She's not told me no.*

Gently my hands rest on her shoulders. When she doesn't pull away, I get a better purchase and turn her around to face me. There's a bemused expression on her face as I lower my lips to hers.

For a moment, it's just the faintest of touches. As I'd warned her, one of my hands twists into her windblown hair, the other descends to her waist and I pull her into my body. With a firm grip, I press with my tongue, requesting silently that she open for me.

She sighs and relents. Now it's tongues touching, sliding together sensuously.

I notice she fits in my arms perfectly. The feel of her, being able to taste her, to breathe in the feminine flowery perfume of her shampoo is as intoxicating as any drug.

I tighten my hold, making my kiss more demanding. She gasps, and presses into me asking for more.

I comply, every part of me tingling, coming alive for the first time in years. A brief encounter with a club girl holds nothing to this. My cock is so hard, it's painfully throbbing.

I raise my mouth slightly, enough to tell her, "See what you fuckin' do to me, babe?" My hand against her waist pulls her to me so she can be left in no doubt. "Don't care what you think about yourself, it's what I think that matters. I think you're one of the sexiest women I've ever met."

"I'm old," she says. "Lost, you're…"

"I'm fifty, babe. Hardly boy toy material. And you're what?"

"Fifty-three," she replies, honestly. "But you could have your choice—"

I grasp her silky locks, holding on tightly, forcing her to look up to see the sincerity in my face. "Yeah, I've got a choice. And you're it." At the flicker of worry in her eyes, I add, "Appreciate it's been a long time for you, babe, so we're going to take this slowly. I'm not a kid just wanting to get his rocks off. When I take you to bed, you're going to know it means something. I'm willing to wait until you're ready."

"Lost, I don't, I couldn't do a one-night stand. If… if I go to bed with someone, it would have to mean something, and I'm in no position to start an affair." I feel the tug against my hand as she tries to turn away, but my grasp is too tight. She's forced to look into my eyes as she says, "I never thought, never expected… Damn, I'm putting this badly. I didn't come away with Dan looking for romance, I get that vicariously through the books that I read. So no, I can't let this go any further. I like you, respect you, perhaps too much. Perhaps for the wrong reasons as you came out of nowhere and saved me. But in a few days, I'll be gone, and if I give in to you, you'd be just one more person who it would hurt to leave." She stops to take a breath.

"Don't want to see you go, babe." I take my chance to speak. "But I won't push you into something you don't want, not until we know how the land lies. I've got a feeling that once I'm inside you, I'll never want to leave. Then waving as you drive off into the sunset, well, you wouldn't be the only person that would hurt." It's my turn to pause, and then continue, "I've got to be honest, babe. You're right to be cautious. Believe me, I'm not a good bet for a happily ever after." I chuckle softly. "I don't mean that in a freedom loving biker way. I mean, I've been there, done that. I know I'll fuck up. Won't be me that wants to walk away."

I loosen my hold, and she takes the opportunity to turn her back on me. "Neither of us seems to be in a position to make promises, Lost." She glances back over her shoulder. "That kiss… I don't think I've ever been kissed like that before. Your passion…"

It makes me wonder about the bastard of a man she married. What kind of caress is she used to, and how much has she missed out on?

She's staring away from me again. "I can't deny I want you.

But I can't go into something without risking my heart. I can't separate physical feelings from emotions. I know…" her breath catches, "I know this is only a pleasant interlude in what's become of my life. The compound is an oasis where I can catch my breath, and you're giving me my chance to speak to Beth before leaving again, and this time, maybe forever."

Damn, now she's put it so starkly it brings everything into sharp focus in my mind. It might be the stupidest decision of my life, but I can't let her go. "No." I might be risking my club, my life. Her… But I can't let her walk away. Sure, for me it would be another loss, something I'd feel deep down inside would have been worth keeping and certainly not the first time it's happened to me. For her though? "No. We'll get Alder off your back. It's him that's going six feet under, babe. You're going nowhere."

Her pleasure in the day has gone, and she shakes her head. "I can't ask that. He's too dangerous."

"You're not asking," I contradict. "But I am. I'm asking that you stay and take a stand. For you, for Dan, for Beth. And, maybe, for us. For however long you want me."

CHAPTER FOURTEEN

Patsy

It's peaceful here. Hot, but not unbearable as Lost has parked under the shade provided by a tree. A gentle breeze is blowing. On the bike it had been cooling, here in the foothills, it's warm.

I walk back to the barrier and rest my forearms on it again thinking hard. Phil had died when his car had exploded. Of course, as I'd no connection with him for years, the police hadn't involved me, and I knew little more than I'd read in the newspaper. So far as I'm aware, they remain with no clues as to who was responsible for the explosion which killed him. The timing though, that it coincided with the Satan's Devils rescuing Beth, I'm ninety-nine percent certain that Demon and the Colorado chapter of the Satan's Devils were the ones who eliminated my ex. Neither Dan, Beth nor I had mourned his passing. His death had left the world a better place. In the end, he'd proven he was a worse man than I'd ever imagined, seeing Beth not as a daughter, but as a commodity he could make money from, uncaring if she were heading for a life of suffering.

I hadn't asked a straight question, knowing I wouldn't get a response. Sharing, admitting was not the way of the Devils. In truth, if I knew who was responsible, I'd probably have shaken his hand.

If Phil had been a bad man, Alder? Well he's something else. More evil, more devious, richer and clearly powerful. The Devils might have been able to take an unsuspecting Phil Foster out, but Alder? Not only will he be better protected, after Phil's death, he'll be on his guard. He's already underground, hiding from the feds. I'm not even certain the Devils could find him.

Lost has basically told me he'd kill a man, so I'd have my life and family again. That he'd offered himself in the process, well, I've got to push that to the back of my mind. Sorting out my life and that of my children takes precedence now. A few short months back, I was a woman happy with her small business and living a quiet life. If anyone had told me I'd condone not just one actual but a second possible murder, I'd have laughed in their face. But that's what I seem to be doing.

Lost looks uneasy, like admitting he'd kill a man to remove him from my life might have upset me. It hasn't. What woman wouldn't want a man to do all in his power to keep them safe? But what if he fails? What if I decide to take a stand, as he calls it, and lose my life, his, and my children's as well? Alder wouldn't stop until he was satisfied. I don't even know what he wants. Me found, certainly, me dead, possibly.

I'm the one he's looking for. Not Dan. So that presents another option which Lost hasn't considered. I could go, disappear, all by myself. Cad, Demon's computer guy in Colorado could get me a new ID. Dan, well, he's dead. He can stay here and be safe, especially if Lost watches out for him. If I leave, only I will suffer. If I stay, I risk everyone's lives.

I hadn't lied when I'd told Lost I've been out on a few dates, but no man I'd seen more than once or twice. Beth had been nine when the hell that had become my marriage had ended, and Connor just four. My life revolved around them and their activities. Sometimes I felt I was an unpaid taxi service, always in demand. But I didn't resent it, these were my kids, I gave them life, and that gave me the responsibility of bringing them up the best that I could. Beth used to encourage me to get a life for myself, babysitting Connor once she was old enough on the rare occasions I did go out.

But I'm a boring homemaker whose hobby is sewing. I was picky with men, always had been, stupidly holding out for a happy ever after. The few men I met seemed to want something short term, or ran when they heard I had kids, thinking I was after a substitute father. Or they saw me as a desperate woman who they wouldn't need to work hard at to get into bed.

I'd never met one who I'd felt any real attraction for. Men my age were balding, had pot bellies, and looked tired.

Lost though, well, he could pass for a man ten years younger. He's kept himself in shape, still has a mass of hair, and that beard… I didn't realise how attractive one was until I saw his. His eyes are sharp and miss nothing, which begs the question, *What does he see in me?*

I admit I've aged well. Without bragging, I know I compare fairly well against some women who've lived the same number of years, and I'm more confident in my outward looks now than I was when I was a gangly teen. My waist is only an inch thicker than thirty years ago, my hair is long and thick, and while bringing up two kids on my own should have caused worry lines aplenty, my face is still fairly smooth. But it's the parts that don't show that are what worry me. My breasts are no longer perky and firm, and my stomach is flabby. Cellulite rules my thighs and butt, and my skin is creased.

What does Lost look like under his clothes?

I'll probably never find out.

At the age of fifty-three, life has been cruel enough to present me with a man that for the first time ever makes me understand the sexual attraction I've read about in books. But the problem is, I'd been honest when I told him, I'd not be able to separate my emotions from any physical activity. If I'm going to risk my heart, it will be with a man who's prepared to give a relationship a try, not who's trying something new for one or two nights.

And what was that strange enigmatic statement, *that it would be me who'd be the one to end it.* Why? What's he hiding?

He's right in that we should go slow, but we haven't got time. Unless, I stay. Problem is, it wouldn't be just me facing the music.

"I don't know what to do," I tell him at last. "Alder left my son for dead; he deserves death himself for that." I turn to look at him so he can appreciate the honesty in my eyes, letting him see I'd kill the man with my own bare hands if it were possible. "I'm just scared to stay. Alder's powerful. We don't know where he is, where he'd be coming from, let alone what he actually wants. If I stay and take him on, someone else may get hurt."

His eyes sharpen. "What exactly are we talking about here, Patsy?"

I take in a lungful of the sweet fresh air. "Dan can stay. Alder isn't looking for him. I trust you, Lost. You can keep an eye out for him, and he could build a new life here. I could go, Alder would lose my trail. Problem over."

He growls. "Problem far from over. You'd lose both your kids."

"But they'll be safe. And that's all that matters."

"If you go, you'll hurt. If you go…" He breaks off.

"If I go, what?"

"Forget it." He shakes his head dismissively.

"Forget what? What is it, Lost?"

Suddenly he stalks toward me. "If you go, I'll fucking hurt. For years I thought I didn't want or need another woman in my life until I met you and that got knocked on the head. I want you, Patsy, I've told you that. But not just for one night. I want to take you out, date you, get to know you and then, if you agree, take you to my bed and fuck you the way you deserve. I want to discover how you taste on my tongue, the sounds you make when you come. I want your thighs squeezing my head. I want you to come over and over again, and then, only then, will I feed my cock into your pussy and feel you clamp down and orgasm over my dick making me lose control too."

My eyes widen in desire and shock as he spouts promises in words no man has ever used in front of me before.

Phil had never gone down on me. My only knowledge of the act is hearing people talk, reading posts which made me giggle on social media, or from books. I wasn't quite sure what I'd feel about participating in that act until Lost mentioned doing those things to me. While mentally I hadn't leaped on board, apparently my body already has as my legs have pressed together.

I'd married Phil when I was twenty-six years old, after he'd taken my virginity and gave me Beth in return. Sex was okay, enough not to object when Phil was in the mood, but not earth-shattering either, just something to do before you fell asleep at night. The picture Lost is painting, well, I haven't felt my stomach clench this way in years, if ever, and I can feel myself becoming wet. *I want that.* Shouldn't I, as a woman, experience sex like Lost's describing just once in my life? Before I'm an old hag and it's too late.

As if he knows I'm weakening, he tells me again, "I want you, Patsy. I can't remember when I ever fuckin' wanted a woman so much."

I'm completely lost for words. The image he's placed in my head of him and me, naked in bed, is seriously affecting my brain-to-mouth coordination.

"Too much," he murmurs as though to himself. "Knew I'd fuck this up." He shrugs and walks back to his bike. He leans over it for a moment, his hands on the seat, his arms rigid and head bowed. He breathes in a deep breath, then glances back. "Come on, I'll take you home."

I know he's misunderstood. Running over to him, I take hold

of his arm. "It's not you. It's not what you said. Lost. If I could, I'd stay with you. You're attracted to me, and heaven help me, but I'm attracted to you. I want, God, do I want everything you said. But we can't start anything. It's wrong timing. If Alder didn't know where I was…"

"You'd stay?" He raises an eyebrow. "If Alder wasn't in the picture, you'd consider staying with me?"

Again I gaze at his face, reading honesty there, and decide to be truthful in return. "If Alder hadn't reared his head, I'd be more cautious than I am. And you, I suspect, wouldn't have come on so strong to me." I pause and look back over the Pacific again. "It's like people heading off to war. Making decisions, wanting to act in the now in case they don't get that chance again."

He smirks. "Do you want to act in the now, Patsy?"

For once in my life, I'm tempted to take the chance. If I didn't, would I regret it all my life? "*If*," I put an emphasis on the word, "if I were staying, I might. My children are grown. I can't live my life based around them anymore, it wouldn't be fair to them." My arms automatically wrap around me. "It's a scary thought, Lost. I was burned, badly, by Phil. He was so charming when we met, I thought I'd won the jackpot." I try to find the words to explain why I was ever taken in by the man. "I was never the popular girl. I was shy and nervous, so I wasn't asked out by many boys. I didn't go to college, instead I worked a number of low-paying jobs. Like Beth, I still lived at home with my mom. My dad had died when I was young."

"Your mom still alive?"

"She died shortly before Connor was born. She was in a car crash."

"I'm sorry."

I shake my head. The loss of the best confidant in my life was still hard to come to terms with. "I'd had a good relationship with her, just like the one I had with Beth. Mom had always told me of the great love she'd shared with my father, and in some ways I think she was my role model, and I wanted to duplicate how she'd lived. So, if a man asked me out, I was always trying to see if he could be the love of my life. I never found him."

"How the fuck did you end up with a man like Phil?"

"Partly me, partly him. He was the most charming man I'd ever met, Lost. Confident, funny, he made me feel like I was the centre of his world. Until he took my virginity."

His eyes widen. "Are you saying you've only ever been with one man?"

"Sad, isn't it? But yes. I'd been cautious until I met him, more cautious after."

He shakes his head and heaves a sigh. "Why the fuck did you marry him, Patsy?"

"Because I fell pregnant. It was a shock for both of us, but he stepped up to do the right thing. At the time, he was establishing his position as an accountant and it helped him to have stability at home, made him seem more reliable or something." I turn away from him, my mind going back to the past. "He wasn't my dad." I give a mirthless laugh. "The charming man I'd first met wasn't the one I ended up with. He always knew better than everyone, and certainly better than me. He was egotistical. Everything was about him and how clever he was. He could be cruel without trying."

"But you stayed with him?"

"I was his wife. I had Beth. It's what you do, isn't it? Try to make your marriage work. He didn't want more kids, but Connor came along anyway. I suppose it was having a baby again that occupied my time, and I didn't pay attention to how he was changing and what he was becoming. He'd always been secretive, but it had gotten worse. He'd become shifty, and I knew he was spending more money than we had coming in. That's when I suspected. When the cops turned up, I knew."

"That's when you left him?"

I nod. "I took my opportunity, Lost. I took advantage of a man when he was down. He'd been money laundering. Somehow he'd gotten away with it and wasn't charged, but he lost his job, and the police were just waiting for him to step out of line. It was his moment of weakness, and I took it. Whether I'd ever truly loved him, there was nothing left at that point. I couldn't live with a man who I was certain would go to prison at any time. I was going to end up alone and wanted that to be on my terms. So, I asked him to leave."

"And he did?" Lost's voice has changed, has become hardened. "Did he suggest he could change?"

"I didn't give him the chance." I think back, trying to find something to justify what I'd done. All the arguments we'd had. His promises that I hadn't believed, his vows to go straight. "I couldn't, Lost. I may not have been in love with the man, but I would have stood by him if he'd lost his job through no fault of his own. He hated that I didn't support him and that I didn't stand up for him. He thought that's what I should have done because his ring was on my finger. But I had to look after myself, and my children."

A shuttered look comes over Lost's eyes. Something I've said has resonated with him. "You had to look out for yourself," he says, quietly, his body tense. Then he snaps. "He spiralled downward after that? Did you ever think that had you supported him, he might not have gone totally bad? That you might have been a stabilising influence on him?"

"Lost?" I'm confused. *Why does he sound like he's taking my ex's side?* "I spent years turning a blind eye to his behaviour as I was trying to make our marriage work. He was always on his downward spiral, as you call it, but he was getting worse. He didn't care who he hurt, only how much he could get away with. He was the only thing that mattered in his world."

Lost is shaking his head, and I notice his body looks tense. He's viewing the scenery but clearly not seeing it.

"Lost…?"

"We better get back."

The man who'd brought me here has disappeared, and a stranger is standing in his place. The man who'd said things to me which caused a visceral reaction, who'd made me feel desired for the first time in my life is gone. Phil had tried, of course, that's how he got me into his bed. While it hadn't been earth-shattering, it hadn't been terrible, so I'd kept going back. But he'd never spoken to me the way Lost had. Somehow, with him, I'd known it wouldn't be sex with the lights off.

Now he's changed. It's clear he doesn't want me. How can a man switch on and switch off in the blink of an eye? It sounds like he blames me. But I did nothing wrong. He hadn't been there, hadn't seen the cruelty that was always there, hidden just below the surface. Phil had managed to keep it under wraps, but I'd seen enough to not want to be in the vicinity once he let the monster out.

Like a wounded animal I try to defend myself. "Phil wasn't a good man. If I hadn't had fallen pregnant, I'd never have married him. But I turned a blind eye to all that as marriage was expected, wasn't it? He was already bad, Lost. I didn't make him that way. All the signs were there, and then he met Alder… It was him he was laundering money for."

"Maybe if you'd fuckin' tried harder, you could have stopped him."

The air resonates with the sound of my hand slapping his face.

Lost's face has gone completely blank as my hand covers my mouth. *I have just hit the president of a one-percenter motorcycle club. Is he going to retaliate?*

Time seems to stretch as I wait to see what Lost will do.

Eventually the statue in front of me comes to life. He turns and walks to his bike, with a terse instruction thrown over his shoulder.

"Get on."

I do. I look down to see if there is something to hold on to with my hands, but while he must be furious, he still cares about my safety as he reaches back, takes hold of my wrists and pulls my arms firmly around his waist.

Even before the engine roars to life, I can feel his body vibrating.

Any joy in the ride is completely gone. The miles back seem twice as long as they had on the journey here, and there's only one thought in my head. *I'm glad I didn't let things go further with Lost.* He's obviously not that man I was beginning to fall for.

Why had the man shown me something I wanted to reach out for and grab with both hands, then almost immediately snatched it back?

CHAPTER FIFTEEN

Lost

I*'ve fucked up.*

Should have fucking expected it.

"Whisky. No not a fuckin' glass, the bottle." I hold out my hand to Wrangler who looks startled at my tone of voice, me being a man who can usually hold on to his temper.

Taking it, shaking my head at the glass, I stomp across the clubroom and ascend the stairs. When I reach my room, I enter, close the door behind me then turn the key in the lock.

Damn it!

That ride back had been awful, the worst of my life. Neither I nor my passenger wanted to be there, or be forced into such close proximity. On my part, I hadn't been able to get back fast enough, but some sense I hadn't completely lost had made me drive carefully, knowing I had a new passenger behind me.

She'd hit me for fuck's sake.

Raising the bottle to my lips, I take a long swig.

Told you you'd fuck up. You always do. You ruin everything you touch. This is only the start of it. Soon the club will see you for the fraud that you are. You smell that? That's the skin on your back charring as they burn that tattoo off.

"Get out of my head!" I roar, throwing myself on my bed. I'm still holding the bottle and it spills.

Great. Now I'm covered in whisky. Luckily, there's still enough left in the bottle. I take another swig.

I could scream at the universe I'm not going to fuck up, but no one would believe me. Because I do, and I always did.

How could everything have gone to shit?

One minute, I thought I was persuading Patsy to stay. She'd been unable to hide her arousal at the dirty talk I threw at her when I hadn't held back exactly what I'd do to her if I had her in my bed. Her expressive eyes had showed almost every thought. When at first I'd heard I'd only be the second man to ever have her, I was going to make sure I'd be her last. It was on my lips to beg her to give us a chance, to stay in San Diego.

Then she had to tell me about that asshole of an ex. He was evil, twisted. *I* know that. Yet the way she was describing her marriage, particularly the end of it, pushed every button I had.

Patsy's not Kim.

But she'd sounded like her. She'd even admitted she'd kicked a man who was down.

She'd made it sound as though Phil Foster had been like me, oblivious to how his marriage actually was. When he'd needed support, he'd been offered none either.

A woman doesn't make a man good, her absence doesn't make a man bad.

But it can destroy him.

I gave my all to Kim and our marriage. We didn't have kids, thank fuck for that, but we had a nice house, we weren't hard up. I was the man who brought flowers home for no reason other than to see a smile on her face. I was the man who never left the toilet seat up, always looking to her comfort and happiness. Looking back, I was the one trying.

It hadn't mattered. Kim's lips curving up was the only thanks I needed.

Expected to be late home for dinner? I'd arrange to bring takeout back or surprise her by booking a table at her favourite restaurant even if I was exhausted from a long working day, tired from building up my business and looking after the livelihoods of those depending on me for their wages.

A party out with her friends? I'd never missed those, even though they were tedious, and I found it hard to talk to some of her acquaintances, finding them pretentious. It made her happy and that was all I wanted.

I supported her when she got bored with her job, quit it, and took time to find what she really wanted to do with her life. Charity work? Well, I worked harder to make up for us losing her wages.

New bed? New couch? New curtains for the house? Again, I just put more hours in. I fucking loved that woman. Why else did I exist other than to ensure her contentment?

Until I fucked up. Until I needed her support. Until I needed her to be my rock. When I looked for understanding, I got blame. When I asked her for help, she refused me.

It was then I found out what she truly thought of me. I'd been her mistake; she should never have married me. I could never give her what she would want, even if she gave me time to get back on my feet. Asking her to get a paying job to help out? I had to have been kidding.

I fought, God, how I'd fought for the marriage I thought we'd had, only to find it had all been smoke and mirrors.

I'd fought for my business, fought to keep our home. The last straw came when we lost the house, that's when I lost her as well. And, of course, I lost my last available money. Her comfort had to be assured, didn't it, her lawyers had asked me. I think the colloquial saying is that she took me to the cleaners, but I didn't resent her. Not then. She blamed me and she was right. I'd fucked up her life.

I gave her everything I had left.

I had nothing.

I was standing, one hand on the seat of my motorcycle, the last thing I owned apart from the clothes on my back. The car had gone with my wife, but not the bike she tried to make me sell. Something in me made me hang on to it.

Automatically I turned out my pockets.

A wallet, empty of bills, a few odd coins, and bits of plastic which would no longer be accepted, a few receipts and a pen.

I could write a will.

I glanced at my bike. On autopilot, I'd removed the key, on impulse, I'd put it back in the ignition, mentally wishing whoever found it good luck, and that they'd get some enjoyment out of it.

I patted the seat. I'd had some good times on this bike, times when I just needed to ride and clear my head. Now though, symbolically, and just like me, the tank was virtually empty.

"Goodbye, old friend," I whispered quietly.

Double tapping the seat once again, I turned and started to make my way down the beach.

It was a good day for surfing, high breakers were rolling in. Further up where a lifeguard patrolled, the beach looked busy. But not right here. I'd chosen this spot carefully.

My boots left an imprint in the sand, idly my brain wondered how long this last vestige of me would remain.

The sound from the breaking waves was loud, crashing and roaring as they landed on the seashore and then receded as though trying to drag the beach into the water. It was a beautiful day, the sun glinting off the blue ocean, sparkling like stars at night. The wind though, that whipped up sand.

Was that a bike I heard? Not mine, the sound was different to that. No matter, I ignored my idle curiosity and walked closer to the edge, my boots now sinking into the dampened sand.

"Nice day for a swim," a gravelly voice called out from behind me. "You going in?" The voice drew closer.

"I can't swim," I replied automatically.

"You live in California and you can't fuckin' swim?" Whoever it was, sounded amused.

I shrugged. Kim had made me build her a pool, but as I'd never learned as a kid, hadn't used it. I'd grown up poor in a trailer.

"That your bike up there?"

It was. I shrugged. "Yeah."

"Kind of day it might be better to go for a ride than taking a dive into the ocean."

I breathed in deep, just wishing the disembodied voice would go away. It sounded like he'd moved even nearer and was standing right behind me, the sound of his boots hitting sand had been inaudible. I'd let the air I'd just taken in out as a sigh. "Tank's empty," I told him. Much like me.

"Like that, is it?" There was more of a snap in his voice.

"What's it to you?" I swung around at last to find I was confronted with a man about the same height as me, with a snake tattoo winding around his neck. He was well muscled, better built than me. I'd maybe got a few more years under my belt, not many though. My eyes took in his leather vest. There was a badge sewn onto it with the word Snake and below that, one that denoted he was the VP.

Instead of answering my question, he asked one of me. "So, you're just going to walk into the ocean? You think that will be easy, man?" He took out a pack of smokes and offered one to me. As I shook my head, a lighter appeared in one of his hands. He cupped the other around the flame so the wind wouldn't blow it out, then soon the tip of his cigarette glowed red. I just hoped he'd smoke it fast and leave me alone.

"I wonder what it will feel like?" Snake took a drag and puffed out smoke. "Will your lungs burn, do you think? You'll want to give up, try not to fight for your life, but some instinct for survival will make you gasp for air, but your mouth and nose will fill with saltwater instead. How long will you last? Will you try

to hold on to that final amount of air as your limbs thrash, trying to keep you afloat? Will you regret it when it's too late? Or, will you give in peacefully? I've always wondered what drowning was actually like."

"What do you care?" I snarled, not much liking the picture he was painting. Wasn't death by drowning supposed to be easy? The only part I wasn't looking forward to was the bit where the whole of my life flashed in front of my eyes. I could have done without reminders of that.

His shoulders rose and fell. "Nothing to me, man. Me? I'd prefer a bullet to my head. Quick and painless."

"I knew a man once. Shot himself. He survived. He was a vegetable, but still, he lived." I had and he did. I shuddered. With my luck and track record, that would be me.

"I wouldn't miss," Snake said, sure of himself. "That's the way I'd like to go, but hey, that's my preference."

I just wanted him to leave, but Snake lowered himself to the ground, and pulled up his knees, getting himself comfortable. I glanced down raising an eyebrow.

"Go on, then." He jerked his head toward the water.

"What?" Surely, he'd try and stop me?

He nodded toward the ocean. "Never seen a man drown himself before."

He was proposing to sit there and casually watch me die? I gritted my teeth. "Kind of wanted to do this alone."

Snake shrugged again. "Seems it's shouldn't matter to you. I won't interfere." He waved his hand toward the ocean. "You go do your thing. Don't worry about me."

I had no fucking idea why, but the thought that he was going to be sitting, smoking, observing, as I took my final breath made it impossible for me to turn and walk into the ocean.

Perhaps, if I waited long enough, he'd get bored and leave.

But it seemed he could read minds. "Take your time. I've got no place to be."

Fuck it.

The waves continued to crash onto the beach. Minutes passed with no further word from him or me.

Damn. Why, I didn't know. I'd reached the end of my tether. There was no way back, but I couldn't end my life with an audience, which made no damn fucking sense.

With a large exhaled breath I started stomping my way up the beach, idly wondering how far the fumes in my tank were going to take me.

"Hey, wait up."

Angrily, I paused. Hadn't he ruined my life enough for one day? Or, to be more precise, my death.

"Get on your bike and follow me."

I was about to tell him to get lost, when I realised, for the first time in weeks, months, maybe, someone was giving me a direction in which to head.

I laughed, mirthlessly. "Don't know what destination you've got in mind, but doubt I'll get there." I tapped my tank. "No gas."

"Gas station 'bout a mile away."

Wishing I could swallow the bile that rose with my admission, I said tersely, "No money."

"Take it as an advance."

I looked at him as if he'd gone mad.

For the hundredth time, he shrugged. "Prospects don't get much. They get a place to sleep, food to eat. Have to do all the shit jobs. Of course, we'll need to check you out first, but if you pass and will give everything you've got to the club, we'll have your back." His face grew serious and stern. "You've gotta be prepared to die for the club man, but hey, you were prepared to do that for less." Another expression change, this time to a grin. "Well, Lost, what have you got to lose?"

"Lost?"

"Never seen a man looking more fuckin' lost before. Guess you've picked up a road name already."

I owed everything to Snake from that point on. While I didn't know it right then, he'd given me a reason to live, and I repaid him by giving my all to the club. I'd lost everything that was important to me, but thanks to him, I did find something worth dying for. Brothers who had my back which, in turn, restored my desire for life.

Raising the bottle to my lips again, feeling the burn of the liquor smoothing its way down my throat, I muse. It hadn't bothered Snake at all that day. As I'd come to know him, I'd realised he'd have watched me walk into that ocean without lifting a finger to save me. That cigarette would have been smoked down to the stub as he'd watched me drown, just like a rat in a science experiment.

Had he set me up from that day?

No. I've thought about it a lot. He'd known nothing about me then. But as he came to know my history, he knew I'd be useful to him. When the Prez had died five years back, Snake had taken his place, and I'd become his perfect patsy as VP.

And, as always, I'd fucked up.

My only excuse in not seeing Snake had gone bad was down to how much I owed him. I hadn't consciously turned a blind eye, but certainly hadn't lifted the carpet to see what might have been swept underneath. I'd given the man my complete trust, probably influenced that he, a decade and a half earlier, had breathed life back into me. I'd trusted him, not knowing I was putting my faith in the wrong man.

When Snake had turned against the club, I'd been one of the last people to believe it.

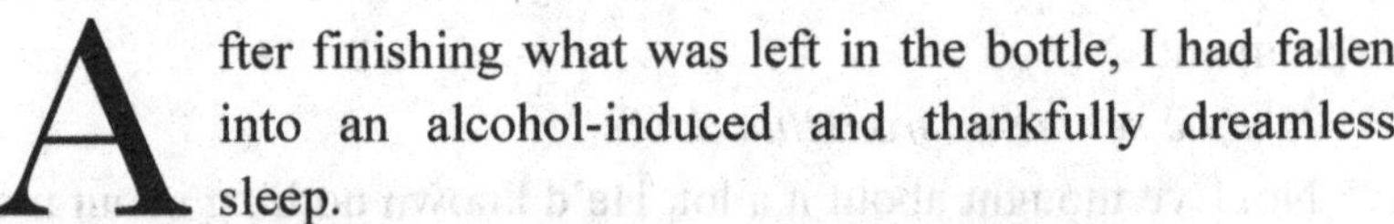

CHAPTER SIXTEEN

Lost

After finishing what was left in the bottle, I had fallen into an alcohol-induced and thankfully dreamless sleep.

I'm woken by a loud banging on the door, and someone trying the handle. *Won't work. I locked it last night.*

Why?

Christ. I groan as the events of yesterday come back into my head, and the memory of how much I fucked up with Patsy. *Gotta apologise.* Yeah, give her the old 'it's not you it's me' talk.

"Lost, Brother, you there?" The doorknob rattles again.

I swing my legs off the bed. *Fuck, my head hurts.* With a glare toward the whisky bottle as though it's its fault I drank it, I lurch to the door, then when it's open, lean against the frame.

"Wow, Brother." Dart steps back, wafting the air away with his hand. "Laid one on last night, didn't you? You fuckin' reek."

I glance down at my t-shirt where most of the spilled whisky landed. "Too much, yeah, but not as much as you're thinking. I'm wearing most of it."

Dart chuckles. "Thank fuck. Look, grab a fresh shirt and

come downstairs. Token's got Demon on a secure line. Patsy's chomping at the bit to talk to Beth, but Demon wanted to speak to us first."

My VP stays at the door as I walk back into the room, tearing my filthy t-shirt over my head as I do. Opening a drawer, I take a clean one out.

"What's the time?"

"Ten."

Fuck. I never sleep so late. Caused by the whisky, obviously. I stretch, then slip my clean shirt over my head, raking my fingers through my hair.

"You look like shit, Brother," my VP helpfully observes.

It will have to do. No time to take a shower but… "Just give me two minutes and I'll be down."

I divert into the bathroom for a much-needed piss, which I do in the unmanly manner of sitting down so I can save time brushing my teeth and getting rid of my whisky-fouled morning breath at the same time.

Ignoring the men using jackhammers in my skull, I race downstairs.

Patsy's in the clubroom, her eyes widening at my dishevelled state. She looks like she's hesitating to even speak to me, but in the end can't stop herself asking tightly, "Beth…?"

I hold up my hand. "Soon, Patsy. Demon needs to update me on something first. I'll come get you as soon as I can, okay?"

Then ignoring anything else she's got to say, and having no time to attempt an apology, I head straight for my office.

Token picks up the phone. "Demon said to call him back. We ran out of small talk waiting for you."

I nod as he hits the numbers. "You know anything?"

"Not yet. Demon wanted to wait for you."

The call connects.

"Lost?"

"I'm here, along with Dart and Token. What you got, Demon?"

The Colorado prez doesn't waste time. "Got Beef and Ink here with me as well as Cad." He pauses, and I hear him take a breath. "As Beth's the one with the authority to open the safe deposit box on her mother's behalf, Ink had to bring her in on the fact that we were interested as to what was inside. Well, you know women. She was curious as fuck after Ink told her, so she took the morning off work. Ink and she were at the bank as soon as it opened."

"You going to tell me there was nothing there?" As usual, I expect to be disappointed. Had to be too simple to get answers straight off the bat.

"Gonna tell you the opposite, Brother. There was shit there. An envelope buried right at the bottom."

"What was in it? What have you found?" I sit up straighter, my hangover all but forgotten. I notice the sparks of interest in my brothers' eyes. "Demon, don't keep us hanging. What have you discovered?"

"Nothing as yet."

What? "What the fuck d'you mean, Demon? What was it, an empty envelope with nothing inside? Any address written on it?" Anything at-fucking-all would help at this point. But there was something about the way he said it that makes me suspect he's toying with me. I glare at the phone. "Spit it out, Demon."

He snorts. It comes down the line clearly. "Not yanking your chain, Brother, just can't give you much right now. The envelope was tucked into a folder containing Phil's will. Well, that's obsolete now, but Patsy had clearly overlooked taking it out. Maybe she didn't want to take responsibility for it—"

"Demon," I growl.

He puts me out of my misery. "There were three floppy discs inside. Cad's been working on getting into that shit."

Floppy discs? I haven't seen one of those in years. "They

password locked or something?" Surely Cad could break that. Token would be able to.

"Hey, Lost, it's Cad here." I hear Demon's tech guy's voice and raise my chin though he can't see me. "We're talking about shit from twenty years back. Had to find what they were written in first, then I had to get Windows 95 emulated on a laptop."

"And?" Dart prompts, getting as impatient as me.

Token, I notice, looks as excited as a historian would be hearing a description of archaeological finds from an ancient dig. "What did you find, Cad?"

"Not a lot, those discs aren't capable of holding much shit, a few kilobytes each is all. Just given it to Prez now."

Demon's voice comes back on the line. "There's some shit we need to get our heads around, two plans which we're trying to decipher. Fuck knows what they are right now. The other is a scanned newspaper article, referring to the disappearance of a group of women. Could be Phil suspected, or knew, Alder had a hand in that. Cad needs to dig into the old records to put the pieces together."

My headache recedes as my brain kicks into gear. "You reckon he wants that shit, that's why he's after Patsy? So she can give him the contents of that envelope? Phil's insurance policy?"

"Could be just that. Might mean nothing to us, but, yeah, might to him."

"You think it would get him off her back if she just handed it over?" Is there a simple way to get her free and clear?

Another pause. "Wish it were that easy, Brother. Beef and I have been discussing it. If Alder thinks that she's been moved under WitSec, then he might think she's already given it to the feds."

"In which case it wouldn't matter whether or not he found her." I'm trying to join dots, which isn't easy with my whisky befuddled head, so Demon gets there a bit quicker.

"What if it's not just what was in the box, but something she has in her head? What if she knows something which Alder doesn't want her spilling?"

That's the most likely, but what could she know? From what I've seen of her, if she'd come across evidence of wrongdoing, she'd have gone straight to the police. She'd left her husband at the first sniff he'd done something criminal. *How could I have blamed her for that?*

"Who were the women who disappeared?" I ask. "Any evidence of trafficking?"

"A group of students out on a hike. This is an initial report about them. Not even sure whether they were ever found, but if not, yeah, that's my bet."

"Okay." I try to switch into business mode. "I'll speak to Patsy. If she knows anything, she doesn't know she does, if that makes sense. But it's worth picking her brain. You take any precautions opening that box up?"

Another voice enters the conversation. "Yeah," comes from Ink. "We took photos of before, after and during. Don't know if it would stand up in court, but the time stamps are all there. We did what we could to avoid accusations of evidence tampering."

I nod, as Demon says, "Ahead of you, Lost. Right now we don't know if this is worth anything, but there might come a time when Patsy needs to testify when Foster put the information in there. Ask Patsy about anything that happened around that time, jog her memory. If she watched the news, she might recall something about those girls going missing."

She might. If she'll even give me the time of day after what I said to her yesterday. Will she trust a man who set out to seduce her and ended up blaming her for something another woman did?

"I'll talk to her." Or get Dart to if she gives me the cold shoulder. "Can you send what you've got to Token? I'll get him working on it as well."

"Already done," Cad replies.

"We need to explore both avenues," Demon states. "These

plans must mean something, otherwise, why leave them there? And those girls… there's something we're missing. In the meantime, how do we keep Patsy safe? My gut feel is that we relocate her."

Exactly what I don't want to do. Surprisingly, I have back up.

"Not a good option," Ink's voice sounds down the line. "Beth's about to talk to her. I won't bother asking her to keep her news a secret. Even if she tries, I reckon Patsy will guess. It was different when she wasn't able to speak to her mother, but when she calls her, Beth won't be able to stop telling her mom that we're having a baby."

There's no point arguing about it. Once Patsy knows she's going to be a grandmother as an actual fact and not a hypothetical possibility somewhere off in the future, she's going to want to be there for her daughter. And Beth will need her mom for support. Even if they're not living in the same place, they'll want to be able to pick up the phone and talk.

"Beth doesn't know what we found," Ink reassures me.

"On that line, it's up to you how much you tell Patsy," Demon suggests. "We need to know if she's got info that can shed light on this shit, so you may need to come clean to her."

There's a murmuring of voices in the background.

"I'll leave this with you for now, Lost. You take a moment to think how to play it from your end, and we'll catch up soon."

"Lost?" Demon's voice is replaced by another.

"Yeah, Ink?"

"Beth's outside and I know she's hopping with impatience right now wanting to talk to her mother. You got Patsy ready on your end?"

"I think she's just as eager. You get Beth in, and I'll get Patsy."

Dart points to himself, then to the door, indicating he'll go get her. I nod as he stands—probably the best idea. She may not be talking to me.

"Windows 95," Token breathes out as the VP disappears. "Heard about it. Never seen it on an actual machine."

I slap him lightly around the head. "You're just a baby," I tease. "What did you use when you started?"

"A Mac of course. Never saw a PC until much later."

Probably when studying for his degree. Like me, he's got a background in computer science, though that shit is all behind me now. Programming would probably need a set of skills which I lost long ago. I've been impressed with Token's ability though.

Token vacates his seat and again the door opens. As he walks out, an eager Patsy runs in. She looks around almost as if expecting to see her daughter sitting in the room.

"Patsy's here. I'm taking my phone off speaker." I do so and pass it over to her.

As she takes it, her eyes gleam, and her attention is immediately on the voice of her daughter and she has no time for me. I get up to leave and give her some privacy, only hearing before I close the door the start of her conversation.

"Ink? Beth? You're both there? It's so good to hear your voices." Her voice is breathy, excited.

I stand outside my office door, replaying the conversation with Demon. I don't know how long I go over and over what Ink had found, and what could be the significance. Long enough that I'm still there when I hear an excited shriek from behind me. I take it that the young couple have just shared their news. Patsy knows her daughter is pregnant.

I lean my head back against the wall, thinking back to the past.

It had been me who'd wanted children, Kim hadn't. It wasn't until later I'd realised she needed all the attention on herself and hadn't wanted to share what she had with anyone, not even her own flesh and blood. It was a blessing we hadn't had any considering the acrimonious end to our marriage. It would have been far worse had we been embroiled in custody battles and co-parenting rights.

Patsy sacrificed her own happiness to make sure her kids had a good life. Is still doing it, distancing herself from Beth to support Dan. She's so far removed from my ex it's hard to imagine how different they are, yet there I was, comparing them yesterday. I hit the heel of my hand to my forehead as I realise how stupid I've been.

For a second, I imagine how I'd be feeling were I to hear I had a grandchild on the way. Happy wouldn't begin to describe it. A new generation, a new kid to spoil, but then, that was never in anyone's plans for my life.

I can only blame myself. I fucked up by marrying the wrong woman, though right up to the end I thought she was my Mrs Right, with the obvious disappointment about the lack of children. Then I fucked up even my apparent sham of a happy marriage along with everything else. It hadn't been until long after she'd taken the last of what I had, I discovered I'd never had a chance. Kim had been fucking somebody else for most of the time we'd been married. My fault, of course, I'd left her alone too much. Left her alone so I could earn money to give her the good things in life.

Seventeen years ago, I followed Snake up the driveway that led to the clubhouse. One year later I received my patch, and then was allowed to fuck the women in the club. After a year's abstinence, well, more than that as I'd not wet my dick since my wife had left, I took advantage. Club girls came, club girls went, so many I can't remember all their faces. They were mainly anonymous asses and tits. Sex on tap became boring after a while, or maybe I was just growing older. I still had urges, still went with the whores from time to time, but I'd come to find relieving any pressure in my dick in the shower was just as good a release as any that the club girls gave me.

Before I'd been so fucking stupid yesterday, I'd meant every word I'd said to Patsy. She's the only woman who's really interested me since my wife. Everything tells me the two women are about as different as anyone could be, yet my fucked-up brain expects her to behave the same way. One hint, and I was accusing her of all the wrong things.

What should I do now? Leave her be? Or try to repair the damage I did yesterday?

My whisky hangover is returning with a vengeance. With my office in use for the time being, I take myself off to the solitude of our currently empty meeting room and think, coming up with a strategy. Once Patsy's finished her conversation, I'll speak to her and get her to dig deep inside her head for any information she might have lodged there.

Of course, if she won't give me the time of day, I might have to deploy my backup plan and get Dart to talk to her.

I sit on my chair at the head of the table, put one ankle on the opposite knee, fold my arms over my chest and allow my chin to drop. I couldn't ask for a better VP than Dart. Now there's a man who didn't know his own value until he was asked to step up. He'd come here temporarily to help the club sort through the mess Snake and the traitors who'd sided with him had left. You can't find not just one snake but nine in the nest without everyone becoming unsettled.

Dart proved his worth, was so successful, we didn't lose a single member. While I thought they'd made the crazy decision to put me in the top seat, he'd thought they'd made an equally ridiculous choice to set him up as VP. The result was, both Dart and I, with knowledge of our own deficiencies, had been more determined to do right by the club. The difference between us was that Dart was exactly who we all saw him as, reliable, dependable and trustworthy.

It's a privilege to be voted into one of the top spots. I stare down at the seat at the end, my original chair among the rest of the non-officer members, the place I'd always expected to remain in. My eyes glaze.

The conversation had been muted, Brothers were still coming to terms with Bird's untimely death. If they were saying anything, they were talking somberly. We were all shocked, it had been hard to take in.

As the VP, Snake had slid into the chair I'm sitting on now, taking Bird's seat but had not assumed he had the title as he opened the meeting.

"Need a new prez," he'd said. "Nominees?"

Men had looked at each other, but Snake had always done a good job. Supported Bird and had all our backs as needed. I wasn't surprised his was the only name put forward, and the vote wasn't really necessary as everyone said yes.

Was it only with hindsight, that now looking back there were times when Snake had made me uneasy? Times when I wasn't certain he'd be good for the club? Bird had been like an elder statesman, taking time to think things through. Hard as nails but making sure whatever he did was to the benefit of all the members. He'd had a good head for business, which I could admire. Snake, on the other hand, was more impulsive, and had to be reined in every now and again. I recall I'd wondered who'd do that now Bird was no longer there to restrain him.

What happened next though, well, that was the surprising part which I hadn't seen coming.

"I nominate Lost as my VP."

"What?" I'd sat stunned at Snake's words which had taken a moment to sink in. I waited for the burst of laughter that never came.

Instead Salem had raised his hand. "Seconded."

I'd looked around, expecting someone to object, to say how ridiculous it was to put me in a position of authority. But no one did. That night I'd sewn a new patch on my cut, half full of pride and half worried to death that I wasn't up to the job.

Had Snake used me? Yeah, hindsight is a wonderful thing. While I'd been oblivious at the time, I know now that he had. Then, I'd thought we'd come to a good division of labour, playing to both our strengths. He'd abdicated the day to day running of the club and our businesses to me and I was happy to take it on. He became focused on seeking out new opportunities and ventures. What I hadn't had was an inkling of just what kind of shit he'd been exploring. How deep his desire was to take the club forward in a whole different direction, or should that be back? Drugs and taking out the president of the mother chapter had been his pet projects.

All this was planned under my nose and without my being any the wiser. Sighing deeply, I still don't understand how he'd managed to keep me in the dark. I was his perfect fall guy, running the club, keeping everything above board, while secret meetings took place and arrangements made. Yeah, some VP I was. Didn't smell anything rotten at all.

When Snake and Poke had been dealt with, I expected to be sent out bad myself. My crime? Allowing the wool to be pulled over my eyes, being completely oblivious.

I shake my head. I'd been prepared to lose my patch over being so blind and stupid. Christ, it's strange how things turn out.

The San Diego chapter needed leadership, needed people at the helm to steer them the right way and sail them into less-troubled water. I was determined to do as good a job as I could, or, until they came to their senses and realised they'd made a mistake.

What started that train of thought? Oh, yeah. Dart. Nah. I couldn't think of a better right-hand man. We make a good team. He's someone I depend on. I would never keep secrets from him, nor him from me.

We trust each other.

I'd never truly trusted Snake, but I owed him for saving my life, even though I'd always known it hadn't mattered a damn to him. If I'd proceeded to walk to my death that day, he'd have just watched on with curiosity.

Instead, he'd given me my club.

So, I'll do my best as prez to pay not him, but the Satan's Devils back.

CHAPTER SEVENTEEN

Patsy

When we'd returned to the compound yesterday, I'd clumsily got off Lost's bike. I certainly didn't feel I could take the liberty of steadying myself on his shoulder, and he didn't offer his hand to help. Almost before I'd straightened, still sitting astride, he'd walked back his bike into its parking slot, then strode past without giving me another look.

Bemused, I just stood staring after him for a moment.

Well, damn the man. If he thinks Phil was redeemable, he's completely wrong. Guess it's best I found out who Lost actually was before I had done something stupid and jumped into his bed. One thing's for certain, he's lost his chance. If he comes sniffing around me again, I'll tell him to get lost.

Uncertain of my position now I've apparently angered the prez, I'd taken the same direction as he had and entered the clubhouse. Lost had been by the bar demanding a bottle of whisky. Again, he ignored me as he walked smartly to the stairs and disappeared up them.

My head was spinning having seen two sides to the man. I'd gone out with a man I called a friend but returned home with a stranger. The change had been so swift, I was unable to predict what was going to happen now. I was half expecting, half waiting for him to return and ask me to leave. I had a speech prepared, begging him to give sanctuary to Dan. Earlier, Lost had almost persuaded me with him fighting by my side there was a chance I could regain my family. Clearly, there's no chance of that now.

But though I waited, Lost hadn't come back down. Neither did anyone else appear to give me my marching instructions.

A reprieve? As the hours passed, I gathered it must be. For tonight, anyway.

A woman had appeared by my side, introducing herself as Eva. I was surprised when she unashamedly admitted she was a sweet butt. In the Pueblo club, the club girls had kept themselves to themselves, or to the men. But Eva had approached me in a friendly, *do you want company* way.

She was easy to talk to. I recalled Alex had mentioned her before, and that she was a nurse. It didn't take long for her to start telling me about her nine-year-old son. She and her ex share custody, and it appears, quite amicably. Whenever she hasn't got her son with her, she lives at the club. She's quite open about having sex with the bikers. It's clearly something she enjoys and feels no shame making herself available to them. The contrast between me, who's only ever been with one man in my life, and her with her vast experience couldn't be starker.

Despite my concerns about Lost and his strange reaction earlier, and Eva's and my diverse outlook on the opposite sex, talking to her made me feel more at home. As I started to relax, I found myself giggling as she pointed out the men, then leaned in to give me some inside knowledge on what they do best. It made me look at them in a different light for certain. It was when she was conveying some secrets about Kink, airily waving her hand at him, that the man himself caught my eye. He shook his head in amusement and gave me a wink. I glowed red, realising he was all too well aware of the sort of details Eva must have been sharing.

I tried to rid myself of the image came into my head of Lost tying me up with rope. *That boat has sailed now, whether or not that was ever in the cards.*

Unlike in Colorado where the club girls, or sweet butts as the men call them, tend to make themselves scarce, here Tits, Cindy and Pearl walk around like they own the place. Last night I'd seen them strutting half naked as though advertising their wares. Nothing was hidden, and I couldn't see how I'd ever thought I could compare. Why would Lost go for a middle-aged frump when he could have the choice of these girls?

I'd had a front-row seat where it was difficult to avoid seeing one of the men getting a blow job out in the open. Pizza had just been delivered, and I'd found it quite distracting trying to eat while he was giving a running commentary on how he was about to come and instructing her to swallow every fucking drop.

Eva had explained to me it was different when Alex was there—everyone was inclined to be more discreet when the only old lady was present, especially when she had their children with her. It had apparently not taken long for the VP to get them to behave. She'd giggled, remembering. Eva referred to Alex's son Tyler as the junior prospect which I thought was delightful, and my questioning about his title led her to tell me the young boy's story, and his fight with sickle cell disease. She'd confided his original cut, given to him when he'd been six, had long been consigned to the back of the wardrobe as it had to be replaced once a year at least. Tyler is now a normal healthy growing boy, and like kids his age, is shooting up fast. I ended up looking forward to meeting him and seeing him in his famous cut. Then my face had fallen as I realised, I probably wouldn't get a chance.

Dan had returned with Salem who he'd been helping out while I'd been absent today. He seemed to be getting on like a house on fire with many of the men, even seemed to be making friends. He'd spent a bit of time around Ink and his brothers in the Colorado chapter, so knew what to expect. Although bikers were not regarded as particularly upright citizens, I knew enough about Beth's man's club to know they were about family and respect, and in comparison with the man who sired him, were far better men. I've seen nothing to suggest the San Diego club was any different. If I end up leaving Dan here, I won't have any worries in that respect.

When Eva left me, I wondered whether I should just go upstairs, but Dan beckoned me over, and by his side, I met a few more of the men. The hardest part was remembering all their names. Pennywise and Salem handles were easy. Apparently when they'd prospected, the prez at the time had had a thing about Stephen King. Scribe was so named as he had for years been supposedly writing a book, but no one had seen anything of it. He was their secretary as he could at least spell.

Smoker had introduced himself, and you could tell when he was in the room. He was usually coughing. After a particularly heavy bout, Eva had appeared and gone over to him, looking concerned. He hadn't sounded a well man to me but suspect it's down to all the cigarettes. I notice he'd go outside, then come back in reeking of smoke. My creased brow had gotten Salem to confide that due to Tyler's prior bad health, the clubroom is, nowadays, surprisingly smoke-free.

All the time I was listening to the men, I kept flicking my eyes toward the stairs, hoping and equally dreading seeing Lost again. But he never reappeared. I'd found the whole atmosphere welcoming, and I had enjoyed the evening's insight into his world. Or would have done, were it not for my concerns about what the future now held for me.

I couldn't understand what had turned Lost, like a switch being thrown from potential lover to a man who seemed to regard me with hate. While at first I'd been bristling, I wondered now whether I'd poorly worded something which he had taken the wrong way. I knew deep in my soul there was nothing I could have said or done to make Phil step off the path he was intent on going down. I had no choice but to make sure he dragged neither me nor the kids down it with him. But maybe it hadn't come over that way.

Misinterpretation or not, I was going to need an apology for the words Lost had thrown at me and the way he'd treated me.

I was certain any chance of even a happily for now with Lost is dead and gone, but I'd prefer to leave on good terms, not bad. I needed to talk to him to at least clear the air, but that night I didn't get my chance. I went to bed with my head full of lost opportunities, and with no idea of how to set things right.

This morning I'd woken up excited about the promised phone call with Beth. Hopefully, we'd be able to talk for a while as I'm sure we've got a lot to catch up on. I want to hear what she and Ink have done to the house, what changes they've made, and how she's enjoying living with her man. I know my daughter, once she starts, she'll tell me everything. I doubt our phone call will be short.

I've been on tenterhooks all morning, happily anticipating one conversation which can't come soon enough, while also dreading confronting Lost. Having slept on it, I realise primarily I'm angry. His mood swing yesterday had been dizzying.

When he'd at last emerged and walked past mid-morning looking like he'd been dragged from the wrong side of his bed, he'd walked past with his head bowed, not even pausing to give me the time of day before heading off to take a phone call.

He hates me.

I felt sad and annoyed at the same time, all my good feelings anticipating speaking to my daughter swept away.

It's quiet. Boring. The men are at work. I'd offered to help the prospect tidying, but he brushed me off, saying it was his job to handle. Alex hasn't turned up, and Dan's gone with Salem to the auto-shop. I while away the time on my tablet, idly swiping through clothing designs and other sites which might help me with my business.

Finally, when I've almost reached the end of my tether, I get the summons I was waiting for. It was time to go and speak to Beth.

Last time I spoke to her I felt guilty as hell even though I'd taken what I'd hoped were the right precautions. I watch television and knew burner phones were hard to trace. Knowing I was doing something I shouldn't have done had made me feel tense, now I know with good reason. It had been a hurried call just to check in with her to see that things were all well. Three or four minutes at best.

Today, I'm told, the phones have been checked both at the San Diego end by Token, and by Cad in Colorado. I've been assured the connection is secure. There's no rush, and we can take our time. I'm determined to make the most of it.

After the initial excitement, both Beth and I burst into tears and can hardly get out a word. Ink's chuckling in the background saying the call was supposed to make us both happy, not upset. His gentle chiding helps us to pull ourselves together.

I make light of the reason Connor and I are at the San Diego club, and just listen to Beth prattle on, as expected, about all the changes Ink and she have done to my house. It doesn't upset me that my home for so long is being usurped and altered by them. It had been in need of an update. I just wish I could see the new kitchen and appliances they'd had installed. Her choice of granite counters sounds great.

I wonder if she's already run out of things to say as it goes quiet on their end. Then Beth speaks again, her voice growing husky.

"We've got some news for you, Mom."

"Go on, tell me."

I think I'm prepared for anything until she rushes it out. "Ink and I are expecting a baby. It's early days, I'm just over two months along."

"You're pregnant?" I shriek into the phone.

"We didn't plan for it, but it happened. We're both over the moon, Mom. Except…" Her voice breaks. I don't need to be a genius to work out what isn't being said.

Except I'm thousands of miles away and can't be there for her. If I leave again, I may never be able to speak to her again. I won't be there for the birth, won't be able to hold my granddaughter or grandson. The implications flood through me. I try to hold back the tears, but Beth knows me too well.

"Mom…" And then she's sobbing.

Ink's deep voice takes over. "This is a fucked-up situation, but I know Demon's working hard to find some way to resolve it. Hang on to hope, Patsy. That's all we can do. We'll find some way to keep in contact, send pictures, I don't know. Dress up in disguise and bring the baby to meet you."

"You can't do that." My sensible side takes over. "Alder's after me, Ink. He seems to accept Connor is dead, so it has to be me he's after. He could do anything, take Beth, take the baby… I wouldn't put anything past him."

"Talk to Lost, Patsy, there are things he needs to tell you."

"Tell us, Ink." Beth's voice sounds stronger. "I should know things which affect me or Mom."

"Club business," Ink says firmly and decisively.

"Ink!"

"Was there anything in that safe deposit box?" I ask, not expecting a positive answer.

"I don't know," Beth complains. "Ink pushed me aside and looked through himself."

"Talk to Lost," Ink instructs again.

I hear a murmured discussion with Beth's voice rising, but Ink's clearly not giving in. With an audible huff, Beth addresses me again. "It's been good to catch up with you, Mom."

"You too, Beth. I'll try to call again." I'll make sure of that before I move on. Something I think is inevitable, whatever help Lost was going to offer, the chance seems to have gone. "Look after yourself, and Ink? You treat her like glass."

"Already doing that, Patsy," Ink reassures me.

It's then we start with the 'I love yous' over and over, both Beth and I renewing our tears over what should be happy news. I can't be there at the exact time I want to be, and she, so used to sharing everything with her mom, wants.

I know Beth's got other pregnant women around her, Ink by her side and his brothers too, but it's not like having your mother with you. I'd always envisaged being at least close by, watching my daughter growing larger, helping her through any difficulties and sharing the joy as she puts together a nursery. Pregnancy is a strain for any woman, and I like to think I could have supported her. Now I'm not sure when I'll even talk to her again. There'll be a hundred things she'll want to ask me, like how she and Dan were as babies.

I think it's Ink who finally ends the call. Neither Beth nor I want to sever the connection.

I sit in Lost's office, barely aware of where I am. Crying so hard, I don't hear the door open or realise that someone's come in until I feel strong masculine arms around me.

"Hush," says Lost, stroking my hair and pulling me into his chest. "Hush, babe. It will be alright, I promise you."

I don't know whether I even like him right now, but that doesn't seem to stop me taking the comfort he offers. I hold him tight and sob into his chest. He doesn't seem to mind my tears soaking into his shirt.

He allows me to cry until I'm hiccuping and coming back to myself.

"She's pregnant," I sob. "I should be happy."

"I know," he replies simply. "I know, babe."

"You know?" He knows I'm upset, or he already knew Beth's expecting a baby?

"Yeah. Demon told me a few days ago. It wasn't my place to tell you. Beth and Ink needed to share their news themselves."

I suppose that makes sense, but I hate the thought of him knowing before me.

He passes me one final tissue, then waits for me to dab the last of my tears away and blow my nose in a very unladylike manner. Why do women cry? It never does anything but give you a headache and, in my case, blotched skin and red eyes which are sore for hours after. I'm not a pretty crier.

Lost stares at me as I do my mop up, refraining from commenting on how bad I look. Instead, his hand gently brushes my hair back from my face as he quietly says, "We need to talk."

I'm wrung dry, unable to sustain my anger. He's right, we do need a discussion, about what had happened between us and where that puts me now. About whether he's still going to help me. The man who comforted me just then is not the man who I returned to the clubhouse with yesterday afternoon. His changing moods has my already aching head spinning. "I don't understand what happened yesterday…" I turn my watery, swollen eyes toward him.

"Yesterday isn't what we really need to talk about." He sounds and looks serious. "But you're right, we need to get that out of the way first." His eyes close briefly. When he opens them again, they're narrowed and full of pain. "I fucked up, Patsy. I took my past out on you. I'm sorry. I know I said some fuckin' hateful things to you." He huffs. "I don't even know why I went there. It wasn't you who should have borne the brunt of what I was feeling."

I kind of felt that at the time. That I was being compared to someone else, someone who'd hurt him in the past. I could tell him he was a jerk and that I could no longer trust him. I could tell him I'm not interested because he'd hurt me too much, but

I don't. Instead I comment, "I said something that triggered you."

He's still stroking my hair, I like it. A little too much if I'm honest. I want to keep him talking so he doesn't stop. As he looks like he's gathering his thoughts, I tell him mine. While I'd been crying, I knew I couldn't do this, either to me or to Beth. I couldn't run from my problems, whatever they are. I need to face them head-on. I need to do everything possible so my future entwines with that of my daughter again.

"Lost," I get in before he can start speaking, "you made me feel like a woman again. You made it sound like you cared. Then you lost it, and to me, there seemed to be no reason." As he opens his mouth, I shake my head. "I need to be there for Beth. I need to be able to contact her whenever I want, even if I can't physically be with her. Sure, she could do without me, but she'd do better with her mom's support. If you think there's a chance we can get the better of Alder, then that's what I want to do. If you're still prepared to help."

He pulls away slightly and looks at me carefully. "You want to stay and fight? Stand up to him?"

"If that's what I have to do, yes. I thought I could be content knowing Beth had Ink and she was happy, but I'm broken in two. I want to be there for Dan, but I need to have contact with Beth too. She needs me. She needs her mom."

"They both need you." His stare becomes intense. "I promise I'll do everything in my power so you can have the life you want Patsy. I… I also want to be there for you."

I shake my head. "How can I trust you after yesterday? You hurt me, Lost. Dangled something in front of me then snatched it away, and I don't understand why. I can't do this alone; I need your help, but I can't depend on you. I can't walk on eggshells wondering whether any word I say is going to be the wrong one."

He stands, brushes his hands back through his hair, then tugs at his beard. "What I needed to talk to you about is about Alder. But I want you to trust me, babe. So first, I need to come clean with you." His face becomes shuttered. "Perhaps I also ought to warn you that everything I touch turns sour, Patsy. Perhaps you're better staying away from me. I have a track record of fuckin' things up. It's all I seem to do." He's berating himself, but something tells me he truly believes it.

"What do you mean? You're the president of this club and I know enough about bikers to know that means everyone here has faith in you. They must have voted you in."

He shrugs. "I've known from the start that they shouldn't have. Even tried to tell them that, but they still wanted me at the head of the table. Fuck knows why."

I'm puzzled. He seems so in control, so confident. Now he's showing me another side, his vulnerability. I frown. Should I take heed of his warning? As far as I can see, he's the only one I can call on to help. While I'd love to return to Colorado, I can't do anything that might put Beth in danger, she's already been through too much. Has Lost really left a raft of failures in his wake? Is he cautioning me with good reason? If he really is prone to making mistakes, then perhaps I'm wrong to hitch my hopes to his wagon. Yet, I think, staring at him, I might not know him well, but, disregarding his strange behaviour yesterday, so far, he's not led me wrong. He rescued me from a stalker, and has extended his club's protection to me and Dan. If I judge by results and actions, I'm not wrong to have faith in this man.

On the other hand, maybe I'm blinded by my attraction to him. Maybe I'm clutching at straws. Yesterday I wanted to explore what could be between us, but today, my sensible head says I'm not sure.

But if he's the only man capable of providing me with the assistance I need, what he's telling me doesn't exactly fill me with confidence. Why does he expect everything to go south? I need to dig deeper.

"Lost, tell me, please. Why don't you trust yourself?"

He turns back to me and those piercing eyes meet mine. "Because I fuck things up. It's what I do, Patsy. I can't change my nature. I ruin people's lives."

"Whose lives?" I'm both curious and worried.

"You really want to know?"

CHAPTER EIGHTEEN

Lost

"You really want to know?" I ask her, my words coming out a little harsher than I intended. I've no problem with telling her about my past, it's no secret, just something I don't often bring up. I do know, however, once I tell her, if I haven't already blown it by my behaviour yesterday, I'll definitely lose any chance I might have had to explore this attraction between us.

When she nods, I take a deep breath. She needs to know, needs to understand that she should run a mile rather than trust my judgement.

I stand and start to pace, exposing my soul easier if I keep moving. Once I start, my whole damn fucked-up life spills out. "I left college with a degree in computer science and a head full of ideas. I went to several conferences and teamed up with some people who were developing a PDA, remember those? Personal Data Assistants. They were a revelation when they came in. Long before smart phones, for the first time you could carry your data with you in a handheld device. They had word processing functions, spreadsheets, a microphone and speakers. It was the new thing. Exciting." I pause to shake my head. *How stupid had I been?*

I see Patsy's listening intently, so I continue. "After I graduated, I got talking to those same people again. They liked my ideas and wanted to run with them. Well, I knew best, didn't I? I knew from their interest that I was onto a winner. I was in a good place financially, my grandfather had died and left me a bit of money—that had come as a surprise, he'd never shared it when he was alive. So I decided to put my windfall into starting up my own company. I employed a couple of programmers and we began developing applications which would run on those PDAs. I was bringing in a lot of money and became ambitious as the future looked bright. To keep up with demand, I had to employ more people. I ended up with a staff of twenty-five—fifteen developers and programmers, the rest were sales and administration." I close my eyes, my lips curving slightly as I remember the good old days. I like to think I was a good boss and had built a great team. One big happy family.

"The problem was, I'd banked everything on one platform, one technology. The big companies were pandering to the public who were clamouring for more and had far more money to invest in research than I had myself. The world didn't want to carry a phone *and* a PDA with them. Smarter people than I saw which way the wind was blowing and combined the two technologies. It culminated in things like the iPhone which was eventually launched in 2007."

"Your company couldn't keep up?"

I raise my chin and lower it. "I went bust because I'd failed to make the right decisions. So tied up in making the best applications I could for one device, I lacked the foresight to keep up with the rest. The platform we were using wasn't popular anymore. We tried to change, but not only had I left it too late, I was a small fuckin' fish in a pond which was dominated by big players. I borrowed money, put everything I owned into the business, but it all went belly-up and I had to let my staff go. Twenty-five people out of employment because I'd made wrong decisions." There had been Bob, Jonathan, Anthony, Sylvia… the list goes on. All people depending on me, who'd fought beside me to pull us back up, but in the end, I let them all down.

"I had to sell my house to pay back the loan." I glance her way, trying to judge her expression. "My wife, of course, left me."

She goes still. "Your wife left you?"

My shoulders rise and fall. "I'd failed her too. We could no longer keep our heads above water. I could no longer support her. I had barely anything left at all. I managed to keep back enough to set her up with a small apartment, but she'd lost her house."

"What did you do?" she asks tersely, her jaw clenched. "Where did you live?"

Yeah. I had expected how this would go. Not a good track record, a man who couldn't provide for his family, who let down everyone who depended on him, including his wife.

"That's when the old prez, Snake, well, he was VP then, but it was he who found me. Brought me here as a prospect as I had nowhere else to go, and nothing to my name except an old motorbike which had next to no gas in the tank. I went from a man with dreams to a man with no home, no money in my wallet. Snake told me I was lost, and that's how I picked up my road name." I don't tell her how Snake found me, or that he'd effectively saved my life.

Patsy stands. I know she's going to walk out and leave now she understands what a fuck up I am. Instead, she walks over to me. I notice there are twin spots of red on her cheeks.

"You gave what you had to a wife who walked out because your business failed? Did you have kids?"

"No, no children."

"Did she work?"

I bark a short laugh. "No. Things got so dire I had to ask her to find something, but obviously she wasn't happy about it."

Her jaw clenches tight. "She complained when she had to get a job?"

I shrug again. "Yeah. She depended on me to support her. I was a disappointment, I failed her."

Those blotches of red on her face deepen, and her finger prods me in the chest. "Listen here, Lost. You were not a failure. Businesses come and go all the time. Technology moves on. No one can predict the way things will head, what will become popular. Sure, your business ran into the ground but that wasn't something you could help. It could have gone the other way; you could have come up with the next best thing since sliced bread. And, it was a time when big technology companies were wiping out the small guys. That wasn't your fault. As for your wife? She sounds like a terrible human being. She was the one who failed you. A woman should stay by her man's side." She sighs, clarifying what she's said. "I couldn't stay with Phil as he was dragging us down into something I couldn't let the kids and me be a part of. If he'd lost his job through no fault of his own, I'd have supported him, but he didn't. He lost it as he made the decision to do something illegal, and then carried on as he found it was lucrative."

"You had to get out, I can see that," I tell her quickly. "I'm so fuckin' sorry I ever compared you."

"Do you still see her?"

"Kim?" I snort. "No. I contacted her shortly after I joined the Devils. Er, let's say she didn't approve of my life choices. Oh, and she'd already found someone else. In fact, he'd been waiting in the wings for a while. Well, let's just say when the penny finally dropped, I realised he hadn't spent all that time waiting."

Her hand comes up and touches my cheek. "You know what you've just told me? You've told me what a good man you are. How people can depend on you as you'd never knowingly let them down. You've shown me you're loyal. Every word that's come out of your mouth has told me I'm right to trust you."

"I'll fuck up..." I look down, then back up. "I fucked up yesterday. That's what I do, Patsy, I—"

I don't know whether it's to shut me up or if there's some other reason, but she rises on tiptoes and her hand curls around the back of my head. She forces my head down, hell, I go willingly, and now her mouth is on mine.

The kiss is every bit as good as yesterday's. It also causes the same reaction as my cock starts to swell. The temptation to use the privacy of my office and put my hands on that ass I long to hold is almost overwhelming. But I'm stopped by the memory of what I'm really here for.

I don't pull away, not immediately. When I do reluctantly separate my lips from hers, I still haven't had enough of her.

"I should never have compared you. You're the complete opposite of Kim. I feel I've been waiting my whole life for someone like you." With my head still bowed, I tentatively ask, "Have I fucked up irrevocably, babe? Or will you give me another chance? Will you stay, see if there's something between us?"

"I still don't see what you see in me, Lost." One corner of her mouth rises. "You know Snake gave you the wrong name, don't you?" At my raised eyebrow, she continues, "You found your place here, didn't you? You should have been called Found."

My eyes go wide, her observation making me chuckle. I stroke her hair again, the silkiness under my fingers a texture I'll never get tired of. "Maybe," I tell her, "but being Lost is all I know." I grow serious. "Patsy, if you're serious about trying to put this trouble with Alder behind you once and for all, I need to ask you some questions. There are matters we should discuss before we talk about you and me, and whether what we have between us has a chance of developing." I hate to have to do this, but it's important.

"Serious stuff?"

"Yeah."

She sits back down again. Her hands are held open, gesturing she'll be an open book to me. But before I can speak, she asks something of me. "I don't like calling you Lost. Not now I know it's not fitting. What's your real name?"

"My government name? Fuck, it's been so long since anyone's called me it. I don't mind you knowing it babe, but I'm not that man anymore. Who I was, was Conan. Conan Holmes."

"Conan." Fuck, the way she breathes it out does something to me. "Well then," she smiles and then tries it again. "Conan, what do you need from me?"

I hate the name, but it seems not when it falls from her lips. And what do I want?

You. In my bed. Spread open and waiting for me. Or on the desk, I'm not fussy. But instead of telling her those thoughts, I get to the matter I should be concentrating on. "How well did you know Alder?"

"Not well. I knew his wife better. Jenny was Phil's sister, so we saw her and Alder quite a lot."

"Did you get along with her?"

Her short laugh holds no mirth. "I didn't have much of a chance. Alder was possessive. He was the kind of man who didn't want her to go anywhere without him. She wasn't even allowed to go out for coffee with me, so I never saw her without him. I think he hit her. I saw traces of a black eye once." She grimaces. "We went out for a meal with them not long before her death. As girls do, we went to the bathroom together. She confided in me that she was making plans to leave him. I offered my help if there was anything I could do. He was evil, and as I said, I'm certain he was abusive."

"Did you help her leave?" Could that be what Alder had against her? Has he been holding a grudge all these years?

She looks sad. “I didn’t get a chance. She drowned shortly after.”

I hadn’t been aware of that; just knew she was out of the picture. “Was there anything suspicious about her death?”

She looks down at her hands, then back up. “Of course, you always wonder. But she’d been drinking a lot. Married to a man like Alder would do that to a girl. She was found with a high level of alcohol in her body and dead in their pool. Alder had supposedly been with Phil at the time. I did speak to Phil about it, she was his sister after all, but he said I was being ridiculous, that it was an accident pure and simple.”

Had Alder murdered his wife? “Did Phil get on with his sister?”

“He got on better with Alder,” she scoffs. “He had no time for Jenny. But then, he didn’t for anybody. Remember, he was quite happy that Alder was going to kill Connor. He himself was going to traffic Beth. He was so narcissistic—all he cares about is himself. He doesn’t give a damn about anyone, not even people of his blood.”

“So even if he knew Alder murdered his sister, he wouldn’t have raised a fuss? He gave him an alibi?”

Patsy tilts her head to one side. “You’re making me try to remember things that happened to me in another life. Yes. The police questioned Phil who’d confirmed Alder had been with him. I knew Jenny wasn’t happy in her marriage, and she could have known too much. It might have been convenient for Alder to get rid of her, but I don’t know if he knew she was planning to leave. It’s just as likely it was an accident, or that she killed herself. The police ruled it an accidental death while under the influence of alcohol.”

I consider that for a moment. Whether Alder had a hand in the death of his wife is probably a moot point twenty years on, not able to be proven. But Patsy said she might have known too much, which begs another question.

"Did you know stuff? Did Phil talk in front of you?" I'm wondering what she could hold in her head.

She gives a negative shrug. "Phil was careful never to share anything with me. Any phone calls he made were from his home office so I couldn't overhear anything. It was why I was so shocked when it all came to light. I'd seen changes in his behaviour, he'd become more secretive, sharper, but I never knew what he was doing." Tapping her fingers to her lips, she adds, "But Jenny used to tell me things about Alder when we got a moment by ourselves, which wasn't often, only when we escaped to the bathroom when we were all out together. It was usually to distract me talking about her bruises."

We could be getting somewhere. "What things?" I probe.

She chuckles. "One that made us both laugh. That Alder had this idea of building a tunnel. Complete fantasy of course."

What? "A tunnel for what? And where from and to?"

"She'd just overheard him refer to it. She knew no more. Not where it was, or what it was for."

"Was he actually building it?"

Now she sucks her bottom lip into her mouth, her brow furrowed. "I think Jenny said he was trying to get the money together. Back then, he was small fry. He didn't even live in a fancy house, so the idea of him coming up with the cash for a large project like that was a joke."

"Did Jenny know how he was earning his money?" I prompt.

"She suspected he was into drugs. Not using but dealing. I was more worried he'd involve Phil, but when I tried to ask him about it, all Phil said was he was giving him a hand with his accounts."

I sit back. How much does Alder know about his dead wife's conversations with his sister-in-law? If he knows anything at all, it's probably too much. A muscle ticks in my jaw as I realise I need to speak to Token about the plans that were found. Was it too off the mark to wonder whether they were for a tunnel? One which ended up being built? One which Alder wouldn't want to be found?

If I add in that Alder's found a way to get drugs undetected over the border, it's not too far off course and wouldn't be the first time the Border Security has been circumvented in that way. It could also be how Alder has managed to stay hidden with a ready-made escape route out of the States.

The border between the United States and Mexico is treated as a challenge by smugglers who always seem to find ways around, under or over it. Tunnels certainly aren't unheard of. Could, in the intervening years, Alder had gotten such a structure constructed? They don't just happen overnight. First, they have to be dug out and the logistics of removing earth, sand and rock isn't simple. Then they need to be shored up and have some kind of ventilation and lighting. To remain undetected for long, they can't simply start and end a few yards either side of the border. They have to be long, with the entrance and exit both hidden.

"Did you ever mention Alder's tunnelling plans to anyone?" I finally ask.

"No. It had only been a casual conversation in the bathroom. I didn't even think they were concrete plans. I'm certain Alder wouldn't be aware Jenny had even mentioned it. I didn't tell Phil. As soon as Phil left, I put him and Alder's illegal activities right out of my head—I had my children to focus on. Jenny was dead by then, Lost. I didn't know if Alder's plans were anything more than a pipe dream in his head."

CHAPTER NINETEEN

Patsy

I listened to Lost and heard how he'd taken things on his shoulders that he should never have done. In the half-century that I have lived, there's been rapid change. Even to me, a technologically challenged person, I've noticed the pace of technological developments. Lost wasn't the first or last person to be burned. Nowadays the market seems dominated by just a few platforms, many others were probably lost along the way. He'd done well, was successful for a time, but then, as so many others, couldn't compete with the big boys.

Rather than be concerned he'd gone the wrong way, I had been impressed that none of his regret was for his personal loss. No, Lost's concerns were all for his staff who'd lost their jobs, and for that bitch of a wife. He'd given her everything he had, kept nothing for himself. I had my own suspicions of how low he'd sunk that day he'd met Snake. I might not know Kim, his ex, but already, I hate her.

Every word Lost said that he thought reflected badly on himself, just showed me what a good man he was. Caring, not for his own comfort, but for others. Instead of pushing me away, it gave me confidence that he'd move heaven and earth to keep me safe. The only risk was he wouldn't look out for himself.

I've no doubt that's why he was voted in as president of the club. Everything he'd do would be for the good of his men. Every decision he'd take would be well considered and thought out. I've seen how the men look up to him and now understand why, even if Lost can't see it himself.

If Phil had been like Lost, I'd have followed him through fire, never giving up on the man I married and professed to love. But unlike Lost, Phil's driving force had been personal greed. The two men couldn't be more different.

Even if Phil had been an upright citizen when we'd broken up, I still wouldn't have stripped him of everything he owned. Even when she'd left him, Lost had given Kim every penny and lost himself while doing so.

Lost is a man who doesn't know his own worth, who's let his prior experiences rule the rest of his life. What happened has shaped him, made him cautious, made him always think twice. That doesn't make him weak, it makes him a man you can trust.

He's now quiet, working through in his head what I'd told him about Alder and the strange information given to me by Alder's wife. Something I said had resonated.

"What are you thinking, Lost?"

He gives me a shuttered look. I find it annoying. It's the same look I've seen on Demon's face back in Colorado.

"If you're going to tell me it's club business, well, don't. My daughter's partner is a member of your club, and I've been around bikers and heard the term. Sure there are things you can keep to yourself, but not when it concerns me and my life." I take a deep breath. "You asked if I was going to stay around and explore what's between us, but I can't if you treat me like the little woman who needs to be protected. I need to be part of the decision-making process, and for that I need to know what's going on. Not," I add fast, seeing the expression coming onto his face, "that I don't trust you, but because it's not the way I tick."

A small grin appears as he throws me a look of respect. He leans in closer and winks. "I kinda like the way you tick, Patsy." Then, again, he moves back. His mouth flattens, then he stuns me, and he dives straight in. "Ink and Beth found shit in that safe deposit box—old info on floppy disk drives of all things. Cad, from Colorado, managed to extract it. Token should be looking at it now. Apparently, there were plans but what they were for wasn't immediately obvious." He pauses and looks at me. "We think this could be the insurance Phil hid from Alder."

The air leaves my lungs in a whoosh. "He must have put that there when we were still married." I think aloud. "Why didn't he take it when he left me?"

"You don't use the safe deposit box, there was nothing recent in it. I suspect he thought you'd never look for it, and that perhaps it was the safest place he could have put it. If you found them, why would you look for info on a floppy disc?"

"Phil knew I wouldn't pry. I didn't want to know anything about him or what he did. So yeah, if I had found it, I'd probably have contacted him and asked if it was his." Well, it wouldn't be anyone else's. His previous words sink in. "You need to understand what was on those discs?" My mind whirrs. "Have I helped?"

"I'm not sure, Patsy. Maybe reaching too far here, but if Alder was thinking of building a tunnel, he wouldn't want anyone to discover it. If Phil knew about it, that would certainly be insurance he could hold over Alder's head. I need to talk to Token, but yeah, it's possible."

"So Alder just wants what's in the box. Why not give it to him?"

Lost rolls his head as if his neck muscles are stiff. "First, we can't offer it up, as then he'd know that you'd found it. Maybe had someone look and interpret it. That puts you in danger.

Second, if we approach Alder, he'll know we know he's looking for you, and that you've got resources at your disposal and are protected. We need to have a plan to deal with him first."

I smile, then hide it, thinking how right I'd been. Lost isn't a man to jump into action without thinking carefully about what's best to be done.

"So what do you suggest?"

Lost tilts his head and looks deep in thought. "Alder's getting drugs into the country, we know that. Dan was responsible for cutting off some of his routes, but Alder would probably have been able to set up new ones. Even new markets. We know the demand is, unfortunately there."

"But if he can't sell where he used to, wouldn't that have dealt his business a blow?"

Lost looks at me as if I'm being a bit dense. "Alder's got a way of bringing kilos of heroin and fuck knows what else into the States. You reckon he can't establish a new distribution network? I suspect Dan would have dented, but not significantly damaged his operation."

"Spell it out for me, Lost. What are you thinking?"

"What if Alder did build his tunnel? What if that's the way he's getting the shit in?"

"But if you find it, what then? Shut it down? Alder will just find another way. It would make him angry to have to do that again, but it wouldn't finish him."

Lost shakes his head. "No, you're right. But there are ways of using the info. If we know where the tunnel is, then we might be able to use that to find him or smoke him out. Even knowing how he's getting his drugs in is a feather in our cap. I don't know, we could threaten to blow it up unless he comes out of hiding and meets with us, then..."

Then they'd deal with Alder. But he wouldn't come unprepared. I'm so scared of what might happen. I don't want to lose Lost now. Surely, though, it's unlikely. "But we don't know where it could be. The border's what, two thousand miles in length? The tunnel entrance could be anywhere and will be well hidden." I bite my lip.

Lost looks thoughtful. "You're right, of course. It's like looking for a needle in a haystack. And we don't even know if it exists." He turns fully so he's looking straight at me. "There's another option for us. That's to use you as bait. Draw him out and take him down. That's your problem solved for good." He raises a quizzical eyebrow as if he's testing the waters out.

I go completely still.

I'm a seamstress, a housewife. I've never physically fought for anything in my life.

Lost sees my concern and rushes to reassure me. "Babe, we can dangle you in front of him, but you don't actually need to be there. We can lure him somewhere, maybe the house you and Dan are living in. He'll turn up expecting to find you, but it would be us waiting instead."

"My house is in a residential area, Lost. You can't have a firefight there. There'd be too many witnesses."

Lost stares at me.

"What?"

He chuckles. "You don't mind us killing him, babe, you just don't want us to get caught. Maybe you're more suited to this lifestyle than I first thought."

His words make me smile. Maybe he's right. But it's the thought of my daughter and her pregnancy that's driving me. You don't come between a woman and her child, however old she might be.

"Have you any other thoughts, Lost?"

He reaches out his hand and his fingers toy with a strand of my hair. The air around us seems to crackle as if there's static electricity. My insides clench as I catch the heat of desire in his eyes.

"Dangerous question to ask, if you don't want to hear the answer."

I take the hand stroking my hair in mine, tightening my fingers and pulling it away. "I'm talking about what we do about Alder."

"I'm thinking about keeping you safe. Keeping you close to my side so no one can ever hurt you."

My stomach tightens at his words which seem more than anyone has ever offered me before, but that won't solve my problems. "I still won't be able to see Beth."

His eyes close briefly, and I think he's making an effort to pull himself back to the matter at hand. "We could involve the feds. Give them everything. The evidence we found, the possibility Alder's bringing drugs in via a tunnel."

"But we don't actually know that. It's, as you said, just a possibility. Something that never materialised. An expressed wish that never came to reality."

"Then I think we ought to find out." He holds out his hand. "Ready to come see where Token's got to?"

I let him take my hand, feeling his large calloused fingers wrap around my much smaller softer ones, making me feel for once, petite. As he leads me out of his office and along to the room where their tech guy apparently holes up, I realise that, as I'd requested, he's including, not excluding, me from matters that affect my life so much.

If I were ever going to be with another man for any length of time, I'd want to be his partner, someone he can come home to and discuss what's gone right or wrong with his day, and a sounding board for those times when he's got problems. Somehow I suspect that his ex-wife Kim hadn't encouraged him to do that. From the little he's told me, she seems like someone totally wrapped up in herself. While he was silently fighting to stay on top of his life, where was she? Having an affair going by what he'd said.

I know there would always be things coming under the heading club business, but surely not everything about his club would be kept under wraps?

Perhaps for now, I should just be content he's not shutting me out.

He raps on Token's door, opening it only when a voice calls out.

Token looks up with a grin. "Don't know why you do that, Prez. You can always walk straight in."

"Wouldn't be the first time I've caught you with a sweet butt sucking your dick," Lost retorts. "While I don't mind, I brought company."

From what I'd seen the night before, I'm sure Lost probably wouldn't be surprised by anything his men get up to.

Token doesn't seem bothered. "She was under my desk," he retorts. "It helps me think." His attention switches to me. "Hi, Patsy." Token gives me a little finger wave.

Lost grabs a chair and places it in front of me, then takes one for himself. "What you got? Anything new on those plans?"

Token throws a not too subtle look my way, but Lost inclines his head then raises it again. He grimaces. "Cad and I have been wracking our brains." He turns his screen around so it's pointing at me and Lost.

Lost sits forward. "This is it?"

"One of them, then there's this…" Token taps at the keyboard and another plan comes into view.

Lost examines them for a moment, his brow furrowed as he looks on. Then he suggests, "Superimpose them."

Token's lips press together. He swings the screen back around and starts tapping again, then uses the mouse, looking like he's dragging something across. He stares at the result, then shakes his head.

"Well I'll be fucked," he says, turning it so we can see. "It at least looks like something. But, what?"

"An engine?" I ask. Not that I'd know. But it's circular and looks like something I've seen some place.

"Not like any I've come across," Token offers.

"Nor me." Lost leans back in the chair and stretches his legs out, crossing them at the ankles. Next, he folds his arms. "What if I said, a tunnel?"

"Tunnel?" Token looks confused. If it were a man other than his president sitting in front of him, I reckon he'd scoff. "Nah, it can't be. Dimensions are wrong, they…" His voice trails off and he looks again at the screen. "You know what it could be? Ventilation."

Lost unfolds his arms and sits up straight, examining the plan more carefully. "What's this?"

There are a long string of letters and numbers. When the plans were separate, they'd be odd letters scattered across the screen with big gaps between them. Now they've been combined, they come together in lines.

Token narrows his eyes, and his lips thin. Then with a sudden movement, he takes the screen back and calls up something else.

Lost stands, leans over the desk, then sits back down. "Something else was in that box, Patsy. A newspaper article about a group of women who disappeared. Phil ever mention anything like that? Can you recall it at all? I know it's twenty years back." He nods at Token. Token presses a few keys and a printer whirrs. Shortly, I'm holding the article in my hands.

I examine it. Six pretty young women looking like a group of high school students standing posed for a photo, kitted out with hiking gear. I don't recognise the location at all. Quickly I scan the words, in my periphery vision, I notice Token picking up his phone.

"Hey, Cad. How you doing, Brother…? Yeah, me too…. I was getting nowhere either until Prez made a suggestion. Superimpose the plans… you doing it…? Yeah. That's right. Lost mentioned there could be a tunnel involved…" Token breaks off and looks at Lost. "Drug smuggling?"

Lost nods. "Likely," he replies.

"Yeah." Token's speaking back into the phone. "Smuggling anyway. Maybe even girls if that article's connected in any way… Yeah. If this was Phil's insurance, there's something here that Alder didn't want him to have... Yeah… Keep digging, okay. Speak later, Brother."

I read the article again. Nothing sparks any memory at all. I turn toward Lost. "You think Alder had anything to do with the disappearance of these girls, and that Phil knew about it?"

"It's possible," Lost says, sighing out the words. "Could Phil have been involved?"

"No." It doesn't take me long to come up with an answer. "Twenty years back, he might have been dabbling in stuff for Alder, but that would have been to do with his accounts. He might have found out about something which he could hold over his brother-in-law, but I'm certain he wasn't getting his hands that dirty at that point."

"This is all we got." Lost's lips press together momentarily. "Any connecting information died along with Phil." He takes the printout from my hand and looks at it himself.

"I haven't been able to track it back." Token shakes his head, his brow creasing as if in some way he's failed. "It's a scanned photocopy. I can't even tell where in the country it is, what newspaper it might be, or what the original story was. No date either. All we know is it's at least twenty-two years old, not even whether the girls turned up or not."

"The girls aren't even named," I point out.

"There's not much to go on." Token shrugs. "I've been running traces but so far nothing's turned up."

"No mention of the school either. Sloppy reporting."

"Or there's more." Leaning over I tap the bottom of the page. "The article isn't complete, maybe the detail wasn't important."

"Or, maybe that's the important bit that's missing." Lost is shaking his head.

"Can I see that again?" Lost passes it over to me.

I stare at it and then look up at the string of letters and numbers on the screen. I read, a lot. Before I got hooked on MC novels, I read crime, mysteries and suspense. I also have the benefit of being the ex-wife of the man who left this article there. Mentally I add up the number of lines on the page. Then, glance back at the screen.

Feeling eyes burning into me, I look up to see Token staring, a focused look on his face. "Whatcha got, Patsy?"

Raising and lowering my shoulders, I feel a bit crazy. Surely it wouldn't be as easy as that? I'm embarrassed to let them know what I'm thinking.

"At this point, I'm stumped," Token admits. "Anything is better than nothing."

"Rather follow a red herring than none at all," Lost encourages from my side.

Grimacing slightly, I let them in on my thoughts. "Phil was intrigued by codes. Used to read about that enigma machine, you know? The one used in World War II. He devoured anything he could read about it. What if these strings of numbers are code, and this article is the key?"

Token's eyes go wide. "You think?" He calls up the image of the article and loads it on one monitor.

"There are fifty-three lines on this page. The biggest number on the plans is fifty-three."

Token looks carefully, comparing both. "There's no pattern that I can see. Sure, here, look? That could be a line number, what the word begins with, then the number of letters in, but the next one doesn't fit the same pattern."

"I'm sorry."

"It was worth a try." Lost takes hold of my hand and gives it a comforting squeeze.

"No, Patsy. I think you've got something here. I've been chasing my tail trying to find the origin of the article, and I couldn't see how it could be an insurance policy with no names, places or dates. So what else could it be? A fuckin' key."

Lost looks from me to Token, then back again. "Your birthdate," he snaps, impatiently. "Phil's too, and Beth and Dan's."

Token grabs a pen and writes them down as I recite them off, adding the date of Phil's sister's for good measure.

"Wedding day?" Token asks.

I tell him that too, whereas I normally try to forget the hastily organised affair before my pregnancy had begun to show.

Token nods toward his prez. "Why don't you leave this with me? I'll get a program running to sort through all the combinations. I'll give it to Cad as well. Could be something, maybe not, but it's worth investigating for sure."

CHAPTER TWENTY

Lost

"You did good there, Patsy," I tell her as we leave Token to work his magic. "Hey, you okay?"

She's leaning her back against the wall of the hallway and her eyes have closed. She takes a deep breath before opening them and focusing on me once more. "I don't know." Her voice breaks. "Four months ago, I was living a normal life. My son, yeah, he was a problem, but I thought, in time, he'd turn his life around. He just had to get away from his monster of a father…" She breaks off and puts her palms against her face. "Beth and I were jogging along well enough together, thinking nothing would ever change." She offers a half-smile. "I was anxious for Beth when she met Ink. Not because he was a biker, well, I suppose it did have something to do with that, but the lifestyle, you know? Beth's an all-in type of girl though she tried to pretend she could do casual, but I knew her better than that. If I'd had any expectations, it would have been I'd have ended up nursing Beth's broken heart."

I notice Patsy's staring at the pictures of past and present members of the club on the opposite wall. Some are serious, most are comical poses. Salem and Pennywise both have their middle fingers up, and Kink's tongue is stuck out. There are lighter patches on the nicotine stained wall, where nine photos had to be removed. Though we'd tried to space out those remaining as the new ones were added, you can still see the evidence of our shadowy past. The men might have gone, but still evidence of them lingers. For the first time in days, I wonder what Shark had been doing in San Diego. With everything else, he's been pushed out of my mind, but there's been no further sightings so maybe I can lock him back into my mental box once again.

"Beth didn't end up disappointed," I remind her, not knowing where she's going with this. "Ink was serious."

She nods. "Thank God. I couldn't have left Beth without knowing she was loved and cared for. But, Lost? How did I get here? I thought I was coming with Dan for his sake. But it's not him who's in danger, it's me. As for this tunnel stuff and freaking coded messages? Christ, I feel like I'm living in some kind of movie."

I hold out my hand, she takes it. Leading her into the clubroom, I notice how time has moved on. The space is filling up with men coming back from their day jobs. I realise I haven't eaten all day.

"Want some food?"

At my question, she purses her lips and thinks. "I ought to, I suppose. I kind of forgot to feel hungry with everything else that's been going on."

"Come on." I lead the way into the kitchen.

"Hi, Patsy. Lost." Eva turns away from the stove and smiles. "Are you hungry?" At my nod, she continues, "I've got some burgers here if you want something fast. Or Cindy's got a casserole going but that won't be ready for a little while."

I glance down at Patsy, who shrugs. "Burger's fine."

As Eva busies herself getting out buns and making our sandwiches, Patsy tugs at my arm. I lower my head so I can hear her softly spoken question.

"The club girls cook?"

Eva overhears and laughs. "Those that can, do. Er, Tits, we don't really trust since the time she got the salt and sugar muddled up. Sure was a weird lasagne that time."

"She did it on purpose," saunters in another girl who continues her explanation, "to get out of having to help. How's my casserole looking?"

"Bubbling," Eva tells her.

Cindy turns to Patsy. "I'm Cindy. I don't think we've been introduced."

"Er, Patsy."

From her slight hesitation, I gather Patsy may not have spoken to, but has definitely seen Cindy, and probably Pearl and Tits in action. I'm pleased Cindy gives her a genuine smile, which she would have been unlikely to do if Patsy had been younger. I've seen the club girls running off competition before. They can be possessive about their bikers. Of course, it could be a different matter if they see I'm serious about her, but maybe not. It's rare nowadays I partake of their services.

Eva's pointing and asking if we want this or that, then passing over condiments so we can prepare our snacks as we want. As we sit down to eat, Cindy struts off.

A loud booming voice precedes its owner into the kitchen. "Hey, Eva? You there, woman? I've got a cock that needs sucking."

Seconds later, I'm slapping Patsy's back to help her stop choking.

"Salem," I growl, as the man making the request comes into sight.

He looks completely unrepentant, even when he spots Patsy seated beside me. He's sporting a smirk as he raises an eyebrow toward Eva who giggles, then sends an apologetic look Patsy's way before she lets the enforcer put his arm around her and leads her off. Probably not very far, no one's particularly shy in the clubroom.

It had been a shock to me that first time Snake had brought me to the clubhouse. I can still remember it now. I'd been granted a new lease on life, even if at the time I didn't know whether I wanted it, whether it was just too damn hard making the effort to stay alive. Maybe if I'd been taken under the wing of a civilian, I'd have returned to my option of taking the easy way out. But I was immediately immersed in a different lifestyle, something I'd never dreamed would become my way of life. I'd been introduced to men who were fiercely protective of each other, rough and rowdy. They would never seek death out, but with the knowledge that Satan might choose any day to take them, they were determined to live a full life before they died. Hence their anything goes way of living.

As a prospect, I'd been tested hard—almost given no time to think which at the time was exactly what I needed. I was run ragged, falling into my bed and going out like a light when my day's duties were finally completed. Tinder, who I'd prospected beside and had shown me the ropes, including passing off the more unpleasant stuff he didn't like, had patched in shortly after, leaving me as the sole grunt they had. Tinder. Yeah. He was another one who threw his lot in with Snake and who's now out bad.

The point is, for an outsider, our way of life can be hard to swallow. I'm slightly concerned about Patsy's reaction. Only a short time ago, she was reminding me about her normal life and how much she missed it, so I spare Patsy a glance, surprised to see she's trying not to laugh.

"Tell me," she pulls her eyes back from the doorway which Eva and Salem had just disappeared through. "do you normally starve? And does anything ever get cooked? Oh, and, please reassure me, the girls do wash their hands."

I can't resist pulling her to me, her head resting against my chest. "Snake, the old prez, well his mom used to run the kitchen while he was around, but she left at the same time he did." I don't tell her he ended up six feet under. "Since then, we're just grateful anyone does anything at all. Tried getting the prospects to cook but seems like their genetic makeup isn't right. It's a woman's job after all."

I feel her tense, then she glances up and sees me grinning, and must remember the breakfast I made for her in her house. Seeing I'm yanking her chain, she slaps me lightly.

"Lost!"

I can't resist her. She looks so damn cute as she bites her lip as she tries to maintain her mock annoyance. Lowering my head, I press my mouth to hers, sucking her lip into mine instead. She moans softly, her burger forgotten, and her arms come around my neck. I'm just starting to enjoy myself when another voice interrupts.

"Mom!"

Patsy jumps away from me like a cat who's been scalded. Guilt is written all over her face as she turns to face her son.

"I, er…" Dan brushes his hair back from his face, then the corners of his mouth rise. "Fuck, Mom. How long has this been going on?"

"Nothing's going on," Patsy replies primly.

"Yeah? Well Lost eating your face just now suggests you're a liar." Now he's grinning widely.

"We just… we were just…" Patsy stammers. "We weren't…"

I put my arm back around her and pull her back in, ignoring her reluctance. "Patsy and I are getting to know each other," I tell her son, using my serious tone. "Don't know where it's going, even if it's going anywhere, but I like your mom, and I hope she reciprocates."

Dan kicks out a chair and sits on it. He looks from Patsy to me, then back again. "Mom, I'm happy as fuck if you've found someone. Hell," this time both hands brush back his hair, "it just took me by surprise. I'm happy for you. Just do me one favour, limit the public displays of affection when I'm around."

Patsy is still feeling uncomfortable. "Dan, I, there's a lot going on. I—"

"Mom, I mean it," her son interrupts. "Honestly. I don't mind. Just be sure Lost is what you want, and Lost?"

I cock my eyebrow.

"You ever hurt her…" he leaves the rest unsaid.

"I'll try not to." It's all I can promise.

Dan gives me a sharp nod. "What's new?" he asks.

Patsy looks at me for confirmation. "It's alright," I tell her. "Dan, listen to what your mom has got to say. If you've any thoughts or it triggers any memories, let me know?" I release Patsy, taking her hand and giving it a squeeze one last time. "I need to talk to Dart. I'll catch up with you as soon as we have any news."

She gives me a weak smile, then turns to her son. As I push up and away from the table, I hear her quietly starting to update him. I don't have any real hopes he can shed light on things that happened when he was a babe in arms, but he spent four years close to his father, and something may come to his mind.

Dart's on the phone as I pass him, so I wave with my hand and indicate my office. He holds up one hand with his fingers splayed which I interpret as he'll be there in five.

In fact it's four, I realise, checking my old-fashioned clock on the wall as he enters and pulls out the chair in front of the desk.

"What do you reckon to this tunnel idea?" he asks.

"Token's spoken to you?" At his nod, I continue, "It's information that's over twenty years old." Picking up a pen out of habit, I use it, not to write, but to tap at my lips. "We know there are tunnels. They tend to be dug, used for a few months, then discovered and shut down."

"There's a tunnelling task force, isn't there? Working on tip-offs. I think they're kept busy."

It's my turn to move my head up and down. "What are the chances that Alder's got a tunnel that's been undiscovered all this time?"

Instead of answering me, Dart asks a question of his own. "I've been thinking about Alder coming after Patsy. If he thinks she's been moved under WitSec, it's possible the reason he wants to catch up with her is to see what they know."

I press my lips together as I think. "What would she be able to tell them? If she'd found Phil's insurance, how would she be able to discover what was on those floppy disc drives? Unless she had a very old computer at home." Patsy might be many things, but I don't get the impression she's up on technology. "As for the code, how could she read it?"

Dart's brow furrows as he thinks. "But he wants her found. Why?"

"Maybe he thinks Dan told her something before he 'died.'" I use air quotes. "He did go to her house a couple of times."

"True." I nod. My pen still taps at my lips. "I still think there's something we're missing."

"Okay." Dart leans back in his chair and kicks out his legs, resting his feet on my desk, crossing them at the ankles.

I glare at him, but he smirks and leaves his boots where they are. Really, I don't give a damn. The desk is old and already marked, and if it helps with his thought process, I'm not going to argue.

"Let's think about this. The information is over twenty years old. But what if it was a pipe dream back then, and the tunnel was only constructed recently?"

"For a start, we don't know if there is a tunnel." I play devil's advocate. "And in twenty years he might have changed his plans or location."

"Maybe he had the perfect site in mind, one that's remained hidden all these years. Or," Dart swings his legs back down and sits forward again, "maybe it's a backup location. What if the information Dan gave him fucked up his current routes, so he's had to use something else? Maybe he's resurrected an old way of getting drugs in and out."

"What else could it be, Dart?" True to my name, I'm totally lost for any explanation. Does it all hinge on data that's been gathering dust for two decades, or is it something Patsy knows now? Until we've got more information, I'm stumped as to how to progress. Am I right to keep Patsy close by, or should we create a new identity and move her? Is she safe here? Or am I putting her at greater risk?

Dart sweeps his long hair back as though preparing to fasten it in a ponytail but just holds it there. "All this started with an anonymous message. If we hadn't gotten that, we'd have never known Patsy was in danger."

I shudder at Dart's reminder. If we hadn't known, Alder would already have his hands on her. With that network of his, she wouldn't have evaded him for long. I owe whoever it was that messaged us. I make a mental note to check with Token whether he's been able to find out any more. Maybe there's more information to come our way if we only knew who the fucker was who sent it.

"Then there's Shark."

My eyes widen. "You think he's got a part to play in this?"

Dart's shoulders rise and fall. "No fuckin' idea. It seems unlikely. But why rear his head after three years? Coincidence? Probably. But it can't be dismissed."

It's easier to list what we don't know than what we do. We know Patsy is in danger, but we don't know why. We know we got a message, but not who from, and we've seen Shark who shouldn't be anywhere near San Diego, so what the hell was he doing being spotted close by?

"Fuck."

"Yeah," Dart says. "That about sums it up."

CHAPTER TWENTY-ONE

Patsy

"So, you and Lost?" Dan raises a quizzical eyebrow at me.

"There's nothing much to tell," I begin, trying to get my own thoughts together. "I like him, Dan." *When he's not being an ass.* Though after he'd explained about his ex, I could see why my comments had caused the reaction they had. But if Lost has deep trust issues about women, then there'll be no future for us. I've lived too long to force a man into the person I want him to be, or for me to change to become the woman he wants. I'd tried enough with Phil to know that doesn't work. There's no point in having a picture of an ideal man in your mind and pretending the one you're with can be moulded into that. I like Lost, as I've told Dan, but the jury's still out on whether we can make anything between us work. And, of course, Alder could come between us, upsetting any plans we might make.

"Well, I didn't expect you to be eating the face of a man you didn't like."

"Dan!" I flick my hand in his direction, seeing him grinning widely. I sigh. "It's early days. At your age, you'd see a girl you like, and your focus is getting her into bed—"

"That's an age thing?" Dan interrupts with a snort. "With you being my mom, the thought might turn my stomach, but I reckon Lost wants to do just that."

"Dan!" Once again, he shocks me.

"And you don't? Want him like that?"

Perhaps I wouldn't be as embarrassed if I were speaking to my daughter rather than my son, or maybe I would. Are moms even supposed to have sex lives? "Dan, whether he does or not, or whether I do, the thing is, I don't want something that's only a fling. If I want a man, I'd like to know it could lead somewhere."

"I didn't see you push him away."

I'm not explaining myself well. "What I'm saying, Dan, is that I need time to understand who Lost is before acting on any attraction. So, it's far too early to say if there's anything between us."

He tilts his head to one side, regarding me carefully for a moment, then barks a laugh. "You're right. I'm not looking for a relationship, but if a girl showed she was willing to put out, I'd take her up on it. But Lost? I get a different vibe from him, Mom. I don't reckon he'd use you."

I'm certain he wouldn't, but I've been wrong before. "It's hardly a good time to start a relationship, Dan." Taking a breath, I dismiss the subject of what's going on with me and the MC prez, and instead, resume the update which Dan had interrupted as soon as Lost was out of earshot. When I finish, his jaw is tight.

He shakes his head. "This shit that was found is over twenty years old?"

I nod.

"You really think this is Phil's insurance I heard him talking about?"

Resting my elbows on the table, I stare at him. "Truthfully, I think everyone is clutching at straws. It all seems so farfetched. Can you remember anything that might shed light on this at all?"

But Dan doesn't get the chance to answer. Before he can even open his mouth, two women come back into the kitchen. One, with reddened cheeks who makes me blush. I find I can't quite look Eva in the eye, knowing exactly why her lips look swollen. The second goes straight to the oven, clearly to check if her meal is cooked. I wave my hand and Dan picks up my signal.

We move the conversation outside.

When we're sat on a picnic bench shaded by a tree, Dan stares out at the magnificent view, before he says, "I'm wracking my brains trying to think of anything that would help. I can't."

"What were you able to tell the feds, Dan?"

"I knew where the drugs entered the country, how they got to Colorado." He pauses, and his eyes close. "Certainly nothing about a tunnel. I told them about his modified trucks, and which crossing points they used, and the routes he would take across the country. Enough so he wasn't able to smuggle them in that way anymore. The main thing was, I could finger him as the man behind it."

"Where is Alder now?" I muse. "He's gone underground, otherwise the feds would already have run him down."

"Agent Caruso told me they'd confiscated his assets. He's lost his house, and the damage I've done to his business, well, he'll have to be building that back up from scratch."

I do some thinking myself. "When I saw him at the funeral, he didn't ask me anything."

"Perhaps," Dan muses, "he didn't think he'd needed to at the time."

"But Phil was already dead," I remind him.

"At that point, the feds hadn't made their move, though. Alder was making sure I was dead. That was the reason he turned up."

Something isn't right. Something that no one has mentioned before. I think we were just stunned to find out it was me Alder was searching for and not my son. "If he thinks you're dead, how does he think the feds got the information to close him down?"

Dan looks like a light bulb's just gone off in his head. "What if Phil's insurance policy was something else? What if Alder thinks Phil left details of his operation with you, to be used at the time of his untimely death?"

I just stare at him, realising we've all been looking at this upside down. If Alder truly believes my son is dead, then who spoke to the feds? "But why me? I'm the last person who Phil would have shared anything with. Anything given to me, I'd just hand to the cops."

"Exactly." Dan grins widely. "Phil could have left a letter or something with his lawyer. Phil dies, the letter comes to you, you hand it over and the feds close in. Then you pack up and run." His face falls. "If you hadn't have moved with me, then maybe Alder wouldn't have become suspicious."

I cover his hand with mine. "Or it's the best thing I could have done. If those are Alder's suspicions, then if I'd stayed, he could have taken me at any time." I wait for that to sink in. "Jesus, Dan. You're right. It all makes sense. Alder wants revenge—"

"Or he wants to find out how much damage was done. If I were Alder, I'd want to know exactly what the feds were told. What if he's got more routes that Phil knew about but not me? He'd have to know whether they were safe to use, or whether they were being staked out to catch him red-fuckin'-handed."

I breathe in deeply. That's the only thing that makes sense. I regard my son almost with fresh eyes. It's been years, if ever, since I've sat and brainstormed ideas with him. Maybe he's not so academic as Beth, but he's far from stupid.

"Hey. I've been looking everywhere for you." Lost comes over and joins us. When he sits on the bench alongside me, Dan raises an eyebrow and grins.

I ignore him, turning instead to Lost. "We've come up with an idea of why Alder is so desperate to find me."

Dan takes over. "Phil told Alder he had insurance. What you found on the floppy discs may or may not have been part of it, but all Alder knows is that after Phil was killed, the feds swooped in and destroyed his drug running organisation." Lost nods his head. "By then, I was already dead." Dan proceeds to fill him in on the thoughts we've just been having.

When he's finished, Lost's eyes have gone wide as he looks at each of us in turn, digesting what we've told him. After a moment, he raises his chin. "Makes more sense than anything else we've come up with." He taps on the picnic bench. Once, twice, then he seems to come to a decision. "I'll take this back to Token. If you're right, those floppies don't hold anything that's going to move this forward. Alder's chasing fictional information that he thinks resides in your head." He rests his hand against my cheek, his eyes full of compassion.

There's no easy escape from Alder. If there's no tunnel to find, Lost loses a bargaining chip. I hadn't really hoped that anything would come from twenty-year-old information.

"We'll sort it, Patsy. Somehow we'll draw Alder out."

"How?"

Instead of answering my question, a shuttered look comes over Lost's face.

"You promised, Lost," I remind him, my voice a low growl. If I don't say anything, he's likely to start labelling everything club business.

"Fuck, woman." He turns his head, one side of his mouth turned up. "You're going to be a pain in my ass, aren't you?"

Dan chuckles. "You bet she is." He winks at me.

Lost shakes his head, then starts to speak. "Okay. It doesn't hurt us if Token keeps doing what he's doing, even if he doesn't turn up anything useful. We can't discount the information that we did find in that box, nor that Alder knew of its existence. That could still be what he wants. There are hundreds of what-ifs and assumptions here. But, and here's the first one, what if Alder had a tunnel dug years back like his wife suggested to you Patsy? He might have stopped using it, or I don't know, part fell in? It was close to being discovered? Hell, could have been discovered and blocked off. But what if he needs to find a new route into the country? If he's desperate, he might go back to revisit one he originally used."

"But where would a tunnel be?" I ask. "We know border control is always looking for tunnels. Surely they would have come across something that old?"

"If it's stayed hidden that long, maybe Alder thinks it's a safe route?" Dan raises an eyebrow.

"But something that safe would have been used before and not abandoned." Lost taps the wood again, a gesture that seems to help him think.

"What if the feds did find it?" I suggest. "What if they watched it for years, then gave up?"

"It would have been destroyed." Lost dismisses my suggestion, then stills. "Unless they didn't find it, but they got too close. Alder moved operations because it was too risky. Now, with no other choice, maybe he's opening it back up."

"He wasn't using a tunnel when I knew him," Dan puts in. "He had couriers crossing the border."

"But his network has been broken up?" Lost questions Dan who raises his chin.

"I don't know what the feds actually did, but I gave them enough information."

Lost rakes his fingers through his hair. "Going back to your other point. Alder wants to know what Patsy knows. It is possible he thinks that there was some 'in case of my death' message left somewhere that Phil would have gotten to you, Patsy."

"That makes sense," I tell him, though it is worrying. "More so than a fictional tunnel he might have dug."

Lost fills his lungs and looks at my son before turning back to me. "Any thought of you leaving has got to be put out of your head, Patsy. We didn't have a clue why Alder had you in his sights, now we've come up with something that gives us a clearer picture and it's one I don't like. You're fuckin' important to Alder, and he won't stop if he thinks it was you who spoke to the feds, and he'll want to know exactly what was said. You're staying here, with me. So I can protect you."

I've never thought of myself as weak, but I've never been challenged before and the thought of leaning on Lost is comforting. But the more important I am to Alder, the more desperate he'll be to find me. If he does, anyone protecting me will be in danger. If I leave, Lost and Dan will be safe. I don't give Lost a response; he won't like the thoughts in my head.

"Hey, Dan!"

"Salem?" Dan swings around as he answers.

"Got something you might want to see." The enforcer's standing by the back door.

Dan grins. "I'll be right there." He waves a goodbye to me and Lost as he stands and leaves.

Lost smiles at me. "Salem seems to have taken your boy under his wing. Said he was impressed with him today."

I return his expression. "He was excited about helping out in your shop."

"As long as he stays out of sight, Salem will be happy with an extra pair of hands. He likes mechanical shit?"

"He seems to have taken to it. I don't think he's ever had a chance to work with his hands." Except for beating people up, I remember.

"Lost, Patsy? Cindy's got food on the table. You coming inside?"

It's Eva. Lost queries me with a tilt of his head. When I nod, he pulls me to my feet.

As we enter the kitchen, Lost pulls out a chair, and gentlemen like, holds it as I sit down. He then takes the one beside me. I look around slightly nervous, wondering if people notice I seem to be monopolising his attention, but no one remarks on it, nor seems to find it strange.

I have to admit to being dubious about eating something a club girl has prepared, but it turns out to be a tasty casserole. Even though I'd not long eaten a burger, my stomach makes some room.

I've had a chance to eat about half when Smoker, who's sitting at the opposite end of the table, has a coughing fit.

Once he's regained his breath, Lost points at him, and tells him in a tone full of authority, "You're going to the doctor."

"No point, Prez," Smoker objects.

Lost growls. "You do as I—"

"No point," Smoker interrupts and repeats, his eyes hardening as he regards his prez. "I already been."

"And?" Eva pauses on the way to seat herself, her plate held in mid-air.

Smoker looks around, seeming to note who's there. I recognise Grumbler, Bones, Blaze, Dusty, Brakes, Snips and Reboot. Eventually he takes a breath, coughs again, then once recovered, shrugs. "Lung cancer," he informs everybody.

There's a shocked silence around the table. Lost puts down his fork. "When the fuck do you start treatment? And why the fuck are you still smoking? You stop that shit right now," he snarls.

Smoker looks around. "I ain't doing either."

"You fuckin' what?" Lost's half out of his seat, leaning forward.

The older man looks annoyed. "My body, my life, ain't it?" He challenges everyone who's looking at him in disbelief. "With treatment, they give me around a year. Without?" He shrugs. "A few months. Seems a no-brainer. I don't have a family, except for my MC one. I'll lose that if I can't ride. So," he pulls his shoulders back, "I've made my decision. I'll live my life, enjoy my cigarettes, and leave fate up to mother nature."

Eva glares at Lost and puts down her untouched plate, resting her hand on Smoker's shoulder. "When did you find out?" she asks.

"Yesterday," Smoker replies.

Her eyes signal a message toward Lost. I interpret it as saying he should give the old man some time. Maybe if he thinks about it a bit longer, he'll decide to fight.

I don't think I'd give up. If there was a chance of even just a few months longer, I'd take it. But that's because I'd want to spend longer with those I loved.

Glancing around the table, I can see by the expressions—some stunned, some hurt—that while Smoker might not realise it right now, his loss will devastate them just as much as if they lost someone related by blood.

CHAPTER TWENTY-TWO

Lost

After Smoker's announcement, I completely lose my appetite. I try one more mouthful, but it feels like cardboard in my mouth. Regrets run through my mind. Why had we not forced Smoker to give up his habit? Deep down, I know the reason.

In the MC, we pride ourselves on riding free and making our own paths in life. Who am I to criticise if a man who knew the risks kept on chain smoking? Who didn't seek help with his health until it was too late? I'm gutted that he doesn't feel he has to try for us, that he can't see how hurt we are, but as he said, it's his life. If it's true that he would only extend it a few months, why spend those suffering the effects of chemical and radiation therapies?

Me? I'd fight for life. Or, I qualify, that's what I think now. How could I put myself in another's shoes? Smoker believes he has no one around him who'd grieve. He's wrong. He's got the whole of the Satan's Devils MC.

I know what Eva had tried to convey by that silent message she sent to me. Smoker is still coming to terms with the news he received yesterday. His initial reaction may change. One thing I know, we've got to approach this carefully. Any direct approach would have the man digging in his heels.

Shrugging off the disruption he's wrought, Smoker takes the plate a moist-eyed Cindy offers to him and starts to dig in. I watch him for a moment as he smacks his lips appreciatively, as though relishing the little things in life. I vow there and then, if I can't change his mind, I'll make sure we do everything we can to make the most of whatever time he's got left. Grumbler might have some ideas; he's known Smoker probably the longest.

Patsy taps my arm to get my attention, but before I can complete my turn in her direction, my phone pings. Taking it out, I read the message.

Token: Have you got a minute?

I don't bother to respond. I pull my plate toward me and start to stand. "Sorry, Patsy, I need to go. I'll catch up with you later." My words are innocent, but my eyes catch hers and hold them for a moment blazing out a more intense suggestion. As her cheeks redden, I suspect she's gotten the message. If nothing else, I could do with a heavy make-out session later, if only to affirm that I'm still healthy and alive.

Though I'm reluctant to leave Patsy, I'm not unhappy to exit the room where I'm leaving one of my members with a problem I'm helpless to solve. I pause at the bar and take a bottle of beer from Curtis, then proceed to Token's office.

I rap on the door, but immediately enter as I'm expected. "Whatcha got?" I ask as I sit opposite his array of monitors.

Token meets my eyes and puts his hand to his face, drawing it down from his nose to his chin. "Fucker's been in contact again."

"The mysterious guy in the wind? Any clue where he's from?"

"Outer Mongolia? Timbuktu? Who the fuck knows?" Token shakes his head. "Got no idea where he is, or even if it is a man."

Leaving aside the who and where for now, I prompt, "What did he/she/it say?"

"They," Token corrects my pronoun with a grin. "Get with the program. If they're not a male or female, they're a they."

"Token." I put a bite of menace into my growl.

"Ok." As Token's face falls, I start to realise his messing around was a delaying tactic. "He's broken the code for me."

Not pointing out he's chosen a particular pronoun, I widen my eyes.

"Hacked straight into my system as though it was child's play." Token thumps his hand down on his desk, glaring at his monitor as if the equipment had betrayed him.

I breathe in deeply, then exhale a loud breath. No one really knows what my skills are, or were, they're well past their sell by date. Snake had asked basic questions, but only to enable him to discount I'd any connection with law enforcement. While I was prospecting, I was instructed to fetch, carry, clean, dig holes and bury bodies, no questions asked, and none directed toward me. By the time I'd earned my patch, the brothers knew everything about me they needed to know—that they could trust me to have their backs. Many members have pasts they want left buried. I wasn't unusual in that. Snake knew I'd fucked up my business but hadn't cared to ask what business that was.

Token, though, he's guessed my background if not how I was involved, purely due to my interest in his security system and the privacy and antivirus software he uses. I've been impressed to be honest. So it's worrying as fuck that someone could break in so easily.

"You sure it's our end?" I query. "Cad's got the same info. Or the email—"

"Encrypted." He gives me a look akin to that which he'd used had I given him instruction on how to boil water. "Anything between Cad and me is sent well protected. And yes, it's us. He's actually circled some of the info while I was watching. Oh, and he added this. I was able to screen shot it. Whenever he posts something it disappears within seconds." He turns one of the monitors toward me, the message states:

Don't be too concerned. We *can* get into Fort Knox.

I bark an incredulous laugh. "I presume he means virtually and not in reality?"

Token shakes his head and rolls his eyes. "Right now, I wouldn't be too sure."

"Two things I want from you." I pull at my forefinger. "First, if he helped break the code, what was the result? And two," I pull at my second finger, "if he, she or they are so fuckin' brilliant, why aren't they doing this themselves?"

"I'm pretty certain I can work it out," he replies. "It's coordinates, but one digit missing from both the longitude and latitude. See?" He points to his screen. "That's what's circled – the gap. Why it's missing don't ask me, but old Phil didn't want to make it easy."

I start to suggest, "You can—"

Another roll of his eyes. "I've already got a program running to go through all the permutations and check what makes sense. I presume if there is a tunnel, that this could be the start and end points?" When I nod, he continues, "As to your second question, why us? Maybe we were just closest? Maybe he is in Timbuktu and nowhere near us. Or maybe he likes seeing us squirm and do his work for him."

I lean toward the latter myself. If he/she/it or they were so fucking clever, why weren't they doing more to help? "Can you make contact with him?"

Token's head moves left then right. "Wish I fuckin' could."

"You get the feeling he could help more?"

Token grimaces then admits, "Put it this way, I got a feeling he can crack the code and find out the locations faster than me."

I lean back my head, rolling it on my neck. "Which suggests he's not close. But what's the benefit to him, helping us out?"

Token looks annoyed. "He's making me feel stupid." His hand thumps down on the desk, making the monitors jump. "Maybe he knows it's dangerous and doesn't like taking risks. Or it could be a trap and he's setting us up. He could already have the coordinates; we turn up and walk straight into the arms of the feds."

"Could it be Alder himself?" I wonder aloud.

He's quiet for a moment, sifting through the facts. "Alder could employ an expert but what's the point? He'd know where his fuckin' tunnel starts and ends. He could have sent us the information in far easier ways."

"True," I agree. "Unless he's playing an elaborate game. He wants Patsy, and I suspect he'd have tried to take her if he knew where she was. And we wouldn't have this information if she hadn't remembered the safe deposit box. So we discount Alder. And this fucker isn't a loner, he said 'we', which suggests he's working with someone else, maybe even a team."

His eyes come to meet mine. "Still feel I'm letting you down, Prez."

"Nah. In no way are you letting me down, Token. You don't know what setup this guy or people have. You're limited as to what you can use." My voice is firm, willing him to believe me. "If someone's providing info that's useful, use it. The only thing that concerns me is locking our systems down so he can't fuckin' get in in the first place."

"Firewalls be damned, Prez, I don't trust them now. I already moved the club stuff onto a separate server, Prez. One that's not connected to the internet," he reminds me.

I'm not surprised it's the first thing he's done. I would have too.

"And there's no way you can start a two-way dialogue? I feel we're being drip fed pieces." I can understand Token's frustration. It's as though we're being toyed with. If there's someone out there two steps ahead of us, I'd like to save time and talk to them.

"I've tried," Token replies. "But I can't get a hold of anything when the messages come through. I've never seen anything like it before. I've done all I can. Protected our shit while keeping a channel open. What I will say is, so far, this guy has not led us wrong."

I muse, half to myself, "Who the fuck can it be?"

Token shrugs. He looks as confused as I am.

Who would want to help us? Someone who also wants Alder stopped? Seems likely. But who, other than the feds, would want that? And the feds would act on the information, not pass it our way.

"I'm going upstairs. Let me know if you come up with anything."

"Sure thing." Even before I reach the door, Token's turned his attention back to the screens in front of him.

The clubroom is in full evening swing by the time I step out of Token's office. Eva looks very comfortable on Pennywise's lap. She's an exhibitionist and isn't at all bothered his fingers are on her clit and she's about to come in front of everyone. Her head is thrown back in abandon, her cheeks are red, and her eyes squeezed shut as Pennywise's hand keeps working. He catches me looking and winks.

I raise my chin back. Not my thing, but hey, to each their own.

Turning I spy Pearl on the stripper pole. I take a moment to appreciate that Alex's lessons are paying off. Her fluidity is amazing. I'm not the only one entranced. By the look of it, she'll be fighting a few brothers off in a minute. Tits is missing but is probably engaged elsewhere. Cindy is, no, was, with Snips as he's just pulled out, expertly tying off the condom.

Most of the brothers are drinking or playing pool. Smoker's not around, but even if he was, it's too soon to broach any serious conversation with him and right now I don't know how to approach it. Making a mental note to leave it a couple of days, I continue to look around.

Dan is deep in conversation with Salem, but there's no sign of Patsy. Given the non-PG displays, it's not surprising. Expecting I'll find her in the room we've assigned to her, I continue to the stairs and climb up.

At my knock, there's a short delay, then the door opens, Patsy holding onto it.

I smirk. "You're safe here, babe."

She looks self-conscious. "I don't know how your men get when they've had a few drinks, Lost. I don't want them to stumble into my room."

"They're not going to mistake you for a sweet butt, babe." I realise immediately I could have phrased that better.

Her face twists. "Of course, they're not."

I growl, my hand curling around her neck, holding her captive. My swift action breaks her hold on the door. "Babe. You're far too classy to be one of them. You cover too much skin. But if you want to bare that in the privacy of my room? Hell, you could rival them any day."

Her eyes widen. In shock or horror, I can't be certain. "Well, you'll be disappointed if you expect a body like theirs. I'm no spring chicken, Lost. I've stretch lines, sagging skin…"

"So have I," I respond, remorselessly. "You want to compare cellulite, then I'm up for that. Though I tell you, there are far better things I'd like to be doing." When her eyes light, I press my case home. "I want my mouth on your pussy, babe. Can't fuckin' wait to taste you."

"Lost!" She tries to pull back, but I've got a tight hold on her.

"But if that's going too fast, I'd be content with just my lips on your mouth. You set the speed and the direction." I stare at the aforementioned lips as I speak, noticing how she bites them, and I feel my dick swell in my pants. "If you just want to kiss, so be it." An image of what Pennywise had just been doing comes into my mind. "Or, I could make you come with my fingers, feel you orgasm all over my hand."

Her breathing has sped up. "Lost," she says my name again.

I continue to taunt her. "When you're nice, wet and ready, I could bend you over my bed, sink my cock into your pussy while my hands clutch at your ass."

In a clear attempt to put distance between us, she asks a little sharply, "Is this how you were with your wife? Because I'm not used to someone vocalising what they want."

If her mention of Kim was to throw cold water on me, it doesn't work. It's her I'm focusing on. "Nah. Sex in my marriage was pretty boring and vanilla—missionary position most of the time. Back then I was too tied up with work to put enough effort into it. Now, I know different. Let's just say, you don't live in the clubhouse without getting inspiration."

Her hands push at my chest. "You want to treat me like a sweet butt."

"Maybe," I admit. "But not because I've practiced with them. Any time I've gone with them, and it's not been that often, it's been to get the job over and done quickly. I may have been saving ideas up for when I met someone who I wanted to take my time with."

"I—I…"

"I want this," I tell her. "I've made it clear exactly what I desire, but I'll give you time to get with the program. You just want to hug? We'll do that. Kiss? My lips are yours. Explore our bodies? Fuck yeah. Fuck? Only if you're ready and want it."

Her face goes through a myriad of emotions.

Giving her a moment, I glance into the room she's been assigned. It's bare, impersonal. Doing anything here wouldn't come close to romantic.

"Come to my room, Patsy."

"I can't," she breathes.

"What else have you got to do?" Moving her to one side, I walk past her, and pick up her e-reader that's lying on the bed.

"Lost!" She runs over, but I hold it up high.

My eyes stare upwards and squint, making out what I can without the aid of my glasses. The text catches my eye.

"Like beards?"

"No."

"Gonna like 'em after this." With that, he dove forward, shoving his face between her thighs. After a quick inhale of her sweet fucking scent, he latched his mouth onto her clit and sucked hard.

She cried out as her hips shot off the bed. Separating her pussy with two fingers in a V, he ate her like a melting soft-serve ice cream cone.

She tasted just as good as one, too.

"Who writes this shit?" Still holding the device high, I glance down. Her face is bright red.

"Jeannie St. James," she replies after a pause.

"Ah ha. Might want to read this myself. What's the book called?"

"*Down & Dirty: Dawg*. It's the seventh in the Dirty Angel MC series." She huffs out the information as though she's reluctant to share.

"Phil had a beard?"

"Lost!" Her eyes go wide, then in a small voice she replies, "No."

I file two facts away. One, she's turned on by books about clubs like mine, and second, well… I continue to read on.

She was pink, hot, and slick. He barely paid attention to her loud moans and encouragement. Her fingers dug painfully into his hair and she shoved his face deeper into her pussy, grinding her hips against his face until her juices coated his lips and beard.

Raising an eyebrow and glancing down, I smirk at her, pointedly moving my hand to the hair covering my chin. She swallows and her flush deepens. Then I raise my eyes once again.

"Lost. You give me that, now."

"I was just getting into it," I protest. "Maybe getting myself some ideas."

She stops trying to physically take it from me, instead stepping back, placing her hands on her hips. "Conan Holmes. You give my e-reader back right now."

"Uh oh." I grin. "Mom's voice." I lower my hands and give it to her, but the damage has already been done. I now know the kind of stuff she reads and presumably enjoys.

CHAPTER TWENTY-THREE

Patsy

While Lost disappears to yet another meeting, I'm drawn into a conversation with Eva, moving it out of the kitchen and into the clubroom when she starts to talk about Smoker's sad declaration at dinner. When Pennywise walks past, he taps her on the shoulder. As she turns, he jerks his head.

Eva smiles at him, then nods. Then to me offers an apology and suggests that we'll pick this conversation back up another time. My eyes, for want of something better to do, follow her as she enthusiastically trails after the biker as he crosses the room. I can see why she's so eager. Pennywise is a handsome man, aquiline features, shoulder-length almost jet-black hair, and dark brown eyes who could easily be a model on the cover of any of the biker romance stories I read. He fills out his jeans to perfection, and the t-shirt he wears struggles to contain his well-defined muscles. I suspect shirtless he'd be hot as sin. He pulls her down on his lap, her back toward his front, then, without wasting a moment, one of his hands finds her breast, the other has expertly unzipped her shorts and disappears inside.

Oh my.

I swing around feeling my face burning red. But in that direction things aren't looking much better. Scribe is fondling Cindy's ass and pushing her back toward a couch. To my right, Pearl is swinging herself around the pole which would have been fine, except the top half of her is naked, and her modesty only covered by a thong so tiny, nothing is left to the imagination. From the hungry looks on the faces of the men watching her, even that wasn't going to stay on long.

Moving stiffly, worried about being a voyeur, I make my way as nonchalantly as I can over to the stairs, resisting the urge to run up them once I get there. I suspect if anyone wanted to describe me at that moment, I'd have looked like a dog running away with its tail between its legs.

Reaching my room, I see by the clock radio next to the bed that it's only half past nine. Far too early to go to bed. Wishing I'd had the foresight to bring a glass of wine—or a bottle—up with me, I decide to watch television, only to find the remote doesn't work, and I'm not venturing downstairs in search of new batteries.

Instead, I decide to read.

Damn, this book is hot. I find myself lost in a world eerily similar to the one I'm in, but different as well. Wow, that biker. Oh, is he going to…? My fingers flick the page, my whole concentration on the words forming images in my brain as I find, yes, he really is.

Rap Rappity rap.

I almost squeal as I'm interrupted at the good part. I glare at the door, wondering who it is. Dan is more of a knock-knock man, and a 'Mom, are you decent in there?'.

Remembering the free-living style these bikers have, I decide to open the door with care. As I do, I'm surprised to see Lost standing there. His smirk and opening words show me he's interpreted the reason I'm hanging onto the door.

I'm fifty-three, not over the hill, and when I take the time I think I scrub up pretty well. I thought I knew Lost was attracted to me, but perhaps I was wrong. He takes the winds completely out of my sails when he tells me I wouldn't be mistaken for a club girl. Not that I'd ever want to be, but hey, it's not nice to have it pointed out that you're not attractive anymore.

"Of course, they're not," I agree, scorn showing on my face. No, none of his men would look twice at me.

I wonder what I should do, find out what he wants in case he's brought news, or shut the door and go back to my fictional hero who knows exactly the right thing to say. It only takes an instant for those considerations to cross my mind, as equally quickly, Lost's hand is around the back of my neck, holding me captive.

When he explains how I'd misinterpreted his words, my hopes rise again. This time, it's me that dashes them, pointing out all the reasons I could never compare with the club girls.

Then, I can barely get breath into my lungs as Lost starts to spout all those dirty words. Words that painted a picture of things I could expect if I could only be brave enough to say yes.

A kiss? His lips on mine again, I'd like that for sure.

His mouth? *There?* What would that be like?

His fingers? Touching me there. Oh God, yes.

It's all too much. I feel myself growing wetter with every word. I get scared and do what I immediately know I'll never forgive myself for. I mention his wife.

But even that doesn't deter him. I make my protests, *surely I shouldn't want this?* For a moment I think I've fallen asleep and have mistaken my dreams for real. Then he pushes past me and *damn it*, he picks up my e-reader, the inked text on the fake page open at the section he'd interrupted me at. *That section.* The one I was reading that had already made me hot and bothered, primed to hear the exact offers he'd just made.

"Lost. You give me that now."

"I was just getting into it. Maybe getting myself some ideas." He touches his beard.

Oh no. That's the part I just read. Like the girl in the book, I wasn't particularly enamoured of whiskers on a man's chin, but what would it feel like if it were Lost's face, there, in between my thighs?

Utterly mortified he's found my secret pleasure, I want the ground to open up and swallow me. Unable to physically wrest my e-reader from him, I take my best mom stance and resort to using his full name, just as I would admonish Dan or Beth.

This time it works, he hands me the device, but instead of letting go, his large hands cover mine as I reach to take it.

"Patsy." He breathes the word in that sexy tone. "Why don't you take that leap? You can trust me. You dictate how far we'll go."

The warmth from his calloused skin is playing havoc with my emotions. Tingles shoot to my core.

As if he knows, he presses his advantage. "Come to my room, Patsy." His voice is deep, almost commanding.

"Why don't we stay here?" This room isn't particularly inviting, but it's my temporary home. Something I can control.

He looks around with disdain. "Whether this will end up with you in my bed Patsy, I'm going to at least take my time with your lips on mine. Want to be in more comfortable surroundings."

I can't argue with that. I bite my lip, noticing he shifts from one foot to the other as I do so. I glance up at him through my eyelashes, noticing his expression. If he was still cockily smirking, if he looked sure of himself, *of me*, I may have said no. But he looks uncertain, as if maybe he's pressed too hard and rather than reeling me in, has pushed me away.

Maybe it is time. Maybe I should step back from the responsible middle-aged woman I usually am. Whether there's any future or not, maybe I should just let go and take something for me for once. If Lost can back up even half of what he's said, I'm in for a very enjoyable time.

I take a breath and leap. "Have you got wine?"

"Wine?" he repeats, looking confused. Then he grins. "Sure, I can get a prospect to bring up a bottle. I think there's some behind the bar." He unwraps his hands, puts my e-reader down, and reaches for me again.

Feeling as nervous as a teenager about to have her first time, heaven help me, I come to a decision with one last objection. "Just let me get changed."

His eyes rake me from head to toe. I'm dressed in what I normally wear to bed, sleep shorts and a tank top, no bra. He lazily raises an eyebrow. "Don't bother on my account, babe."

He's not going to let me put on my armour. But truth be told, I'm covered in more than I'd wear at the beach. While there's no doubt my lack of clothing might provide easy access to wandering hands, I'm certain Lost is speaking the truth, and if I withhold my consent, those appendages of his will behave.

My last delaying tactic having failed, I let him take my hand. For some reason, it's trembling.

His room is at the end of the corridor. As he opens the door, I step inside. Immediately I'm taken aback.

"Wow, you weren't kidding." His is much nicer than mine. Twice the size at least, divided into a bedroom space and a comfortable seating area with a television and music system. There's a turntable and a shelf taken up with old-fashioned LPs. A desk with a laptop and papers spread out over the top is off to one side. Because of its size there are two windows, being at the end of the block it's double aspect, offering two different views. One, out across the front of the compound, and the other looking down over the city and I can see the ocean in the distance. "This is nice," I tell him.

He gives a dismissive shrug. "I'm comfortable here." Taking out his phone, he places my request for wine, then grimaces, and turns to me. "No wine. But Wrangler can rustle up a jug of margaritas if you want that?"

Sounds good to me. I nod, then cross to the window, looking out at the view. Within moments, I feel a heat at my back, then I'm surrounded by his arms.

"You can see for miles."

"Uh-huh," he remarks, nuzzling my neck, making me tilt my head to the side, his gentle touch sending sensations flooding through me as he finds the pulse point and sucks gently.

Before my legs go completely weak, suddenly wanting to take the initiative, I pull out of his grasp and swing around, placing my palms against his cheeks, applying pressure so he understands what I want and brings down his mouth to meet mine.

His kiss is sinful, full of promise. First his arms hold me to him, both around my waist, then one slips down, palming my ass and holding me against him.

My God. He's hard. And if that bulge is anything to go by, his cock is large, like the rest of him.

His tongue demands entry and invades, mine meets his. I love his taste, can't get enough of him. This close I can smell a lemony scent tinged with the aroma of leather. Rising on tiptoe, I try to get closer though there's not much distance between us.

When the knock sounds on the door, Lost curses, and steps back. "Stay right here," he warns, before crossing the room. Without opening the door fully, he takes something then closes it, then settles the jug of margaritas down, before coming back and taking me again into his arms. "Now, where were we?"

I feel emboldened, and point to his lips, then touch mine. "I believe we were kissing."

"Hmm mmm." He rubs his beard against my face. "We were, weren't we?" The surprisingly soft beard tickles rather than scratches. "That book you were reading? Reckon that fella's got a beard like mine?"

Jesus. I hope he has. And that the effect he had on that woman's pussy is the same effect Lost will have on mine. Mine? I'm rushing things here even though they're only in my head.

Or, perhaps, Lost is on the same wavelength. "Want to find out, Patsy?"

I haven't touched a drink yet tonight, so it's him I must be drunk on. Because heaven help me, here in his room, so close to his bed, there's nothing else I want more. Taking things slow be damned. For once in my life, I want sex as it's written about in books, to see if any of that could be real. If I leave here tomorrow, I'd rather know what it could be like, than think forever that I might have lost my one chance to find out.

I raise my hand, smooth it down his cheek, then brazenly tug at his beard. "Why don't you show me?"

His eyes darken as his pupils dilate. "You sure, babe?"

I swallow hard once, then twice. "I'm sure."

CHAPTER TWENTY-FOUR

Patsy

I'*m sure*. I might have had plans to take this slowly, but hell, life's for living, isn't it? Even if this is just the once, I should reach out and take what he's offering.

When his hands move, his fingers closing around the bottom hem of my tank, any remaining uncertainty flees. Only one insecurity remains. I'd prefer to leave my clothes on and turn off the light.

He's moving too fast. *Slow, I need slow.* I'm turned on, but not enough to bare my not-as-young-as-it-was body to him. But it's as if he knows. All he's doing is pulling it away from my skin, so his hands, not his eyes, can explore.

Cautiously, his hands roam higher until he cups my breasts in his hands. Feeling him fondling and weighing them, I blush once more, knowing they're not perky or as firm as they once were.

But his sigh of appreciation is reassuring, as are his words. "Fuckin' perfect babe. Are you sensitive?"

I'm just about to reply, I'm not sure. I was once, but I've had two kids and after my nipples were used for the purpose nature intended, I don't regard them as sexual anymore. But the light fluttering almost not-there touch by the back of his hands, has those tight nubs hardening. My back imperceptibly straightens, pushing my breasts into his hold, providing the signal he seems to have been waiting for.

He closes his fingers and thumbs around my nipples, gently rolling them, his question answered by my moan as a shooting sensation goes straight to my groin.

"Want my mouth on these, Patsy." He pauses, giving me time to offer some objection.

Stopping him now is the furthest thought from my mind. When I utter no complaint, he raises my t-shirt and drops his mouth down.

Oh my. His hands were one thing, his mouth another. He's gentle, not rough, his soft tongue almost a teasing touch, as though he's read my mind, and knows exactly what I like.

I roll my head back as he moves his attention from one nipple to the other, his hands continuing to massage and plump. He nips gently with his teeth, and once again I moan. I'm only vaguely aware that he's taking my top off until I feel the material brushing over my face.

Automatically, my arms cross over my chest.

My eyes, which had closed without me being aware, flick open to find him staring at me. His chest is rising and falling, and the tick in his jaw shows he's holding himself back tightly. Slowly, my hands once again drop away, the reaction being him licking his lips, and his mouth curving.

This is one-sided.

Boldly, I step forward. My hands find the bottom of his shirt and I begin tugging it up. He bends, and raises his arms, allowing me to slide it off.

I get the first sight of Lost's naked chest.

He's a man, not a boy. He has a mass of chest hair which like that on his head is greying. His skin, while not the shiny smoothness of youth, is pulled tight over a spectacular array of muscles. He even has that delicious V I've seen in pictures and have read about, but never have had an example of in front of me. My eyes follow it down to the bulge I'd felt but not yet feasted my eyes on. My hands itch to reach out, undo his button and zipper and expose it to me, but my brain prevents me taking such a liberty.

"Jeez, woman," Lost hisses through his teeth. "Babe, I can feel your eyes burning into me. Not showing you the goods, not yet. I'm likely to go off like a fuckin' rocket once you put your hands on me, and I'm not that young anymore. If I'm gonna come tonight, it's going to be in your sweet pussy."

Oh, please, yes. It's my turn to lick my lips.

"Jesus." Smirking, he places his hands on my biceps, and gently turns me and pushes me backward to the bed. When the back of my knees hit it, he uses that sexy growl of his and says, "Get on, Patsy."

I hoist myself up, then shuffle on my butt until I'm in the middle of the comforter. He climbs on, then stalks me on his knees. He hooks his thumbs into the waistband of my sleep shorts and focuses his eyes on me.

"Tell me you want this, Patsy. Tell me you want to feel what my beard can do to your pussy."

Oh hell to the yes.

"Words, Patsy."

"Yes."

Needing no further encouragement, he pulls down my shorts, baring my pussy to his eyes. Turning my head to the side, I avoid looking at his face. My stomach isn't anything to write home about, I hadn't lied about cellulite. I could do with losing a few pounds, but hey, I like my food. My muscles aren't as firm as I'd like…

"Stop cataloguing your faults, babe. You look fuckin' perfect to me."

Bravely I turn in time to see him lower his head, his face growing pinched as his nostrils flare. *He's smelling me?*

"Fuck, babe. You smell like heaven."

I feel awkward as he spreads my knees, baring me to him, uncomfortable as he sits back and stares in an intense way I've only experienced in gynaecological examinations.

"You promised me the beard," I remind him, embarrassed at how he's looking at me.

"I did, didn't I?" He continues to feast his eyes on my pussy. "You really never had anyone go down on you before?" When I shake my head, he continues, "So, you haven't got a point of comparison, have you?"

I suppose I haven't. I decide to toy with him. "Should I try it with a beardless man first?"

It was my tone of delivery. A suggestion offered in a matter-of-fact way as if I was giving it serious consideration that gets a look of shocked surprise on his face.

He launches himself forward, hovering over me. "Only if I fuckin' shave my face," he tells me. "This is mine, okay? All fuckin' mine."

His sudden burst of possessiveness is hot. My skin burns as he exhales a heated breath.

So, okay, I won't be looking for another man. That thought, that command, my immediate agreement to it, doesn't worry me one bit. I doubt he's going to disappoint.

"Say you're mine, Patsy. I want to hear it from your lips."

I want to tell him that maybe I should try out the goods before committing to anything, but already I know, what Lost is offering is so much more than I've ever had before. As his eyes stare into mine intently, I bite back my saucy comment, realising at my age, at this time in my life, I couldn't have envisaged a man like this would want me. I should reach out and grab the chance with both hands.

But still I hesitate. "We don't even know where I'll be this time tomorrow, in a week, in a month…"

"You're in my bed. And I'm going to move heaven and earth to make sure that's where you're going to stay, Patsy. Fuck, woman, I haven't even had you yet, but my mind is made up. I want you. However long you want me to be yours."

It's far too soon to make forever promises even if I didn't have a crime boss intent on finding me. But I can't deny there's a connection with Lost that if things work out, I'd like to explore further. Sure, he can be an ass, but at least it seems when he is, he has the guts to admit it.

"Yours," I breathe out, realising it's the only response I can make, knowing it's right for this moment.

He lowers his head, taking my lips in a kiss that leaves me bruised and feeling thoroughly ravished, and I love every minute of it. Then, finally, he moves down and satisfies my curiosity as to what difference a beard makes. Well, having no experience, I can make no comparison, but as his mouth works my clit, I have an insight into what the women in the books I read find so enthralling about oral sex.

Sex with my ex had been polite. He wasn't selfish, using his fingers to bring me off before moving on to the main event. I hadn't been surprised that I didn't orgasm with him inside me, my reading showing it was not uncommon at all. Magazine articles were full of women needing clitoral manipulation to get off, and I'd been too embarrassed to ask Phil for extra help.

But I'd had pleasure and had enjoyed the closeness of the physical connection with a man. Even though his choice of position was limited to one, and it had only ever been with the lights off. I'd thought that was the most I could expect from sex.

I was wrong, I think now, as Lost licks, sucks, nibbles and runs that beard over my clit, then changes things up just when I think I'm going to reach the peak I'm striving for, by moving down and thrusting his tongue inside me.

I never really thought about the differences between tongues and fingers, never appreciated how different the former would feel. But I already know I'm going to be addicted, and hope

Lost's been truthful about how much he enjoys it, as I'm going to want to experience this, a lot.

"Fuck, you taste good. Hope you're enjoying this, babe, as I'm going to be down here for a while."

"Mmm mmm." It seems I'm unable to make a coherent response.

This time, when he moves his mouth back to my clit, he starts to push one of his thick fingers inside me.

"Fuck me, you're tight," he comments, easing it in then out, gliding through my wetness which I worry isn't as sufficient as it once was. "Hold on," he tells me when I tense at the intrusion. Pushing himself up, he leans over and opens a bedside table, and takes something out.

My eyes widen, then shut. I turn my head to the side as he opens a tube of lube. I'm embarrassed, never needing to use that before, but then the last time I had sex, I was two decades younger.

"Babe?" he queries. "Look at me." When I do, he continues, "What's up?"

"That's not sexy," I cry out, unable to stop myself.

"Babe," he reproaches me. "I'm big, you're tight. It's been fuckin' years for you. Neither of us are as young as we were. And I need to ask you, I'm clean, but do I need a condom or not? What's your preference?"

I suppose we need to have this conversation, and maybe should have had it before. "Lost, I…" my voice falters. Telling him the symptoms of my age creeping up on me doesn't seem the right time or place. It's an admission that while my mind is as excited as any teenager embarking on a new romance, my body isn't able to keep up.

"Patsy," he interrupts. "If you're expecting a young stud who can go for repeat rounds and keep it up all night, then you're going to be disappointed. I've not got the stamina I had once and I'm not ashamed to admit it."

"I'm going through menopause," I tell him fast, as though ripping off a Band-Aid. "It's been months since I had a period, but I don't know if I'm still at risk of falling pregnant or not.

"Condom it is then, babe, unless," he looks at me and winks, "you want to take a risk."

A baby at my age? My horrified expression gives him the response he needs. "I'd love to fuck you bare, Patsy. But that's got to wait. If I were younger, I'd love a baby, but now? Hell, I'll just have to enjoy our grandkids."

Ours. That word, that indication that we could have a future, the suggestion that I'll have a man by my side when my children give me grandbabies, I know I'd like that.

"And for now," he picks up the lube again, "we make our own sexy, babe." With that, he again lowers his head, lapping my natural lubricant I am still producing, feeling him licking me clean, then he raises his head, grinning broadly.

Glancing down, I see his beard glistening with my juices. Another wink, then he's back, attacking and teasing my clit, making my thighs clench against him, my stomach muscles flutter, my mouth open wide as the most powerful orgasm I've ever had makes me see stars.

He continues to lick and suck and I feel his fingers push inside, this time, with no resistance, and some part of my brain realises he must have applied a generous amount of lube. Then I'm incapable of rational thinking as he finds a place inside me that I hadn't believed existed.

An internal pressure, another suck to my clit and I'm screaming aloud.

I feel him lift away from my body and force myself to open my eyes and watch as he lowers the zipper of his jeans.

Seeing me staring, he slides off the bed and, tortuously slowly, eases out of his pants, pulling his underwear down at the same time, allowing his cock, surrounded by greying pubic hair to jut free and proud.

I gulp, more than grateful he's applied the lubricant now. His eyes are locked on mine. In turn, I'm mesmerised as he tears open a condom with his teeth, then smooths the latex down. When he's covered that part of his anatomy, he squeezes another large dollop of lube onto his hand, and applies it to the outside of the condom, catching my eye and smirking as he treats me to a show, gliding his hand up and down slowly.

The knowledge I need it is an unwelcome reminder of how my body's changing with age. Lost's casual acceptance, his willingness to adapt, takes the awkwardness away. His slow masturbation is heating me more.

"Ready for me?" He leans over me once more, his lips brushing across mine. His biceps thicken, as he takes his weight on his arms.

"So ready," I breathe.

He folds down to one elbow, freeing a hand which he uses to guide his hard cock to my entrance, then slowly, he starts to push in. It's my turn to hiss at the invasion, a feeling I've not experienced in years.

His face is a mask of concentration as he pulls up one of my legs, opening me more fully. His mouth thins, his eyes squeeze closed as he gains ground with small advances and then retreating.

When he starts massaging my clit, I jerk, my action taking more of him inside me. He opens an eye, grins, and rotates his hips, pushing forward as he does so. If that's not made him bottom out inside me, I'm worried about how much more I could take.

"Fuck, babe. You feel so good, like I've died and gone to heaven."

CHAPTER TWENTY-FIVE

Lost

She's as tight as an untried virgin, or what I suspect one would feel like. As I bottom out inside her, and she squeezes around me, I can't remember anything feeling this good before. When I tell her I feel like I'd died and found my own slice of heaven, she looks shocked.

As am I, when her fist bumps my arms. "Don't you dare die on me now, Lost. Will you please move for God's sake?"

I can't help it, I laugh. Fuck, the touch of fun she's bringing to a physical action elevates it to a place I've not visited before.

"Like this?" I draw out slightly, mentally mapping that spot I'd found which I'm pretty sure by her reaction was uncharted territory for her. When I push back in, I aim for it carefully, reading by her gasp and startled expression I've not missed my mark.

I do it again, adding that swivel to my hips, a sharp thrust that has her gasping, clutching at me, her head thrown back.

"Can you take more?" I ask, finding it hard to hold myself back, but the last thing I want to do is to hurt her.

"Give me what you've got," she demands.

I quicken my pace, upping my game. As I start to put more

effort into it, hammering into her, I realise I won't be able to keep this up for long, she feels so damn good. While I've not gone without for the same number of years as she has, it's been more than one since I was last inside a woman, and never one like her. I can feel those telltale signs, my balls drawing up and my cock so hard it's ready to blow, but I'm not leaving her behind when I go over. I rub furiously on her nub of nerves, rewarded when I feel her muscles tense, her eyes close and her mouth opens wide.

"Eyes. Look at me, babe," I growl. "Want to see you come."

"I won't come," she warns me. "No need to wait."

Fuck, yeah, she will. That's if I've got anything to do with it. I grit my teeth, my body vibrating with the effort as I hold myself back while making sure I hit that spot every damn time.

"Lost?" she cries out as her pussy starts clenching. "Lost?" she wails as if realising her body's no longer under her control.

I'm about to lose it, so I pinch her clit, rotate my hips and call on every fucking trick in my repertoire. Lowering my face, I suck hard on a nipple and bite it.

"Lost!" This time her voice screams my name loudly. Her hands clutch at the comforter, her eyes close and her body all but jerks off the bed.

That's it. I can hold back no longer. Her pulsating cunt takes me over with her. Cum shoots from my dick into the condom, spurt after spurt as I make up for months of abstinence myself.

I continue pushing my dick into her, little jerks until my cock is sated and starts to soften, until I've extended her pleasure and there's nothing left for her to milk anymore.

"Patsy?" I ask, when her eyes remain squeezed tightly shut. "Hey, babe," I ask again, seeing a tear emerge.

"I just… Lost, that was… Lost?"

Letting my cock slide out, holding the condom to me, I lean forward so I can take her mouth. She reacts tiredly to my kiss.

I'm no longer ravishing her lips, just caressing them in an outpouring of emotion caused by the act we both shared.

"Yeah, babe. That was..." I struggle to describe it myself, then think, darn, why do we have to? Why put a name to something so perfect? "I'm just going to deal with this."

Patsy murmurs something unintelligible, which I interpret as agreement as I go to the bathroom and dispose of the condom and give my cock a quick rinse in the sink. Taking a washcloth, I wet it in warm water, then return to the bed. Patsy's still lying just how I left her, limbs akimbo. When I gently wash the lube and her juices away, she sighs. Retracing my steps, I throw the used cloth in the laundry bin.

All the time, I'm thinking.

I don't want her to leave and go back to her own room. I want to hold her in my arms all night. Kim hadn't been a cuddler, but I am, and I'd hazard a guess that Patsy is too. I'm trying to frame the right words to say to convince her to spend the night, but when I get back into the bedroom, I have to smother my laughter.

Patsy's turned onto her side with the comforter pulled over her. Her eyes are closed, and her gentle breathing suggests she's already succumbed to sleep.

I don't hesitate before sliding in behind her, pausing for just a moment then think, *fuck it*, and take the risk of moving closer to her, and draping my arm over her naked chest. She sighs with contentment and unconsciously presses back against me.

Perfect. There's nothing better than the feeling of skin on skin, I muse, noting sleepily as we spoon, we fit as though we were made for each other.

Like any man after a momentous release, I'm sleepy as fuck. It doesn't take long before I join her in slumber.

I sleep like the fucking dead. Snake doesn't appear in my nightmares, in fact, I have no dreams at all. I'm dead to the world until I'm woken by a loud rap on my door, followed by a voice.

"You in there, Prez? We need you."

"Yeah, Toke. I'll be there in a sec."

"What's going on?" Patsy jerks awake, turning to me with wide eyes, as if rapidly trying to work out where she is, and what I'm doing there.

Before I answer, I lower my face, intent on kissing her.

She tries to move away, covering her mouth. "Morning breath."

"Don't give a fuck," I tell her, my hand gripping her chin. "Give me those lips, babe." She complies, and I partake. Sure, we could probably have done with brushing our teeth first, but I couldn't resist. Long before I've had my fill of her, I pull away. "Gotta run, babe."

"Lost," she calls as I stand. "I didn't mean to fall asleep." She bites her lip, looking remorseful.

"Babe, don't fuckin' apologise. Best sleep I've ever had with you in my arms."

She focuses on my morning wood, jutting out and fully erect. "You really got to go right now?" Then, having been so bold, she lowers her eyes.

I chuckle. "If I could stay, I would. But if Token's got news for me, I need to hear it. You're good to stay here, babe."

"I might," she counters. "Your bed is so comfortable."

It should be. I spent a fortune on that mattress hoping it would banish my bad dreams. Seems all I needed was the company of one special woman to make it work for me. I make a decision on the spot.

"Move your stuff in here, babe."

"What?" She pushes her bed hair out of her face, and sits up, hugging the comforter against her.

I shrug. "I want you in my bed, Patsy." I told her she was mine, but I don't think she believed it. "We're not teenagers, babe. We don't have to tiptoe around pretending this isn't what it is. I want to go to sleep with you in my arms every night, after I've fucked you senseless that is."

"Wow," she states, breathily. "You say it how it is."

Again my shoulders rise and fall, and my mouth curves up in a grin. "Up to you, babe. But I've said my bit."

"I might be leaving…"

She might, but if I get my way, she won't.

"If I move my stuff in, sleep with you every night, it will make it harder to go."

That right there is my hope. But first I've got to make sure it's safe for her, that she doesn't need to run anymore. That starts with me getting my ass moving. "I'll make this right," I promise her, as I open the drawer, finding a clean t-shirt and underwear, then, show her my ass as I walk toward the bathroom.

It's only minutes later that I return, showered and dressed. I've been thinking of arguments I could use to get her to stay with me, but for now I'll need to keep those to myself.

She's fast asleep.

I exit the room, closing the door quietly. The first person I see is Dan.

"Have you seen Mom?" He's exiting her room. "She's not downstairs, and not in there." He waves his hand behind him.

"She's sleeping," I tell him truthfully, my head jerking toward the door I've just come out of. I raise an eyebrow toward him in challenge. Best get this out in the open right now.

His eyes go wide. "She… You… My mom, Lost?"

For a moment I tense my muscles in preparation for a fist. But then, his expression relaxes, and he looks resigned. "Don't hurt her, Lost. She, er, with my dad, she hasn't had a good record with relationships."

I could brush him off, but I don't. "Dan, look, Patsy's spoken to me about Phil. He was wrong for her from the start. If I do anything, it will be to show her what she's been missing. This isn't a casual thing for me, nor, I hope, for her. I want her to stay, and if she does, my desire is to make this permanent."

"It's what she deserves, Lost. But…" his words trail off.

"But am I the right man for her?" It's a question I can't answer. I want to say yes, but at the root of it, I'm Lost. Mindful I'm late to meet Token, I start moving my feet. As I pass him, my hand lands on his shoulder. "Only time will tell." Time, and whether I can get rid of Alder.

Speeding up my steps, I go quickly to Token's office. Computers whir, but the man himself is nowhere in sight. I exit again and spy Wrangler.

"They're in church," he calls out.

Church? I haven't called a meeting. Knowing I'm not yet senile, and I won't have forgotten, I continue to the meeting room, mystified that they've taken the unusual step of assembling without me. I'm curious, not concerned.

At least they've waited to start their discussion. Brothers are milling around, drinking coffee or even beer. Dart's hovering near the doorway.

"Prez," he leans in and speaks into my ear, "Token's got some info. He brought it to me as you were," he pauses, grins, then continues, "otherwise engaged. I thought you'd want everyone in on this."

"How did you know I was 'otherwise engaged'?" I use air quotes for emphasis.

Dart chuckles. "Seemed likely. Patsy wasn't in her room, Dan couldn't find her, and you overslept. Thought it might have been because you overexerted yourself. You've got to be careful at your age, you know."

"My age?" I growl menacingly. "Could still whip your fuckin' ass."

He laughs, "Sure, old man," then ducks to evade my playful fist. He walks off to his seat leaving me mock glaring at him.

See? This is why Dart and I make a good team, the ability to joke with each other without causing offence.

He's not the only one. As I make my way to the head of the table, Salem, who's already in his seat, leans back on his chair balancing with one foot against the table and calls out, "We gonna discuss this, Prez?"

Puzzled, I tilt my head to the side and pause my step.

"If you're proposing taking an ol' lady… Ouch."

The last is in response to my playful slap around his head.

I take my seat and wait a moment for the table to settle. Waving the gavel rather than banging it, I kick off, not with my request to hear Token's news, but something else instead.

"Seems I can't have any privacy around here. Yeah, Patsy and I are getting into something, but it's too soon to say where it will go. I'd appreciate some respect."

"Aw, Prez." Pennywise doesn't look as contrite as his words suggest. "We don't mean anything by it."

"Yeah, we do," Salem objects. "Prez doesn't spend the night with a woman, so I'm guessing he's serious about her. If they get together, she'll be our first lady. *If* we vote her in that is."

She'd make a fucking amazing one, I'm sure of that. And just why is what I tell them. "If that happens, she'd do great. She's already brought up two moody teenagers, I'm sure she'll be able to handle you assholes." Now Salem's given voice to it, I decide I like the sound of the handle 'ol' lady' being applied to Patsy. But to make that happen… This time I do bang the gavel. "Token, what you got?"

CHAPTER TWENTY-SIX

Lost

"Got locations from the coordinates," Token begins. "One's in Tijuana, and the other is this side of the border."

"Where?" Salem butts in.

"A fuckin' Mexican restaurant."

"I could eat Mexican," Bones suggests. "Should we go check it out?"

"Whoa." I hold up my hands. "No one's just running off. We need to discuss this. First, that info is twenty-plus years old, and second, if the drugs are delivered to those premises, it's unlikely they'll be in plain sight. Can't search while they're open for business, and they're unlikely to offer to show us around."

"Still, it might be worth checking out," Dart suggests. "If it's a front, we might be able to gain some info without giving away our suspicions."

"According to Trip Advisor, it's good, but not fantastic. Top marks for service and value for money, as for the food itself the reviews are a bit mixed, but nothing more or less than most other restaurants," Token enlightens us. "Some folks love it, some hate it."

"So they're doing what they can to appear legit," I surmise. "How long has it been in business?"

"Twenty years."

"Exactly? Or thereabouts?"

"Exactly," Token confirms.

Hmm. Two years later than our information was dated. Still, it had been just plans. Maybe Alder took time to get his shit together.

"Has it always been in the same hands?" Dart poses his reasonable question. I tilt my head.

"Family business," Token replies. "Looks like a son runs it now. Maybe the father retired."

"Any police interest?" Scribe comes up with a good question. We all look to Token expecting him to already have the answer. While I was enjoying myself with Patsy, he'll have been up all night digging deeper and deeper. I notice his eyes look red and tired.

"No. The only unusual thing is zero reports. Even the best run restaurants have problems in that length of time. Someone leaving without paying, or a brawl in the parking lot. There's zilch from this place though."

"They'd handle that shit themselves if they were into something shady," Snips observes, scratching an itch on his nose.

Brakes looks at him sideways. "Or they're lucky and haven't had trouble."

"In twenty years it would seem unlikely," I suggest. "What's the locale like?" I raise my eyebrow at Token.

"Not the best area, a Hispanic enclave for the most part. The businesses around are nine-to-five, nowhere else that would be open into the night. There is an auto-shop just behind it. Let's just say, from the reviews, it wouldn't give our shop a run for its money."

Interesting. A place with an excuse to have activity after hours, and no one around to question it.

"I still say we need to go check it out," Bones insists, sniffing loudly.

I don't disagree, but I'm doubtful whether we'd find anything useful. If they've been running a drug trade through the restaurant for two decades, they'll be polished as fuck. I wait for the treasurer to blow his nose, then address him. "And I still ask what would that give us? Okay, so you'd get fed, maybe visit the heads. But they're not going to have shit out in the open, and I doubt there'd be a trapdoor in plain sight."

Bones bristles a little at my dismissal.

"You just want a free meal," Pennywise observes.

"Bones would do anything for a good chili." Brakes and Pennywise exchange fist bumps.

Snips snorts.

Strangely, it's Smoker who raises his hand. "I'll go." He might have been going to say more but is overcome by a bout of coughing. As Pennywise opens his mouth, Smoker recovers, holds up his hand, and continues, "I'll dress as a homeless man, hang around their dumpster, maybe even beg for a few scraps."

I stare at Smoker. It's not a bad idea, of anyone he pulls it off. He's got grey shaggy hair that never looks styled, a long beard that's always plaited and hangs down to his paunch. He's pale and thin, which I now know is from his illness. "It could be dangerous," I warn.

"Look," Smoker's husky voice deepens, "let's not beat around the fuckin' bush. I won't be around much longer. Let me work for the club while I can. My lungs are fucked, but there's nothing wrong with my eyesight and hearing. As for danger? I've got the least to lose of anyone."

There's a second of silence while we digest that. It's hard hearing.

"But your cough…" Pennywise observes.

"If anyone was sending someone in incognito, they wouldn't

send someone with a fuckin' hacking cough. It will add to the authenticity. Might even get me a bit of sympathy."

"I don't like anyone going alone without backup," I object.

Smoker turns his red eyes to me. "I gotta get used to it. Where I'm headed, I won't have company."

Another reminder that Smoker is dying makes brothers shift awkwardly. I realise my resolve to talk to the man about getting treatment would probably just be wasted words. He seems resigned and resolute that he's not going to extend his life laid up sick with radiation treatments, or surgery which might not even work. Maybe I'd be the same, wanting to do something useful rather than just sitting around waiting.

My lips press together. "Okay," I say at last. "You go in, Smoker. See what you can pick up. But," I point my index finger toward him, "you don't take risks, you don't draw attention to yourself."

Smoker nods. "I know Token's probably seen images from Google Earth, but there's no substitute for checking shit out on the ground. This auto-shop might be a cover for shifting the shit that comes through the tunnel if it's close. It's a way of storing transport at least. I'd like to check out the access points."

"We don't know, Smoker, if anything's coming through the tunnel, or even if the tunnel is actually there." Dart is talking sense. "Just keep your eyes out for anything suspicious."

"I'll go in tonight."

"I'll drop you off in a cage," Pennywise, now on board, tells him. "You going to be able to walk a block? Won't be able to take you to the front door."

"I can do it," Smoker insists. "And yeah, didn't want to take my bike. Might be a bit of a giveaway." He winks, then coughs.

"What are we going to do if we find there is a tunnel?" Grumbler, quiet up until now, asks.

Niran jumps in. "There's a tunnel task force. Could report it anonymously, then sit back and watch Alder's operation take a big hit."

It's an attractive option. Border control would be all over that shit, but it wouldn't serve my purpose. "I want Alder," I tell them straight. "Niran's suggestion has merit, but unless Alder's there at the time of a raid, he'll get away scot-free yet again."

"Getting Alder off Patsy's back is what we are doing this for." Dart backs me up, his eyes roaming the table in challenge.

Blaze is shaking his head. "How do we get from finding his tunnel to taking out Alder? That's what I can't understand."

That's the part I haven't quite got yet.

"We find out if there really is a tunnel they're transporting drugs through. Then, I say we question the staff."

Salem's made a good point, but it's Kink who points out the flaws. "What if they are paid to turn a blind eye? The staff might not be involved at all." He gestures at Token. "From the reviews, they run a business most people like. The motherfuckers involved in drug smuggling are unlikely to be able to carry that off."

"Then I say we stake the place out," Snips offers. "After hours, when the staff go home."

"I can check for vantage points we could use when I go tonight."

I nod at Smoker's suggestion and take it up myself. "We wait for Smoker's report. We can learn a lot from how he's treated, what he can see, and how we might get eyes on this place. If they are running a second business, they might just run him off." My eyes flick to Smoker's in warning. He nods back. If challenged, he'll leave it. "As for Alder, I need something to get his attention and smoke him out."

"Threatening to blow up his tunnel might do that."

"Or just the suggestion of involving Border Security might get him moving." I exchange a glance with Dart. "Dan fucked up one of his routes. If this is his backup operation, doubt he'll want the feds to close this one down."

"But would he appear in person?" Dusty challenges clasping his hands and placing them on the tabletop. "Even if you threatened him? He's not stupid, else he wouldn't have remained hidden this long."

"And what if he's hiding in Mexico?" Scribe asks, looking around.

"We could use the tunnel to go to him," Reboot pronounces, then swings around at the snort from beside him. "What?"

"You'd crawl through a tunnel? Not me, man." Keeper shudders.

"I have enough problems riding in a cage." Deuce also looks dubious.

I have to admit, the claustrophobic idea doesn't appeal to me either. I eye the table, realising we've got off topic a tad, and unproductive discussions are just going to go around and around if I don't bring a halt to it. "Right, let's cut to the chase. Token will keep doing what he does, digging into the data and the background of this Mexican eatery." An idea comes to me. "Hey, Pennywise. How about you eating out tonight? Then you'll be close by if Smoker hits any problems."

Our expert sniper shakes his head. "Can't stomach Mexican food, Prez. It gives me the runs."

"I'll go," Niran suggests. "I love a good fajita."

"Want me as well?" Reboot offers. "I could do with a decent meal."

Niran and Reboot bump fists together.

"Okay." Niran's solid and Reboot's been patched in nearly three years now. I feel happier that I know Smoker will have someone at his back should things go south.

"Want us to hang around tomorrow in case you want to call church?"

"No can do, Brother." Blaze addresses Brakes. "I've got a large piece to work on tomorrow, too late to reschedule now."

Blaze manages our tattoo parlour, and as it's Monday tomorrow, most will need to be at work.

"If there's a need, we'll meet in the evening. I'll catch up with Niran, Reboot, Smoker and Token first thing and we'll take it from there. Any more questions or other business we need to discuss now?"

"Yeah, anyone got any clothes that could pass for homeless shit?" Smoker ignores Salem's comment of just what he's wearing would work.

Keeper makes a suggestion. "They don't need to be dirty, but ill-fitting would do, as if you'd raided a charity store. What about something of Bones?"

Bones is about the same height as Smoker, but broader. Smoker nods, acknowledging that would do.

"I got a sweatshirt that's full of holes," Salem offers.

"As long as it doesn't stink of your armpits," Smoker retorts.

Salem makes a show of sniffing said body area, while we all groan.

I bang the gavel. "Church dismissed." Then, I stay seated while the brothers file out. All except one, that is.

"So," Dart turns his head in my direction. "How are things between you and Patsy?"

Dart's my VP and my friend. I lean back on my chair, locking my hands behind my head. "I was married before," I begin, slowly. "Kim and I were a mistake from the start. Oh, I was head over heels in love with her, blinded to all her faults. I ignored everything that was wrong between us, so intent on making our relationship work. Never saw I was attempting the impossible until it was over." I don't really need to explain, I'd discussed my ex at length with him one night when I'd had too much to drink.

Dart raises his chin in encouragement.

"Never saw myself risking another relationship, once burned, forever shy of commitment. But Patsy? There was an instant attraction there, even more so than with Kim. Last night proved we're more than compatible. I don't know her thoughts, Dart, but I know mine. I want her, and already can't see myself saying goodbye to her. She's the one I've been waiting for. Crazy, huh?"

"Nah, not crazy." Dart places his elbows on the table. "I knew with Alex the first time I saw her dancing but kidded myself I didn't want her. Held out until, well, you know what happened, you were there, Lost. I stopped myself because it was ridiculous. She was nothing I'd ever looked at before. I knew she'd want a man who offered commitment, and I was so damn scared of tying myself down, I nearly lost her before I got my head out of my ass."

He's right. I'd been there and watched the car-crash beginnings to their relationship.

"If Patsy wasn't intent on running, maybe I'd take this slower. But the thought of losing her, of never knowing where she is or what she's doing has focused my attention. I want her, Dart. Want her to be my ol' lady."

"So Salem had it right? You're claiming her?"

"Two-way street, ain't it, Brother? Don't know her views on that as of yet." I told her she was mine, but doubt she realised I meant it, putting it down to being in the throes of passion at the time. "She might need more time to get her head around it."

He's thoughtful for a moment. "From what I've seen of her, she'd make a good first lady."

"Would it put Alex's nose out of joint?"

"Hell no. Alex already likes her. And you know my ol' lady, she's not like that. From what I've seen of Patsy, she'd never lord it over her, or any of us."

She wouldn't. I'm certain of that.

"As far as you're concerned, Lost, I think you need someone in your corner. Sure, you've got us, but I can vouch for having someone to come home to, someone who listens when you want to rant. And," he winks, "who knows how to suck your cock just the way you like it."

Just like that he has me imagining Patsy's lips around my cock. Christ, looks like it takes nothing to get my dick swelling where she's involved. Now I'm wondering whether she's ever given head before, or whether I'd need to instruct her. I really have no objection to being her first.

But I agree. Someone like Patsy—someone who *is* Patsy, would ground me. Give me a purpose to get up every day. Make me want to be a better man.

Now, I've just got to persuade her.

CHAPTER TWENTY-SEVEN

Patsy

Lost's bed is comfortable, the mattress supportive and yet still soft, the comforter cosy in the air-conditioned coolness of the room. Best of all, it smells of him.

I knew he would have stayed with me if he got his wishes granted, but Token's summons had woken us, and I knew he couldn't refuse. I'd tried to entice him, but his club comes first. As it rightly should. He'd worn me out last night, giving my body a workout it hadn't had for many years so I'd fallen back asleep. When I awaken the second time, I miss him. It dawns on me maybe too much.

Perhaps it's best I have a few moments alone to process what's happened between us.

On a sexual level, how can I begin to describe it? Lost's way of making love is demanding, controlling and boy, did it work. There was no way my previous experience could match up. My orgasms were so powerful, for a few seconds I wasn't sure I was going to survive them, and oh, that beard. I've no desire to try a clean-shaven man, certain they wouldn't match up. As I stretch my legs, relishing the slight soreness that tells me it hadn't all been a dream, I know I want more, if only to check the first time wasn't a fluke. Yeah, sure. Conduct an experiment, why not?

Why not? Because I'm already addicted to his touch.

Even now it might be too late. I was stupid to jump into bed with him. If I want to walk away with my feelings unscathed, there must never be a repeat. But oh, how he's spoiled me. I doubt I'll ever find a man like Lost again. No other man would measure up. It's not just his prowess in bed, it was his personality and how easy he'd made everything. I'd felt embarrassed, awkward, uncertain, but he'd taken all my worries away.

I hadn't felt like a menopausal woman in his arms. I'd felt ageless, cherished and loved.

Loved? Too soon, no way. Lost had told me I was his, but he only meant last night, didn't he? I know my own feelings, could he be feeling the same way?

My feelings?

I pull his pillow toward me, breathing in the scent of the man. I've never been particularly enamoured of a man's perfume before, and if I'm honest, I do smell his sweat. But it's his pheromones clinging to the material that are doing something to me, and instead of a turn-off, it's a turn-on, twinned with the memory of what we had been doing. I wish I could steal his sheet, take it with me so he'd be with me every day.

Take it with me, because yes, I have to leave. Leave, I must, before I sink deeper into the pool of desire and affection that I feel toward Lost. Get away, before I admit what I feel could be love. Initially I'd had feelings for my ex, what I already feel for Lost surpasses them.

He asked me to move my things into his room.

What's worrying is how much I want to. To fall asleep in his arms each night after making love, well, there's nothing more I'd rather do.

There are too many reasons why I can't.

Yesterday, I'd had information thrown at me from all directions. Suggestions, ideas, outrageous thoughts that made me feel I'd been dropped into the middle of an action movie. One thing after another coming at me fast, it had been too hard to compute.

Now, I lay back, sifting through, trying to get everything straight in my head. It all circles around to one thing—everyone would be better off if I went away.

I start to rise, then stop. *No. Think this through. Don't act rashly.*

I'm totally out of my depth and not afraid to admit it. I'm a housewife, mother and I sew clothes. I've never even handled a gun in my life. The only fights I've ever seen have been staged and filmed, or violence I've seen on the news. In real life, I suspect they'd be terrifying. I don't want my son or the man who made love to me in the midst of something like that. Nor do I want Lost's men to be pulled into something because of me. They've got their own quirks, but I'm beginning to like them.

I'm the one Alder's after. If I leave, everyone here will be safe.

Tears prick at the back of my eyes. *I don't want to leave.* I just don't see what else I can do. The only thing I'm firm on is that whatever decision I make has to be acted on today, while I'm still able to tear myself away from the man who's come to mean so much to me in such a short time.

Tear myself away? Rip my heart into shreds is more like it. This time, it won't just be a daughter I'm leaving behind, it will be Dan, and Lost. *But they'll be safe.*

Angrily I wipe my eyes dry, knowing I've no choice. I have to go now, before it becomes too great a temptation to spend more nights in Lost's bed.

What does Alder want from me? If only I knew, maybe I could give it to him then stay. Or maybe leaving won't be forever. Maybe Alder will get arrested and be put away, and then I'll be able to return and maybe have my happily ever after.

I will survive. I've spent eighteen years on my own, bringing up my children with no one to support me. I did it and never complained. I don't know what it's like to have someone to lean on. I can do what's necessary again, even though it would hurt me. At least I won't have the pain of being responsible for the death of anyone close to me. I wouldn't be able to bear seeing the light fade from Lost's eyes.

My decision is made. I'm leaving. Today.

I use Lost's shower, use his toiletries too, knowing I'll smell of his body wash, at least until I bathe myself again. The water washes away my tears and I try to plant a smile on my face as I retreat to my room, using my own toothbrush to clean my teeth. Half of me wishes Lost will come out of his meeting, see what I'm doing and stop me, but the rest of me knows it's me who's bringing trouble down onto his head.

Before I can have second thoughts, I pack my bag, mentally running through everything I need to do.

One of the members drove my car to the compound, so I've transportation at least. My son. What do I do about him? How can I tell him goodbye? He'll want to come with me, and I can't let him. Alder is after me, not him. What about Beth? If I call her to say goodbye, she'll play on the pregnancy card and try to persuade me to stay. She'll tell Ink, who'll tell Lost.

Beth's got Ink, her friends too. Mel's about to give birth herself, she'll be able to help Beth through. Violet too. She'll be fine.

Will she? Will Dan?

But I can't send Lost to his death. What if Alder brings his fight to the compound? Dan might die too. If Alder's got so many contacts in San Diego, it's only a matter of time before he sees Dan around. He can't stay locked up on the compound for the rest of his life. Somehow I've got to draw Alder's attention away.

I've got no choice. What's the happiness of a woman in her mid-fifties against the health and wellbeing of her children?

They'll be safe if I go, that's all I want. Dan can stay dead to the world and build a new life for himself. Lost will help him. Though we haven't discussed it at length, I know he would.

Dan. I can't leave without trying to explain to him. I'll just have to make him see sense, that it will be better for everyone if I leave on my own. If I slip up again, and Alder finds me, it will only be me who pays the price.

I carry my bag down the stairs, guilty as any teenager trying to creep out of her parents' house unseen, but all the members appear to be in their meeting with Lost, and there's only a prospect behind the bar. Prospects, I've learned, obey orders and don't ask questions. Not that I expect him to dance to my tune, but at least he should ignore what I'm doing.

Dan's not around. Setting my bag down out of sight, I ascend the stairs again, only to find he's not in his room either.

With a sigh, I return to the clubroom and now I do approach Wrangler.

"Do you know where Dan, my son, is?"

"Yes, ma'am. He's in the next hangar. I overheard Salem asking him if he'd do a job."

The hangar they're clearing out so they can do custom work there. I'm not surprised, Dan seems to enjoy tinkering with bikes. Perhaps they'll give him a job, and he can go to college. The world is his oyster if I can lure Alder away from him.

I'd expected to have to confront him, but now he's out of the way, perhaps I'll take this reprieve.

"Have you got a paper and pen?"

Behind the bar, Wrangler sinks to his haunches and then rises, my requested items in his hand. Taking the page torn from a notebook, I go to a table and start to write. It's hard to say goodbye, but knowing any words would be inadequate, a few sentences will have to suffice.

I fold the paper, then pass it to Wrangler. "This is for Dan. Please give it to my son."

Then, I pick up my bag.

"Where are you going?" the prospect asks, his brow furrowed.

"Just to my house to collect some more stuff." I try to heft the bag as though it's empty. Crossing my fingers behind my back, I add, "Lost knows all about it."

Then, with my head held high, I exit the clubroom, taking my keys out of my purse, and walk to my car.

I worry someone might be manning the gate, but I'm in luck. There's no one there and it slides open as I approach it. No last obstacle to impede my escape. I sigh with relief as I drive through. I'm free.

My jubilation is short lived. *What do I do now?*

The only thing I can do. Drive. But where? I try to get excited that I can go anywhere I want, but I can't even think of a direction in which I should be headed.

I like the ocean, and the warmer climate. Maybe I should make my way across the southern states, maybe all the way to Florida. I'll drive as far as I can each day, and perhaps I'll come across somewhere that will appeal to me as a place to settle down. The only limiting thing will be my dwindling money.

I need to earn. I'll need to work, keep posting my designs to my website. At least the company that is currently buying them will hopefully continue. I can work anywhere.

I point my car east on I-8 and put my foot to the metal, well, obeying the speed limits of course.

As I drive, the immensity of what I'm doing hits me. I'm running as I couldn't get attached to Lost. Or any more than I have already. One more night in his bed, and I wouldn't have left. I regret last night, considering it would have been better to live my life without knowing the pleasure I could find with Lost. On the other hand, though, I'm grateful to have experienced it, and to have the memory to hold on to for the rest of time.

Oh God, what have I done? I've left Beth without a word. I didn't have the guts to face Dan either.

I've been a fool. I didn't speak to anyone as they'd all have told me this is the wrong thing to do.

Should I turn back?

I pull off the road at the next rest stop, trying to park away from the trailer outfits against which my car looks tiny. I try to make myself think rationally.

If I go back now, I'll never have the strength to leave again. I know myself too well. Lost will know what I've done by now and will do everything short of tying me to his bed to prevent me—actually I wouldn't put that past him. Dan will pressure me by saying my place is with him now and will use Beth's condition to persuade me.

I tap my hands on the steering wheel. *What do I do?*

It comes back to the question, what does Alder want from me?

However hard I think back, Phil never told me or even hinted about what he and Alder were into. He didn't even share the names of his legitimate clients with me, let alone details of plans he and his brother-in-law had. The information that was left in the safe deposit box is ancient history now, it has to be. It all comes down to Alder thinking it was me who dropped him in it to the feds and not knowing exactly what I shared with them.

What if I do make it to Florida? What would I do there? Settle down, live a new life. How could I be happy without my family around me? Never knowing what's happening in their lives and always looking behind me.

I'm unhappy now and will probably be that way for the rest of my life. I can't see me ever finding peace again having left everything I love behind me.

The beginnings of an idea form in my mind. I'll get far enough away then try to make contact with Alder. God knows how, the feds couldn't find him. But if I slipped up again, and this time deliberately, maybe I could draw him out? Find out what he wants, then… Well, let's be honest, he might kill me. But there's a chance I might make him see that I've no information that can harm him, and never have. Maybe there's a chance I'll see my family and Lost again. It's worth the risk. Without them, I've not much to live for.

I sob. Dan, Beth and Lost. Can I really survive never seeing them again?

I sob again. I won't survive. Not if I've given up everything that means anything to me. Have I been foolish? Should I have leaned on Lost? But for eighteen years, longer if I'm honest, I've relied on no one but myself. The thought of passing over my safety into someone else's hands is scary.

I seem to be frozen. I can't move forward; I can't go back. I don't know what the hell to do for the best.

I can't even drive on. I wouldn't be able to see the road through my tears.

CHAPTER TWENTY-EIGHT

Lost

Dart stands, patting his pockets to check he's got everything with him. "I've got a woman and family to get home to."

I raise my chin toward him, realising I've been speaking about myself, and haven't enquired about his. "Baby doing well?"

He grimaces slightly. "She's teething, which means we're not sleeping."

There are some benefits to not having children it would seem. "Bring her to the compound soon, Dart. Been a while since I've seen my niece." Might not have my own kids, but I can be a relative by proxy.

"She gets spoiled rotten when she's here," he complains, but the curve of his lips shows not seriously.

"Hey, Prez?" Token's at the door. "Patsy's gone."

"Gone?" I swing around, trying to interpret the words in any way that could suggest he didn't mean them to sound as they had. But one look at his face and I feel as though someone's poured ice cold water down my back.

"Yeah." Token's nostrils flare as he pushes a prospect into the room. "Fucker here didn't think to stop her."

"I didn't know," Wrangler wails his defence. "She said you knew, Lost. There was no reason to tell anyone. She left a note for her son."

No note for me? I hold out my hand and snap, "Give it to me."

He does. It only takes a few seconds to peruse it.

Darling Dan

I'm so sorry to leave without talking, but I know you'd try and dissuade me. I can't have you or Lost, or the MC putting themselves in danger. Please don't try to find me. Speak to Lost, he'll help you get sorted I'm certain.

Tell Beth I love her, but this is for the best.

I love you, Dan, always remember that. Wherever I end up, I'll be thinking of you. Thinking of both you and Beth.

Tell Lost... Tell Lost I'll never forget him.

Your ever-loving mom xxx

Goddamnit! I'm glad I intercepted the note, Dan would be distraught to read it. Why the hell had she taken off?

I have my suspicions, but they're not for examination now. Now we've got to find her.

Taking my phone out of my cut, I try to call her.

"No good, Prez," Token says. "I've traced her phone, she left it here."

"Fuck!" I roar, slamming my fist down on the table. "How the hell do we find her now? Did she say anything, Prospect, about where she was headed?"

Wrangler shuffles, looks down at his feet, then when he looks up it seems to have dawned on him how badly he fucked up, and can already see the chances of him getting patched in are fading into the distance. "I didn't ask," he mumbles. "I didn't think. Sorry, Prez."

Sorry isn't going to cut it. Dart's looking from the prospect then back to me, his eyes wide open in horror. He's been here before when Alex disappeared. At least I know Patsy hasn't been kidnapped by her crazy ex.

"Who let her out the fuckin' gate?" *Could someone more intelligent than Wrangler have stopped her? Is there a chance she's still here?*

Wrangler shifts awkwardly. "Sorry, Prez. I was behind the bar and watching the monitors. I opened it for her."

"Lost, Brother. I'm so fuckin' sorry…" For once Dart is at a loss for words. His expression directed toward the prospect shows he's also questioning how he could have been so stupid.

I'm at a complete loss. My impulse is to rush after her. But where? I could put my fist in Wrangler's face, but how would that help?

"What are we waiting for?" Token asks, his expression not what I would have expected.

"What do you fuckin' suggest we do, Toke? Send search parties out in every fuckin' direction? How long has she fucking been gone?"

Wrangler brightens at a question he can answer. "About an hour."

"Then I suggest we go get her. If we hurry, we can catch up to her."

"If it were that fuckin' easy…" I again catch the strange, almost self-satisfied expression on Token's face. My lips press together and my eyes narrow. "What do you know that I don't?"

Token shrugs. "Only that I put a tracker on her car."

"Which she might have already swapped for another, or a rental." Patsy's not stupid, she'd known enough to buy a burner phone.

"Not when I've already frozen her bank accounts. I suspected she might do something stupid."

I could kiss the fucking asshole. "What are we fuckin' waiting for then?"

Dart rushes past me. I'm hot on his heels as he enters the clubroom and whistles loudly. "Patsy's gone. We're bringing her back. Who's with us?"

It seems quite a few. Salem puts down his undrunk beer, Pennywise slurps back some of his before slamming the bottle onto the table. Scribe, Dusty and Blaze stand. Grumbler, Bones, Kink and Snips are already running out to their bikes.

"I'll go in the truck with Wrangler," Token suggests. "I can track her, you all follow."

Suits me. Quicker we get to wherever we're heading, the faster I can bring my woman home. And this time I'll make damn sure she's never leaving again, even if I have to tie her to my fucking bed.

I don't have to tell them how to ride in formation. Getting into position behind the truck, I take the lead, Dart at my side. Grumbler and Salem fall into place behind us. Next come Bones and Snips, and the others, then Blaze at the rear as road captain.

I'm not surprised when Token leads us up I-8 heading east, not that I knew which direction she'd run in, but expected it to be one of the major routes out of the city. We've only left San Diego about fifty miles behind when right indicator of the truck I'm following comes on. A flick of my eyes shows it's a rest stop, and I wave my hand over my head.

A brief, unlikely concern, that somehow she searched the car and found the tracker Token had planted there is quickly dismissed. I've more faith in my brother's ability to hide it than hers to find it in a casual search, even if she knew it was there. Then any fear disappears when I spot her car, and her sitting in the driver's seat.

As if I'd given them instruction, the bikes surround the car, blocking any escape. Then I'm cutting my engine, sweeping my leg over the bike and running to her door. It's locked.

She's sitting, open-mouthed, and I can see from here, her

eyes are red and raw from crying. Rapping on the window, I indicate the door handle when I have her attention.

A moment passes, then it unlocks. I wrench it open, crouch down and pull the sobbing woman into my arms. All the admonishments I was going to say are wiped from my mind. All the reasons why what she was doing was crazy, go unsaid.

Her hands grip the sides of my cut. "I'm sorry," she wails. "I didn't want you to get hurt."

Again I bite back any comment about how I can look after myself, as a comparison shoots through my head. Kim only ever thought of herself. Patsy is putting me and her family first because she's more worried about everyone else. Instead of telling her how stupid she's been, I open my mouth and set some things straight.

"I told you, you are mine, Patsy. Perhaps you didn't get what I meant. You're mine to love, mine to cherish, and mine to protect." As she shakes her head, I place my fingers under her chin. "I get that you're scared, Patsy. I'll back off a bit if you need more time. I overwhelmed you last night, didn't I?"

"Last night was perfect, Lost. But it showed what you were coming to mean to me." A tear rolls down her cheek, she wipes it away. "If you died…"

"Babe, listen to me. I'm an MC prez, I ride with the Satan's Devils MC. We're not just one chapter, babe. You already know that. You know Demon would have my back if I need him. And not only Colorado. If I put out the word, I'll have another hundred bikers here within a day. There's not a problem too big that I and my brothers can't solve. I'll keep you safe, I promise you, babe, and neither my brothers nor I will take unnecessary risks."

This time, when her eyes turn toward mine, there's a glimmer of hope in them. "Lost, I… I stopped because I knew what I was doing was wrong. I had this idea maybe I could get Alder to follow me, confront him, find out what he wants from me."

My eyes widen in fear at the thought of her doing it alone, while at the root of it, she's got the makings of a plan. But Patsy facing him without backup? Hell to the no. The very idea makes my skin feel like it's breaking out in hives. "We'll talk, okay? We'll work something out. We'll get you free of Alder once and for all. But together, babe. Not having you going off on your own."

"Prez," my name is snapped. I glance around at Token. "What?"

He jerks his head. Dart comes up to take my place by Patsy's side, as I walk a few steps away. "What you got?" I repeat.

"Fucker's playing with us."

"Who?"

"I got a message."

This is like pulling teeth. "Who from?"

"My bank," Token emotionlessly informs me.

If he's pulled me away to tell me he's gone overdrawn, I'll lay him out cold. But it's Token. I just stare and wait.

"You know addresses can be hidden, yeah? This message isn't from my bank at all. It's from the fucker that seems to be able to hack into anything I touch."

He's got my interest now. "What's it say?"

Instead of replying, he shows me:

You took your time. I'll leave the woman to you now.

What the fuck? Immediately I look around. I'm just about to tell the guys to fan out and find whoever's got fuckin' eyes on us, but there's only one way to enter this rest stop or leave. Trees and bushes have grown up high, so there's no nearby high ground he could be spying from. He must be close. Close enough that I can almost taste his discovery. Maybe in one of the parked-up trucks, but his message said he was about to leave, and I can't hear an engine starting.

But Token stops me with a gesture of his hand. He's pointing up into the air.

The drone, hovering above us, dips, spins, then, after it's weird approximation of a salute, rises and soars, heading away to fuck knows where.

The air rushes out of my lungs, but I'm still not giving up. "How far can those things fly?" I snap, watching until it disappears over a rise.

"Legally, you should stay close enough to keep it in view. But I doubt that fucker cares about legality at all. He could be anywhere, a few feet, yards, or a fuckin' mile." Token sounds like he's talking through gritted teeth. Then when he too stops looking up, he shakes his head. "Only thing I got from that was that whoever it is had eyes on her too."

There's only one thing that makes any sense, even though it sounds crazy. "He's protecting her."

Token does his characteristic shrug. "She's important to him. Does he want to keep her safe for her own sake? Or is there a purpose she can serve?"

I don't like there being anyone sniffing around Patsy, whatever reason he has, good or bad. He wants to talk to her? He'll have to have words with me first. "How did he know she'd taken off in the first place?"

"Obviously hacked into the same tracking app that I use." Token sounds disgusted. "One thing I will say, Lost. This guy is better than me."

"Or he's got more resources at his disposal." I slap Token on the back. "He let us know he was here, and I want to know why. He could easily have spied on her, on us, without us being aware."

Token stops me as I'm about to walk off. "There's more to think about, Prez. Why was he watching her? Was he going to step in and help if she got into trouble?" Token jerks his head toward the big eighteen wheelers parked up. "A lone woman, with only flimsy locked doors."

I had noticed and had been going to talk to her about that.

But, upset as she was, I expect she'd needed to get off the road without analysing how safe it was first.

"He was close enough to offer assistance if she got into trouble?" I ask, again, looking around.

Token shakes his head. "No, but he's probably tracking my fuckin' phone. He knew we were on our way."

He'd let us see the drone. Was that just to show us the technology he was able to use? I feel sorry for Token, I know he feels he's letting me down. "He's not hiding from us. And, it looks like he's on our side."

"Yeah." Token closes his eyes then opens them again. "But hell, this is all fucked up. I deal in data, hate things coming at me from the side."

I can fully understand where he's coming from. My world was all binary code once. Ones and zeros which all added up to make sense.

Turning, I notice Dart's got Patsy out of the car, and she's dabbing at her eyes with a tissue. Fuck, I hate to see women cry, and particularly mine. Recently, she's had cause to be upset far too much.

"Let's get back to the compound." I pat Token on the back again. "That drone has reminded me eyes can be anywhere. I don't like Patsy being out in the open."

I walk away, going to Patsy and Dart. "Babe, you're on the back of my bike." I want her where I can feel her, know that she's close. It's lucky I've still got the spare helmet in my saddlebag. Getting it out, I hand it to her along with the bandana and sunglasses she'd previously used.

"My car…?"

"Prospect!" All I need do is point, and he's holding out his hand for her keys. Wrangler's sheepish look reminds me how he fucked up. I hate disappointing any man, but I'll be watching him extra carefully now. If he can't demonstrate basic fucking common sense, he won't be getting his patch. Sure, she might have told him I already knew, but he should have fucking checked.

Token nods as though I've asked a question and swings himself up into the driver's seat of the truck.

As Patsy gets on behind me, her arms, without encouragement, come around my waist and hold me tight. Then, once everyone's back on their rides, I start my engine.

This time I'm in the lead, brothers behind me once again in formation, but the cages follow bringing up the rear. I only breathe easier once we're back.

It's not just me. It's only when we're through the gates of the compound that I feel tension seep from Patsy.

The thought that I might have lost her forever turns my gut sour. If Token hadn't thought to put a tracker on her car, I might never have found her. That someone other than us was also able to trace where she went, helps not one iota. That's a mystery that needs to be solved.

I tap her leg, she dismounts, then I walk my bike back and park. When I've swung my leg over the seat, I catch her eye.

"We need to talk."

She bites her lip and looks down.

"Come." I hold out my hand, then lead her into the clubhouse, through the clubroom and up the stairs to my bedroom, the room I'd give anything to think of as ours.

Avoiding the bed, I take her to the comfy sofa. Sitting, I tug her, overbalancing her so she all but falls into my lap, an oomph coming from her mouth. Wrapping my arms around her, I just hold her tight.

We sit like that for a few minutes, our breathing falling into a pattern where our chests rise and fall in unison. It's symbolic, reminding me we've got to get our heads onto the same page, and I can't risk her running off again. Despite that it's club business, it involves her. I go against every ingrained instinct and begin to talk to her.

"Things are moving forward, babe. I know it probably feels to you that we're treading water, but we've got a direction to swim in now. The numbers from the plans in the safe deposit box of yours were coordinates of two locations. One this side in San Diego, and one the Mexican side of the border. That strongly suggests there's something linking the two, and as there's no road, it points to a tunnel. Smoker, Niran and Reboot are going tonight to check it out."

"Isn't that dangerous?" Of course her first worry is the risk to someone else.

"Nah. This end is a Mexican restaurant. The only danger they'll be in is risking a case of food poisoning. They're only going to see how the land lies."

As I wanted, she huffs a laugh. "You think there really is a tunnel and that after all these years, he's still using it?"

"We don't know anything, babe. It's just worth checking out. Dan's info cut off one of his routes, it's possible he's resurrected this one, or could have been using it all this time." I take a breath and tell her the rest. "There's a bit of a mystery. Someone, and we don't know who, is hacking into our systems."

"But you'd make sure they're secure, wouldn't you? Aren't you a computer genius or something?"

Chuckling, I explain, "I've been out of the game too long to have much input, but Toke's a good man. He's tearing his hair out as he's up against someone better. Thing is, it was an anonymous message that sent me to you in the first place, and," I pause, then admit, "It wasn't only us that were able to track your car."

I watch the blood drain from her face. "Alder?" she breathes.

"No, babe," I rush to reassure her. "It seems to be someone with your best interest at heart. But they've got technical skills I can't help but admire, and not knowing who, or why, has unnerved me a little." Her brow furrows in confusion, but I can't tell her anything more.

I just hold her while she shivers and reassure her. "You're safe here now. We can lockdown the compound so it's watertight if we have to."

"Who could it be?"

"Have you any ideas, Patsy? Any family? Any friend, anyone who might have access to advanced technology who'd be trying to keep you safe?"

"There's no one," she says fast. "My parents were only children, and so am I. My friends don't have skills like that. I don't even know anyone that's an expert in computers except for Cad in Pueblo, but Demon would bring you in on that. You think this strange person is on my side? Not wanting to hurt me? Surely that's nothing to worry about?" She pauses, then adds, almost hopefully, "Could it be the cops or the feds?"

"No, I'm pretty sure it's not the authorities. It's just that I don't like mysteries," I tell her. "But on the face of it, no. It's not a concern."

I didn't think she'd have answers for me, but it was worth a try. She'd tensed when I told her about the strange contacts but relaxes again against me now.

"You shouldn't have left, Patsy."

"I still think it was for the best. It's me Alder is after. You just told me you're sending your men into danger, and the other mystery of someone else watching me. I'm the common denominator. If I go, everyone's safe."

I didn't want to have to spell it out to her, but there's something she's missing. "Demon's got Beth covered, but there's always a chance something will go wrong."

She narrows her eyes. "What do you mean, he's got Beth covered?"

"Either Ink or a prospect is always with her." I pinch the bridge of my nose. "Patsy, what draws a mother out of the woodwork faster than a bullet flies?" When her mouth opens in terror, I continue, "Need me to spell it out? That her daughter, her only surviving child as far as Alder knows, is being threatened or hurt."

"But…"

I hate the look of panic I've just put on her face. "There's only one way to deal with this babe. You want everyone safe, that's my aim as well. But to reach that outcome, Alder has to be dealt with. The common denominator, as you put it, is him, not you."

She considers my words quietly for a moment. "I've been stupid, haven't I? I thought it all through, but I never considered that. That he'd use others to find me."

"Should have spoken to me, babe." I sigh, thinking I know why she didn't. "You acted on impulse, didn't you?" I go for the jugular. "Tell me, babe. What made you leave? Today of all days?"

Her head comes up, her eyes meet mine, then she looks away fast.

"You scared, Patsy?"

"Of course I am. Alder wants me for some reason. Now, you say he could use my family to get to me, and there's someone else who knows where I am. Of course, I'm freaking scared."

"Nah, those are reasons for staying," I refute, "not for leaving. Did I push you too hard last night?"

She counters with her own question. "What you said, when you found me? That I was yours." I just wait for her to continue, and she doesn't disappoint. "I'm starting to have feelings for you, Lost."

Without being conceited, I knew that was at the heart of her problems. "Babe." I turn her head so she's forced to look at me. "Maybe our marriages have shown us what we don't want so we find it easier to recognise what we do when we find it. I was attracted to you the first moment I saw you. When I got to know who you were, I began to fall fast. You've got me under your spell, Patsy. Sure, it's happened fast, but to hell with societal precepts. If you want me to say it first, I will. I love you, Patsy."

"It's too soon," she protests. "And look at the baggage I come with."

"Who's to say it's too soon?" I counter. "What do you feel for me?" I press.

"I can't drag you into something we might not survive."

"What do you feel?" I ask again, holding onto her chin so she can't look away.

"You want me to say it? You want me to voice what's impossible this soon?" she cries out. "You want me to tell you that driving away, I didn't want to live without you. You want me to say what I don't want to admit to myself?"

I answer none of her questions. Just stare into her eyes.

"You make my heart race. You brighten up the room when you walk in. You make me feel safe, protected and cherished. I want to sleep in your bed, in your arms, wake up with you every day. You… you… It's too soon, but I love you, Lost."

Thank fuck. I can't hold back any longer, and my lips find hers. Our mouths meld together, our teeth meet, our tongues advance and retreat as passion sweeps through us both.

I thought I'd loved Kim. I hadn't known what love was. It's not feeling you'd do anything for the other person in your life, it's the knowledge that they'd reciprocate in the same way. Patsy was prepared to risk everything to keep me safe, not recognising that I'd do the same.

Eventually we pull away, and I rest my forehead against hers. "We'll sort this out," I promise her. "We'll get rid of the threat of Alder and be able to make a future together."

CHAPTER TWENTY-NINE

Lost

Our kiss had had the predictable reaction on my cock, and Patsy noticed. Neither of us objected when I suggested bringing him out to play. It was what we both needed, to get as close as humanly possible. Quickly, we'd removed the boundary of clothing between us and came together in the way that a man and a woman in love should.

Last night had been fun, we'd joked around. Today, we'd made love silently. Our hands touching, fingers exploring, eyes meeting, our bodies moving together saying with just physical responses all that we had to say. I worshipped her, showing the truth of the emotion I'd told her I'd felt for her. That couple of hours when I'd feared I might never see her again accelerating the declaration that I hadn't expected to utter today. It was clear her risking our relationship had focused her mind in the same way.

After, sated, we dozed together. I fell asleep, with my woman in my arms.

"Lost, you okay, babe? You were tossing and turning."

I open my eyes to see Patsy staring down, her brow

furrowed. I try to grasp the vestiges of my dream, but it's rapidly fading.

"Just a dream," I tell her, cupping my hand around her cheek. Unromantically, my stomach chooses that moment to growl loudly. Chuckling, I sit up. "You hungry, babe?"

Her eyes examine my face as though checking I'm really alright, then her face relaxes. "Starving," she replies, lazily.

I tap her ass. "Well, let's get showered and go grab something."

"I need to speak to Dan." Her eyes widen as she realises she'd forgotten about him. "Lost, what do I say to him? How do I explain?"

"I doubt he knows anything," I reassure her. "My men won't say a thing about what's gone on, and I didn't see him when we returned. I suspect he's oblivious to the fact you were missing." If he'd known, I'd have expected him to have beaten my door down by now.

"I was going to leave him, Lost. I left him a note…"

"Which Wrangler gave to me." Belatedly. He shouldn't have waited.

"So he might not know?" When I nod, she relaxes a little.

I let her shower first. I might be getting older, but if I shared the water with her, I'm certain my cock would be up for another round. That it wasn't only my stomach protesting the lack of sustenance persuaded me this was not the time.

She's quicker than I expected, and is soon out, dressed again in the same clothes. I take only a minute or so, and then we're ready to go.

Wrapping my arm around her, we descend to the clubroom.

"Mom." Dan raises his bottle of beer as he greets her, proving he's totally unaware that she left the compound today. "Lost? Can I have a word?"

"Sure," I reply to him. "Just need to get your mom fed first."

Token's the first person I see as I enter the kitchen. I give him a chin lift.

"You hungry?" Pearl asks. "I made a chicken pasta bake earlier."

When I nod, she starts to serve up two plates. I move to take them from her, which puts what's happening at the other end of the table in my sights. Inwardly I groan, turning to get Patsy out of there, but I'm not fast enough. Her eyes are already fixated on the scene.

Kink's seated at the table, on the floor beside him kneels a very naked young woman. The only thing she's wearing is a blindfold and a collar and attached to that is a leash which Kink has wrapped loosely around his fist.

I turn, opening my mouth to offer some kind of explanation —fuck knows what—but halt as I see Patsy's lips curve.

Kink loads his fork and completely oblivious to his audience, speaks to the girl by his side. "Open your mouth." When she does, he places the fork in her mouth, and she closes her lips around the food offered.

I clear my throat, and Kink catches my eye and grins.

"Kink's got a new pet," Token says, unnecessarily.

The only reaction Patsy shows is to take her plate from me with thanks, then she tilts her head toward the clubroom. I take mine and follow her out, embarrassed as fuck on her behalf, but to my surprise, she puts her plate down and then covers her face as she laughs.

"Does that happen often?"

"A bit," I tell her, cautiously.

"I did wonder how he got his handle." She chuckles and then picks up her fork. "Anything else I should be aware of?"

"Not like that. We only have one Kink," I tell her. *Thank fuck.* But again my woman goes up in my estimation. Another might have run from the club screaming.

Dan walks across. "Can I join you?"

I nod, he sits down. He waits until we've cleaned our plates, then gets down to what he wants to discuss. He looks first at his mom, then at me. Then he takes a breath. "How do you become a prospect, Lost?"

I hear Patsy's indrawn breath. Do I wait to find out her opinion before answering her son's question? But he's twenty-two, not a kid anymore, and while her views should be taken into account, he's his own man. I decide to treat him like I'd do anyone.

"You hang around, show your interest. You ever ride a motorcycle?"

"I have." His face twists. "I don't have a licence though."

"Well, you'll have to do that properly, and get yourself a bike. Prospecting's not fuckin' easy, I'll tell you that straight. You have to do everything that's asked of you, however outlandish it may seem. You snap to it without question." I narrow my eyes. "You know why we do that?"

"So you can see what a man's made of?"

He's partially right, but there's a lot more to it. "So every man here knows they can trust you to have their back, to prove your loyalty to the club. It's not easy, there are failures. You sulk or object or question shit, and you won't get patched in."

Patsy sits forward. "I thought you wanted to go to college."

Before Dan can answer, I interrupt, "He could still do that. If he wants to work in our shop, for example, we can take him on as an apprentice, he can study and get his certificates done."

"You'd do that?" Dan asks, a gleam appearing in his eyes.

"It will need to be voted on, but I don't see a problem. If you're serious, that is."

Dan shrugs. "I like the club, like the lifestyle. I enjoy the work too. I'm serious, Lost."

Patsy's looking concerned. Damn. I don't want to go against her wishes, but Dan should at least have a chance to prove himself as a hang-around if that's what he wants. If she doesn't want her son associated with an outlaw MC, what does that say about the future I want between her and me?

But I've misjudged her. She turns to me. "Is it safe, Lost? Dan's been here on the compound, but he'll have to go out if he joins you. He can't be confined to the compound for life. What if Alder finds him? Won't that bring trouble to the club?"

It's not her son's choices she's worried about. Again, she's concerned about us. I regard her carefully for a moment, realising she's been a mom for so long, it would appear she never considers herself.

"I told you, babe, we'll deal with it. We'll come out the other side."

She looks dubious, and hell, if she were to ask, I couldn't come up with a plan. That idea of using her to draw Alder out is something I need to ponder on. Not putting her in danger, of course, but a word in the right ear could get Alder in the right place at the right time. Then we could end his sorry life and the world would be a lot better for it. It would have to be carefully done, of course. We'd need a plan that was watertight.

Salem wanders over and joins us. Taking the makings of a joint out of his pocket, he starts to roll one up. I see Patsy flinch in case he questions her about earlier, but I know he's not going to do that. Anything he wants to know, he'll ask me later in private. Instead, he raises his chin at Dan.

"You did some good work getting the hangar ready," he acknowledges. "Got more done than I expected."

"When are you planning on moving the custom work here?" I ask.

"Need to get some more equipment set up, then we're good to go. Next week, perhaps?"

"How d'ya feel about taking on an apprentice?" I nod at Dan.

Salem eyes him carefully, his sharp eyes causing the young man to squirm. "Dan? Sure."

A bark of laughter interrupts us, as I turn, I too join in huffing a laugh. Smoker's beard, for once out of its braided confines hangs like a shaggy untamed bush. He's put some kind of grease in his hair as well, making him look unwashed. His top is torn and stretches tightly across what I notice is a scrawny chest. I hadn't noticed how much weight he's lost recently, which probably explains why Bones' jeans hang low and heavy on him, clearly needing that piece of rope that serves as a belt to hold them up.

Niran, minus his cut, is in a crisp white button-up shirt which contrasts blindingly against the dark brown of his skin.

"For fuck's sake, don't spill chili down that."

Niran shows his middle finger to Blaze, as I turn my attention to Reboot. Yeah, he's scrubbed up clean enough too. Just two citizen friends out for a meal, nothing to make them stand out.

With back slaps and calls of 'go find shit out', they leave. Already I'm eager for them to return so I can see what they uncover. I hate this, too many question marks and too few full stops.

The evening progresses like most others in the clubhouse. Okay, so luckily it's not every day Kink passes leading his naked chick, crawling on all fours, back to his room, but often enough that it doesn't raise eyebrows. Well, except for the woman sitting opposite me, but her expression is one of amusement and not trepidation. The girls come out to play, Pearl again demonstrating her skill on the pole while Cindy disappears with Dusty, and Tits sinks to her knees in front of Bones. Eva, I remember, has custody of her kid this weekend, so she won't be here.

I'd half expected Patsy to want to escape upstairs, but when I ask if she plays pool, then finding out she's never tried, I offer to teach her, and she accepts. She seems to be learning to avert her eyes at tableaus she doesn't want to look at, though I do catch her sneaking the odd glimpse at Tits' head bobbing up and down on the treasurer's lap. It's not with disgust, I notice, hiding my grin, but with interest.

I show her how to hold the cue stick, and how to sink a ball. She hits a few simple ones, jumping up and down on the spot when a ball goes into a pocket. Then the remaining balls aren't at all well placed, and she needs help.

Moving behind her, I lean over, my chest over her back, covering her hands with mine and positioning her so she's got a chance of doing this right, and taking the opportunity to whisper into her ear.

"You ever given head, babe?"

She squeals and I wince as the tip of the cue goes into the felt, but luckily doesn't tear it.

"Is that a yes or a no?" I chuckle.

"No," she hisses firmly back.

"No, you haven't? Or no you don't want to? Give me a clue here, babe."

She turns and licks her fucking lips. "No, I've never tried it."

Damn. "Jeez." I reach down, needing to inch my cock over a bit to give it some space. Patsy's eyes are watching my action.

"Um…"

"Fuck, woman." I pull her into my arms. "You see what you do to me?" I take her hand, placing it over my throbbing appendage.

"We're in public, Lost."

"Don't fuckin' care," I respond, almost laughing out loud taking into account what's going on around.

"Well I'm not getting on my knees here," she tells me, primly.

I, of course, read what she's left unsaid. That she will when we get upstairs.

My intention had been to wait until Niran, Reboot and Smoker returned, anxious to hear what, if anything, they might have found out. Now I'm torn. I've a woman, not just any woman, but Patsy, all but offering to suck my cock. Do I act like the MC prez and wait for my men to return? Or say fuck it, quite literally in this case?

I'm so engrossed in the options vying for top position in my head, I totally miss the opening of the clubhouse door until my name is shouted.

"Prez!"

Niran's voice is in that tone that he needs my attention now.

"Hold that thought," I direct at Patsy, then turn, my attention on club business now. One look at Niran's face, and I'm pointing him toward the meeting room. "Church," I call out.

Dart's gone home for the night, Kink's probably tied up, or more accurately, has someone tied, and some of the other brothers have disappeared with the whores, but those who are still here disengage themselves from whatever, or whoever, they were doing, and follow me into church.

Niran is so agitated he doesn't even sit down. But he stops his pacing, places his hands on the back of the chair and leans forward.

"Where are Reboot and Smoker?" I snap, worried we're a member down.

"Outside," he informs us, brushing one of his hands over his short black hair, then, ceasing that action he slams his fist down, "with Shark. Fuckin' Shark was there. Before he had a chance to recognise Reboot, we managed to take him down. Thought you might want words with him, Prez."

"Fuckin' Shark?"

"Shark, you sure, Brother?"

Various loudly voiced expressions of disbelief and exclamations come from all around. As, up to now, there had been no further sightings of him, I think we'd all assumed he'd left town.

Words? Of course I fucking want to talk to him. He was warned what would happen if he ever showed his face in the city again.

CHAPTER THIRTY

Lost

"Where is he now?" I ask Niran sharply.

"Told Smoker and Reboot to take him to the brig."

The brig, named so far back no one can remember who came up with it now, is our place we take people we want to question. Vegas and Colorado have basements, Tucson their storeroom where Snake met his end, and we've converted and soundproofed a portioned off area at the end of our second hangar. I presume it was an old member with a Navy background who gave it the title, but whatever, it stuck.

"Any idea what he was doing there?" Salem asks.

At last, Niran pulls out a chair and sits down. He seems to have calmed a little, enough to explain what went down. "Reboot and I went into the restaurant, got seated. Ordered from the menu. I went to the bathroom to check the place out, but couldn't tell much, or see anything untoward. Standard down-market restaurant, though have to admit, the food was top notch. I'm pretty certain though, if you asked to see their papers, most of the staff would magically disappear."

It's San Diego. Not surprising this close to the border a business employs illegals. They can pay them far less for a start. A Mexican restaurant isn't going to raise suspicions by being staffed by Hispanics.

"Saw nothing that resembled a trapdoor. Of course, I couldn't ask to inspect the kitchen or storerooms but kept my ear open. Should have taken someone who understands more than a smattering of Spanish, I suppose, but doubt they'd speak freely in any case." Niran shakes his head. "If it's a front, it's a good cover. Smoker may have gotten more."

I hadn't expected Niran to return saying he'd seen drugs passing hands. Drugs coming through tunnels are measured in tens if not hundreds of kilos, and not just an ounce sold by a street dealer. If drugs are coming through, they'll be moved on. A restaurant does get lots of deliveries, boxes in, boxes out, could be a good way of getting product into the United States.

"They do deliveries?" Grumbler asks.

When Niran nods, Grumbler raises his eyebrow toward me. Hmm, he could be onto something. Those scooters could be carrying something other than food in those insulated boxes.

"Where does Shark come in?" Salem rasps out, his thoughts being on our traitor.

Niran raises his chin. "He doesn't know me. I heard his name, but he was out bad before my time. Reboot had just been a prospect, but he'd been there."

Shark had been particularly hard on the prospects; it didn't surprise me Reboot recognised him fast.

"Shark spot him?" I need to know what damage was done. If Shark had kicked off, the restaurant would be warned, looking for a reason our members were there, without cuts, having a meal.

"Nah. Reboot recognised him, thought fast, then positioned himself so his back was toward the man. I wanted to watch for a while. Easily saw Shark wasn't a customer, no, he had another reason to be there. He seemed particularly friendly with the man who appeared to be the manager."

"Pick anything up?" Pennywise asks.

"Couldn't overhear. Not without making myself obvious. Shark took a pack of cigarettes out and was tossing a lighter in his hand, clearly preparing to go out for a smoke. I left Reboot where he was, told him to settle up when Shark was out of sight. I was worried about him stumbling across Smoker, so I went out the front, walked around the place and managed to find Smoker and warn him." Niran pauses and looks around. "Lucky I did. Shark came out the back entrance when he lit up, would have walked smack into him. Smoker approached from the shadows and asked him if he could get a cigarette. Shark didn't take much notice of a homeless man, and Smoker kept his head down. But the fucker wasn't going to give anyone shit, except, playing the big man, dole out a beatdown on a helpless man. Played right into our hands. As he went after Smoker to teach him a lesson, I hit him over the head. He went down. Reboot joined us by then." Niran shrugs. "Brought the truck around to the rear of the place, zip-tied him and gagged him with duct tape and brought him here."

"He wake up?"

Niran nods. "Halfway back. Couldn't do much more than thrash around. Had to stop Reboot from hitting him again. I thought you wouldn't want him concussed, or, not until we learn what he knows, and what the fuck he was doing there."

They'd done good.

"Anyone see him disappear?"

"Nah," Niran replies to the sergeant-at-arms.

I wonder if Shark's disappearance will ring alarm bells. We don't want that business getting twitchy and closing down, not until we know more about what goes on there. The fact that one of our out bad members was hanging around is highly suspicious.

Damn it. Should I have asked more questions about Shark at the time? Tried to hunt him down? It was all too easy to accept he'd only made a fleeting visit to this town. Anyone with a brain in his skull wouldn't stick around long, not with the Satan's Devils' price on his head.

"Can't believe how cocky that fucker is. Never fuckin' dreamed he'd still be hanging around." Kink, who's walked in during Niran's explanation and who's thankfully left his 'pet' of the day behind in his room, comments. I have two thoughts, one whether he's left the girl tied to his bed, and the second, at least I wasn't the only one to not have paid too much attention to Shark rearing his head.

I stand. "Not going to get answers until we're face-to-face. Who's coming to speak to Shark?" I'm not surprised when everyone gets to their feet. "Salem, call Dart," I request.

"Want everyone in on this, Prez?"

Looking around, I count up the absentees. Scribe is missing, Keeper too. And Bones and Snips. "Yeah, tell them what's going down." I doubt there will be anyone who wants to miss out.

As I walk across the clubroom, Patsy catches my eye. I detour one moment, resting my hand against her cheek. "Go to bed, babe. I'll be awhile."

"You going to be okay, Lost?"

"Sure." For a fleeting moment I'm torn between wanting to question Shark and going upstairs with her.

"You coming, Prez?" Grumbler pauses.

"Yeah." I bend, brushing my lips over the woman who's crept into my heart. Then, knowing club business comes before getting my needs met, I match my steps to those of the sergeant-at-arms, and walk beside him to the hangar a short distance away from the clubhouse. As we proceed to the back, I take note that the custom auto-shop is starting to take shape. Workbenches and metal drawers which will contain a myriad of tools are being set up. One area is curtained off with plastic sheeting, presumably for spray jobs. Once Salem gets an idea in his head, it's not long before he brings it to life.

Then we arrive. Grumbler opens the door, then steps back to let me precede him inside.

In true Satan's Devils' fashion, Shark is restrained, his hands tied above him, his feet only just touching the ground.

My eyes are caught by Smoker who's sat himself down. It's clear the evening's activities have taken it out of him, as he looks pale, and his eyes are half-closed, his breathing sounds laboured and his hand rests over his chest. Perhaps I should have insisted he stayed home. But suggesting he's not up to this is probably a worse option as far as he's concerned. I'll just have to keep a close eye on him.

Suddenly, there's a bark of laughter. The man, for whom this should be no laughing matter, is chuckling like a fucking loon.

"Oh, man. Now I'm fuckin' glad that I was sent out bad." Shark's got his eyes fixed on my cut. "Couldn't they do better than you? Snake always told us what a loser you were."

You're going to fuck up. Think you're an MC prez? Think again. Shaking my head, I try to rid myself of Snake's voice, but instead it chuckles. *Even a loser like Shark sees what a fuck-up you are.*

For a moment, I'm frozen to the spot. I'm not sure what I would have done had Grumbler not growled loudly from my side, getting Shark's attention turned on him. "You? Sergeant-at-arms? Fuck. It gets worse. You aren't fit to shine Poke's fuckin' boots, let alone wear them."

"You want to have a go at me now?" Bones walks menacingly closer. "When they made me fuckin' treasurer, I discovered the hundred ways DJ was cooking the books. Siphoning off money to start your enterprise, stealing from the members."

"But you didn't know what DJ was doing at the time." Shark's still laughing. "All you did was moan about your light payouts. Not one of you could fuckin' see what was happening in front of your nose."

Pennywise makes a sound in his throat that alerts me I'd better take the initiative away from the strung-up man. But seeing him has brought all my doubts that I'm the right man for this job flooding back.

Taking a breath, I summon my inner strength, willing up the MC prez inside me. While I've so far had a fairly quiet three years, concentrating on keeping the club happy and together rather than coming down hard on discipline, I had had years of watching Snake ply his trade. And, on at least one memorable occasion, witnessed how Drummer, our mother chapter prez performed. I'm not totally bereft of ideas.

Walking behind Shark, who's still staring and smirking at the men he used to ride alongside, I take my knife out of its sheath, and slice through the shirt he's wearing. At least Shark has the sense to fall. silent as the Satan's Devils' full back patch tattoo comes into sight.

"You were sent out bad," I remind him, my voice deceptively calm. "You were to get that blacked out."

"I was getting around to it," Shark protests.

I walk back around to face him, our insignia on the traitor's back more than I can stomach. "You were told the consequences if you didn't. You know what? We can help you with that. Get that fucker burned off right now."

Shark's eyes flick warily around the room, but if he's looking for any sympathy or someone to appeal to, he's not going to find it. The club had suffered too much. He meets my eyes, his narrow. "You haven't got the guts." I suppose you have to admire a man who tries. In answer, I raise an eyebrow. It's effective, as he swallows. "We were brothers once," he appeals.

"Kind of hard to worm your way back in after you've insulted the prez and sergeant-at-arms," a voice behind me reminds him. "If that's what you were trying to do."

I turn and nod a greeting at Dart. "Well said, VP." I deliberately taunt Shark with Dart's position in the club.

Shark, though, spits. "Me? Want to come back? Fuck no. Not while he," he jerks his head my way, "is at the top of the table." He spares a moment to look around, his eyes landing on the men one by one, before settling on Salem. "You should have been prez, Sal. How the fuck could you stand back and let this loser take your spot?"

It's the first time anyone's suggested Salem should be sat in my chair, or in my hearing at least. I cast an interested eye the enforcer's way and incline my chin to show he's free to answer as he wants.

Salem runs his hands over a wicked-looking knife he's taken out, as if testing how sharp it is. He stares at the steel as though giving serious consideration to the matter at hand, before lazily looking up. "Thing is, Shark, what you could never understand, is that some of us like working to our strengths and not endeavouring to take more than we deserve. I'm the enforcer, suits me just fine. Never wanted anything more. And, if you thought by flattering me, I'd go easy on you, hear this. You think you can sweet-talk me by insulting a man I look up to, a man I'm more than happy to give my all to support, then you are fuckin' wrong." Salem's tone and rising volume shows how annoyed he is.

A sensible man would shut up right now and not continue to taunt the person capable of bringing him a world of pain. Shark does shut his mouth, showing he may have a couple of brain cells left after all.

There's a bench behind me, I lean on it, folding my arms. I purse my lips, and stare at the man strung up in front of me, then cast my eyes around the room. It's clear everyone's deferring to me to take the lead. Shark and the dead man in my head might challenge my authority, but they're in the minority.

Finally, I draw in a breath and exhale. "You know how this is going to go, Shark. The only choice you might get is whether we burn or slice that tat off. But believe you me, it's coming off today."

Shark's paled, but a trace of his cockiness remains. "Snake said you wouldn't survive in an MC. Not without him to lead. I don't believe you're going to do that."

"Perhaps I've changed. Or," I shrug, "perhaps Snake was right. I don't much care for the scent of burning flesh, nor copious amounts of blood. And perhaps my sensitive ears can't stand the screams." I pause, then add, "Maybe I can be persuaded to instruct Blaze to get his stuff and do what you should have done all along. Black that tat out."

Shark narrows his eyes and a calculating look comes into them. "Yeah?" he says at last, having considered the less painful option. "And how could I persuade you to do that?"

I don't promise him anything. He'll be leaving here in a box whatever I, or he, says. But let him think there might be a glimmer of hope, that I might go easy on him as I'm not the man Snake was.

You're not, Snake's voice helpfully confirms.

My internal conservation makes me snap. "Answer my questions, and then we may have something to discuss."

I feel movement as my brothers step closer, as though not wanting to miss any of Shark's explanation of what he's been up to since he's been gone.

I kick it off. "What are you doing back in San Diego?"

"Making a living," he throws back.

I growl. "If this is going to be like pulling teeth, Shark, I'll let Salem soften you up. You've seen his handiwork before, and I can assure you he's not gone soft."

The enforcer moves forward, half turns and gives me a wink out of sight of Shark. "You might want to step out, Prez, there's going to be blood."

Shark shudders. Yes, he's seen Salem at work. So have I, and it's not pretty. But he gets results.

Suddenly our captive decides that he does want to talk. "When you sent us out bad, you sent us away with nothing. No club wanted us, we lost our home, our brothers. We lost everything." For the first time an emotion other than sneering comes into his voice. There's no need to explain, any of us would be able to imagine the pain of leaving the brotherhood behind. His eyes again flick to Salem, then back to me. "I had to look after me. Find a way to survive. Snake had been meeting with drug dealers, setting deals up, I was present at some of them. Even with Snake dead, they still wanted to work with the MC, well, you stopped all that. Fuckin' stupid." He rolls his eyes. "Have you any idea how much the club could have gotten from that deal?"

"Dirty money," Dart growls. He indicates the men around him. "The stuff you were proposing to peddle kills people, splits families up. Men liable to go to prison if they're caught carrying or gunned down by rivals. Money? Fuck that."

"Snake had it all sorted," Shark insists. "He wasn't proposing we'd stand around selling it on street corners. Nah, he had contacts. He went straight to the top. Took me with him."

As muscle probably. I'm sure Shark hadn't been as important as it appears he thinks he was. An idea hits me. Too outlandish, surely? I don't dive in, wanting to explore a little more first.

For fuck's sake, get on with it. I'd have had him begging for his life by now.

Again I push Snake's voice to the background, preferring to get Shark to talk while he still has some teeth. Once I release Salem and the boys on him, there won't be much left. I focus back on him.

"What was this deal Snake made? What did it entail?"

Again, Shark scoffs, his eyes flicking around the room. "Do you think it's a good idea to hear all that you lost? All those fuckin' dollars you could have had in the bank? Your brothers might change their minds on you Lost. It's all down to you. Your fuckin' fault you didn't hear Snake out." He takes another look up at the ceiling and back down. "It was simple. We'd have taken possession of the drugs when they came over the border. Transported them to where they'd be sold."

Simple sure. Transporting kilos of Mexican horse or whatever else they were buying and selling. It's one easy way to get arrested or dead. But I pretend interest and tinge my voice with a touch of regret. "And where would they be sold, where would the club have gotten them to?"

"Wherever there was a hunger. California, Arizona, Colorado."

I feel Dart stiffen beside me, but whatever's itching at him, he keeps to himself. Pretty certain he knows I'll be on the same wavelength, but asking too much too soon will put Shark on his guard. "How did the drugs come over the border?"

Shark grins. "I'll tell you everything if you promise to let me walk away."

I can't promise him that. Truth is, Shark's never going to be putting one foot in front of the other again. The love he used to have from his brothers has long since turned to hatred, but perhaps the time has come to use more than words.

"Need Salem to encourage you?" I start to raise my hand to gesture to the enforcer.

Words come from Shark's mouth in a rush. "I don't know. But I do know it's all stopped recently. Somehow the feds knew how to close that shit down." Shark clearly wants to stay out of Salem's reach.

I shake my head. He was just berating us for not going ahead with Snake's deal while in the next breath telling us we were right.

A drug operation brought down recently? I fight hard to keep my face impassive, though inside there's a kernel of excitement bubbling. *He's got to be talking about Alder.* Christ. We wanted to get hold of someone with knowledge of Alder's operation. Could he just have dropped into our hands? I force myself to be patient.

Another sideways glance at Dart which is returned with a chin lift shows he's also thinking the same way as me.

Taking a chance, I come straight out with it, speaking as casually as possible. "So how long have you been working with Alder?"

At fucking last. I'd have gotten that info hours ago. Didn't you learn anything from me, Lost?

I fucking learned that you would kill a man before he told you anything.

I'd seen Snake's temper flare more than once. Partly why I'm taking this slow. Dangling the glimpse of a future in front of Shark if only he tells me everything he knows.

Fuckin' pussy.

A shake of my head to clear it and I focus on Shark again. His eyes have widened, and the first sign of fear shows. *He's scared of Alder.*

"For fuck's sake." Dart dips his head toward me. When I nod, he continues, "There's no point denying you know him. Why the fuck do you think we were at the restaurant tonight?"

"But, but…" Shark flusters. "But you said… Fuck." It's like watching a penny drop. Trouble is, if we ask direct, he'll clam up. As it is, we're left with picking up clues from the little he allows to drop. "I'm not telling you anything about Alder."

"Good," I tell him, sounding approving. "Alder likes a man who can keep his mouth shut."

Shark's eyes land on me. "You're working with him?" he asks, incredulously.

I hear a strangled cough from behind me. Swinging around, I see Pennywise trying not to laugh. He mouths at me, *He's fucking stupid.* I tend to agree.

Shark was never the brightest of the bunch, he proved that when he threw in his lot with Snake. Now, his chin drops to his chest. "You won't touch drugs." I open my mouth to kid him that maybe we've changed our minds. That the club needs money, but Shark continues working it out in his head.

"You won't touch drugs, so you know it's other merchandise instead."

I resist turning to see the expression on Dart's, or anyone's face. Instead, I take Dart's lead. "Yeah." I raise my chin. "The merchandise being brought in via the tunnel."

Shark's head snaps up. "You know about that? But Alder never said. Never mentioned the Devils." Shark doesn't seem to know what to believe. "Hey, let me down. Sounds like we're both on the same side."

"Maybe the same side, but not the same point in the pecking order," I tell him. "That Alder didn't tell you about us suggests he doesn't think you're as significant as you think." That gets him. Leaning back once again, I cross my feet at my ankles, and smile. Shark never paid enough attention to me to realise my expression is fake. "Or, as you were a Satan's Devil once, still have our tat on your back, he assumes we're all working together."

"Together. Yes. We can work together. The next shipment's important, that's probably why he wants us all on board. And yes, I still have my patch."

The patch he won't have much longer.

"What do you know about it being important?" Dart asks with a quick glance in my direction. He also spares a warning look at the men who are getting restless.

Shark seems to be trying to weigh up what he knows that we don't, and vice versa. In the end, he settles on what sounds like the truth. "I don't know. I've seen immigrants coming in having paid top dollar, of course, and bitches and kids going out. Pretty boys, too, but you'll know all about that."

I hear the intake of breath all around me. We were on the wrong track, there is a tunnel, but it's not being used from what I thought. Sounds to me like Alder's found a trade to supplement the loss of income from his drugs. Maybe he's been doing it all along—people trafficking, one way or another. I doubt any of those immigrants coming through that tunnel end up where they expect, and as for people going in the opposite direction, my stomach churns when I think about what's happening to them.

"We," I indicate the men standing around me. As I do, I notice the expressions on their faces, in the main disgust, some, like Pennywise, dismay that this was a man they once called brother. "We," I begin again, "know what part we have to play. But so we don't trip over each other, what precisely is your role, Shark?"

Again he puffs out his chest. The man's so stupid, he thinks we're all in this together. "I get the merchandise onto the transport. Stop any making a break for freedom. See? They've paid to get into the States and expect it to be the end of their journey. They want to go meet up with family in some cases, so I need to persuade them to stick around. Alder has other plans for them."

Yeah. As I suspected, Alder makes a fortune out of people possibly giving him their last cent for the promise of a new life in America. Well, on the whole, illegal immigration doesn't bother me, I don't abide by citizen's laws. What doesn't sit well is people who take advantage. Wives could be meeting up with husbands or kids, their parents or other family. Instead, my bet is that they'll find themselves used as slave labour instead.

"You gonna let me down now?" Shark asks hopefully. "I've told you everything."

Not quite. "Which shipment are you waiting on?" Dart asks casually. "Tonight's?"

"Nah, Tuesday." He stills. "You mean, there's one tonight? But it's Sunday. Enrico never mentioned that."

Dart slams the heel of his hand against his head. "Fuck me, my bad. I can't remember what day of the week it is."

I give a good-natured chuckle while Shark's expression makes him look like he's working with a bunch of amateurs. "How many on your team, Shark?"

"Why do you want to know?"

"I'm just wondering how many I'll need to send along."

He thinks for a moment, then answers, "Me and Enrico deal with it."

"Just the two of you?" I'm genuinely surprised.

Shark gives an unpleasant smirk. "Doesn't take many when they're weak and unarmed, and you're carrying guns and tasers."

Welcome to the good ol' US of A. Guns and fucking tasers.

"We're new to this." I'm wondering how long I can string him along. "Interested in meeting the top man himself. Will Alder be there?"

"Sometimes he is, sometimes he stays in Mexico. If he's stateside, he occasionally wants to see what new stock he's got."

I'll just have to hope he's curious tomorrow. *It's an important shipment.* I don't know why, but hope there's a chance if it is, he'll be there to check it all goes well.

"Look, that's it. I can't tell you anything else. Seeing as we're both on the same side, are you going to untie me now?"

I eye him thoughtfully for a moment. Then smile and nod. "Yeah, Shark, you've told us everything. Salem?" I wave the enforcer forward as though I'm going to instruct him to let Shark down, then hold up my hand to halt him. "Oh, first. We've been asked to watch out for a Patsy Foster. What do you know about her?"

Shark shakes his head. "Not a clue, only what you've been told I suspect. Just that Alder wants her found."

I eye him for a moment, wondering if I've got all I'm going to get. I think it is, in comparison to what the enforcer can do, my interrogation methods are tame. So I do what any good manager does, I use the skills at my disposal.

"All yours, Salem."

Shark grins, then his face starts to fall as instead of approaching him to untie the ropes, Salem instead approaches the workbench and walks back to the out bad member carrying some tools, and a bottle.

It's when the brandy hits the man's back that he starts to scream. "You can't do this. Alder needs me. I've got to be there."

"Is that right?" Salem asks, setting the blowtorch alight.

"Yeah!" Shark yells. "You know him. If I'm not there..." his voice trails off as he realises if he doesn't turn up it will be because he'll be somewhere Alder and no one else will be able to hurt him.

Salem stares at me. I reckon we've got all we're going to get, but I hold up my hand to ask one more thing.

"Where are Tinder, DJ, Crow, Rattler and Bastard? They working with Alder too?"

"I've no fuckin' idea!" Shark cries out what I think is a truthful response. "We went separate ways."

I'm grateful that the brig is soundproofed as Shark's screams grow louder and louder, then he's begging, crying, whimpering as the blowtorch does its work. Every member stares on, none of us turn away. It's a brutal reminder that allegiance to the MC is everything. Betray the club and you don't get a second chance.

I hadn't lied. I don't like the smell of burned flesh, nor do I particularly like screams that almost burst my eardrum, and blood, well, if it's not mine, it's not so bad. I just don't much like getting it on me. But I know what I need to do.

I make a gesture, and one by one all club members advance on Shark, taking their revenge on the man who let them down.

There's not much left of the man by the time I put the bullet into his head.

"Took you fuckin' long enough. Should have pulled out a few teeth. Let Salem loose..."

"I got results," I mentally confront the image of Snake.

"Not like me."

No. Not like him. Just because I don't do things the same way, doesn't make me less of a prez. Why should I spend my life comparing myself to a man I've no desire to emulate?

CHAPTER THIRTY-ONE

Patsy

"I overheard something." Dan approaches me as Lost leaves the clubroom, his eyes following all the members as they walk out.

I stack the cue sticks away, ready to be used by someone else, fully intent on doing what Lost suggested and waiting for him in his room. *Naked? On my knees?* I've never wanted a man's dick in my mouth before, I mean, they pee out of it for Christ's sake. But for some reason my mouth waters thinking about his. If his mouth on me had blown my mind, could I return the favour, give him as much pleasure as he'd given me?

Distracted by the thoughts in my head, I speak in an off-handed manner to my son. "Yeah? What?"

"That you fuckin' ran." His growl gets my full attention. As I turn to him, he continues, "You were going to leave me without a word."

"I left a note," I object, flustered. He wasn't supposed to know about my mistake. I try to justify my actions. "Alder wants me, Dan. If I'd gone away, left a trail away from the club, then everyone here would be safe. I didn't want to put anyone here in danger."

Dan stares, then breathes out loudly. "For fuck's sake, Mom. Don't you know anything about this MC yet? They protect their own, and you're Lost's, Mom, aren't you?"

I suppose in his eyes I am. "Dan, I've never felt this way about a man before, and it scares the hell out of me. What if I stay and he ends up dead?"

"He won't," Dan assures me, his eyes like steel. "And if you were determined to leave, why the hell didn't you ask me to come with you?"

"You'd have been fine."

"Of course, I'd have been fine." He rolls his eyes. "But you intended to set off on your own completely unprotected. I should have gone with you."

He's standing straight, his body taut, and I suddenly realise something. My son is a grown man, and in his eyes, I don't need to protect him anymore. He sees himself in the role of protector himself. If he joins the MC, he'll fit right in.

I lower my eyes, understanding how much I've wronged him. "I'm sorry. But I'm here now. Lost brought me back."

"Thank fuck for that. Mom, promise me. Never, ever run off again. If you even think about it, talk with me first. If you do think that's the only answer, then I'll come with you."

"But you've got the chance of a new life here. A new family, Dan."

"Don't give a fuck. Blood comes first, Mom. For years I didn't behave like your son, and I'd like the opportunity to put that to rights."

"You already have." I raise my eyes to meet his again. "I know you've seen the worst of people and have put that behind you. When you were younger, if you said you were going to join an MC, I'd have acted like I did when you left to go with Phil. But I know what you're getting into. Prospecting will be hard work and will try you, but I've no doubt you'll get through. I'm proud that you're going to give it a go."

"You don't think it's all about living the life and free pussy?" He raises an eyebrow.

"Dan!" I admonish. "I'm your mom. I don't want to think about that. And if I'm staying here with Lost, I hope you'll be more discreet than some of the brothers."

He smirks but doesn't give me the answer I want. I bat his arm. "Anyway, prospects have to stay clear of the club girls until they get patched in."

"Don't remind me." His face falls.

"Anyway, the difference is, when you left to go with Phil, it was because you thought his life was easy."

"It wasn't." He grimaces. "No one wanted me there. I was the son, the heir, or so they believed. No one had my back when push came to shove. But here? It's all about proving myself, but this time with a purpose. I've got a chance of becoming part of a team, and that's what I want."

"I'm sorry I tried to leave." I revert back to the reason he came over. "I wasn't really thinking, Dan. Lost, well, he overwhelmed me, and I panicked I suppose."

"Overwhelmed you?" He grins. "Fucked you, I think."

Did he really say that? "Dan, I… *Dan!*"

He elbows me gently in the ribs. "I don't mind, Mom. Just as long as you keep it in your room and don't put on a display in the clubroom." As I splutter, he continues, "Seriously, I think Lost is the best thing to ever happen to you. Give it a chance, Mom. Let Lost put this right and get Alder behind you." His eyes fill with mirth again. "I wonder what Beth will say? Like daughter, like mother, you've snared yourself a biker."

Despite myself, I laugh. It's the last thing I ever expected. But despite him being an MC prez, Lost is a good man.

"Want a drink?"

I've had enough. "No, I was going to bed." My expression challenges him to question whether it's my own or Lost's, but luckily, he refrains from comment.

Instead he leans in, kissing my cheek. "Have a good *sleep*, Mom. I'll hang around with the prospects and see if I can pick up a few tips."

I make my way to the stairs as Dan goes and true to his word, props himself against the bar and starts a discussion with Curtis.

I enter Lost's room feeling like an intruder. Standing in the doorway, I'm undecided about whether I should really be here or not.

I stare around the room. There's no doubt it's a comfortable, if very masculine, space. If Lost and I are really together, will this be where we will live? I don't need much, just a space where I can work, and I'm sure Lost will find me a corner for that. A bed, sofa and television are the basics for sure. But I do like to cook, and while there's a kitchen downstairs, it's normally in use preparing meals for all of the brothers, and I'm not sure I'd want to do that. Apart from the fact he lives in just one room, I can hear music throbbing up through the floorboards. He's always on call, subject to a knock on the door summoning him at all hours. This isn't a place where he can switch off.

Would he live off compound? I know that Dart does. Should I even ask him? I need to take the man as he is and not try to change him. But if I don't, I'd have to change myself, and perhaps I'm too old to do that. I like having my own space, loved my old house with a garden which was great for entertaining in the summer months.

Am I thinking too much like Kim, his ex, did? Thinking only of myself. The thought is disturbing.

The only thing that should matter is that we're together. If I love the man, I should be able to do that anywhere. I look around again, trying to ignore the thump of the beat in the background. *I can make this work.* I'll have to. I'm already committed to Lost.

Love the man, love the club. That's something I've read in my books. And there will be more advantages than disadvantages being with Lost, I'm certain of that.

Viewing the room more positively as my new home has me moving my feet and closing the door behind me. I go into the shower and once again, using Lost's shower gel, wash away the grime of the day. Then, with the towel wrapped tightly around me, I delve into the bag that I'd packed earlier on today. For a moment I pause, realising I'd been crazy to leave, that a life spent running away is no way to live. I suspect I'd have realised that before too long and returned, even if I had gotten away.

But Lost had come after me. He'd cared enough to find me. That gives me a warm feeling inside.

I start digging through my clothes again, hoping to find something sexy, but nothing's magically appeared since I threw it all in.

I could slide into his bed naked. Lost would be happy enough with that. But as I'm alone, I feel a little unnerved and want at least some armour around me. *What if there's a fire alarm or something?* But nothing I've got in my bag seems suitable. Eyeing Lost's drawers, I go over and open them. The first has an assortment of underwear and socks, but the second proves more fruitful. I pull out a much-worn t-shirt with *Satan's Devils MC San Diego* printed on it. It reminds me of him, so I put it on. It drowns me, reaching down to mid-thigh.

I laugh at myself for thinking I could be ready on my knees when Lost returns but realise I could be waiting a while. I have no idea how long he'll be gone, or what he's doing right now.

The bed looks tempting and, as I already know, is comfortable. Lifting the comforter, I slide under it. I yawn. It's been a long day and I was stressed out for much of it. I close my eyes, just to rest them for a short while.

This pillow is so soft yet somehow so supportive...

"It's alright," I hear a voice murmur. "It's late, just go back to sleep."

I haven't even the energy to wake up properly, only vaguely conscious that a strong, familiar arm is being draped across me.

When I do manage to rouse myself, sunlight is shining through the curtains and Lost is awake and staring down into my eyes. My first thought is that he clearly needs less sleep than I do.

Unable to resist, I raise my hand, placing it against his bearded face. "What time did you come to bed?"

His brow furrows. "No idea, but it was late." His mouth quirks. "I see someone's stolen my t-shirt."

I grin. "Do you mind?"

"Mind? Fuck no. I like you in it." His hand moves up and down my arm.

I shift over, moving in closer to him. He doesn't disappoint, taking my lips in a scorching kiss, before resting his forehead against mine, saying, apologetically, "I'd love to take this further, Patsy, but I've got things I need to get done."

Clearly reluctant, he pushes away from me.

As he searches through his drawers for fresh clothes, I start to pry. "Did you have a good meeting yesterday?"

He swings around. I've surprised him. For a moment, I doubt he's going to reply. "Niran came across a man, Shark, at that eatery they were checking out." His eyes lock with mine. "Shark's one of the traitors that sided with Snake. Seems he's back stirring up trouble. Had a chat with him to find out what he knew."

"Oh." I suspect I don't want to know the details of how that conversation went.

I start again. "What did you find out?"

Lost shakes his head, then comes over and takes my hand, squeezing it gently. "Shark was working for Alder, but he had no information on why Alder wants you, Patsy. We did find out Alder's not running drugs, or not through the tunnel."

I pick through what he's just said. "There is a tunnel?" He raises his chin. "But he's given drug running up?" It's my turn to frown. "Oh God, Lost. That's why he wants his revenge. Dan's info must have shut his whole trade down."

But again Lost moves his head side to side. "No, he's not out of pocket and I suspect he's still got a hand in that game. But the tunnel is used for another purpose." He pauses, grimaces, then admits, "People trafficking."

He's just woken me up and sleepily I'm having difficulty waking up. *There actually is a tunnel?* That was the last thing I expected. *People trafficking?* "So Phil wasn't working alone?" My eyes narrow. "Dan got the impression it was Phil's project, and not something Alder condoned." Then I start adding two and two together. "Phil knew of the tunnel's existence, or, at least, the plans. He said he was going to take Beth out of the country. What if he was the one who set the trafficking route up, and Alder's taken it over now?"

"It could be," Lost agrees, staring at a blank wall as he pulls his thoughts together. "But I wouldn't have thought Phil had enough clout or money for that. I've no idea how long Alder's been in this particular trade. He could have built the tunnel for bringing drugs through and then changed its use to something else." He's quiet for a moment. "I've got to go meet with the men now, babe."

I've started to be able to read him. The way his face tightens and his jaw clenches puts my senses on high alert. "You're going to do something dangerous, aren't you?"

Instead of answering, he justifies himself. "Got to shut this down, Patsy. If we're lucky, we might now have a way to draw Alder out."

My hands go to my face. "When?"

His lips press together, and I realise he's not going to say anything more.

I sit upright, pulling his t-shirt around me. "Lost, please. I don't want to lose you. Just let it drop."

"Can't Patsy." He turns those vibrant eyes on me. "Whether you're involved or not, this has to stop."

"Then report it to the authorities. They can deal with it." Anything but Lost risking himself.

"They might close his tunnel down, but they won't get Alder. He'll just start up somewhere else. Trust me, Patsy."

"What if you tell Alder where I am? Draw him out? Catch him that way."

"No. Not putting you at risk." He eyes me for a moment. "Need to be able to trust you, babe. If you've got any ideas about exposing yourself, making yourself bait, I'll put a fucking prospect on you. Or," he softens his words with a wink, "I'll see if Kink's got a spare set of handcuffs I can use." His eyes land on the rail on his headboard.

Handcuffs. Why did he have to go there? Handcuffed to Lost's bed? His being able to do whatever he wants to me? I admit to thoughts no woman of my age should have.

Lost's eyes gleam. "You see possibilities with that, babe? Because I sure do."

Is he able to see inside my head?

For a moment he's silent, then his expression changes again. "Can I trust you?" He slips back into MC prez mode, leaving my lover to one side.

I open my mouth to argue, preferring to face the firing squad myself, but I know when to stop. It's clear nothing I can say will change the course of action he's decided on. While I hate it, all I can do is offer support.

I nod. "I'll not do anything without speaking with you." It's the same promise I gave to my son. "Just be careful."

"I will." He again looks at me carefully with heat in his eyes. "I've got something to live for now."

Preening slightly, I push for him to expand on his comment, even simpering a little as I ask impudently, "Like what?"

He leans in closer. “Like that promised blow job.”

He’s still chuckling, presumably at the expression on my face, when he disappears into the bathroom.

CHAPTER THIRTY-TWO

Lost

I remain smiling as I finish my day's preparations and fully dressed, leave my room. Patsy's face at my declaration had been a picture to remember. Her mock shock had made me laugh. At least my comment had broken the tension.

Look at us. Our feelings already so deep for the other, we'd both be prepared to sacrifice ourselves for each other. Truth is, with Patsy waiting for me, and me still not having felt her lips around my cock, make me more determined than ever to return to her without so much as a scratch. Knowing what I already do about my soon-to-be old lady, that goes for all my men too. She wouldn't appreciate me leaving anyone behind.

Now we've got to prepare and minimise all risk.

As I appear, Dart whistles loudly and points toward the meeting room. A subdued crowd follows me in.

I wait until all the seats are filled, then immediately get started.

"With all the excitement yesterday, we heard Niran's account but nothing from Reboot and Smoker. Let's rectify that now." As my eyes fall on the last man I've named, I notice he's looking particularly pale today. His chest moves fast as though he's taking in shallow and frequent breaths. At the very least the man might require oxygen. I'll have to ask. In my view, he's got weeks, not months, unless he accepts some help.

It's he who first raises his fingers. I raise my chin toward him. "They didn't suspect me, Prez." He pauses and starts hacking. Pennywise gets up, walks down the table, and puts a sealed bottle of water in front of him. Smoker opens it, gives a grateful nod of thanks, and drinks some. His voice sounds hoarse and noticeably weaker than normal when he continues. "So," he waves disparagingly at his chest, "I couldn't stay quiet. A man came out to have a smoke. Hispanic. He investigated who was making all that noise. I bummed a cigarette, and he asked me if I was hungry. I said yes, not thinking anything of it, but wanting to keep up my cover." He takes another few sips of his water. "He finishes his smoke and goes back inside. Comes out with a tortilla filled with some good shit."

"Nice fella," Salem observes. "Get anything out of him?"

"Nah. When I thanked him, he told me he knew what it was like to be hungry. Then he disappeared before I could question him."

It would have been hard even if the guy had stayed to chat. What could Smoker have asked? *Hey, you got the entrance to a tunnel around here?*

"While I was eating, I nosed around. That auto-shop place? There's a back entrance facing the restaurant. The area between the two premises looks like it's used quite a lot, a well-trodden path. Could be the workers like Mexican food for lunch, or—"

"Or they use the shop for cover for the trucks transporting the immigrants out." Bones sniffs and glances at me.

I'd like to get into that shop and check it out. "Any lights on there? Anyone working late?"

Smoker shakes his head. "All locked and closed up. I got as close as I could but saw nothing to indicate anyone around."

I raise my chin toward the man who's coughing once again. He'd done good, and I convey that with my nod.

"We could go tonight, Lost? See what more we can find. After hours when the restaurant has closed up."

I nod at Dart, then look around. "Whose lock-picking skills are up to speed?"

"I'll go." Token's raising his hand. "In case they've got alarms and shit, I can jam the signal."

"We'll go." Salem knocks his fist against Pennywise's bunched knuckles.

"How many do you need, Prez?"

I think for a moment. If we turn up in force, it's more likely we could be spotted. "Me, Token, Niran and Salem." I pause and glance around. "Dart, you take Grumbler, Blaze and Kink and see if you can find anything in the restaurant. Pennywise, can you take up a spot and keep an eye out for us?"

"Want me to go loaded?"

"Yeah." Pennywise is a sniper with super powerful sights on his rifle. He's often our lookout being able to spot trouble from a long way out.

"You're not leaving me out, Prez." Smoker speaks up. "They fed me last night. Won't raise questions if I hang around again tonight. Vagrants will always go back if there's food around. I'll have eyes on the ground before closing, see if anything's moving you need to be given advance warning of."

"Good idea." I'd rather he spent the evening in bed, but I'm not going to insult him with that suggestion. "But you stay out of trouble, Smoker, you hear?"

He gives a slight raise of his chin.

"What about us, Prez?" Reboot indicates himself and Keeper. I notice Scribe and Dusty are looking at me too.

"Not tonight," I say, then to counter their looks of disappointment add, "We all heard Shark, it's tomorrow it's going down. That's when we'll need all boots on the ground. A small group of us have more chance of staying unseen. Too many, and we might get noticed and they may change their plans." I change subject but continue addressing myself to Reboot. "We heard Niran's impression of the place, you notice anything about the restaurant itself?"

"I'd eat there again," Reboot informs us. "Good food, and the service was fine. I didn't get the impression the staff were the type to be involved in people smuggling."

"And what do people smugglers look like?" Deuce challenges him.

Niran frowns and jumps in to back him up. "Of course, it's hard to tell what's behind a smile, but they seemed genuine. As Reboot said, the service was good. Waitstaff paid their customers attention, little things like plates being removed as soon as you finish eating, fresh drinks offered when your glass was empty. Of course, we had to leave when Shark raised his head, but that's what I observed while I was there."

"What time do they close?" If the restaurant staff are not involved, perhaps it's after hours when Alder's minions come out from underground. Maybe literally, in this case.

"Eleven pm," Reboot says. "I checked."

"Tonight is about reconnaissance." I level my best prez stare at each of the men who'll be accompanying me. "We're not going in to confront anyone. If someone's there, if possible, we watch, observe, but don't engage."

"Aw shucks, Prez." Salem flexes his hands, his knuckles cracking audibly. "You spoil all the fun."

"They've got an alarm," Niran puts in, keeping the discussion on track. "I noticed that. Token's the expert, but to me, it looked quite sophisticated."

"We'll step carefully," Token agrees. "Did you see what the make was?" When Niran nods and names a popular brand, the technical guy smiles. "Only a few local firms install those systems. I'll hack into their databases and see exactly what they've got. Oh, and Prez? Got those new toys I'd like to try out."

My brow furrows, then I raise my chin and grin. "Okay, get them handed out, Toke."

"Oooh. We getting new toys?" Kink asks.

"Not the ones you're used to," Reboot quips.

"Bluetooth earbuds," Token explains. "I'll hook us all up on the same line. Keep communications open all the time. That way if anyone spots anything, they can warn everyone immediately."

"Fuck. I'll have Pennywise barking in my ear all the time," Salem complains, receiving a middle finger pointed at him from the aforementioned man.

"Right." For once, I bang the gavel. "That's all we can plan for tonight. An information-seeking mission. Tomorrow we'll make our move."

"And what move is that?" Grumbler asks.

All eyes are on me.

For the last three years I've not had to do much more than keep our businesses going and men fed and happy. This is the first time I've really been tested. I'm used to men looking to me for advice on whether we should start a custom motorcycle business or take on a new tattoo artist.

I've been a member of the MC for many years. I'm no stranger to death or violence. Last night was the first time I was directly responsible for ordering a man's death, and I'd slept like a newborn baby after. Shark was a traitor, and there was only one way to deal with him.

Today, I'm being asked to make decisions that will put my men in danger. Tonight, we won't engage, if necessary, we'll make a retreat. Tomorrow's a different matter.

Admit it. I named you right. You're lost. You've got no answers. Everyone is looking at you to lead them and you're just going to let them down.

Shaking my head to clear it, I do what I've always done, taken people through my thought processes.

"I want Alder." I state that so there can be no misunderstanding. Taking Alder down is the only reason the club is involved in this. All eyes are still watching me. "From what Shark said, we might get lucky and catch him there tomorrow night. If he isn't? Well, somehow we've got to draw him out."

"How?" Grumbler asks. I notice he doesn't offer a solution.

I've an idea in my head. "We send him a message. If this is a two-way operation tomorrow night, we can expect immigrants coming in, and people to be trafficked taken out. We liberate all of them."

Dart frowns. "Sometimes traffickers target people they want. It happened in Tucson. Drummer's old lady, Sam, got onto their lists. Shark mentioned something important. Maybe the whole contingent, or one or two, were particularly chosen? We just set them free, they could still be in danger of being picked up."

He's made a good point. "The women, kids, hell, men? Boys?" I run through who's likely. "We'll drop them at the local hospital. Fuck knows they'll be in need of medical attention, if only mentally. They can contact the authorities and they can take it from there. My focus is Alder."

Smoker sits back, his hands in the pockets of his cut. "So we don't wear our colours. Go in incognito, else we'll have the law banging our door down."

"Mask. Balaclavas." I look around at everyone. "Smoker's right, so make sure no one sees anything to recognise you."

Smoker's on a roll now. "Or why not bring them here to the compound? You could use them as bait, hold them hostage until Alder meets up with you."

"Complicated as shit, Brother." I shake my head. "The compound's not set up for fuck knows how many women." And all desperate to get home I would expect.

"Your ol' lady could be in charge of them." Smoker raises his eyebrow.

I open my mouth to tell him firstly, she's not been accepted officially as my old lady, and secondly, that she wouldn't do that, but then I reconsider. Patsy very well might. While I haven't asked her, I reckon she'd do whatever was needed. Her compassion and understanding, the way she put others before herself was all part of her attraction. But despite all that, if I thought she wouldn't be able to hack it as the old lady of an MC prez, I would have left well enough alone.

"Why don't you just come out and get us to vote on it?" Dart leans back in his chair, linking his hands behind his head. "You want her as your old lady, don't you?"

"I, er…" How exactly do I do this? We've got, and had, a lack of old ladies around here. Dart is the only one who has an old lady, and Alex had come with him from Tucson.

"Look, you just fuckin' ask for a vote." Dart's chuckling at me. "Tell you what, I'll do it as you've got a horse in this race. All those in favour of Prez taking Patsy as his old lady, say, aye."

A chorus of agreement sounds.

"Anyone say nay?"

Silence.

"Okay." I grin widely, nodding my thanks to my VP. "Seems I've got an old lady if she agrees. But we're not bringing the women back to the compound."

Smoker sighs deeply, then when his coughing fit ends, says regretfully, "Shame, some of them could have been whores looking for a new place to start over."

"Should have known you just wanted to get your dick wet, old man." Snips, sitting next to him, bumps his fist against Smoker's arm lightly.

"You fuckin' kidding, Brother?" Bones stares down the table at him. "Fuckin' would probably kill you."

Silence descends, broken only by Smoker's cough and Bones sniffing.

Smoker breaks it himself, catching the treasurer's eye and saying with a wink, "Can think of worse ways to go."

Dart clears his throat. "Back on topic. How are we going to smoke Alder out?"

Grumbler leans forward, resting his chin on his clasped hands. "Tell him we want a slice of his business?"

It's a good suggestion. I raise my chin. "He's using the tunnel, we know that. His drug route was shut down by the feds according to Shark. Presumably, Dan's knowledge did a lot of damage."

"Or Alder doesn't know exactly what the feds know and could expect them to set a trap."

Dart's right. Alder would be hesitant about using any of his established routes, as the feds could be waiting for him anywhere. But Dan didn't know about the tunnel. Presumably by steering clear of the drugs for now—he probably can't even know which suppliers are being watched—Alders' got a need for a new trade. In flesh. "That's why he resurrected an old route."

"Or maybe Phil used it all along?" This comes from the normally quiet Dusty. When I raise my eyebrow at him, he continues, "Could be he thought Patsy might be in the know about it. If he had to stop one business because of the knowledge Dan had, maybe he wants her out of the way just in case Phil told her about his plans."

That could make sense. Well, nothing else has so far.

"So we could hold our knowledge of the existence of his tunnel for ransom." Salem grins, showing his teeth. "I like that idea."

I do, too. "We tell him we want part of his business, or hush money to keep us quiet about it at least. If he doesn't meet to discuss it, we'll inform the tunnel task force or whatever it's called. He loses everything or gains a partner."

"And after that meet, we'll make sure he's dead."

It could work.

A kernel of excitement flickers inside me. From the first time I knew Patsy was in danger, I now have a pathway to ending it once and for all.

"Why don't we contact him now?" Reboot asks. "Why put ourselves in danger?"

If only it was as easy as that. "I don't know how to contact him," I explain. Maybe that was a question I should have asked Shark. Too late now. "Throwing a wrench into his smooth-running works will get his attention."

Again I glance around, studying the faces of every man present. They elected me to lead them, part of which is keeping them safe. Maybe it's not just Reboot who's concerned about the danger implicit in what I've proposed we do. "This isn't our fight, this is mine. I want Alder taken out, but that's because I want my old lady to be free."

"Stop right there, Prez." Smoker raises his hand. "I don't like anything I hear about this Alder. He's fucking up my town. Drugs were bad enough, but this trafficking he's got going on?" He raps his knuckles on the table. "I, for one, want him taken down."

"Goes for me too." Pennywise nods at Smoker.

"Me three."

Others follow Salem's comment.

"Been fuckin' boring lately," Bones observes. "I'd like a chance to crack some heads together."

I'd comment they weren't taking this seriously, but while their words may be lighthearted, their expressions are not.

My VP's shaking his head. I cock an eyebrow toward him.

"What you're forgetting, Prez, is that Patsy's not just your ol' lady. Even without that, she'd be club. She's part of the MC because her daughter is our Colorado brother's ol' lady, and Demon, prez of that club, charged us with looking out for her."

I draw in a breath. He's right, but I'd overlooked that fact. Some of the guilt of including my brothers in what feels like a personal fight drifts away. If we stepped back, Demon would probably come in to fill the gap. One way or another, Alder was going to meet his end via the Satan's Devils. Like Salem had earlier, I stretch my hands, making my knuckles crack and grin. "Well, let's get down to the details then."

We take a few minutes to agree what time we're going to head out tonight, then I dismiss them all, sitting back in my chair for a moment. I need some time to go over the plans in my head, thinking of what I might have missed, and what could come up and take us from the blind side.

It all hinges on what we find out. Plans laid can be altered once we know the lay of the land. While I search in the depths of my mind, I can't think of anything more I can do now.

You've forgotten something. Shut up, I tell the voice in my head. *You've not considered everything. You're lost before you start. I'll be seeing you soon.*

Abruptly I stand, kicking at my chair. Problem is, there's a large part of me that wonders whether the virtual Snake who haunts me is right. Have I forgotten something? Would I let the others down so badly they'll destroy my cut and burn the tat off my back? Or, maybe I'll just take a bullet in the head.

What if I'm about to lead my men into a war that we can't win?

No. I slam both palms down on the table. No, I won't. I may not trust myself, but I trust them. I couldn't ask for a better man than Dart to be at my right hand. Salem, Grumbler, Bones and Pennywise know what they're doing, and I can depend on them. Niran, well, he'll step up as the sergeant-at-arms if Grumbler ever steps down. And Keeper, Deuce and Reboot were all patched in by me, and I wouldn't have brought them on board if I didn't think they'd make the grade.

I may be the prez, may ride at the head, but this club is more than one man. If I were taking the wrong direction, Dart would let me know.

That's what was missing between me and Snake. Snake always knew which way to head, and never turned back even when he knew he was wrong. He didn't need to take advice from anyone. Fuck knows he hadn't let me in on the plans that ended up with him dead.

I stand up straight. Snake was wrong. Having doubts, asking questions isn't a sign of weakness, but a sign of strength. Snake was weak, thinking he was always right. It's that that had led to his death. For now, I'm still alive. And rather than being responsible for the decimation of my club, I'm determined to lead them right.

"You'll fuck up."

"Get away, Snake."

A manic chuckle. "You know I'm right. Lost. That's what you are. You'll always lose in the end."

I won't fuck up. Or I'll die trying not to. What I have now, my brothers, my club, my woman, far too important to make a mistake.

"They'll all see through you in the end."

But they won't. They'll see a man doing his best. My business was always my sole responsibility, that was the error I'd made. My mistake had been to take everything on my own shoulders, including the success, or as it turned out, the failure of my marriage. This time, I'll be sharing the burden, club-wise and with my ol' lady. Patsy will be there with me one hundred percent.

"You were the one who thought you could go it alone, Snake. You were the one with the ideas that didn't pan out. You were the one who the club kicked out."

"No, you'll fuck up."

"Yeah, I might. But never as badly as you."

The shadowy figure shimmers. "You..." For once he sounds

uncertain of himself. "I made you, Lost. You'd be dead without me."

"Maybe so. But I could have died the day we met, and you would have happily sat and watched and wouldn't have lifted a finger to stop my drowning. I was never anything to you, was I, Snake?"

"You'll fuck up."

"Get lost, Snake. Go back and sup with the Devil."

Snake starts to shimmer.

I'm strong. Stronger than he was. He always put himself first. The difference between us is I know I come last. I'd choose my woman, my brothers and club before myself.

For once, I advance on the shadowy figure, and it's he who steps back. Pointing my finger at him, I snarl, "You're dead, Snake. I'm alive. I'll never have my patch burned off. I'll be a Satan's Devil when I die."

Flames start flickering, a cleansing fire burning, the effect like paper charring gradually blackening his image. His mouth opens in a silent scream as the fires of Hell consume him completely and there's nothing of him left.

He's gone. The air suddenly seems easier to breathe as though I've banished him once and for all.

I'm me. My own man. Maybe I'm called Lost, and maybe I always will be, but maybe being Lost doesn't mean that I am.

One side of my mouth turns up, then the other, feeling like a weight has been lifted off me. I let plans for the night settle onto the back burner as I remember I've got another, and far pleasanter matter to address.

At last I exit the meeting room and go to find my woman.

CHAPTER THIRTY-THREE

Patsy

When my son nudges me in the side, I turn to see Lost striding toward me like a man on a mission.

"I think you're wanted, Mom," Dan tells me, his face split in a wide grin.

"We need to talk." Lost sounds as serious as that look on his face.

I swallow and jerk my head up and down. "Of course."

"Upstairs." His word is barked, short and direct, but not stated cruelly. He's clearly got something on his mind.

"We'll talk later," I throw at my son, before following in the direction Lost has already started going in. "Is something wrong?" I ask quietly, as I catch up with him.

"What? No." He pauses mid-step, turning to face me. "Just need to ask you something."

Well, it can't be about Alder or this mess, else he'd probably have brought it up in front of my son. Unless it's about Dan. It's urgent, whatever it is. As Lost resumes his steps, I try to keep up with his long strides.

We come to his door, he opens it, then gentleman-like steps back to let me enter before him.

I'm no sooner inside when his hands come to my arms and he swings me around to face him.

"Want those lips now." His mouth comes down, I raise my head, going on tiptoe to meet him.

One of his hands curls around my neck, that possessive, controlling touch I love. Our tongues duel, and I can't get enough, addicted to his taste and the feeling of his mouth moving against mine. His smell of leather and man so comforting, making me feel like I've come home.

At last he pulls back, bending slightly so his cheek rests against mine. "Fuck, Patsy. I've missed you."

"It's only been a couple of hours," I remind him.

"Only?" He smiles, then pulls away and takes my hand, leading me over to his sofa, and indicating I should sit down.

"Babe? The brothers have voted. You're my official ol' lady now."

My eyes widen. "I thought we'd wait until we knew what I was doing."

"We do. It's settled. You're mine and you're staying with me now."

I grimace, wanting nothing more. "But Alder's still out there."

He nods. "But now we've got a plan for taking him out. Before you ask, it doesn't involve you, babe. You won't need to play a part."

"But it's dangerous?"

The shuttered look that comes over his eyes shows he can't hide that it might.

For a moment, I'm undecided, and eye him carefully. I could continue to protest, but I messed up yesterday. I couldn't go and leave him and my children behind. I'd rather die than live without them, I know that now. I could make his life difficult by insisting he step back and let this thing with Alder drop, but that would mean constantly looking over our shoulders, and Alder's not a man to give up. If he can't find me, he could go after my pregnant daughter, and if he discovers my son's alive, he'd kill him for real.

I make the only possible decision, to trust my man. *My man.* It has a lovely ring to it.

So instead of protesting, I ask, "Do I get my own cut?"

Air whooshes in through his teeth at the words he clearly didn't expect. "Fuck, babe. You with my cut saying you're my property?" He half closes his eyes. "I can picture it now. You, naked, wearing just my leather, and me fuckin' you hard."

Seems I don't have any objection to that. I squirm a little in the seat.

He opens his eyes. "Must admit I thought you'd argue about the word property."

"Don't forget I have a daughter who's an old lady," I remind him. "At first it was hard to get my head around, but it's like a wedding ring, isn't it? A biker promise to his old lady."

"You want that as well, Patsy? You want my ring on your finger and do it legally?"

For a moment, I stare down at my hands, naked of adornment, which is how I like them. "I was married before, Lost. A ring, a marriage certificate is no guarantee of anything—no vows spoken in front of an officiant promises they'll be followed when all the fuss dies down."

"My experience is pretty similar," Lost agrees.

"I don't need all the trimmings now, Lost. You and me, promises given to each other, seem to mean so much more."

He sits down beside me, pulling me into his arms. "I will make a vow. I vow you'll never regret this. I vow to treat you right every day, and always come home to you at night." He pauses, then winks. "And I vow to ride you as much and as hard as my bike."

I chuckle, and taking his hand, bring it to my lips and kiss it. "I vow to support you as I should as your old lady and," I release his hand, slip out of his grip and start easing myself down to the floor, "learn how to give you a blow job."

The effect of my words is slightly ruined by both of my knees cracking loudly as they hit the ground.

Lost snorts, I giggle. It's just a reminder neither of us are that young anymore.

"Babe..."

But any objection is swallowed as I put my hands to the buttons holding the fly of his jeans together. Undoing them, I free him from his underwear, and pull his already hard cock out.

"You don't have to do this," he offers, but I can tell his heart isn't behind his words.

"I told you, I've never done this before, so I don't know if I'll be any good at it."

He leans his head back, closes his eyes, and makes me an offer. "Just do what you're comfortable doing, Patsy. Your hands on me alone is fuckin' incredible."

I've never spent time examining a man's cock before. Sure I've felt it, sometimes Phil liked me to jerk him off, but to map it with my eyes, to realise there was an odd beauty to the organ that seemed to be stuck on to the body as an afterthought.

Lost's arises through a thatch of neatly trimmed grey wiry hair, in a sea of white skin. Pushing his t-shirt higher, his belly is tanned, a marked line showing where his underwear lies. His cock is a deep reddish colour contrasting with both shades of skin.

Purple veins protrude. Feeling brave, I reach forward and lick them, tracing them with my tongue. Lost hisses. I use my hands to slide up and down his length, marvelling at his size. No wonder he makes me feel so full when he's inside me. As I stroke him, a drop of precum appears on the tip. Feeling brave, I lick it off. It tastes salty, not too unpleasant.

Summoning up even more courage, I put my mouth over the crown and suck.

"Jeez!" Lost all but jumps off the couch.

He's far too big for me to take much of him in, but I take what I can before I feel like I'm going to gag. As I work my lips, tongue and hands simultaneously, his cock twitches and thickens.

If he comes, do I swallow? I'm not sure I'm ready for that.

Suddenly I feel his hands resting gently on the back of my head, guiding me as I bob up and down on his cock.

"Babe. You have no fuckin' idea what you're doing to me." His voice is thick, his words sounding forced out. "Babe, that's fuckin' amazing. Fuck, babe."

I redouble my efforts wanting to make him feel as good as he had when he went down on me. His hips are thrusting gently as he uses my mouth. That he's enjoying what I'm doing makes me feel powerful.

"Babe, I'm getting close. Gonna come one way or another." His voice has gone husky and breathless.

I'm still undecided, but knowing he's loving the feeling of my lips around his dick, don't want to stop or pull back. Leaving one hand on his cock which feels like velvet-covered steel, I move the other to fondle his balls, a movement that makes him breathe in deeply.

"Babe," he warns.

Then he swells and warmth floods my mouth. I swallow rapidly, it's sour, odd. Not exactly unpleasant, but not quite nice either.

"Oh fuck me," he breathes out. "Babe."

I open my eyes, not having realised I'd closed them. His eyes, half-hooded, are on mine. "Fuck." He takes in air, his lungs rising as if he's recovering now. He leans forward, his hands cupping my cheeks, his thumbs stroking my skin. "You look absolutely beautiful, Patsy."

I feel I look a mess. My eyes are watering, my cheeks are red and my lips must be swollen.

"Thank you," he says at length. Then, putting his strong arms around me, pulls me up to again sit beside him on the couch.

"I didn't know what I was doing."

He chuckles softly. "If I were a bad man, I'd tell you you haven't got it quite right. That you need more practice. A *lot* more." He stares at me and winks. "But I'm not a bad man, so I'll just tell you this. It was fuckin' perfect, babe."

"I'm sure you've had better." I have to remember he's been with experienced whores.

"No," he refutes. "I know what you're thinking, Patsy, and you're wrong. It's not technique, it's not being able to deep throat a man, or whether you swallow or not. It's the connection between two people who want to pleasure each other that makes it so good."

I eye him and give him an impudent grin. "Seems like the pleasure was a bit one-sided to me."

"Hmm," he chuckles softly. "You're right, I've been remiss."

He can move fast for a man of his age and size. Before I can take a second breath, I'm on my back and my pants have been torn away, along with my underwear. Then he's returning the favour and it's not long before he makes my hands scrabble for purchase against the cushions and I scream.

It's later, when we've both cleaned ourselves up and recovered, that he takes hold of my hand and squeezes it.

"I'll be late to bed tonight. Just telling you so you don't worry."

"Is it anything to do with Alder?" Air whistles as I draw it in through my teeth. "Lost…"

His free hand cups my face. "Babe, there's going to be times that I'll pull the club-business card, being able to say nothing more than when I expect to be back."

I'm starting to realise why the women in Pueblo hated those two words so much. While I know from my daughter that's it's for my safety as much as his, that what I don't know can't incriminate me, him or the club, I hadn't realised I'm going to have to learn how to curb my tongue and not insist on him telling me exactly where he's going and why.

I take a deep breath and physically push all the questions bar one back down. "Are you going to get hurt, Lost?"

"Not if I can help it, babe."

"Lost…"

"Hush." He pulls me to him again. This time our kiss isn't ravaging, but sweet, full of emotion.

"Come back to me, Lost."

I hate it at that moment. I hate it more when shortly, dressed as though he's going on some type of raid, he leaves me. I hadn't tried to argue with him anymore, knowing there was nothing I could say that would stop him.

I agreed to be his old lady, to wear his property cut.

All I can do is just hope that he comes back safely, with his club along with him.

CHAPTER THIRTY-FOUR

Lost

Christ. Patsy might have been new to the experience, but that blow job had been hot. Her hesitant fumbling had made more of an impression on me than any encounter with any of the club girls. I'd tried to hold back, preferring to come inside her, but ended up taking my own selfish pleasure. I'd given her warning, but she'd swallowed. I'm not quite sure she'll go that far again in the future, but damn. Did I say it was hot?

Of course, I returned the favour, which I enjoyed almost as much. Seeing the normally put together woman lose all inhibition was just as rewarding.

Pleasant memories go through my head as I get ready for our outing tonight. Patsy's eyes had hardened when she saw me dressing all in black, sliding knives into my belt and ankle sheath, and placing my gun in my holster, but refrained from saying another word, just pulling me close and giving me a kiss to remember.

Now I put her out of my head and focus on what I'm doing, and currently that's sitting in a truck a block out from the Mexican restaurant which is, hopefully, closed up for the night.

"Pennywise?" I ask.

Through the power of technology, he speaks right into my ear. "All clear. Looks like no one's home at the auto-shop. All dark and quiet. Smoker's lying low. He reported the restaurant has closed. They stayed to clean up, then left. All lights are out." Pennywise has found a place to perch on the top of one of the high-rise buildings. Fuck knows exactly where he is, or how he managed to get there, but he can cover both premises from his spot.

"Far as I know, Prez, everyone's left." Smoker's voice comes through loud and clear.

"I'm good to go on the security system." Token's disembodied voice is next, he too had gone ahead. "They've got cameras, but I've hacked in and got some footage going on a loop, and I've remotely disabled the alarm."

"You sure?" I ask.

"We'll soon know," his response comes. The best I can expect.

"Grumbler's ready to pick the lock when you give the go ahead," Dart informs me, his voice sounding tinny.

"What about the auto-shop?" That's my focus tonight.

"I'm there now," Token speaks again. "Basic alarm which I'll deal with once we're inside."

"Wait until we're there as backup," I warn him.

"Copy that, Prez," Token says back.

I've got faith in the man, but hell, my skin prickles at the thought he may not have been successful and soon we'll hear the blaring of alarms ringing out. For that reason, I've parked the truck close. Curtis will stay with it and come get us should we need to make a fast getaway. Hopefully, if they see us, they'll just think a gang broke in to steal tools.

Dart with Grumbler, Blaze and Kink are in another truck on the other side of the block near the restaurant. They've got Wrangler as a getaway driver, and I just hope he uses his brains tonight and doesn't fuck anything up.

"Dart? We're ready to move."

"Copy that, Prez," Dart says professionally, then adds with more familiarity, "Take care, Lost."

You too, Brother. You too.

I don't need to tell the men to be silent. We get out of the truck, pushing the doors closed gently so they engage with just soft clicks. We certainly don't need sounds of slamming to alert people to our presence. Curtis drives off to wait out of sight as Salem and Niran follow me around the back of the shop to the staff entrance.

Token's there and waiting, with him a number of high- and low-tech tools, a lockpick and skeleton key, and a device which should help reveal the combination to disable the alarm.

I hold up three fingers, then lower them one by one.

We're inside.

I hold my breath and stand back, letting Token use his skills on the device screwed to the wall. It seems a lifetime but in reality is less than a minute before he turns around. "Done, Prez."

I'm not the only one to exhale my breath loudly. "Okay, fan out. Look around. Pennywise, is the coast still clear?"

"Not even a mouse moving," he replies. With the powerful scope that he's got he's probably not exaggerating what he can and can't see.

I head to the office, Token with me. He fires up an ancient looking and grubby PC, while by the beam from my flashlight, I look through the paperwork. There doesn't seem to be anything that shows it's anything other than a legit business, but as a front, they'd need to be seen to be doing the work.

I glance at Token who shakes his head. "It's clean as a whistle, Prez. I'd guess they're prepared if they ever have a visit from men carrying a search warrant."

Unless we're wrong, and they're legit and keep their noses clean. "Need Bones to look at anything?" He's good at digging out financial shit that doesn't make sense. He should be, he puts ours in order often enough.

Token points to the screen. "Bookkeeping is good, there's nothing to see here, Prez."

"Prez?" I hold my hand to my ear as Salem's voice comes through. "Out here, in the bays. We found something."

Sparing a brief glance for each other, Token closes down the PC, and I put the paperwork back just how I found it, then go out to see what Salem's found. It's a second before I can see him, and that's only when Niran points down. Looking over into the mechanic's pit, Salem isn't immediately visible, then he appears like a conjuring trick.

"There's a soundproofed room through here."

As he indicates where he'd just emerged from, I jump down.

"Wait." Salem holds up his hand, he points. It looks like the side of any other pit in any auto-shop in town.

"There's something behind it?"

"Sure is."

When I shine my flashlight on him, it shows he's only got his weight on one leg. "You hurt?"

"Accident, Prez. When I jumped down, I slipped on some oil and my leg shot out from under me." He rubs at his backside where he obviously went down. "Wrenched my ankle, but I'll live." Salem brushes away my concern. "When my foot hit the wall, I heard a noise that sounded hollow. Once I knew I was looking for something, I found the mechanism that opens it up."

It, as I find once he opens it to show me, is a room which is heavily padded. There are bunk beds on three sides, six in total. There's barely a foot of clear ground in the middle, and some of that is taken up by a bucket. It doesn't take a genius to work out what we've found.

"Another one here," Niran yells from two pits along. "I've got six bunks here."

"Nothing in the other pits," Token shouts.

"Found the fuckin' tunnel," Dart's voice says grimly in my ear. He reminds me he's been listening to what's been going on over here. "Their operation includes both the restaurant and the auto-shop."

"Jesus." I wipe my hands down my face realising we've got proof now. We're on the right track. Then suddenly, I realise something. "This is a place where people trafficked will be stored. Soundproofed so no one can hear them screaming. And if they're going out tomorrow night…"

"It's possible they'll be bringing them in tonight under cover of darkness."

Else why have a place ready to hold them? I don't bother addressing Salem's comment, just give a terse command. "Everybody out. Now. Dart, you copy?"

"Copy that. We're moving."

"Curtis?"

"I'M ready to swing by and pick you up."

KNOWING my VP will have his end well in hand, we go out the same way we came in, Token taking far too long in my view to rearm the alarm, then we're relocking the door. Salem's limping badly, but when I question him, he again says it's just strained and nothing's broken.

"Movement, Prez," Pennywise suddenly says hastily. "A truck's just arriving out the front. Make that two. Men getting out, coming in your direction."

"Want us there, Prez?" Dart's voice sounds.

"Get the fuck clear and back to the compound," I instruct

him. My aim is for us all to slip away without anyone being any the wiser.

"They're outside the shop now," Pennywise warns.

I wave at my men, not needing to say anything. We'll head to where we can safely get Curtis there with the truck and get gone. Like me, they sidle silently, keeping close to the walls. No problem, we're going to make it… until Salem trips over something and goes down, hard.

"Who's there?" a voice shouts out.

Fuck it. We all freeze, but it looks like we're going to be caught. If we move now, we could be spotted, if we don't move, they'll find us. I freeze, hardly daring to breathe, hoping they'll dismiss the sound as a stray cat hunting. One striding by would be great just now.

A burst of coughing sounds loudly, and Smoker comes around the corner, doubled up trying to get his breath. His coughing fit is genuine, as he's obviously hurried to get here from the restaurant parking lot.

Now they're distracted, I pull Salem out of sight behind a dumpster, Token and Niran too sinking into a crouch.

I peer around the side.

"Who the fuck are you?" A man appears and challenges Smoker, who can't reply as he's struggling to breathe. I count four more men gathering.

"I asked you who the fuck you are?" the angry voice demands.

"I ain't no one," Smoker manages to rasp. "I just…" *cough, cough. Cough, cough, cough.* "I'm just trying to find some food." He manages to straighten and wave his arm toward the restaurant. "They throw out good grub." Then he starts coughing again, bending double. I'm genuinely worried about him. He sounds like he needs medical treatment.

I expect them to tell him to get gone, but they don't actually say anything. It's dark, and I don't think any of us actually see the gun appearing in the man's hand until the bullet's been fired with a soft pop through the silencer attached to the barrel, and Smoker crashes to the ground, his final cough echoing into the silence.

One of the men kicks at his body, but Smoker's gone. He doesn't even flinch.

Niran's hand comes out to grab me, one hand going over my mouth. Grumbler holds me back on my other side.

"There's no helping him," Niran whispers directly into the ear without an earpiece. "He's gone man, that was a head shot. Don't let him die in vain." That Niran's right doesn't sit well with me. Smoker had come to our rescue and had lost his life as a result. But if we confront them now, we could join Smoker, or at best, come out on top and blow our chances of shutting down this operation.

"Now we've got a fuckin' body to get rid of," a newcomer states, approaching the group who just killed Smoker. "Why the fuck did you do that?"

"Don't need any witnesses and look at him. No one will fuckin' miss someone like that. Put him inside. He'll keep until tomorrow, then we can ship him out along with the merchandise and dump the body somewhere." The shooter doesn't sound bothered. "Get the front doors open and the trucks inside, then we can start unloading them."

When they unlock the door and disappear into the auto-shop, with no shouts that we've left signs we've been there, we slip away into the night and I instruct Curtis to come get us with the truck.

"I sent the others back to the compound." I'm surprised to see Dart. "I wanted to make sure you got clear, so came around to meet Curtis. What the fuck happened?"

I realise I hadn't said a word, so Dart's been left in the dark. I hardly want to say it now, knowing it will make it more real.

In the light of a streetlamp, I let him see the distress in my eyes. "Smoker's fuckin' dead." I slam my hand against the bodywork, probably leaving a dent.

"It's my fault," Salem says, rubbing his ankle. "If I hadn't stumbled—"

"It's no one's fuckin' fault except those motherfuckers." Niran, his voice catching, but once again the voice of reason says, "Fuckin' useless pieces of shit who shot a harmless man."

"What happened?" Dart repeats, looking from one of us to the other.

I nod toward Salem. "Salem hurt his leg, stumbled over something when we were getting away. Smoker heard, came around to provide us with cover. They fuckin' killed him for no reason."

It's my fault he's dead. I should have put two and two together before we went in. But how was I to know they had a place for storage? Never in a million years could I have guessed. I thought we'd be clear going in tonight, expecting all the action to take place tomorrow.

A voice crackles in my ear again. "I'm still in place. They've taken two trucks into the auto-shop. Can't see what. They've closed the doors behind them."

Drugs don't need bunks or soundproofing. Their cargo must be the traumatised women Shark was talking about. They'll be crammed into those cells for twenty-four hours. Frightened, scared, and knowing their horrors are only just beginning. I wonder how many of them there are and hoping those cells won't be full to capacity.

I wished we'd killed the motherfuckers when we had our chance, and freed the women.

A hand grips my shoulder making me realise I'd spoken aloud. "Couldn't have done that, Prez." The whites of Niran's eyes are about the only thing I can make out in the dim light as his voice of reasonableness continues, "We'll get our revenge tomorrow night. We'll do it for Smoker. Free the women and blow this operation to smithereens. This shop of horrors won't be used for trafficking again."

He's right. I take a deep breath, trying to calm myself. I couldn't have known anyone would turn up, or that they'd be as cold as to kill an apparently homeless man with no reason.

"Want me to stay on watch?"

Do I? But I doubt Pennywise will find anything useful. Those holding pens, cells, whatever you want to call them, were soundproofed. The men will probably slip away before it gets light, and the shop's mechanics will do a day's work possibly completely unaware who they are working alongside.

"What do we do about Smoker?" Dart sounds grim.

"Get his fuckin' body back tomorrow night." That's when I'll be able to take my revenge. "Let's get back to the compound. Pennywise, you copy?"

"Copy, Prez."

I hate leaving a man behind, even if he can't know what we're doing anymore. Hate losing a man at all. I ride in the truck back to the compound wound up and irate, and I'm not the only one. No one's talking or trying to make conversation. I think we're all stunned. Smoker had given his life for the club. He'd died a hero, and not one of us is going to forget that.

I walk into the clubroom and see the club girls standing around, hopeful they'll be able to provide their services now we've returned. Grabbing a bottle of whisky and a glass, I shout out, "Get yourselves a drink and get into church."

Dart takes the bottle from my hand, pours two shot glasses full, then hands me back one. "Need you sober, Prez."

Yes. Unfortunately, he does. I don't really know why I picked up the whisky in the first place. But Smoker is dead for fuck's sake and his blood is on my hands. The buck stops with the prez.

I take my seat at the head of the table. By now, word has gone around. I'm faced with sombre men wearing various expressions of disbelief, confusion and anger on their faces, or in some cases, a combination of all three.

Snips bangs the table in anger. "What fuckin' happened?" He's the first to break the silence.

Salem stares down the table. "Smoker saw what had to be done and did it." He stares Snips down. "Saved our fuckin' lives and we're not ever going to forget it."

Niran joins in. "No one asked Smoker to put himself in danger." He pauses, shakes his head, then resumes, "He should have gotten away with it. They had no suspicions he was anything other than a homeless man. Should have been easy and they could have just run him off, but they fuckin' killed him."

Pennywise speaks up. "We're working on the assumption they'd brought women in to put in their holding cells. We had no fuckin' idea they were bringing them in tonight until Salem found they were set up for them. Clearly they didn't want anyone hanging around."

It's time I spoke up. "They killed, murdered, Smoker in cold blood. But they weren't suspicious and didn't look for someone else. Look, I should have expected…"

Salem's fist hits the wood. "*I* was there, Prez. How the fuck could you have expected to find what we found? You haven't got a crystal ball that I know of. And if you want to blame anyone, blame me. I was the one who fucked up by not being careful when I jumped down. My ankle gave way, and *I* was the one who made the noise. If I hadn't, we'd have gotten away clean. As it was, if Smoker hadn't appeared, they'd have tracked us down."

"Why didn't you take them out?" At Snips angry cry, I wonder whether we should have taken our revenge there and then. Would it have made everyone feel better?

"No, Prez was right," Grumbler says. "Attacking them wouldn't have brought back Smoker, and it would have fucked up our plans. They're already dead men walking, but it's tomorrow night, well, today now, we'll have them in our sights. The mission will go ahead thanks to our brother who sacrificed his life."

"He didn't know what he was walking into. He couldn't have expected it." He hadn't known they would shoot an unarmed harmless looking man. That's what hurts most, I think, that he hadn't expected it. Didn't know the risk he'd be taking, and that there'd be no more rides on his bike.

"I disagree," Grumbler states firmly, catching my eye. "Smoker had to know how it could have gone down. Fuck, any of us would. And, I hate to say this, brothers," he pauses, and makes sure everyone's listening to him, "Smoker was already a dead man. He'd made the decision to live out his life sentence without trying to prolong it. I've known him a long time," he looks pointedly at Snips, "and I think this is how Smoker would have preferred it. He wouldn't have gone looking for it, but if asked, he would have chosen a quick bullet to the head instead of weeks of unbearable pain and discomfort."

"He wasn't fuckin' suicidal," Snips protests.

"No?" Bones puts in. "Then why the fuck didn't he seek treatment. Nah, I agree with the sergeant-at-arms. If he'd been given the choice, this is how he'd have wanted to go out. As a fuckin' hero, giving his life to save his brothers. That's how we'll always remember him, not as a man who faded away until his death."

I let that sink in for a moment, realising Bones is right. Smoker should have been able to enjoy those last few months he had left, but he was already deteriorating fast. Given the choice, he might have preferred his end to be quick and, I hope, painless. His memory will always live on. He died for this club. And once this is over, will be buried with the full honours he deserves.

Kink tries to stifle a yawn, his action reminding me it's well past the middle of the night, and dawn will soon, if not already, be breaking. Hard to tell in this windowless room. I need men at their best later.

"We'll bring Smoker home when we go in tonight," I tell them, then change tack. "Dart, tell us what you found."

Dart nods at Blaze. "He found the entrance to the tunnel. There's a false floor in the storeroom. Under that is a trapdoor, it's well hidden."

Blaze shrugs. "I was stomping my way around that restaurant. That floor had a different sound. Knew there had to be some easy way for them to open it, found a few loose planks and lifted them up."

Niran raises his hand. "I've been thinking about how to play this tomorrow… tonight. How about a couple of us going there to eat? Aim to get there later on so we'll be there when they close. Then I'll go to the bathroom and hide myself away. That way, I'll already be inside."

"Not you," Salem objects. "Sorry, man, they'd notice you're missing. You kinda stick out."

Niran chuckles good-naturedly, not arguing the point.

"It's a good idea," I acknowledge. "Look, it's been a long ass night. We'll call it a day now. Go raise a glass for Smoker, then get to bed. Need you all with your heads on straight tonight."

Dart turns his head to stare at me, I raise my chin back. We might not have said the words, but our exchange had included a silent promise that we'd lost Smoker, and the Devils aren't going to lose anyone else. Not on my damn watch.

CHAPTER THIRTY-FIVE

Lost

I didn't want to tell Patsy that we'd come back leaving one of our members behind, knowing it would upset her and make her worry about me and the other men. But I knew not hearing it from me would be worse. As soon as she went downstairs, she'd be made aware we'd returned one less.

When I go to bed, I try my hardest not to disturb her, but she must have been sleeping lightly as she awakes.

"Go back to sleep." Bad news can wait.

"I wasn't really sleeping; I was too worried about you. Did everything go alright? Are you okay, Lost?"

Okay. Seems it can't wait. I'm not going to start our relationship by lying to her. "Kind of." I pull my thoughts together. "We achieved what we wanted from tonight." I can give myself a tick for that. "I'm fine, Salem's got a twisted ankle, but that's all the injuries there were. But, babe." In the darkness, I grimace. It seems she can tell, or maybe it was the tone of my voice speaking just those two words.

"What happened, Lost? Tell me."

"Can't tell you the details, but we lost Smoker. Babe, he's dead."

"Smoker… what? Oh my God." She sits bolt upright. "What happened?"

Reaching out my hand, I curl it around the back of her neck, and gently pull her back down, holding her against my chest. "Can't tell you the details."

"Was it anything to do with the cancer?"

Her voice vibrating against my chest is comforting. "No, babe," I admit.

"Oh."

I have to remember, what she doesn't know can't hurt her. This is one of the things she's going to have to accept about this life.

There's a minute of silence, then she asks, "Was it quick? Did he suffer?"

"He didn't even see it coming, babe." And that's the truth. The coward shot him in the back of the head.

Her hand strokes my chest, and I feel wetness on my skin. Something eases inside me, knowing Smoker's got someone shedding tears for him.

"He knew he was dying," I explain. "He'd accepted that. I think he'd already made his peace with whomever he needed to. I'm crushed that he's gone the way he did, yet, in some ways it's a relief to know we're not going to have to watch him suffering." Then I add, "Grumbler thinks it was how he would have wanted it. He saved us, babe. His death had a purpose. He died a fuckin' hero."

She's quiet as though letting that sink in. "Is it finished now? Did you get Alder?"

"No."

Her hands grip me. "Can't you let it drop? Smoker's dead…"

"Got to make sure he didn't die in vain, Patsy. We've started this, and we're going to make sure we finish it. It's our battle as much as yours now."

She's quiet. "When?"

She'll notice when I don't come to bed tonight. Hell, she'll know when she sees the mood in the clubhouse.

"Tonight."

She takes in a deep breath. "I don't know what to say."

"Don't say anything, babe. Things are set in motion and there's nothing you can do to stop them now."

"Okay. But please, take care. You've lost one man already," her voice breaking as she says it.

I know that, and I'll never forget. "Babe, we found out shit tonight. Shit that will help us get organised. This was already dangerous. The information we got will make sure we're not unprepared. I'm not stepping back from this."

"It's because of me…"

"It's because of Smoker." I kiss the top of her head. "The brothers won't stop now, babe." She'll understand but won't like it. I give her something to focus on instead, something she should take the lead on as she's my old lady. "Babe, will you do me a favour? Organise a send-off for Smoker? Eva will help, all the other chapters will need to be invited, but I'd like you to take the lead."

"Conan Holmes," she says carefully, "I will do that, but only if you promise me I won't be doing it for anyone else."

Hopefully there will be more deaths tonight, but none who she'll need to mourn.

I can't give her the words, so I kiss her instead. Despite her lips bringing me comfort, it doesn't stop my mind racing, going over what I've got to do next. When our mouths part, she settles with her head on my chest. It's comforting. My hand automatically caresses her hair. Gradually, her breathing evens while my brain continues to work.

Plan, plan, then plan again. Check every detail and make no assumptions. Not paying enough attention to the auto-shop or considering how they could be set up got Smoker killed tonight.

Patsy stays where she is, her head on my chest.

What will we do if Alder is there?

What will we do if he's not?

How many men will we be facing?

What about the women, will we be able to rescue them, and will they come with us without a fuss?

What exactly will we be walking into?

How can I keep everyone safe?

At some point, pure exhaustion must take over as, when I'm next aware, it's morning. The head on my chest is gone, in fact, other than me, the bed is empty. Reaching for my phone, I see it's late in the morning. Patsy must have let me sleep in. I stretch, then still, as memories of the night before return to me.

Smoker's gone. He's dead.

I sit up, all vestiges of sleep wiped away. Tonight, we'll wreak Satan's Devils' revenge on those responsible for his death.

Not forgotten you, Brother. Nor what you did.

I won't let him down.

I'm surprised I hadn't had a nightmare last night, Snake appearing to admonish me. Maybe it was Patsy's comforting presence that kept him away, or maybe, for once, he had nothing to say to me.

Snake's voice in my head is my own subconscious taunting me and usually delighting in pointing out my mistakes. But I hadn't made one, it was just circumstances I had no control over. What I need to do now is put plans into place that mean nothing tonight is left to chance.

I get myself ready and dressed, grab something to eat, then motion to the men in the clubroom, not surprised everyone is there, ready to meet.

Now we're in church, making our plans as watertight as humanly possible.

"You want me on lookout again?" Pennywise offers, but he doesn't look too happy about it.

I consider him and his offer. As a sniper he'd held his unit's record for hitting a target at fifteen hundred yards. The sights on his rifle are powerful, making him uniquely qualified to watch out for us from a distance. He'd given us a warning last night that saved our lives, but tonight it's going to be different. And Pennywise is also a good man to have beside you in hand-to-hand combat.

"We do need a look out, Prez, but how about Curtis?" Niran suggests. "He's almost through to getting his patch, and he impresses me."

"That's because you're twins," Reboot jokes.

"Yeah, yeah." Niran rolls his eyes. "What's your name again? I get you muddled up as you white folks all look the same."

There are snorts of laughter directed at Reboot who gives a good-natured grin.

"I like Curtis." I stare around the table. "But I need him here. Don't want to leave the compound unguarded."

"Can Dan handle himself?" Grumbler asks.

"I'd say so," Salem replies. "Been talking to him. He used to be the muscle for his father. He's also interested in prospecting."

"Whatcha thinking?" I ask the sergeant-at-arms.

Grumbler looks my way. "Let Curtis come along, see how he does in the field. Dan and Wrangler can hold the fort here."

It's not a bad idea. The more men we have, the easier it will be to take the fuckers that killed Smoker down.

"Wet work tonight, brothers, if we can." Grumbler now turns to the details. "Anyone got a problem with that?"

It seems no one has. I'm happy to avoid bullets if we can. Even silencers aren't good after being fired a few times, and we don't want to draw unwanted attention by re-enacting the shootout at the OK Corral.

We're now down to the details. After some back and forth, accepting some ideas, dismissing others, our plans become concrete.

"You know what you're doing, Reboot?"

"Sure, Prez. Me, Brakes, Keeper and Kink are getting there about ten. We'll stay until we're kicked out at closing time."

"I'll feed my habit." Brakes looks around, making sure everyone is listening. "Deuce will be outside when I come out smoking. If I flick my lighter twice, I'll have information."

"Otherwise you keep out of sight, Deuce, got it?"

Deuce rewards me with a chin lift. He's got it.

"Anyone going to stand in for Smoker?" Salem asks. "Would be useful to have eyes out back."

It would. And now we've lost them. "No, it's too dangerous. Can't introduce another homeless man, that would arouse suspicions."

"And the waitstaff?" Grumbler questions Niran again.

"I honestly can't see how they're involved." He glances at Reboot who backs him up with a raised chin. "Can't be certain of course, but apart from Enrico, the owner, who's in it up to his neck, they don't seem the type."

"So nothing is likely to happen until after closing when they've gone home," I surmise. "But don't take chances. We can't know that for sure. You have your fuckin' eyes on everyone in that restaurant, whether they look innocent or not. Everyone acquainted themselves with that description of Alder?" The four who'll be eating there all nod. I'd had to ask Patsy for the details of what he looked like as Token was unable to come up with a recent picture. She'd seen him last at Connor's funeral. While I suspect it's highly unlikely he'll put in an appearance early in the night, it's good to have the information so we can be on the lookout just in case.

Eventually I feel all questions which could be asked have been brought up, all contingency plans discussed, brothers rehearsed in backup plans B, C, D and fucking E. I'm determined not to have another Smoker on our hands tonight.

It's only then I begin to dismiss church.

"Prez?" Salem interrupts. When I raise my chin, he continues, "You know what Snake was like when he sat in that seat?"

I stiffen, wondering where he's going with this.

Salem glances down the table at the old-timers, giving them chin lifts. "Bird, now, he was someone you could trust and follow. Cautious and careful."

I feel even worse, now thinking my deficiencies as a prez are going to be highlighted. *Have I fucked up? Is this where they replace me as prez?*

Grumbler eyes him thoughtfully. "Lost is something else though, isn't he?"

They can all see what a failure I am.

"Sure fuckin' is," Bones says. "May not like talking something to death, but you know what? Even if we get to Plan Z tonight, I reckon we'll all be fuckin' word perfect."

Dart barks a laugh. "Prez," he addresses me directly, "I think what they're trying to say is that you're not Snake, not Bird, but better than both. You're a fuckin' good man they'd all follow to the ends of the fuckin' earth."

"Now you're putting words in my mouth, VP," Salem objects, then he smirks. "And yeah, though I wouldn't have put it so fuckin' eloquently, that's what I was trying to say." When I go red, thinking how to respond, he adds, "Just wanted to put it out there after what Shark said. Wanted to make sure you knew, Prez, that we chose the best fuckin' man to lead this club, and there's not one man here who doubts that."

"Yeah." Bones sniffs and wipes his nose. When he's returned the grubby rag into his pocket, he continues, "Don't think you know this Lost, but the club met when you went to Tucson along with Snake and Poke on their final one-way trip. Had words about whether we were going to walk away or work to make this club survive. Well, on that we were undecided. What we did know was there was only one man we'd get behind if we were going to give it a shot. Even if Drummer hadn't made the suggestion, that seat was already yours in our eyes."

"You came through," Salem takes over again. "Pulled us together as a functional unit once again. Not sure there's any other man who could have done that. You, with Dart as VP by your side. You care about this fuckin' club, Lost. Care about each of us, whether we live, die, have food in our bellies and enough money to get by. Three years ago, I wasn't certain if I could trust again, but hell, Prez, you showed me I could."

"Goes for all of us, Brother." Brakes speaks up, his words echoed all around.

I'm humbled. Disbelieving. Fuck me, there are even tears in my eyes. But I can't say they are wrong. Snake would have told the men to jump, and that's what they'd have done. But in the right direction or high enough? He didn't give a fuck. I have a personal reason to know he didn't care who lived and who died. In the end, he all but destroyed the club with his selfishness.

But to hear them say they'd already picked me before Drummer had said a word? That their doubts had been whether the club had a future, not that it was me they were worried about riding behind? And then to hear they acknowledged what Dart and I had done when we pulled this club back together. I'm a man. I don't cry. And I'll be damned if I wipe away tears that threaten to fall, but I'm so fucking full of pride.

I have no idea how to respond to their words. I can't express how I'm feeling to hear they've got confidence in me and giving me the assurance that should this go wrong, it won't be for lack of preparation.

"Can we go over Plan Z again as I kind of lost it at Y?" Snips quips, I think to break the emotional overload I don't think I'm the only one to be suffering from.

I try to think of something, anything I could say to respond, but can't find words that will cut it just now.

Dart notices my predicament, or perhaps it's because he

shares my own plight. Instead of a great speech, he bangs his fist over his chest. "For Smoker. For us. Tonight we'll ride. Ride Satan's Devils. Satan's Devils Ride together."

Our battle cry is taken up from every seat.

My ears are still ringing when the meeting finally breaks up.

Word's clearly gone around that something's happening tonight. I was right to warn Patsy as it's obvious. No one would have needed to say anything, it's hard to hide that Smoker hasn't returned, and with brothers disappearing at all hours it's obvious that something's about to go down. Out in the clubroom the sweet butts are noticeably quiet and keeping to themselves. I hear one word whispered time after time, *revenge.* Yes, that's what's expected when we've lost one of our own.

Weapons are being checked and made ready. Wrangler and Curtis are rushing around, making sure hands have beers close by.

I see the man I'm looking for. He's standing alone, looking uncertain. I make my way over there now.

"Dan." I greet him with a chin lift. "Where's your mom?"

"She and Eva are making sandwiches. They thought something quick and easy would suit you tonight."

They're right. No one's in the mood to sit and chat over a plated meal, something they can eat while still making preparations will do well.

"Need to discuss something with you." I point to an empty table, and Dan precedes me to it. When we're sitting down, I continue, "Can't give you the details. But we're all heading out tonight."

I've caught his interest. "How can I help?"

"I need to take Curtis with me. Want you to stay here with Wrangler and keep the compound buttoned down."

He pulls back his shoulders. "I can do that. I won't let you down."

"You got a gun?"

He shakes his head. "Go see Grumbler. He'll see your sorted out. I take it you know how to use one?"

He rolls his eyes. "Sure do."

"Good. When this is over, we'll talk about getting you onboard as a prospect, okay?" The brothers will need to vote on it, but I doubt anyone would raise an objection. And if we patch Curtis in, then we'll be a prospect short and we don't have anyone else waiting.

His eyes have lit up. "I won't let you down, Prez."

"Not your prez quite yet," I tell him with a smile. "But someone's got a new title. Your mom told you she's my official ol' lady?"

"Official?" His eyes go wide. "You got an unofficial one too?"

I make as if I'm going to hit him. He jumps back with a laugh. Then his face falls. "There is no way in hell I'm going to be calling you Dad."

"Thank fuck." I grin back at him.

"Got a minute, Prez?"

I hold up one finger to Pennywise and turn back to Dan. "I'm trusting you. Don't let me down."

"I won't." His reply is spoken seriously. As I get up to go see what Pennywise wants, I notice Dan wasting no time and is hovering, waiting to catch the eye of the sergeant-at-arms.

Pennywise wants to go over something again. He's not the last either. The next few hours pass in a flurry of discussions with one person, then another. I don't mind, the more we go over it, the better prepared we'll be if something goes wrong.

I have to admit I've got more of a spring in my step today. My fears and uncertainties about being the right man for Prez had dissipated when the men showed such faith in me. If they believe in me, maybe it's time I should believe in myself. As I answer questions left, right and centre, I become surer of the outcome tonight. It's too much to hope we'll actually be able to get our hands on Alder, but we'll damage his operation to ensure he sits up and takes notice. Then, when I've got him where I want him, I'll reel him in.

I slap more than a few backs and get mine slapped in return. The mood is one of anticipation, adrenaline starting to build in our veins.

I talk to Curtis with Salem beside me. The prospect seems to take it as an honour he's being included in some of the information we're not sharing with Wrangler, but then, he's been prospecting for longer. I relieve him of the prospecting duties so he's got a chance to get his head around exactly what we need him to do. Hovering, I'm pleased to see him listening carefully to, then asking questions of Salem who I notice is still walking with a fucking limp. But he insists he'll strap it up and will be good to go tonight.

Dan, well, he impresses me too. Though nobody's asked him, seeing Wrangler struggling to keep everyone in fresh beers, he busies himself helping the prospect, replenishing tables and taking away empties and, because of what's coming tonight, we're turning a blind eye to people smoking inside for once, keeping the ash trays clean.

The ash trays that remind me of Smoker.

We're coming to get you, Brother. Not leaving you alone any longer than we can help.

When I snag a sandwich for myself, I take a moment to pull Patsy toward me, and like we spent the night, holding her cheek against my chest for a moment. She gives me strength, and a purpose, allowing me to take comfort from her. Something, someone to come home to. In a brief moment of quiet contemplation, I realise this is what I've been missing all my life.

After a hard day I'd pull myself back up and go home to keep Kim happy and satisfied, seeing that all her needs were met and catered to. Patsy's already showing she's different. She's made sure I've had enough to eat—all my brothers as well come to that, seeing a second round of sandwiches was needed and making them without being asked. She's not asking for information that I'm unable to give her, as though she's decided that now I'm set on a course she won't be able to change it, relieving me of extra pressure of justifying myself to her.

When I finally have to leave, she pulls herself up a little straighter, looks me in the eye and tells me to come back as soon as I can. No pleading, no tears, no begging to change something she can't influence. My eyes linger on her a moment before I walk out the door.

My phone rings as I reach my bike. I take it out and answer it.

"Prez."

"Deuce. What's up?"

"Kink came out for a smoke. I walked past and pretended to tie up my shoelace. He doesn't know what Niran was talking about. The food's crap and the service poor and sloppy. Reboot hasn't been recognised—he says it's a whole different team working tonight, except for the manager. There are three waiters from what he can see, no female waitstaff. And he saw two more in the kitchen when he went to the head."

"Thanks Deuce. That's useful to know. Did Kink have anything else for you?"

"That's it. They're staying as long as they can before they get kicked out."

I end the call and beckon the brothers around me. "Kink's reported back. The staff are all different tonight. Five men and the manager. That's all he's been able to see."

"There were five there last night too." Salem meets my eye. "Five men, including the one who killed Smoker."

"So eleven in total?"

"And whoever's coming with the illegals through the tunnel," I warn them not to forget. But there's seventeen of us not including Curtis, our lookout. Salem's strapping around his ankle has seemed to do the trick, and he's barely limping as he strides to his bike. But he'd have to be half dead before he'd agree to being left behind. I'm just glad I'm not a man down as it looks like we could outnumber them. But I won't be taking that to the bank until we're certain.

CHAPTER THIRTY-SIX

Lost

We've been over our strategy so many times as soon as we arrive at the spot where we're going to park up, men pile out of the trucks or dismount their bikes and assemble in the groups we'd agreed on.

Salem puts himself in charge of distributing guns and extra ammunition, as well as Kevlar vests. The guns had been brought in the trucks to avoid men riding bikes being stopped and found to be carrying, no one wanted to be dragged off to jail tonight. As men took their equipment, they handed over their cuts, more than one folding theirs carefully, and caressing it before giving it up. A lump comes into my throat as I hope all will be riding home wearing their colours by the time we've wrapped this up.

Niran and Grumbler are leading one team who'll be going to the auto-shop. Their part of the plan is to take out the men guarding the captives. When it's safe, they'll free who they find there, get them into the same trucks used by the traffickers, and on my signal, take them to a hospital and drop them off. That part can't happen too early as we want no one to be tipped off while the body count is still rising.

Grumbler himself has insisted he'll take custody of Smoker's body, and I'm happy to assign him that task, knowing he'll treat our fallen brother with the respect he deserves.

I'm accompanying Dart and the rest of the brothers who'll be concentrating on the restaurant itself. Again, our plan is to dispose of the men waiting for whoever's coming through that tunnel tonight. Then, once the trapdoor is opened, the final piece will fall into place.

Will we get Alder? According to Shark, he could be there if he's going to check the merchandise himself, but I think it's unlikely. Still, my heart beats faster at the thought of going home to Patsy and telling her her problems are over forever. *One day soon, if I have my way, I'll be telling her exactly that.*

I wait for the voice in my head warning me I'm going to fuck up, but Snake stays quiet and keeps any dead thoughts he may have to himself. If he appears, I'll just tell him to go fuck himself.

Silent and serious men are waiting for my signal. *This is it.* I enjoy just one more moment of peace before letting all hell loose, in the form of Devils of course, all seeking retribution for the callous loss of one of their own last night.

"All clear?" I ask quietly.

"Clear." Tonight it's Curtis's voice that comes over crisp in my ear.

Then I raise my chin and my hand, and that's all it takes. Around me brothers slide into their pre-agreed formation like well-oiled cogs in a clock.

I'm in the lead of my team with Dart beside me. Keeping to the shadows, we walk down the street, approaching the restaurant with caution. We're taking the chance the operation has run smoothly and undetected for so long, they won't be expecting an attack. Of course, taking Shark out was a risk that his absence might be seen as a warning and that they might be more cautious tonight, but Plan B caters for that.

When we come to the darkened end of the block, I notice it's because tonight the streetlights aren't working. Purposefully for a trade best done out of sight, but also contributing positively to our mission. Dart and I split up. I, with Pennywise, Salem, Token, Deuce and Reboot to guide us once we're inside, approach the back entrance. Dart and his team will go to the front and come in once I give the signal. We're expecting the front door to be locked, but the windows are glass so tonight, in case there's a lookout in place, he'll need to use force to come in rather than taking the time to pick the lock. I'm hopeful the back door will be left unlocked for easy access for those coming from the auto-shop. But if need be, it's dark enough there that Token will be able to work his magic and get us in.

As luck would have it, the door isn't just not secured, it's wide open, and I can hear voices inside.

I stand back, signalling unnecessarily for quiet as words float out to my ears.

"That asshole Shark hasn't turned up again." The accent is Hispanic.

"He could be running late."

"Not the fuckin' first time he's pulled a disappearing trick. Well he's not fuckin' getting his cut from tonight."

I grin in the darkness, glad Shark had proved to be unreliable, and that his non-appearance isn't apparently any cause for concern.

"I left the back door open in case he turns up."

"If he turns up, he'll be running into my fuckin' fist," the man with the accent says.

"I hear you, Enrico," the native English speaker agrees. "I'm going to have a smoke."

"Sure, you've got plenty of time."

I don't need to tell them as Deuce, Token and Reboot follow my lead, pressing our backs against the wall, while Pennywise inches forward moving closer to the door, followed by Salem as back up.

The man coming out with a pack of cigarettes in his hand doesn't have a chance as Pennywise's strong arm pulls him back and expertly slashes his throat. Salem helps his brother carry the body out of sight.

Deuce mimes something, I nod showing it's a good idea. He takes out his own smokes and lights one, then stands with his back to the door. His form is only a silhouette and should buy us a few seconds grace.

"Gordon? Get your ass back in here now."

Deuce puffs on his cigarette making the tip glow orange.

"Did you fuckin' hear me? Enrico wants you." The man appears at the door and takes his final step forward. Salem and Pennywise have retaken their positions, and this time it's Salem who does the honours.

Two down.

"We're going inside," I murmur quietly.

"Copy that," Dart replies from his position out front.

I tap Reboot on the shoulder. He indicates the door, and waves to the right. I just wanted the confirmation as a reminder of where the storeroom with the trapdoor is. Then, I move to the lead and taking a breath, step into the lion's den.

I can hear voices and raucous laughter, loud enough to cover the muffled sound of my boots.

"Who the…?"

The man who's appeared from nowhere makes a move for his gun, but Deuce is faster, moving as quick as lightening to my side, covering the man's mouth with his hand and holding him steady for Pennywise's knife. This time we leave him where he's fallen, no time to move him outside.

I eye a case of bottles and indicate them with my hand. Salem and Deuce take up positions outside the closed storeroom door, while Pennywise, Token and Deuce cover the hallway that leads to the restaurant itself.

"Distraction in two," I speak quietly again.

"Got it, Prez," Dart replies in my ear.

Then after counting the two brief seconds in my head, knock the case off the shelf.

It does the job.

We've taken out three men, but there's Enrico left, and also the men who were laughing. At least two more from the different voices I'd been able to distinguish.

Oh, and the one who comes rushing out of the storeroom, allowing Salem to make his second kill of the night.

Three men come down the hallway. "What the fuck?" Enrico's voice snarls. "You be fuckin' careful, that's my stock…"

He cares about the restaurant?

"I want him alive." I don't have to be quiet anymore.

What we don't want is them shooting. A gunshot would warn their comrades in the auto-shop, that's if by now there's any left breathing, but I can't take the chance there are not as I haven't yet had the all clear from my sergeant-at-arms.

Fuck, but I've a good team around me. Knives flash, punches are thrown, the air punctuated with oomphs and the sound of fists hitting flesh. Then there's the sound of reinforcements making their way in from the front.

By the time Dart arrives Enrico's been overpowered and Pennywise is zip-tying his hands, and the other two men are dead.

"Front of the restaurant is clear," Dart tells me first. "Two men dead." Then looks around and shakes his head. "Could have left something for us." He nods at Token and Salem and the other body at their feet.

"You can have whoever comes up from the tunnel," I tell my VP seriously. Then look around. "Anyone injured?"

As they're assuring me no, the element of surprise and lack of expectation of any threat had made our job easy.

And I'm further relieved to hear, "All clear here," coming in

Grumbler's voice in my ear. "Do you want me to open up the holding pens?"

Pens are where you keep animals. I hate the term that he's used, but that's exactly what they are.

"No, stick to the plan." Like me, I know he'll want whoever's been imprisoned freed as soon as we can, but I can't have screaming and traumatised women stepping in front of a gun. Or running off into the streets of San Diego sounding the alarm. I certainly don't want the cops turning up and finding us surrounded by dead bodies. Quickest way to get a one-way ticket to a different type of pen than the ones Grumbler wants to open.

"Grumbler. You've got a truck coming up the road. Maybe nothing… Nah. It is. It's stopping outside. One, no two men getting out. Doesn't seem to be anyone else."

"On it."

Curtis and Grumbler's voices cease. I'm holding my breath, looking around I see the others doing the same. Then the sergeant-at-arms voice sounds again. "Problem dealt with. Neither of them Alder, Prez. Looked like extra muscle."

"Copy," I confirm.

"Fuckin' murdering assholes." Enrico's been swearing at us for a while, but I'd tuned him out.

Ignoring his protestations, I spit a question at him. "What's the procedure? Who are you expecting through the tunnel? How many of your men?"

"Enough to fuckin' kill you," he rasps out.

I highly doubt that. Instead I turn to Reboot with the intention of telling him to open the trapdoor up when I pause. What if there's a signal they wait for, and not getting it, hustle back through the tunnel instead? I can't afford to miss anything, however small it might seem. I turn again to Enrico. "You want to live? Or die like your men?"

He huffs loudly. "As if you're going to let me walk."

"I might," I tell him. "Or, I might not. But there's a chance I'll be lenient tonight."

"Ain't gonna cooperate with you."

I raise my eyes to Pennywise who flashes his knife. The light glints off it just right. "I'm bored," he tells me lazily. "While we're waiting, can I carve him into bits?" Without waiting for my response, he slices into Enrico's ear. Not deep by any means, but enough to sting and make it bleed. Ears bleed quite copiously, it would seem.

"No, no." Enrico shakes his head as though to ease the sting, the movement sends blood flying around. His eyes go wide, clearly feeling the warmth dribbling down his face. He looks from Pennywise to me in horror. He hadn't seemed worried about a quick death but having body parts cut off doesn't appear attractive to him in the least. "If I help you, you'll let me go, yes?"

"If you don't, I'll let Pennywise alleviate his boredom."

My threat works. "The trapdoor stays shut. They phone me, and I give them the all clear. It's only then it's opened up and I move the planks back. It's bolted from the other side."

Thank fuck he's speaking. If he hadn't, we'd have fucked it up. But I'm suspicious, and take a menacing step closer, my height making me tower above the smaller, though fairly muscular, man. "You wouldn't be lying to me, would you?" My voice comes out as a low growl.

He gulps. "No, *signor*. I'm telling the truth."

"Can you hear without an ear?" Salem asks, conversationally. "I don't know how this shit works."

Pennywise replies in an equally even tone, "Probably the outer ear, yes. But not if I pierce the ear canal."

Reboot flinches, but Enrico screams. "No. I speak truth."

His English seems to be failing him, as is his bodily control. It's Dart who points it out sneeringly, "Man's pissed himself."

Sure enough, there's a wet patch on the front of his jeans. I'm pretty certain a man with such little control of himself is a man literally scared to death. I doubt he'll be lying to me.

"They call. I reply. They open," he tells me again, as if trying to convince me.

"Your men," I ask. "Are they always the same ones?"

Enrico shakes his head. "Mostly, but I sometimes have others. And the men coming through aren't always the same."

That's good news at least. I eye him again. "Your men all Hispanic?" He nods. I glance at who I've got. Brakes is the only one who's half that ethnicity, and he's with Grumbler in the auto-shop.

But then Enrico continues, "Had a couple of blacks working for me when we were running the drug trade."

"Brakes and I are coming across. Dusty's ready to relieve Curtis if that's your plan. He and I can act as Enrico's men."

As Niran's voice sounds in my earpiece, I think for a moment. Having Curtis on lookout is one thing, having him in the thick of everything going down is another.

"He's close to being patched in," Dart reminds me.

"I'll do it." I'd forgotten Curtis's link was still live. "I'm ready, Prez."

"Dusty? Take Curtis's place, will you?" It had taken only a second to decide.

"What happens when they arrive?" Another question to the man whose pants are soaked through and stinking.

Enrico is still eyeing Pennywise warily. "One, two come up through the door. Then the merchandise. One, two more come after."

Niran, Curtis and Brakes arrive and step into the room with the trapdoor. Hastily I go through the plan that I've quickly amended. "Help them up out of the tunnel, put them at ease. Get the immigrants up, then when the final fuckers come through, we'll come in and take them out."

"They'll expect to see me."

Enrico's right. They probably will.

"You'll be in my sights, fucker," Pennywise growls. "One wrong move and I'll torture you for hours."

"Thought that was my job," Salem objects.

"You can help," Pennywise promises.

"Everyone wants to be a fuckin' enforcer." Salem rolls his eyes.

A phone ringing makes more than one of us jump. I nod at Pennywise who reaches into Enrico's pocket and pulls it out. He holds it to the man's bleeding ear and touches his knife to his other.

"They don't come up, you're Pennywise's, you got me?" I ask. When my threat's sunk in, I nod for him to answer.

"Enrico… Yes. We're organised…Yes, now."

I nod at Pennywise who slices through Enrico's zip tie while Niran slides the wood back and forth removing the planks with ease. Then as he steps back, I ease back against the door, finding a viewpoint in the gap offered by the hinges.

There's the sound of a bolt being thrown, then a man appears, grunting with the effort of lifting the wood, raising his chin when Curtis helpfully lends a hand. In a practiced move he pulls himself up and out of the void below. He nods at Enrico and gives little more than a quick unworried glance around, before indicating to someone still below.

A second man appears, taking the helpful hand offered by Niran. He then steps back.

"*Subir.*" He waves down into the tunnel and beckons upwards with his hand.

The next man is more hesitant and looks less athletic, struggling to emerge. Curtis steps forward to help. When the man is standing, he looks around, his eyes wide.

"America?" he asks, the word sounding unnatural on his lips, his voice full of wonder and hope.

When Niran agrees he has indeed reached his destination, the man falls to his knees and kisses the ground. His two escorts share a grin I find I don't like, and silently promise as soon as I get my chance, I'll wipe it off their smarmy faces.

A family appears next, the woman looking tired and weary. She hands up a baby which her husband takes from her. She's weak, needing help from above and below to make it to the top. A child, about six, appears after her. The woman who looks like she's not far from the end of her rope, then reaches for the baby which is placed back carefully in her arms.

One by one they emerge, all showing relief and emotion at having made it safely under the border, reaching the land of hope without being detected, unknowing that it could so easily have been the opposite. If Alder had his way, now they're here, instead of a new life of freedom, they'll be trapped in a hell even worse from whatever they escaped.

There are five men, two women, and the two children. Their condition shows not one of them has had an easy journey.

After the last one, another two men, not guides as they've posed to be, but guards appear.

"Transport ready?" The final man directs his question to Enrico. "Where are the girls?"

Fuck. My eyes widen. *He was expecting them to be ready and waiting.*

Enrico shrugs. "Had to take on new men. They're still learning the ropes. They're on their way now."

"They better fuckin' be," the man growls. "Ain't got time to hang around."

Niran's waiting for my signal, Curtis looking slightly nervous, but then he's never been asked to kill a man before. I need Pennywise and Salem in there and quickly.

Thinking fast, Niran says, "I think I hear them coming now."

It's the opening I want. The men group the immigrants in a corner of the room, shouting at them in Spanish, presumably telling them to stay put. Then, they go toward the door with expectant looks on their faces, clearly prepared for a bunch of intimidated women. Instead it's Salem and Pennywise who are first through the door, heading for the men waiting while Niran and Brakes are already behind their targets closing in. Brakes takes the man closest to him and guns come out. Salem's got his target. Pennywise, his finesse now gone, hacks furiously into the man who's drawing a gun.

The last man standing grabs hold of the six-year-old who now I can tell is a little girl and holds her in front of him. But he hadn't reckoned on her father, who despite his weakened state, throws himself on him. The trio go down and it's Curtis who jumps in, his knife going into the guard's throat.

I must have been holding my breath. I now let in out and suck a deep lungful of oxygen in. I cock my head toward Dart who gives me back a sharp confirmatory nod. They are all dead. Well, all except Enrico, I'm not quite sure what to do with him now. But as rapid Spanish starts flying, and the immigrants look at the scene in horror and us in fright, I realise I need an interpreter.

"Tell them they are safe. Tell them these are bad men who would have kidnapped them and sold them into slavery. Tell them they are free to go now."

Enrico speaks rapidly in Spanish.

I notice Brakes looking on.

"My Spanish is rusty," he tells me. "But I got the gist. He said what you wanted."

The Spanish continues back and forth.

I step forward. "Anyone here speak English?"

One man tentatively holds up his hand. "I try to learn," he attempts.

"You've been tricked," I tell him. "These men were bad. They were going to sell you, not let you walk free."

His eyes widen, letting me know he got the gist. He speaks rapidly to the group surrounding him, and they huddle together.

Realising they don't have any fucking idea what's going to happen to them now, I try to keep my tone friendly. "Have you all got plans? Where were you going from here?"

"We've got a little money." The words rush out. "Not much after paying to get here. That was many *pesos*. Many many *pesos*."

"No, I don't want your money. You're free to leave."

I give them a moment to process the change in their fortunes again. I doubt I can help them. They'll presumably have some sort of idea of what they'd do when they got out this side. Their plans wouldn't have included Alder, and he wouldn't have bothered to arrange them rides, that wasn't on his agenda. Presumably they expected to make their own way once they got here, so that's what I'll leave them to do. If the authorities don't catch them, they'll be able to make their fresh new start. I wonder if it will be anything like as rosy a future as they'd expected, but they'd made their choice.

"I'd appreciate it if you didn't tell anyone about this." It's too much for him, so Enrico, at a nod from me, translates.

"Here." Dart pulls out his wallet and empties it of notes. He passes it to the father of the two children.

Well, I can't be outdone by my VP. I also empty my pockets of cash.

It looks like no one else is going to be left out, and all the immigrants are soon gratefully stuffing the little we were able to scrape up into their pockets.

Then, as Brakes indicates the way to the front door, the man with the family pauses by me and shakes my hand.

"Thank you," he says slowly and carefully. "Thank you."

If we had a common language, I think he'd say more, but his expression, the look of hope in his eyes and the hesitant smile as he holds tightly onto his child speaks volumes. Silently I wish the family well and wonder what will become of them.

After they've left, Grumbler says urgently into my ear, "Can I free the fuckin' women now?"

"You ready as we discussed?" There's a pause before he replies, his tone resigned. "Yes."

I turn to Dart. "Close that trap door and put the floor back down. Keep Enrico occupied. I'm going to the shop."

CHAPTER THIRTY-SEVEN

Lost

If Satan doesn't come calling and I live until I'm a hundred, I don't think I'll ever forget what I found when those rooms which Grumbler, as it turns out quite accurately, called holding pens were finally opened up.

Empty, they looked okay, but now, each filled with eight women, the ten foot by ten foot rooms appear cramped and crowded. They smell, as well. The women only had use of a bucket between them, one in each pen.

Grumbler opens the first, Niran the second. At first, the women don't move, just looked at them with suspicion. And so they might. I fucking hate what I'm doing, but we'd been through it time and time again at church. Immigrants who'll do their best to stay as far as possible from any sign of the authorities are one thing, American citizens are quite different and with them we can't let our faces be seen.

"Come on," Niran says, gentling his normal tone. "Let's get you out of here." His calmness is lost though, to them he's a man wearing a balaclava, probably appearing every bit as bad as the men who brought them here.

The women seem to be undecided, then one, a tall woman

probably in her late twenties or early thirties puts her arms around a couple of girls and pushes them forward. "You don't want to get hurt again," she warns them, making my gut clench. *Again.* I hate that we have to scare them.

Grumbler's encouraging the ones on his side as well, and I can hear his voice break, but he clears his throat to cover it up. As the women appear one by one, shaking with fear, I run my eyes over them all. A couple appear to be in their thirties, one looks to be a pre-teen, and the others are a range of somewhere in between.

For a moment I'm glad my face is covered as I wouldn't be able to hide my look of derision and disgust. Not at the state they're in, they're not to blame for that. But that these women were stolen away from their homes, or even if some were hookers taken from off the street, they didn't deserve to be sold like animals instead of human beings.

They cling to the rungs of the ladder attached to the sides of the pits, climbing slowly as though reluctant. Even when they're at the top, they huddle together as though broken. If I'd been worried about them making a run for it, I now dismiss that thought. These women seem beyond making the attempt. I'm glad Grumbler had the foresight to move the bodies of the men he'd killed. The sight of them would only have traumatised them further.

"Smoker's here."

Oh fuck no. I lean over the edge of the pit, my chest rising and falling as I fight to control my rage. Not only had the women been penned like cattle, half of them had been forced to share their accommodation with a dead man. No wonder they look traumatised. I wonder if there's enough therapy in the world to help them. That Smoker wasn't in the room with the youngest is the only glimmer of light.

"Bring him up." My instruction is terse.

Leaving Brakes and Blaze watching the women, Niran joins

Grumbler back in the pit, then in a fireman's lift brings Smoker up. Reverently they lay him down, crossing his hands over his chest. I stand beside him for a moment, my head bowed, knowing I'd give anything to hear him coughing again. The only blessing is, he looks peaceful.

"I, er, I closed his eyes," the tall woman says hesitantly. "You, he. He was your friend?"

I suppose it's obvious.

"Who are you?" another one asks.

"Hush. They don't like it when we speak," a younger girl says, looking around the others in warning, holding a finger to her lips.

"These are different," one says, softly. "They don't smell the same."

I'd noticed she'd had more help climbing the ladder than the rest but hadn't noticed much else. Now I examine her, I can see she's blind. Her experience must have been doubly terrifying for her.

We need to get them out of here. I need the women gone, so we can get back to support Dart.

"Go to the trucks." Smoker's body, the sight of the blind woman, the whole damn thing has made my voice sharp. I hate it, but the women jump.

We're not here to make friends, I remind myself, nothing more we can do to help them but get them somewhere safe and away from here fast.

"Different but the same," the tall woman snaps. Her back straightening, and any sympathy she might have had for me, gone.

At a signal from Grumbler, the brothers start herding the women toward the trucks. As they approach, most automatically hold out their hands, the youngest one starts weeping. It's then I notice the chains and handcuffs which are waiting for them.

Grumbler tilts his head toward me, I stare for a moment at

this new reminder of how badly these women have been treated. *Guns and tasers,* Shark's words echo in my head.

I clap my hands together, getting their attention on me. "I'm going to have to ask you to get into the trucks one last time. But no chains or fuckin' handcuffs, okay?"

A couple raise their eyes to me, but most stay staring at the ground. It's clear they have no idea they've been rescued. And why the fuck should they? All the men around them are masked.

"We're going to drop you off at a hospital, okay? There you can contact your folks and speak to the authorities. They'll get you home."

The taller woman's face comes up as I say that. Her brow creases as though she's having a hard time comprehending. After a moment, she speaks, "Is this for real?"

"It's a trick," the one who warned them against speaking tells them.

"No trick. Your nightmare is over," I confirm, trying to convey my earnestness with just my eyes and voice.

"You're playing with us," she says. "This *is* a trick."

"No trick, sweetheart." Pennywise steps up beside me.

She glances at the other women who seem to accept her as spokeswoman. "How can we trust you?"

"What option have you got?" Truthfully, I could throw open the door and let them make their own way to where they want. But there's danger lurking in every corner for a group of women left alone walking the streets. I also don't want them to be able to describe this place or its location. Not until I'm sure nothing can link it with us and our activities here tonight. And surely, dropping them off where they can receive medical attention if they need it, seems the best solution.

"Come on," Pennywise encourages her, pointing like I'd done to the two trucks.

It's easy to understand their reluctance.

The women huddle together for a moment, I let them talk.

Inside I'm brimming with frustration, wanting to hurry them up. It won't be long until someone realises the women aren't being escorted back through the tunnel, and I expect that someone to come looking for them.

"Who are you?" the one assisting the blind woman asks. "And why are you masked?"

"Friends," I tell her. "Friends who don't want to be recognised or who need thanks. Who just want to right a wrong."

"People don't act like that," someone else sneers.

"We do." Dart's come to stand beside me, but they don't seem convinced.

I sigh. "You're a group of women who were, what, picked up off the street?" Most of them give slight nods. "Do you know what the man who took you intended to do with you?" I hope I don't have to put it into words, not with the young girl listening. But I can see from their faces they hadn't been kept in the dark. I raise my chin. "Hopefully you'll be safe if you return to your homes, but the trade won't stop. The man behind this, he'll just go on. Snatching girls, keeping them prisoner. Selling them. I want him stopped."

"So why are you hiding your faces?" comes from the tall woman. "If this is a rescue like you say, we should be able to see who you are and thank you. If you were legit, you'd call the cops."

I raise my chin, acknowledging her point. "Sure. But the man I'm after has already got the feds after him, and he's managed to evade them for months. As far as we know, he's holed up in Mexico, maybe further away than that. But his network still works for him. Women keep getting kidnapped and forcefully taken where they don't want to go."

"If you think he's out of reach of the cops and the feds," She looks scornful, "how are you going to bring him down? Who are you, some sort of secret military organisation?"

"Delta force?" one of her companions says, hopefully.

"Nah." I don't bother to fabricate a lie. "This is personal to me."

It's a risk letting them go. Keeping them would be a bargaining chip I could use to bring Alder out of hiding, but one or two I could hide, sixteen? Too many to keep out of sight and not risk escaping, not unless I want to chain them in the same way as their captors, and I'm not stooping to that level.

No, I'm left with the hope that finding his tunnel empty, no girls coming through and no immigrants ending up where he expects them to will send him a message and make him want to talk to me. I'll tempt him with an offer of doing business together. Then, when I do smoke him out, I'll get justice.

Of course it will be justice at the end of my gun. After making him hurt. After the mental anguish my old lady suffered and the physical pain of her son, I won't be leaving it all up to Salem, and will be landing quite a few punches myself.

The tall woman looks around again. Then she speaks to the others. "Come on. What option have we got? What's the worst that can happen? We've had hope dangled in front of us and snatched away? Can't see a purpose in that. So, let's get into the trucks and trust that they're taking us somewhere we want to go."

I wish they were happy, excited to be free. But some are weeping when they get up in the truck for what I know is the final time, helped by Grumbler and Niran. Then Kink and Blaze drive them away.

A few minutes later, Dusty comes back with the other trucks. Reverently we load Smoker into it, and take a second to pay our respects, then Dusty takes off.

We've only just got the big garage doors slid back shut behind them when the voice in my ear speaks.

"Got company, Prez. They're trying to get the trapdoor open."

"On my way."

Everyone left in the auto-shop follows my lead back across to the restaurant.

"What do you want to do?"

"Get Enrico." When he appears, I jerk my head and Salem cuts the zip ties off his hands and frees him. "One word that shouldn't be said," I threaten, "and you're dead."

He gives me a sharp nod.

I stand back. Dusty and Snips pull back the planks and the trapdoor is thrown open.

"What the fuck, Enrico? Where are the bitches?" A voice comes up from below, but no one comes into sight.

He's being cautious.

"They're on their way," Enrico answers. "A bitch tried to run. Once one got loose, they all tried to scatter. Had to lock them all down until they got her back. They're coming across now."

"Who was the stupid asshole that let her run?"

"Hernando," Enrico supplies.

"Fucker's dead." There's the sound of a man huffing as he starts to heave himself up. A Hispanic appears, then another. Then they bend to help a third man out.

A white man comes into sight, his eyes shooting daggers at the restaurant owner. He steps to one side, and two other men come up and flank him. "I might as well inspect what I'm getting now I'm here."

His words, as well as his appearance, confirm my suspicions. *It's Alder himself.*

We've hit the jackpot.

I feel like a kid with all my Christmases coming at once as Salem and Pennywise grab hold of his henchmen, overpowering them and taking them out.

Alder stiffens, looks around in consternation. "You're fucking dead," he tells Enrico. "You didn't warn me!" he roars.

"In his defence," I step forward, "he didn't have much choice. Salem? Search him."

Alder visibly flinches, but with our guns pointed at him holds his arms out to his sides. Salem relieves him of his Glock, then nods to me confirming he's no longer carrying.

"Who the fuck are you?" Alder blusters, shaking Salem's hands off and all but shuddering. "You're going to fucking regret this. Where's my stock?"

"I'm Lost," I introduce myself. "President of the Satan's Devils MC. If by stock you mean the women, I've got them safe."

His eyes narrow. "You're a dead man if you don't give them back."

I allow a smirk to appear on my face. "I don't think you're in a position to argue."

Pressing his lips together, he digests what I've said. For a moment it looks like he's thinking, then, he starts to speak again. "Your MC branching out? You want in on this trade?"

"Could be I want to use the tunnel for my own business." I don't, but it's kind of fun jerking his chain. And there is some method to my madness. "Why don't we go somewhere more comfortable and discuss it?"

It's worded as a suggestion, but he has to realise with his men dead, he's outnumbered, disarmed and left with no alternative. I've got plans for Alder once I get him back to the compound. Suffice to say, he'll never be leaving again. Having seen those traumatised women tonight, I've no doubt Salem will get inventive, and after I've got my shots in, I have no compulsion to hold him back.

I also don't want to hang around long. Dawn will soon be breaking, and I want to be gone before full daylight.

"I can't have the tunnel found," Alder protests. "My operation here is watertight."

"Except, it isn't," I point out. "After you." I indicate the doorway, and tell Dart, "Bring him too." Him is Enrico who doesn't look enthusiastic at the thought of our hospitality.

"I'm not going with you." Alder takes a step back, bringing him closer to the trap door.

"I think you are," Grumbler growls menacingly from behind him. "You can walk or I'll fuckin' carry you."

With his gammy leg I think it will need more than just him, Alder's not a small man. But it seems having Salem's hands on him were enough, as he arranges his features into a defeated scowl, and starts to move toward the doorway.

I follow, working out the logistics of transport in my head, thanking fuck we brought the trucks. I'll be going with Alder as I'm not taking my eyes off him, not when I'm this close to removing the threat to my old lady once and for all. It's not that I don't trust my men, I want to take full responsibility.

"I'll go get the truck," Curtis offers. I thank him with a raise of my chin, and he pushes past.

More leisurely, to give Curtis a few moments head start, we step out of the restaurant and emerge under a sky that's lightening, weak sunlight already filtering through from under a wispy cloud. It's another gorgeous San Diego morning. I scan left and right, but it's still early, and the area is deserted. In the distance there are sounds of the city awakening, and already the noise of engines from the planes flying overhead.

The truck comes into sight. I watch Alder's face; he isn't giving much away. His look is more calculating than defeated.

I can't fucking wait to start getting answers from him, with Salem's help. The most burning one, of course, is why he's been so intent on finding my old lady.

I'm still staring at him when a perfect round hole appears in his forehead, and he drops to the ground.

Pennywise launches forward, immediately feeling for a pulse.

"He's fuckin' dead."

"What the fuck?" Dart leaps forward as Curtis gets out of the truck leaving the engine running. Both join the rest of us standing bemused around the dead body at our feet.

One second, two… Then I start moving. "Get Enrico in the truck."

"What do you want to do with him?" Salem asks.

"Put him in the restaurant then close it up." Just one more dead body that I suspect will be found soon. But we're all wearing gloves and hopefully have left no evidence to connect them to us.

As my instructions are followed, I notice Token staring at his phone. When he shows me the screen there's an alert that's come up. It simply says:

Pennywise is good. I'm better.

"Get back to the fuckin' compound." I don't have a word to describe how furious I am. I don't think I've ever felt this angry in my life.

As I sit in the front seat, and Dart gets in the driver's side as Curtis is watching Enrico in the back, I'm fuming. *Alder's dead.* Quick and clean. He never knew what was happening, never had a chance to suffer my retribution. My hands clench and unclench. *I needed this. Needed to kill him myself.*

Now he can't give me answers.

Now he can't pay for his crimes.

"Church, now," I roar as I enter the clubhouse.

It's an instruction I barely need give as it seems everyone is as angry and discombobulated as I am.

Even as riled as I am, I pause to place my hand briefly on Smoker's chair before going to my seat. He's dead, and the motherfucker who took Alder down stopped me getting my revenge. We might have got the man who pulled the trigger, but not the one who gave the command.

"What the fuck was that, Token?"

He doesn't pretend not to know what I'm talking about.

"Fuck knows, Prez." He slams his hand down. "Asshole has tech skills beyond anything I've seen."

"He's got sniper skills too," Pennywise growls. "That's what he meant. Fuck knows where he took that shot from."

"He was there, waiting," Token agrees. "He knew our every move and was watching and waiting."

I try to calm myself down. "He wanted to take Alder out himself. Why? Didn't he trust us?"

"He can't have believed we'd work with Alder, could he?"

I glance at my VP. "I've no fuckin' idea. Your guess is as good as mine."

"Does it matter?" Niran asks, his tone measured and reasonable. "The man is dead."

What matters is that I didn't get the satisfaction of killing him. Or finding the answer to the mystery he took to his grave.

I bow my head and rub my eyes. Fuck, it's late, or early, whichever way you want to look at it. Maybe Niran is right and I should just let this go. Looking up again, I note the tired looks on the faces around. Not a few are trying to hide their yawns.

"Alder's gone. It's over. Let's go and get some rest."

"What do you want to do about Enrico?"

"I doubt if he's got anything useful to tell us, but tomorrow we'll ask." I raise my hardened eyes. "He condoned and facilitated that business for years. Can't say he deserves any less than being dispatched to Satan."

From the hollers of agreement around me, I almost feel sorry for the restaurant owner/criminal we've currently got in the brig. Brothers were denied taking their revenge out on Alder, so Enrico will suffer instead.

CHAPTER THIRTY-EIGHT

Patsy

"Lost?" I sit upright, glancing at the clock by the side of the bed, noticing it's morning.

I'd tried to wait up for Lost, but he'd been out so late eventually I'd come to bed. I hadn't expected to fall asleep, but it seems like I had.

As Lost removes his cut and then tiredly takes off his t-shirt, boots and jeans, I run my eyes over his body checking for any injury. There are none visible, even though he wears a pained look on his face.

"What happened, Lost?" I'm not certain he's going to talk to me.

Still, without saying a word, he gets into bed, pulling my body against him. It's only when my head is in its normal place, resting on his chest, he begins speaking, and my pillow vibrates.

"Alder's dead."

I gasp. "You killed him?"

He might have chuckled, but there's derision in it instead of mirth. "Nah, babe. Not me. Not my men."

"But he's no longer able to bother me?" As the words sink in, it feels like an enormous weight has been lifted and I hardly dare believe what it means. "I'm free? Dan's free? Dan can go back to being Connor again? Oh my God, Lost. This is amazing news."

"Yeah, I suppose it is."

"You're not happy?" I ask, incredulously.

"He died before I could question him," he replies grumpily. "Now we'll never know why he was after you."

"I don't care. He's gone. That's all that matters to me." He's no longer a threat to me or my family. The implications start to sink in. "I can see Beth. Oh, Lost, do you see what this means? I can be there when my grandchild is born." Impulsively I pull myself up and leaning over, kiss him. "This is the best news you could have given to me."

He gives me a small smile. "I don't like loose ends."

A thought occurs to me. "Is everyone okay? No one hurt?"

"Everyone's fine, babe. It's just been a long night."

He needs his sleep. I snuggle back into position again, but I can feel his heart racing, beating as fast as my own. On my part it's because this man has righted my world. He's done exactly what he said he would do, he's taken on my enemy and kept me safe while he did. Do I feel sorry a man has been killed? A few months ago, I never thought I could be bloodthirsty, but Alder's no normal man. It's only by chance that the Devils found my son and rescued him, otherwise he'd be dead. I could never forgive him for that.

"Patsy." Suddenly Lost moves, and I'm on my back with him looming over me. "I can't sleep," he tells me.

"I may have a remedy to help," I brazenly reply.

"Fuck woman, have you any idea how much you mean to me? And you're all mine now."

His mouth lowers, he takes my lips. Our tongues meet and dance, then he pulls away. Lifting the t-shirt of his that I wore to bed, he pulls it right off, feasting his eyes on my breasts, lavishing attention on my nipples, before telling me, "Gonna eat you out now."

Yes please.

Already familiar with my body he doesn't need long before I'm twisting the sheets in my hands and crying out his name. Then, pausing only to .don a condom, and apply lube, he's inside me.

Both of us sigh.

He proceeds to do what he does so well, that bucking, twisting action with his hips. It's not just his physical prowess, but when he meets my eyes, holding my gaze, signalling all the emotion he feels for me, mine signalling all of mine back, that makes our lovemaking something that could not be bettered.

We come, together. Then clutch at each other, holding each other close. Slowly our heart rates return to normal, then our breathing slows. Held tight in each other's arms, we fall asleep together.

It's an anti-climax in many ways, I think to myself, some hours later. Almost as if the last couple of days hadn't happened. Lost has disappeared to talk to Token in his office, Dan's gone with Salem to the hangar they're converting into a custom bike workshop. Other brothers are hanging around, playing pool or just talking and drinking.

The atmosphere has changed, instead of quiet and secrecy, the men are speaking loudly again, mainly about bikes.

In one corner Pennywise is getting a tattoo on his arm.

The door opens, and a child's cry has me turning around. Alex is walking in, preceded by a young boy I haven't yet met, though who I've heard about, and a fussy baby in her arms. I hurry across to meet her.

"Can I take her?"

"Please do," Alex laughs. "She's teething. Poor kid has had it rough, temperature and a rash. That's why I've not been around for a couple of days. Hey, Tyler. Say hello to Patsy."

Tyler comes over with a swagger that reminds me of Dart.

He stops in front of me and looks me up and down. "Pleased to meetcha," he says at last.

"He's nine, going on an old man." Alex's eyes are full of laughter, but also pride as she looks at her son.

"Can I go find Eva?" Tyler asks.

"Um, I think she's busy right now," I tell them, having seen her go off with Dusty awhile back.

"Hey, Ty. Come here a moment," Blaze calls out, winking at Alex.

When the kid turns and strides across the room, I see the back of the cut he's wearing. I adore it. It reads 'Junior Prospect', just as I'd been told.

"Dart tells me your problems are over," Alex begins, waiting for my nod. "And that you're sticking around. It will be so good to have another old lady here." She views the room, then turns back and winks. "Who do you think we need to work on to increase our numbers? It would be good to have a few more old ladies."

I do the same as her and examine the people in the room, realising in the short time I've been here, these men have become friends. But would any of them be in the market for an old lady? The idea makes me snort. "Do you think anyone would take any of this lot on?"

She giggles. "Let me just go drop this off, and then I'll come back and relieve you of Isla." She waves the bag at me as if to show me what 'this' is.

"I'm fine holding onto her. You take your time." I lower my face and breathe in that unique baby scent, realising that in a few months I'll be able to meet my grandbaby, and no one could stop me now. *I could ring Beth.* I freeze. It had become so ingrained in me that I couldn't, for some insane reason, the thought of contacting her hadn't entered my head. I decide I'll do that as soon as I've handed back Isla.

The television above the bar is on, but no one's paying much attention to it, and I doubt anyone knows even what program is playing, until Pennywise's shout.

Blaze turns the tattoo gun off, and now we can hear what the newscaster is telling us.

"The DEA have today found a tunnel entrance in a restaurant in San Diego. Initial reports show it goes to Tijuana in Mexico. It appears to have been the site of a mass killing earlier today which the DEA are initially putting down as fighting between rival gang members. The tunnel was discovered as a result of an anonymous tip-off. No drugs were found on the premises, but it's likely that drugs were smuggled in this way."

"You practicing to be a grandparent, babe?" Lost puts his arms around me and smiles down at the baby in my arms who's sucking her thumb.

"Did you see that?" I nod toward the television.

"They're always finding tunnels or stopping smugglers," he replies, seeming to be unconcerned.

"Yes, but…"

He cuts off what I was going to say by kissing me. When someone wolf whistles he shows them the finger.

"Fuck, it's like watching your parents," Deuce complains.

"Then look away," Lost replies unrepentantly, and kisses me again.

"Get a room." That's Blaze. "I can't concentrate." He pretends to cover his eyes.

I glare at Kink as he starts to open his mouth. "You can't say anything," I call over to him. "Not when you drag naked women around in here."

Grumbler comes over and slaps Lost's back. "She'll do," he says, with a wide grin on his face. "She'll fuckin' do."

"She will that." Lost cups his hands around my face, then touches his forehead to mine.

When he pulls back, there's an intense look in his eyes. Then he takes a deep breath and reaches for a bag he must have carried out and placed on the table behind him. The bag I saw Alex carrying in earlier. He opens it and takes something out.

It's a leather cut. On the front it has a patch which says 'First Old Lady', and on the reverse, 'Property of Lost'.

It's a moment with all the seriousness of a wedding ceremony but with none of the normal trappings. The television has been switched off and he's distracted me sufficiently I've forgotten what I'd been watching. The room has gone completely silent, so much so you could hear a pin drop. In the periphery of my vision I see Salem and Dan have returned, even the club girls have put in an appearance. But everyone seems to be holding their breath.

"You gonna stay in San Diego, Patsy?"

Lost takes in air and holds it.

I realise I could go back home. But Colorado isn't home anymore. My daughter lives there, but I can visit her any time I want. Home is here. With Lost.

"Yes."

He lets his breath out.

With shaking hands I reach out and Lost reverently holds the cut so I can put my arms through it, then holds onto it until it rests on my shoulders. I know I'll have to thank Alex as it fits perfectly.

"I take you as my ol' lady," Lost says, quietly.

"I take you as my old man," I respond.

"I pronounce you Prez and First Old Lady," Dart calls out.

"I'll drink to that," Dusty quips and raises his bottle.

Lost grimaces for a second, and I wonder what's wrong until he says loudly, "Drink to us, but raise your glasses to Smoker. He should have been here to celebrate with us."

"He is still fuckin' here," Brakes protests. "It will be years before the odour of nicotine fades."

I might not laugh like some of the others, but even I have to smile at the truth in Brake's words. I tell my old man earnestly,

"He'd be happy for us, Lost. You know that." And I'm already planning a send-off for him that no one will forget in a long time.

"I know," he replies softly.

"Hey, who got those patches done? 'Cause they're wrong."

"What the fuck?" Dart steps up to Bones, his posture threatening. "My ol' lady doesn't make mistakes. You need fuckin' glasses?"

Bones looks over at me and winks. "She got it the wrong way around. It should read 'Lost Property', not 'Property of Lost.'"

He cracks up, and a number of others chortle with him. I grin myself. Then going on tiptoe kiss my man's cheek. "He's right. I was lost, and you found me."

"Wrong way around, babe," Lost replies. "I was lost until you found me. Being lost became my way of life. Don't feel lost anymore."

The clubroom door opens again. As everyone's here, we all turn automatically. I freeze to the spot, disbelieving, then my feet are moving, running across the room as two people appear.

I stop right in front of them, hardly daring to credit the evidence of my own eyes. "Bethany?" I start, hesitantly.

Her eyes are wide. "Mom?" Her hands reach out and turn me, reading the back of my cut. "You? Lost? Mom!" she squeals as she turns me back. "Mom? I said you might find yourself a man, but I didn't expect… First old lady?" she recites the words on the front. Then her hands go to her hips. "Uh-huh. I find myself a biker. You had to go one better. You've snagged yourself a prez."

She can't keep the act up. Only a second passes before her arms come around me. As always I marvel I only just come up to her shoulders, and in our normal fashion, or ever since she was a teenager and put on her growth spurt, I let myself be hugged.

"Guess that answers that question, darlin'," Ink drawls. "Patsy's not coming back to Colorado."

Ah. It hits me then that she might have expected me to. "Bethany, I'm sorry. I, well, decisions were made when it seemed I'd never be able to come back. I…"

"Don't be silly, Mom. You've got a new life, and I've got Ink." She links her arms through that of her man. "Everything will work out. We no longer need to ring or visit in secret. We're only a few hours flight away, and you can come stay when the baby is born."

"Try and keep me away. But, how did you know? How did you know it was safe to come?" I realised I'd been so pleased and so shocked, I hadn't questioned her appearance.

"Lost rang Demon early this morning," Ink explains. "We wanted to get the first flight we could manage to get seats on. Beth couldn't wait to see you."

Whereas I'm a bad mom. My first thought hadn't been to contact my daughter. I hadn't even called.

"Mom." Beth's got my mom tone off pat. "If I'd just gotten myself a hot man, I'd have better things to do than check up on my adult daughter."

"It's not that," I fluster. "I haven't got my head around all this yet. It still feels unbelievable that Alder's not out there any longer. Going to take more than a minute for that to settle in my head."

Ink grins at me. "Now you can really enjoy living in California."

"Bethie."

Connor must have come up to us while I'd been fixated on Beth, trying to see whether she was showing yet. She's not, but it won't be long I suspect.

"Give me a hug, Connor."

While my daughter and son, both six-foot-two hug, standing alongside Ink who's taller, I feel petite.

Arms come around me, and I lean back into the chest of my man. "Happy?" he asks.

"I couldn't be happier."

Then when Ink reaches out his hand and Lost and him do some weird handshake involving thumbs interlinked, I realise they've not been properly introduced before.

"This is my… biker-in-law," I remember at the last moment, like me and Lost, they've not tied the knot officially. "And my daughter, Beth."

"Kind of got that," Lost drawls. "You're both welcome."

"Mom, I've been planning it all the way down here." As Ink rolls his eyes, I guess he bore the brunt of whatever she's talking about.

"Planning what?" I prompt.

"Now you can be there, Ink and I will be getting married. Soon, while I can still fit into a nice dress."

Now I'm passed back from Lost to Beth as her arms wrap around me once again. My tears join hers. Happy tears, of course.

To my great delight, Ink and Beth decide to take a mini vacation in California and stay at the club for a few days. I end up grateful for Beth's help, in addition to that of Alex and Eva, when I do take on my formal duties of old lady and I start planning the logistics of Smoker's funeral.

The loss of a Satan's Devils' brother is a big deal, I find, particularly when he lost his life defending his brothers. Not only was everyone in our chapter going to attend but also contingents from Utah, Colorado, Vegas and Arizona. The question of housing them all caused a few headaches, not to mention all the food to be delivered and prepared. Connor helped Wrangler and Curtis with the gallons of beer they delivered, the amount unbelievable, but heaven forbid they should chance running out.

Smoker had served his country many years back, so the Patriot Riders were going to attend to pay respects to their fallen comrade.

There must have been well over a hundred bikes lining the

route as the hearse took Smoker to the crematorium on the day of his funeral. That wasn't his final journey, however, as he returned strapped to the back of Lost's bike, his ashes to be spread in the hills behind the compound. Smoker was home. He was finally at rest.

"You did good," Lost tells me when we've waved the last of the visiting bikers away. The clubhouse seems almost silent now, with just the San Diego men.

"I'm just pleased it's over." Lost doesn't ask me to explain. There's a lot that I'm glad is in my rearview now. Organising and overseeing Smoker's wake had thrown me fully into being the prez's old lady, and I'd been worried about messing it up. I'd been introduced to so many bikers I couldn't remember all the names, except for the scariest one, the prez of the mother chapter, Drummer, whose steely stare had had me at a loss for words. Until his old lady introduced herself, and we were soon discussing her two little boys. Yes, the last couple of days had been stressful, making sure the arrangements all went off without a hitch, which they did, and making Lost proud of me as his old lady, which it seems, I had.

I lean my elbows on the railing, and look out toward the ocean, as the last days and weeks go through my head. Of course, I'm also pleased not to have to worry about Alder. And, there's a tiny part of me, that was pleased when Beth returned to Colorado. I loved seeing her but wanted to spend time with my man.

For the first time in days, Lost and I had time to ourselves, and had come out for what he correctly called, wind therapy.

"Are you okay, Lost?" I know there's something niggling at him.

"I don't like an unsolved mystery," he admits. "One day, Patsy, I'll find out. I'll find the motherfucker who killed Alder."

"Wouldn't it be better to just leave it?" I turn around to face him. "Alder's dead, so's Phil. We've got our life ahead of us."

He looks over my head, out toward the Pacific glistening in the distance. "Drummer's uneasy."

The mention of his name makes me shiver. Nice guy. If he was on your side, that is. I wouldn't want to get on the wrong side of him if he hardened those steely-grey eyes. I admire Sam coping with him.

"Why is he uneasy?"

"Because the same darn thing happened to Demon in Colorado." As I raise my eyes with my brow furrowed, Lost nods. "There was a man, a fucker who dealt in the skin trade, and by that, I'm not meaning fur. Demon's crew caught him. He was taken out with one shot from a sniper rifle before they could deal with him."

"Like Alder?" I'd managed to get the details out of him one night by using my womanly wiles. Seems like my man will do a lot for a blow job.

"Two clubs, two identical hits?" I start to see why Drummer's worried.

"Only good thing is that the fucker seems to be on the right side."

"Yours," I breathe.

But he contradicts, "Not ours, babe. Just not on the side of the fuckers who look on women as commodities."

"What does Demon think?"

Lost shrugs. Whether he knows the Colorado prez's thoughts or not, he's not going to share. Instead, he starts toying with my hair. When he leans in and kisses me, his semi-hard cock makes its presence known against the material of his jeans.

I'm not surprised when his next words are, "Come on, babe. Let's get back. There's something I want to show you."

He takes hold of my hand, I hold back. Laughing I tell him, "I think I might have seen it before."

"Not like this." He tugs me again, making my feet move. "I might have borrowed some things from Kink."

I stop dead. “Like handcuffs?”

“Fuck, babe. You’d like that, wouldn’t you?” His eyes go wide when he turns to face me. Then he’s back around the other way making me walk forward again. “Like ropes, floggers, whips…”

I slide up behind him and put my arms around his waist, but before he can start the engine, I lean forward and speak into his ear. “Just how fast can this thing go?”

EPILOGUE

Stormy

"I'm calling you back, Stormy."

Er, fucking no to that. "I did what had to be done, Pip."

A sigh loaded with exasperation comes down the phone. "No, you fuckin' didn't. You had a task—"

"Which I completed," I say, ire in my voice. "The governor's daughter is back with her family. I hung around. The police collected her from the hospital." I shake my head though. Fuck knows what damage had been done to that young girl. But at least she hadn't been taken over the border and sold.

"I gave you the task."

"I got it done. Lost and his crew were already all over it. We lost track of her coming across the country, but I knew where she was going to end up. They had the manpower, I just helped them along."

"Without them, we'd never have gotten the coordinates."

"Which we had to decipher for them." I sigh myself, not understanding why Pip's all over this.

"You really can't tell, can you?" His voice sounds clipped. "They're Satan's Devils, Stormy."

I let the pause draw out, then complain, "I pointed them in all the right directions."

"You're making a habit of this—"

"I made the kill."

He snorts. "And left them frustrated as hell. You're doing it too often. And enjoying it too much."

Can't argue with his last point. I grin. Then come up with an excuse. "There was a chance they might cut a deal with Alder."

"No there wasn't." Pip's frustration comes down the line. "Two hits. Two clubs. How long until someone puts this together?"

"They needed my help."

"Sure, they needed *our* help. And we gave it to them. But they should have been allowed to take Alder out themselves. You're running the risk of exposing us."

"I'm not," I protest, loudly. "I was nowhere close. I knew I could make the shot and I did."

"Not questioning your fuckin' ability. I question your method. Lost will be going crazy, it was his hit, not yours. No point arguing Stormy. One time, I gave you the benefit of the doubt. Not doing that again. You're coming back to the nest."

"I don't play well with others," I growl.

"Too fuckin' bad. You're going to get your ass home."

COMING SOON

What do you do when your hopes and dreams come literally crashing down around you? When you find one split second, and something that wasn't your fault, stops you taking part in your hobby just when you're nearing the top?

Another rider's misjudgment, and my trial bike competition days were over.

I was angry, I admit it. I love my MC brothers, but they couldn't understand. I could still ride a bike, just no longer in a competitive environment.

Drummer took the decision to give me something else to think about, and temporarily give me some distance from Tucson. It was a simple enough task he assigned me. Make my way, of necessity slowly, to Utah, and check that chapter out.

Sure, the Utah club were friendly enough and never hesitated to support other chapters, but they were secretive. Drummer's instruction was to find out what went on behind closed doors, and for me to return with the assurance they were following the Satan's Devils rules and regulations.

The time on the road would give me a chance to clear my head, my welcome assured at my destination, as they wore the same patch on their backs. Then I'd return home, hopefully with my mood improved.

Neither Drummer or I had anticipated the mishaps along the route.

OTHER WORKS BY MANDA MELLETT

<u>Blood Brothers – A series about sexy dominant sheikhs and their bodyguards</u>

Stolen Lives (#1) Nijad and Cara

Close Protection (#2) Jon and Mia

Second Chances (#3) Kadar and Zoe

Identity Crisis (#4) Sean and Vanessa

Dark Horses (#5) Jasim and Janna

Hard Choices (#6) Aiza

<u>Satan's Devils MC - Arizona Chapter</u>

Turning Wheels (Blood Brothers #3.5, Satan's Devils #1) Wraith and Sophie

Drummer's Beat (#2) Drummer and Sam

Slick Running (#3) Slick and Ella

Targeting Dart (#4) Dart and Alex

Heart Broken (#5) Heart and Marc

Peg's Stand (#6) Peg and Darcy

Rock Bottom (#7) Rock and Becca

Joker's Fool (#8) Joker and Lady

Mouse Trapped (#9) Mouse and Mariana

Blade's Edge (#10) Blade and Tash

Heart Mended: A Satan's Devils MC Novella

Truck Stopped (#11) Truck & Allie

Satan's Devils MC Boxset 1 Books 1-5

Satan’s Devils MC Boxset 2 Books 6-8

Satan’s Devils MC Boxset 3 Books 9-11

Satan’s Devils MC - Colorado Chapter

Paladin’s Hell (#1) Paladin and Jayden

Demon’s Angel (#2) Demon and Violet

Devil’s Due (#3) Beef and Steph

Devil’s Dilemma (#4) Pyro and Mel

Ink’s Devil (#5) Ink and Beth

Devil’s Spawn (#6)

Satan’s Devils MC - Next Generation

1. Amy’s Santa (#1) Wizard and Amy
1. Hawk’s Cry (#2) Hawk and Olivia

ACKNOWLEDGMENTS

Acknowledgements and Author's Note

Almost three years ago I published the fourth in the Satan's Devils MC series, Targeting Dart. In that book, I moved Dart from being a member in the Tucson chapter to rightfully earn his place as VP in San Diego. Lost, the previous VP, was given his chance to take his seat at the head of the table.

I knew Lost had a story to tell, but he was reticent about sharing it with me. It's taken three years to get the truth out of him. I knew from the start he wasn't a cardboard cutout of an MC prez and was going to lead his club differently.

Why had he picked up his handle?

Sometimes books are best left to germinate in the background, and I hope you agree this is the case with this story. When Lost finally started talking, I was excited to learn about his past and the type of man he was, also how despicable a man the previous prez, Snake was.

I've enjoyed writing about San Diego and revisiting it if only in my head. My brother lived in the area for many years and so I've been there a few times. The book starts with a scene at La

Jolla I remember so well, the seals on the beach, the pelicans flying overhead, and the squirrels popping up their heads from the undergrowth, it's so clear, I can almost smell the sea. We will be returning to San Diego in future books. I will be writing about Niran, Pennywise, Salem and, of course, Kink. I found a new group of bikers who I fell in love with writing this story, and I hope you did too.

Hopefully, in the not too far distant future, the events taking place during the writing of this book will be part of history, but I think it's worth noting I wrote this book during the Covid-19 lockdown. It should have been easy, right? Nowhere to go, no one to see—but it was hard to concentrate, and my writing output suffered terribly. My heart breaks for all the lives snuffed out around the world, for family and friends who've lost loved ones, and for everyone who's become ill and who will suffer lasting effects. To date we're not out the other side yet, but I hope that one day soon we will be.

If you've been affected personally by Covid-19, be assured you're in my thoughts—not that that's worth much. But if we come out with anything from the pandemic, I hope it's kindness that prevails.

In time we'll move past this, as I must now do in this note.

A huge shout out and thank you to Jeanne St James. Have you read any of her books? If not, you might want to give them a try. When I was writing the intimate scene between Patsy and Lost, I had the idea of starting it with Patsy reading a sexy scene. I tried writing it myself, but it was obviously in my voice. So Jeanne came to the rescue and allowed me to use a section from one of her books—she'd asked her reader group to come up with some of the sexiest bits of her books. I think you'll agree that scene was hot and led nicely into Lost and Patsy getting together.

Being Lost was a team effort, and due to the haphazard writing process, this time I really did need my eagle-eyed beta readers helping me. Sheri, what can I say? Thank you seems inadequate. Your references back to Targeting Dart and Ink's Devil set me back on the right part more than once. It's certainly not the first time you've stopped me from making a mistake, but you excelled yourself this time. Jo, a new addition to my beta team, proved she has an eye for detail which led me to correct a few things. Jo, never be afraid of offering suggestions, I always want to write the best possible book.

Another special mention goes out to Danena who spent her time off from making hundreds of face masks to read through the book. As normal, she found errors everyone else had missed. I'm forever grateful for your help, and in awe of your generous heart.

Sometimes an author just needs to know the story flows and keeps people's interest, so as usual, thanks to the rest of my great beta team, Tami, Alex, Nicole, Terra, and Zoe.

Again, I've worked with Maggie Kern, who's edited this book and helped me pull a load of isolated thoughts and words together. She's kept me calm, laughed with me and let me rant. I can't thank you enough, Maggie, and hope it won't be too long before I see you again.

A huge thankyou to Golden Czermak of Furious Fotog for the cover photograph, and to the model Christopher Clark for gracing it so nicely. I know the cover has generated a lot of interest in Being Lost. This picture fitted my mental image of Lost to perfection.

Of course, to produce the cover took the magic of Wicked Smart Designs. I love working with Dar, her turnaround speed is amazing, and her work is excellent.

The final stage in the production of a book is proofreading, and this is the first time I've worked with Honey Palomino for this. Thank you Honey, you made some great suggestions. I enjoyed working with you. Now some of you may know Honey better as an author—if you don't, please do check out her Gods of Chaos MC series, I highly recommend them.

Finally, last as always, but definitely not least, thanks to all of you, my wonderful readers who've taken a chance on this book. If it wasn't for your encouragement, I wouldn't keep writing. I have recently received messages and emails telling me how much you like my books, and I love reading every one. A positive message inspires me to write more.

If you've enjoyed this book, please consider writing a review. Reviews are essential to us authors, and I appreciate and read them all.

This book may be done, but don't worry. There'll be another Satan's Devil coming along very soon. In fact, we'll be finding out where Road disappeared to.

STAY IN TOUCH

Email: manda@mandamellett.com

Website: www.mandamellett.com

Sign up for my newsletter to hear about new releases in the Satan's Devils and Blood Brothers series.

Facebook reader group: https://www.facebook.com/groups/mandasbadboys/

ABOUT THE AUTHOR

Manda's life's always seemed a bit weird, starting with a childhood that even today she's still trying to make sense of, then losing her parents in the late teens. Going from the tragic to the bizarre, who else could be unlucky enough to have had two car accidents, neither her fault, one involving a nun, and another involving a police woman?

There isn't enough space to list everything that's happened to Manda, or what she's learned from it. But by using the rich fabric of her personal life, psychology degree, varied work experiences, and amazing characters she's met, Manda is able to populate her books with believable in-depth characters and enjoys pitting them against situations which challenge them. Her books are full of suspense, twists and turns and the unexpected.

Manda lives in the beautiful countryside of Essex in the UK, the area's claim to fame being the Wilkin's Jam Factory at nearby Tiptree. She can usually find jars of jam which remind her of home wherever she goes. As well as writing books and reading, Manda loves walking her dogs and keeping fit. She lives with her husband of over 30 years, who, along with her son, is her greatest fan and supporter.

Manda is thankful that one of the more unusual, and at the time unpleasant, turns her life took, now enables her to spend her time writing. Confirming, in her view, every cloud has a silver lining.

Photo by Carmel Jane Photography

www.ingramcontent.com/pod-product-compliance
Lightning Source LLC
Chambersburg PA
CBHW010345200726
48286CB00016B/2804

* 9 7 8 1 9 1 2 2 8 8 7 3 1 *